More Acclaim for Pipe Dreams

"In this fascinating tale, John Madinger expertly weaves the true crime and mystery fiction genres into a tapestry reminiscent of *In Cold Blood* and *To Kill a Mockingbird*. Written with the elegant prose of a poet, Pipe Dreams masterfully combines historical facts and figures with vivid settings that eloquently capture the shocking and brutal crimes committed in 1931 Hawaii—and still remembered in the Islands today."
—Michael A. Black, *Legends of the West, Dying Art, Cold Fury*

"Madinger nicely interweaves a well-established historical timeline with a professional investigator's sense of detail and a skilled storyteller's vivid imagination. Much like the hopelessly trapped opium smokers that inhabit his story, once you start reading, you're going to find yourself caught up in the all-too-serious question of what is real—and what is not."
—Ken Goddard, *CSI: In Extremis, Balefire*

"Pipe Dreams draws the reader into a dark story of deceit, arrogance, and desperation. The author does a masterful job of portraying the infamous Massie affair, employing his own knowledge and experience as a federal agent to further validate a gripping story."
—Deborah Turrell Atkinson, *Primitive Secrets, Feathers in the Soul*

"A compelling mystery that fictionalizes Hawaii's all-too-real Massie murder case, with well-written and credible characterizations of many of the principals involved."
—Alan Brennert, *Mokoka'i, Honolulu*

"A blend of thriller, historical fiction, and murder mystery, Pipe Dreams offers heart-pounding action laced with well-researched facts detailing the infamous Massie case as it unfolds amid the illegal drug trade of 1930s Territorial Hawaii."
—Gail Baugniet, *Paradise, Passion, Murder; Dark Paradise: Mysteries in the Land of Aloha*

"Madinger effectively draws on his expertise from his own law enforcement past, and he writes with the same vigor that he brought to his previous detective fiction, including the novel *Death on Diamond Head*…this suspenseful, impressive work…successfully and cinematically reinvents a notorious criminal case. A vibrant and riveting fictionalization of real-life crimes and trials in 1930s Hawaii."
—Kirkus Reviews

"Hawaii's infamous Massie case saw a lie lead to murder and ruined lives. The missing piece to the puzzle has always been the 'why'—why did Thalia Massie lie and set the tragic sequence of events in motion? In Pipe Dreams, based upon true events of that case, John Madinger proposes a theory that answers the 'why' and completes a devastating picture of the secret Thalia lied to conceal. If you love mysteries and Hawaii, you'll love Pipe Dreams."
—Mike Farris, *A Death in the Islands*

Pipe Dreams

Pipe Dreams

The Dark Secret Behind
Hawaii's Most Notorious Crime

John Madinger

© 2020 John Madinger

All rights reserved. No part of this book may be reproduced, stored in, or introduced into a retrieval system, or transmitted in any form, or by any means (electronic, mechanical, photocopying, recording, or otherwise) without the prior written permission of the publisher.

This book is a work of historical fiction. Aside from actual people, places and events that appear in the narrative, all names, characters and incidents are products of the author's imagination and are used fictitiously. Any resemblance to actual persons, living or dead, or actual events is purely coincidental.

ISBN 978-1-948011-36-5
Library of Congress Control Number: 2020940191

Photo credits: John Madinger (cover pipe, p. 144 top) Katerina Sisperova/iStock (cover smoke); Lagodka/Dreamstime (cover background); Hawaii State Archives (p. 138 top right, p. 219, p. 141, p. 142 top); UPI/Getty Images (p. 138 bottom right, p. 140 top, p. 143 bottom); US Army (p. 140 bottom); Wikimedia Commons (p. 138 top left); Honolulu Police Department (p. 138 bottom left); Library of Congress/New York Sun Archives (p. 137, p. 142 bottom); Associated Press (p. 143 top); US Navy (p. 144 bottom)

Cover Design: Angela Wu-Ki
Production: Dawn Sakamoto Paiva

Watermark Publishing
1000 Bishop St., Ste. 806
Honolulu, HI 96813
www.bookshawaii.net
info@bookshawaii.net

10 9 8 7 6 5 4 3 2 1

Printed in Korea

To the memory of William K. "Billy" Wells, and to those who served with him in the Federal Bureau of Narcotics, 1930-1968

PROLOGUE

Ala Moana Road, Honolulu, Territory of Hawaii
Sunday, September 13, 1931

It began as a dream, a bad one, hovering at the edge of the beach road in the darkness. When they first saw her, she was nothing more than a pale, vaguely feminine form silhouetted against the brush. Her dress hung on her like a shroud, the green silk bleached a smoky gray by their headlamps, the blood made blacker than a crow's wing.

They slowed their car, and their tired smiles faded as the two couples struggled to grasp the meaning of this small white figure alone on an empty road an hour after midnight. All agreed later that for just an instant they had doubted her humanity.

When they coasted to a stop, they could see it was not a ghost, but a girl with a tangle of light brown hair framing her battered face. As she moved stiffly into the shadows at the side of the car, she became again just a pallid shape probing the shocked occupants of the vehicle with fear-filled eyes.

"Are you white people?" she asked, her voice barely audible above the motor's ticking and the grumbling of surf on a nearby reef. It was a query somehow both alarming and absurd, but they were, and they admitted it. On this assurance alone, she embraced the safety of a car full of strangers and asked to be taken home.

She answered their worried questions in one- and two-word phrases spoken through a haze of pain, saying she had left a party earlier in the evening, walking into Waikiki when a car pulled up and two men dragged her inside.

No, she shook her head; there was no need to tell the police about the men in the car, four Hawaiians who had beaten her as they drove the mile and a half to the lonely place where they had thrown her into the bushes.

"No. No hospital," she said, though anyone could see her wounds were real enough. Blood from her smashed lips spattered the green dress's shoulders and neck. She cradled her face in her slender fingers, hiding cuts and bruises and the broken jaw that made conversation a torture, so they rode quietly for a time, and wondered about the rest of it.

The inevitable question hung between the girl and her rescuers, smoldering ominous and unspoken for most of the drive to Kahawai Street. The two women felt the dread most keenly, and their glances flashed between the girl and each other, wordlessly communicating the awful suspicion that seemed to swell in the silence until one of them, with a daughter of her own, finally summoned the courage to voice it.

No, nothing else had been done to her; she hadn't been "injured" in any other way, the girl insisted. "Just drive me home, please," she begged. "My husband will take care of me."

Following her terse directions, they came to a tidy bungalow in Manoa, that deep, green valley Mark Twain once called "dream haunted." But the driveway was empty and the house dark, staring silently back at her deliverers, barren of the comfort she seemed to expect within. Was she sure they could do no more?

"No, it will be all right," she told them. "My husband will know what to do."

It was 1:25 on the morning it all began.

At that exact moment, Lieutenant (junior grade) Thomas Hedges Massie, United States Navy, was missing a wife and he didn't know what to do. He had last seen her at a party at the Ala Wai Inn, a nightclub on the outskirts of Waikiki, sometime before midnight. Now she wasn't with any of the other Navy couples who had been at the party, she wasn't at home, and above all, she very visibly wasn't with him at the nearby house of another submariner. Lieutenant Massie—short, starched, and serious—found the absence of his spouse irritating, embarrassing and, because he was at his core a very decent young man, deeply worrying.

It wasn't the first time twenty-year-old Thalia had gone off on her own. It wasn't even the first time that weekend. Tommie's colleagues knew her as his "kid bride," a flighty girl who didn't mix well in the Navy's social circles. Earlier that very evening she had caused a scene at the party, exchanging words with—then slapping—another young lieutenant before vanishing into the night. Living with Thalia could be a trial.

Nevertheless, some things an officer and a gentleman simply didn't do, particularly one as thoroughly conscious of his honor and duty as Lieutenant Thomas Hedges Massie. Misplacing a wife was one of those things definitely not done so, at a loss for an answer to the other officers' questions and fretting under the smug and accusatory vibrations from their wives, the unsettled young man once again telephoned his house. This time, he would testify later, someone picked up the receiver.

"Come home," he heard his wife say. "Something awful has happened."

That was how it began. It would end bloody, with lies and lynching, with kidnapping and murder. It would end with three people dead, and the lives of everyone else in Hawaii changed forever.

I've had seven decades to wonder. Would the ending have been different had the lieutenant known his wife as well as I did? And would that story Thalia told have changed if she'd ever seen her husband the way I had? Because I know Thalia Massie was an awful liar, with a secret much darker than the beach road that night.

And decent, honorable little Tommie? Well, Thalia and I were both wrong about him.

Come to find out he did have one killing in him, after all.

CHAPTER 1

Federal Building, Room 213, Honolulu, Territory of Hawaii
Friday, September 11, 1931

The old Hawaiians knew September as part of *kau wela*—the "hot season"—and truthfully it isn't the best time to visit the Islands. I wasn't visiting, though; I had a mission. I had come to join the opium war that September in 1931. The Dollar Line's *SS President Monroe* brought me home on a muggy Friday morning, and the full weight of kau wela fell on me as I walked the two blocks from the steamer pier to the Federal Building, lugging a battered leather suitcase to the second floor.

"Don't just stand there; come on in," a clear voice answered my taps from behind the frosted glass.

I opened the door into a small room crowded with green metal furniture and, in one shadowed corner, a short man in a brown suit. Sunlight pouring in through an open window thrust stark shafts through the fragrant pipe smoke eddying between the filing cabinets. Above the man, a ceiling fan creaked out a tired rhythm, idly shoving around some of the syrupy air that mingled languidly with the smoke.

"Let's see. It's Friday and the *Monroe*'s in, so you must be the new boy," the man said, "reporting immediately on arrival."

"Yes, sir," I agreed. "That's what my orders said. I've got them right here." I felt for the damp papers nestled in my pocket next to the little green *Manual of Instructions for Narcotic Agents and Inspectors*.

"Mmm," he said, tilting his head to one side, appraising me from a different angle. "You can start by cutting out that 'sir' shit. Say, do I look distinguished to you?" He leaned back in his chair, examining with a peeved expression the pipe that had obviously gone out.

"Pardon me?"

"Do I look distinguished? You know. Sophisticated?"

I sneaked a look at the gold lettering on the door to make sure I was really in the right place. Yep, Bureau of Narcotics. "Uh, I suppose."

"No kidding? Maybe my wife's right, after all. She says smoking a pipe makes you look refined. And here all along I figured it was just a line of bull to get me to quit cigarettes," he snorted and stood, stepping out of his corner through the sunbeams.

"Come on in, sit down." He gestured at a wooden desk covered with cardboard boxes and loose file folders. "I'm Billy Wells." He extended his hand, which was strong and callused and full of confidence.

"John, er, Jack Mather," I answered back.

"Yeah, I figured. What's the H for?"

"H?"

"'John H.' It doesn't say on your forms."

"Oh. I don't use it. Just Jack."

"Mmm. Okay, Jack. C.T.—the chief—is out today. He's got grand jury for five or six people, so I'm supposed to fill you in." Wells moved a box off the chair behind what was apparently to be my desk, dropped it onto the floor, and motioned for me to sit. "We got your file in the last mail. Said you're just out of college?"

I confirmed this as he perched himself on the adjacent desk, held the now-cold pipe in one hand, and searched through his coat pockets. "What made you decide on this job, if you don't mind my asking?" he inquired.

"I actually put in for Internal Revenue, mostly because I took business at Stanford," I explained. "This thing came up first, and they told me in San Francisco I could use the accounting here, too."

"It could come in handy on this deal." He pointed the pipe stem at the boxes on and around my desk. "I guess you know that's why you got assigned down here. We're supposed to make some effort to close this thing out, but to tell you the truth, most folks have lost interest. Everybody's moved on, and that probably includes the White Friend."

"The White Friend?"

He stopped rummaging in his pockets and squinted at me. "They didn't tell you anything about the case back in Frisco?"

"No, sir. Not really. I was only in the office for a day, just to pick up my things. They said there was a trial, a smuggling case, but you didn't get everybody. They said there were loose ends still."

Wells finally located the items he'd been hunting: a tobacco pouch and what looked like a small metal hook. He began scraping at the pipe bowl. Tobacco flakes and ash fluttered to the floor.

"I ain't a 'sir,' just Billy. To you and everybody else in Honolulu. And loose *end* is more like it. There's really only one. The white bastard that helped the Chinese get their stuff through Customs."

"The White Friend."

Wells stood and stretched. "That's what the Chinese called him. A couple of the top boys in the organization know who he is, but they're not saying, so we're pretty much stuck."

"But what am I supposed to do?"

"All these boxes. Bank records and the crooks' papers. Somebody somewhere wondered if maybe the answer was somewhere in here. Thought maybe you'd be able to find it." Wells threw a skeptical look at the boxes. "I doubt it, frankly. Whoever the hell he is, I don't think he's stupid enough to leave those kinds of tracks."

"How much dope did he smuggle?"

Wells finished his scraping and checked the pipe, then dipped it into the tobacco pouch. "A couple of tons. A fair bit, I'll give him that."

"A couple of *tons*? My God, he must have made a fortune!"

Wells nodded. "That's for damned sure. He raked in a lot of dough. At least $53,000 we know of. And if he *is* still around, he's probably still raking."

"That's amazing! We can't just let somebody like that get away with it. We've got to do something."

"That's why you're here. But chances are he's moved on, whoever he was. We've got a couple of his boys still out waiting on their appeals, but the rest of the *hui*'s all in O.P. or dead."

"Hui?"

"Opium hui. It's like a group or a partnership. Papers like to call it an opium ring. We got their records; they're in there somewhere." He gestured at a box. "The White Friend worked for the hui."

"Don't we have any idea about who he was?"

Wells used the hook to tamp the tobacco and shook his head. "We're just guessing. Me, I always figured it was a Customs man, or Immigration. Somebody on the docks who could grease the shipments through. Or a cop, maybe; they guard the piers. One of the Chinese talked about a uniform one time, but he couldn't say what kind, so no help."

While Wells ground at the pipe, I churned with the possibilities.

I'd like to tell you that I was consumed with a passion to see justice done, to bring the power of the law down on the White Friend because that's what I promised to do when I took the oath. I'd spent a week on the steamer reading about my new job—not just my manual, but in books like, *Opium: The Demon Flower*; *The Menace of Narcotics*; *Dope*; and *King of the Opium Ring*. All of these had convinced me completely about how demonic and menacing the evil of drug addiction really was, so some of me might have wanted to solve that part of the world's problems. When you're twenty-two, you believe things like that are possible.

Mostly, though, like everyone that age, I just wanted to impress this man and be a hero.

"I'll do whatever I have to, to get this guy," I vowed with what I hoped was a forceful display of iron resolve.

The door banged open but he didn't look away; he was examining me carefully with warm brown eyes. "Yeah?" he asked, not sounding too impressed. "You sure that's a promise you want to keep?"

The man who followed me into our office that morning exactly filled the bottom three-quarters of the doorway. He swept into the room with a wide smile on his square face and the assurance of someone who knows his accustomed welcome is waiting.

"Why, it's the ever-vigilant Inspector Kam of the hard-hitting Vice squad, come to pay a call," Wells announced, grinning and waving at another open desk. Obviously delighted, the imposing detective, whose body was as solid as a *koa* log and about the same shape, plumped himself into a chair and leaned back. He propped both big shoes on the desk, then angled a toothpick into one corner of his mouth and tried without visible success to look serious.

"You been reading my press. Good. You Treasury boys should know you're getting your tax dollars' worth," he grinned. "Who's your friend?"

"Jack Mather, the new man I was telling you about. Jack, this is Kwai Kam. He's in charge of the Vice detail here in town."

I stood and shook Kam's offered hand, one approximately the size of a dictionary and about as hard.

"Good to meet you," he said. "We can use the help. In fact..." He turned to Billy. "You boys might be able to give us a hand tonight. You remember Mr. Woo Loo Soon?"

"Our old friend George. He at it again?"

"Hell, yes. Gonna be a real disappointment to his probation officer."

"Where is he now?"

"Off River Street, just up from Beretania. I was thinking you might be interested. And a Federal beef will carry more weight."

Wells got up and rummaged through a file cabinet, found a file marked "Soon," and tossed it on my desk. "Oh, yeah, I'll take another shot at George. He'll probably draw some time on this one."

Kam shifted his toothpick. "He's a worthless little bastard, but maybe this time we can talk him into giving us something useful. I thought we'd go about eight. It'll be early, but dark; should be getting some business in by then."

"We're indicting Joe Kubey again today. C.T.'s gonna go get him, but I should be around by tonight."

While Wells and Kam began planning, I read the folder he'd given me and listened in, wondering if my new boss intended to take me along, hoping that my education was about to commence.

If so, it would begin on the border with Hell. Soon's place crouched on the ragged edge of what they called Hell's Half-Acre, a very apt description of the tenement and shanty warren that made up one of Honolulu's worst neighborhoods. Just getting to a joint in that part of town called for some finesse: the narrow passageways swarmed with bootleggers, prostitutes, opium smokers, footpads, and assorted alley scum.

We got a good bit of our business out of Hell's Half-Acre over the years, and Kam's Vice squad got even more. The area ideally suited those who ran the opium laydowns—small one-room operations serving a customer or two at a time. The file showed that Soon had haunted the Acre for a decade, moving his joint from rat hole to rat hole—usually, but not always, one step ahead of Kam and the Vice cops.

An opium addict himself, George Soon ran his den to support his own habit, cooked and sold *yen pock* opium pills, and provided the pipe and smoking gear to his customers. The smudged rap sheet in his file said he'd been pinched for opium several times before, including a collar in April. He was already on probation, so another conviction could mean a trip to the federal penitentiary.

They set another meeting for seven o'clock that evening at a chop suey place on Beretania Street, where Kam said there'd "still be time for some noodles before dark." We would cover the four or five blocks to Soon's on foot, and if everything went well, ruin his night.

While they chatted about opium dens and *hop* sellers, I poked through one of the White Friend's boxes. Where, in those neat stacks of canceled checks and bank account statements, was there any link to the dark world they were talking about? And how was I supposed to find it?

River Street near Beretania Street
Friday, September 11

By the time we got to the chop suey house, Kam and another detective, Henry McKeague, had already ordered. The table was covered with plates of food: noodles, fried rice, vegetables, shrimp, and a triple order of Kam's favorite, *char siu* pork, with fragrant steam rising from its candied red edges. He waved his chopsticks at the opposite side of the booth, though it was difficult for him to be expansive; he and McKeague were big men, and wedged in tightly together on the side that faced the door.

As we sat eating, the sky outside slowly darkened. In the cool of the evening, Honolulu prepared for nightfall, a languid, easy time I remembered fondly from my boyhood as the best part of the day. Of course, those warm memories were born in an entirely different part of town, separated by much more than the three short miles between Manoa Valley and the Acre. In this hardscrabble section of the city, a far less romantic day was only beginning.

Honolulu in 1931 had a population of maybe 130,000. The Depression was starting to bite, but people were still working, still fulfilling the grand plan of business magnate Walter Dillingham and the so-called Big Five firms that ran the Islands like the world's biggest company town.

Most of these 130,000 were immigrants or the descendants of people brought to Hawaii to tend the sugar or pineapple plantations, to build railroads or swamp cargo to and from the holds of ships. These were laboring people, and labor they did—long hours at low pay in some of the most difficult jobs imaginable. It was a grinding, sapping lifetime of struggle. Plenty had not-so-fond memories of the time when a *luna*, an overseer with a whip, rode above them in the fields.

Some of these folks turned to opium or alcohol to lift, even for an evening, the crushing weight on their backs, but it always amazed me that more did not. Instead, many like Kam focused on their families, cherishing the nearly universal belief that in Hawaii, times would someday be better for their children.

In Kam's case, this meant better lives for a swarming, happy brood of thirteen, whose raucous welcome could almost overwhelm even their father's massive, stoic form. The first time I visited his house I introduced myself to a dizzying array of young Kams. I couldn't say afterward that I'd actually "met" Kam's family; the experience was more like encountering a celebrating mob or being swept up in a small but joyous riot.

His own work ethic called for him to spend fourteen days on duty before getting a day off, and those were twelve- or fourteen-hour workdays. I don't know where he found the time to make thirteen kids, but he loved each one, and filled time before a raid or waiting on the benches outside a courtroom with stories of this son's or that daughter's exploits. They may have been an interchangeable jumble of names and faces to me, distinguished mostly by size, but each was distinctly perfect in the Inspector's devoted eyes.

"Yeah, but thirteen of them!" I exclaimed.

"A very lucky number for me," he said, reaching for the plate of noodles. "Not that I believe in that superstition crap."

"So, you don't burn the joss papers," Billy teased with a smile.

"True, true. I never burn joss for luck. I have all I need."

"Thirteen kids," I marveled. "That's a lot of luck."

"Take one look at those faces, and tell me I don't already have heaven's blessings," he said reasonably. "And what about you, Jack? You got family here, right?"

"My parents. And a sister at college. Nothing like you."

"Hmmm. You're still a young kid. You get started soon, you can get thirteen, easy."

Billy laughed. "Not on a T-Man's pay."

Kam waved him off. "Family's more important than money. You find a way. Hey, Mather, you related to Auntie Marie? Lives in Nuuanu. I known her since I was a kid."

This was another thing about Honolulu. It was still a small town in many ways, and you seldom went anywhere without running into someone who knew you or your family. "She's my dad's mother."

"Oh, yeah? Your *tutu*, then. Nice lady, that one. Still teaching school?"

"No, she retired. She lives with us now."

"You see her, you tell her Kam said 'hello.'"

The sun went down, and the sky purpled behind Dole's pineapple-shaped water tower. We ate Chinese food and spoke of his family and mine, of growing up in wealthy, green Manoa Valley and in poor Palama flats, and of school papers and admission requirements to Punahou and Iolani, the favored private schools that parents coveted for their children. Kam and his wife had managed to place an older son in Iolani, a boys' school, and he talked of Punahou for a daughter he declared to be "especially promising."

"Here, look. I've got a picture," he said, and pulled the image of a shy-looking schoolgirl from a packet in his coat pocket. McKeague rolled his eyes.

Apparently Kam made this same claim about all of his children at various times. To an outsider, "especially promising" might seem a hopelessly optimistic characterization coming from an uneducated Chinese police officer with no prospects for wealth or advancement in the midst of a worldwide depression. This was, after all, a man whose job regularly took him into the foulest corners of Honolulu, actively searching through the muck for the basest people he could dredge up. Most of his world for much of his life was a place where all of the evidence available to him should have fostered an absolute belief that anything evil was not only possible, it was normal.

Many would be twisted by that sort of reality, yet Kwai Kam was a good man to sit with as he spoke of his children, riffling through their photographs, secure in his conviction that their futures would transcend his own. And as I listened to him, I could see the barriers of race, class, language, and poverty built up over a century and a half fall away, swept aside by a father's love. Maybe the father's dream included the faith that, in a place like Hawaii, anything good was also possible.

But if the Vice officer found time for dreams, he made time for reality. And, when we were full and quiet after an hour of food and talk, when the soft, liquid Hawaiian night cloaked the dreams of cop and criminal, the fine and the mean equally, we packed up a fire axe and a sledge hammer and went looking for trouble in Hell's Half-Acre.

By a quarter past eight, the four of us were safely opposite the decrepit two-story structure that served as George Soon's latest opium salon. We looped around the edges of the slum neighborhood I would learn like my own backyard, crossed and re-crossed Nuuanu Stream, and never moved in a straight line that might reveal our objective.

Billy told me that Soon had made our task much easier by establishing himself on the edge of the worst area, not that he was trying to do the cops any favors. It was more likely he was making life safer for his customers. If he had been in a place like Buckle Lane, Tin Can Alley, the innocuous-sounding but malignant College Walk, or just in the center of Hell's Half-Acre, our task would have been much more difficult.

In the years to come, I would pass hundreds of times through this maze of twisting lanes and passages, cutting through tiny yards enclosed with rough plank fences, unpaved alleys, and tenement hallways all teeming with people. One of those approaches never went unnoticed.

The neighborhood would roil in our wake—a cacophony of barking dogs, startled roosters, and taunting urchins that had to be outdistanced or warned off with vicious but mostly empty threats.

Tonight, though, we slipped unnoticed to a boarded-up garage, this one backing up onto the stream, where we crouched in the weeds, hugging the darker shadow at the side of the building. From our vantage, we could see across to Soon's weathered wooden tenement and back down to Beretania, one of Honolulu's main streets. In the lighted intersection sat the white police ambulance and one of the city's two radio patrol cars. Some uniformed officers moved back and forth in the lamp's glow, working an accident.

"That ain't gonna bother a real *yen shee* man," Kam said, jerking his head at the police cars. "They'll be coming, but we can't see shit from here."

After a brief whispered conference with Billy, Kam announced a change of plans.

"Okay. Jack and I'll go across to the building next door, get up somewhere high where we can see the stairs. When somebody comes, we'll shine the light over here."

I took Billy's flashlight and followed the Inspector across River Street, up some stairs and a ladder to the still-warm corrugated roof of Soon's next-door neighbor. Under their metal lid, I could hear the sounds of the residents—babies crying, people laughing, talking, fighting, all unaware I was right over their heads.

"This ain't too bad. You can see the door, but kind of hard to get down fast," Kam muttered. "Sit tight up here. I'm gonna go down, see if there's a better spot."

As he slid back over the edge, a sliver of light showed at Soon's door. Three people emerged onto the walkway, headed away from me toward the stairwell. Two men supported a woman between them. She seemed reluctant to leave, then half-turned as she reached the top of the stairs before dropping out of sight on the steps.

A few minutes later, Kam was back, telling me this spot would have to do. I told him about the three people leaving, but he'd missed all of them. "No matter," he said confidently. "Plenty more be stopping by tonight. There you go, there's two right now."

He peered at them intently. "Ha. We lucked out. That one in front is Lau Sau. He's hard to miss. I know him good; he stools every now and then for one of the boys on the squad. And that little one is Sammy Akana. Both of 'em are *yen shee loo*," Kam whispered.

I recognized the second man from his clothes; he was one of the two who had just left with the woman, and I told Kam.

"Yeah? Probably went and got some more money," he said as they slipped inside Soon's door. "We'll give 'em a couple minutes to cook up some pills, then go."

In those days, we didn't need a warrant to raid a den, only the knowledge that a crime was being committed on the premises. "*Yen shee loo*" meant "opium man," a smoker, and his presence on the scene gave us what we needed to hit Soon's place.

I tensed up, waiting. "Okay," Kam said, after what seemed like forever. "Give Billy the light."

I flashed the light toward Billy's hiding place and saw him and McKeague erupt out of the shadows and run toward Soon's building. Kam and I scrambled for the edge of the roof, not worried about noise any longer, and dropped down the ladder into a courtyard full of rubbish.

A moment later, we were on Soon's stairs, hearing his door crash above us and Billy's "Police!" Kam plunged through the open door and I stood panting in the threshold, hunting for threats in the gloom. Thick smoke choked the air inside the room. Sickly, pallid light struggled to escape a stubby oil lamp on the floor that threw Kafkaesque shadows on the ceiling and walls. A slightly larger but equally useless kerosene lantern hung on a nail by the door. Its feeble glow rendered the shapes crowded into the dank little space in eerie shades of fish-belly gray.

The smaller man we had seen entering lay on the floor, staring up at us with wide eyes the color of old ivory, holding a bamboo pipe. McKeague had the second *yen shee loo*, a real creep, the one Kam had identified as Lau Sau, by the front of his denim jacket; he was holding him up against the back wall, spinning him, hands moving on his body. Sau, surrendering, muttered "Okay, okay," to the unpainted boards.

The last man, who could only be George Soon, scrambled for a corner. Billy reached for him, and I saw a small object skitter off under the wooden framed bed. Kam, too, caught the movement, and dove for the bed as Billy jerked Soon to his feet. With his prisoner held by the back of the neck, Billy gestured with his free hand for the smoker on the floor to stand, then took the pipe from him as he rose, and handed it to me.

None of the three resisted as they were frisked for weapons. McKeague took a nasty-looking knife from Sau; this and a pair of scissors used for trimming the lamp wicks were the most dangerous items found.

Kam emerged from under the bed, his prize in hand. "Got a can!" he announced triumphantly, and displayed one of the five-*tael* tins I would learn to know so well. He waved it in Soon's face. "Some here. Looks like we got him, Billy."

Billy nodded. "Prison for you, George." Soon sagged in his hands.

When the three were in handcuffs, Kam and Billy gave the room a fast but thorough search. Opium smoking is an involved process, ritualized and much more complex than taking a pill or sticking a needle in your arm. Billy collected all of the paraphernalia associated with the smoking rite on the wooden tray found in every den. Aside from some *yen shee*, the gray, ash-like residue from the pipe, they found no more opium in the room.

McKeague stood over the three prisoners, but they gave no trouble, sitting sullenly next to the open door, staring dully at the floor as the search went on.

"We're about *pau* here, Billy," Kam said, dusting himself off.

"Yeah, we better see about some transportation. Jack, go out and see if those cops are still down the block. Maybe we can snag a ride with them."

I ducked out of the shattered door, and clattered down the stairs. Halfway down, I saw that twenty or more spectators had gathered, watching me descend with upturned faces. Unsure of my reception, I slowed and made sure the badge I'd pinned to my lapel was plainly visible. "Police business," I said as the onlookers parted, their attention shifting between me and the unseen action on the landing above. I was out of the crowd in a moment and into the middle of River Street, and was relieved to see the patrol car still partially blocking the intersection.

I explained our need for a ride to a plainclothesman, dropping Kam's name. The officer said they were almost finished and offered the use of both the ambulance and their radio car. Soon we drove back the short distance to Soon's tenement.

The patrolmen held back the crowd as Billy and Kam brought the prisoners down to the street. "We can probably get everything in the meat wagon," Kam said.

"You can," Billy said. "I ain't riding in that thing. Hank and I'll take this one in the squad car." He pulled Lau Sau by his collar and the rest of us piled our tools and evidence into the ambulance, escaping Hell's Half-Acre by 8:45 p.m.

Back at the office, Billy had McKeague hold our three prisoners in the hallway while he and Kam planned their next step. The two of them murmured together at the chief's desk. Then Billy motioned for me to come closer.

"Sau and I got to talking a little bit in the car on the way down. In fact, I had to shut him up so the driver wouldn't hear."

"Oh, boy. That would've fried it," Kam grimaced.

"Yeah. See, he told me he might have a line into somebody we've been itching to get for quite a while. Need to play this just right, though, or the sons of bitches are gonna wise up and be gone."

"We got to get rid of those other two *lan yeung*, that's the first thing," Kam said, looking toward the hallway where the prisoners sat on the marble floor.

"We can book Soon. Hold him over the weekend. He had the dope when we busted in."

"And Sau and Akana didn't, so we just cut them loose."

"That'll work." Billy turned to me. "Kam and I'll stay here with Sau, squeeze him a little bit. You and Hank walk those other two birds down to the jail. Tell him to book Soon and let Akana go. Then you go on home and I'll call you in the morning, fill you in. Everything goes good, we might be working tomorrow, too."

As I went to the hallway and collected McKeague and the other two, I wondered what Lau Sau had said. Why was Billy so interested in the most repulsive person I'd ever seen in my life?

CHAPTER 2

2850 Kahawai Street, Manoa Valley
Saturday, September 12

On Saturdays, the last bus left Manoa at seven, and both girls knew it. Buses on the Manoa Valley route mostly carried the housekeepers, cooks, and gardeners of the *haole* families who lived in the quiet valley, and if these people worked at all on Saturday, most of them got off by five. Every week, though, a few stragglers gathered in a gossipy little cluster in front of the Japanese grocery on East Manoa Road, sharing stories of their employers or plans for their Sunday as they waited for the last bus.

Beatrice Nakamura should have been with them, but a block away, in the fading light of the little cottage, she sat on the edge of the guest room bed. Her employer stood over her, holding a tumbler of whiskey.

"I'm sure I've told you ten times before, but why don't you remind me what you're supposed to do," Thalia Massie said, sounding sweetly reasonable.

"Change the sheets on the master's bed before he get home Friday."

"And..."

"And on the guest bed, if it get used."

"That's right. Now, how can that be so hard to remember?"

"But Missus, the guest one never get used."

"Of course it did." Thalia waved her glass. "I told you Lieutenant Massie's friend slept in it Tuesday night. I thought you Orientals were so cunning. That's what everyone said. 'Oh, you must get a Japanese girl; they're all so clever.'" She took a sip from her drink. "But I suppose if you were that bright, you wouldn't need to work as a servant, would you?"

Car doors slammed outside; the voices of Tommie's shipmates and their wives called out to the house. Party time. Thalia grimaced and knocked back the rest of the tumbler.

From a hundred yards away, the girls heard the engine of the last bus catch and roar, grinding through the gears as it moved off down the valley toward Honolulu. Beatrice's face flushed. She had a two-mile walk to the main bus line on King Street. She wouldn't be home in Kalihi before ten.

Her captor waited until the sounds of the engine faded completely away. "You have some time now; you can change the bed before you go," she said.

"Thalia, darling, the others are here." Tommie Massie came into the room, unbuttoning his shirt, then stopped in surprise when he saw Bea sitting on the bed. He was a small man, slightly built, and spoke with the accent of his native Kentucky. "Beatrice, what are you doing still here?" he said.

"Missus have more things for me to do."

"What? That's ridiculous. It's almost seven. You'll miss your bus. Whatever it is can wait until Monday. You'd better hurry."

"Bus already went," Bea said. "The last one tonight."

"Oh, for crying out… Thalia, what were you thinking?"

"Tommie, she's not doing as she's told," Thalia whined. "I'm only trying to—"

"Keeping her late on Saturday isn't going to solve it. We're taking two cars; we'll give you a lift down to the bus stop on King Street, Bea. It's on our way."

"Thank you, Lieutenant." Bea stood to gather her sweater and umbrella from a chair in the corner of the room. She didn't look up as she left, but Thalia caught the little smirk and felt the warmth in her fade.

"But Tommie," she tried again, but stopped when he shook his head.

"Darling, I'm sure you thought you were doing the right thing," he said. "But now we're going to be inconvenienced because she's missed the bus. You can see that."

"Make her walk. She needs to be taught. She doesn't listen to me. She never listens. It isn't fair."

"Please don't whine, Thalia. It grates. I'll speak to her," he promised, turning toward the closet. "I'll have her get your gown out for you, the green one I like. Now get ready. You're not dressed yet, and the others are here."

She glared at his back as he opened the closet door, hunting for a shirt to wear under the white jacket, humming to himself, his wife forgotten. Turning smartly, she marched out through the living room, ignoring her guests' greetings, stomped into the kitchen, and looked for the brown glass bottle in the cabinet over the sink.

CHAPTER 3

Federal Building, Room 213
Saturday, September 12

True to his word, Billy called me at home the next morning and told me we had plans for Saturday night. I got down to the office at four, and he was on the phone with the boss when I let myself in. He hung up and it rang again.

"Federal Narcotics. Yeah, Sau, I know who this is." A pause as he lit his pipe, listening. "No kidding? He said he's got it? Okay, tell me where you are; I'm coming over." Wells got directions, which he jotted onto the back of an envelope, then hung up, humming.

"Okay. We're in business," he said, reaching for his hat. "Man, this worked out perfect, you coming in yesterday. Couldn't have planned it any better."

"What's going on?"

"I'll fill you in on the way." I followed him down the hall. "We didn't get a chance to talk much yesterday. You still know your way around town, right?" he said as we got to the car.

"I've been coming home during the summer. It hasn't changed that much."

"Good. You can drive. I'm not keen on it." He tossed me the key and gave the name of a plate lunch place in Liliha, a couple of miles away. "I'll steer you right."

In the car, Billy set to work on his pipe again. "This might work out pretty good," he repeated. "How many people in town know you're with the Bureau?"

"Gee, I don't know. This is the first time I've been back since I graduated. I haven't told anybody except my folks and a neighbor."

"The file said your father works for Walter Dillingham."

"Sort of. He's an engineer on one of the Army projects out by Pearl Harbor. Fort Kamehameha. It's a Dillingham contract."

Wells nodded. "It's probably okay. Anyhow, the thing is, about a month ago we got some information about two Honolulu cops who were running a shakedown scheme. Not our business, except they've got an opium angle. It's kind of funny; they're not really dope peddlers, 'cause they never actually sell anything. It's all just a con game." He shook his head, disgusted.

"Somehow, these two clowns got hold of a bunch of opium tins, the five-tael size. One of 'em, calls himself 'Brown,' we think is a patrolman named William Russell. He goes around finding potential buyers and sets up deals for five or ten cans, arranges a meeting to get the money, then hands over the stuff. Right after he leaves, the second cop, who we know is Russell's pal, Albert Holt, shows up and slaps the cuffs on the buyer. He takes the opium back, gives the guy a warning, and cuts him loose.

"These buyers, they're overjoyed just to be let go. No chance they're gonna make a complaint, even if they figure out later they've been conned. Mostly Chinese. They know what they're doing's illegal as hell, and they don't want to risk problems with any more police."

I maneuvered through a passing shower, slowed with the other cars on the slick pavement, and wondered where he was going with this.

"Here's the problem," Billy continued. "Holt and Russell know C.T. and me. Last couple of years, we've just had a two-man office, and of course they know all the local cops, too. But," he said, looking at me directly. "They don't know you. And the first thing that little shithead Sau told me last night was, he had a line into a guy named Brown who wanted to sell some Lam Kee hop. If this Brown guy is Russell, maybe we'll send you in to rope him."

My qualifications for an undercover assignment were minimal, to say the least. "You know," I hedged, "I'm not exactly trained for that."

"Don't matter," Billy said airily, waving the pipe, which had gone out again. "You got the easy part. Shoot, I could teach a goddamn monkey to do the roper's job." He started to work again on the pipe. "Nah, according to Sau, they trust him already. We'll just run you in there with him."

"I guess I could try it. It sounds okay." I tried to project some confidence.

"We'll see." Billy's tone became more serious now. "If everything goes like we plan it out, which it almost never does, it should be a nice, smooth deal. One thing you'll learn about police work in this town, everybody's pretty easygoing. Hell, most of the time we don't even carry a gun. A few of the Honolulu cops never carry one. But Holt and Russell do." He gazed at me intently, watching what was left of my confidence wilt. "And if this turns out not to be a nice, smooth deal, it could go real bad, real fast.

"And here we are," he said cheerily as I eased up to the curb.

Liliha Street
Saturday, September 12

There are two things you need to know about undercover work, and if you're going to try it, believe me, you need to know them real bad. In September of 1931, I didn't know either one of them.

The first thing is, roping is pure peril. Like Billy said, bad things could happen when your deal went sour. We had a few agents killed that way during my time in the Bureau.

There were other, less deadly hazards. Some agents got hooked on dope or got in money trouble. You have no badge, no uniform, and most of the time no gun. You're out there alone, up to your neck in all the same things that make a life of crime alluring to criminals—fast money, easy women, shady schemes. It's a pit, one you can either climb in or fall in. Ropers often fell.

The key to climbing in and getting back out is not the agent; it's always the informer, and that's the second thing I didn't know. I found out on my second day on the job, from somebody who had already lived up to every one of my expectations about how evil and menacing dope really was—that morose and tubercular Chinese piper, Lau Sau.

Sau was a *yen shee* man, and he looked the part—sallow-faced and cadaverous. His appearance was silent testimony to years on the pipe. Consumption gripped Sau like a vise, plundering air from the diseased lungs he polluted twice daily with opium smoke. He spoke in a raspy wheeze punctuated with wrenching wet, hacking coughs, filtered slightly through a bloody handkerchief he carried tucked into his vest. I had recoiled from him in horror the night before, endlessly grateful when Billy offered to take charge of him in the other car.

Every time I ever saw him, Sau wore the same thing: a uniform that consisted of a filthy black bowler, a long-sleeved gray shirt that might once have aspired to whiteness, and that striped silk vest, the debased remnants of someone's evening attire. Billy's report said Sau was forty-five, but he laughed, "You gotta keep in mind, those are people years. Measure him in dope fiend time, he's 120 or so." Lau Sau looked every day of it.

The report also listed a profusion of grisly scars, vivid memorials to a struggle for survival in that time-twisted world, relics of alley battles from Hong Kong to Honolulu. His eyes, hard chestnuts of challenge and suspicion, moved quickly, always seeking some edge their proprietor could exploit. But his most distinctive feature, aside from the profound impression of imminent expiration, was his nose. The end had been sheared off in some long-ago spasm of violence. Angry red scar tissue capped the remnants, giving him a distinctly pug-like aspect highlighted by a bright cherry spot in the center of his face.

"And what happened to his nose?" I asked, seeing the gaunt piper straighten up at the picnic table where he waited for us.

"I'll let you ask him," Wells said. "It's a good story. I heard it last night, and he ain't shy about telling it."

Stoned (usually) or sober (not if he could help it), Sau traveled in an energy-conserving dawdle; the opium and his bacillus conspired to chain him in a state of perpetual torpor only the darting maroon eyes could escape. They tracked us relentlessly as we approached and sat down with him.

"I get 'em all set for you," Sau rasped. Trying not to lean too close, over the voices of the other diners nearby I strained to catch the words distorted by drugs, disease, language, and the handkerchief. "Supposed to be tonight. This man, Brown, he *hapa haole*?"

"Sure is," Billy said. "Russell's part-white. And he says he's got the hop?"

Sau nodded as vigorously as he could manage. "He say fifty-five dollar, one can. Good deal, that."

"Damn straight. That's how come they get so many buyers, 'cause it's too good to be true. How'd you meet him?"

"Mori-*san*. You know him? He one *pai gow* man down Hotel Street," Sau wheezed. "He take me to Brown."

"Yeah, that'd be Ernest Mori," Billy told me as Sau loafed over to the lunch counter to buy his only meal of the day with Billy's quarter. "Chinatown gambler. Hedges his bets by snitching part-time for Vice, the little shit. I'm thinking he'd be a perfect shill for those two.

"You did good," Billy told Sau when he returned with his stew and rice. "Now, here's how we're gonna do it."

Billy laid out the plan for Sau, whose dancing maroon eyes fixed on me as soon as he heard I'd be going along. Billy sent him on his way with explicit directions on what to do next.

"Got to keep checking on him every time I hear that death rattle of his," Billy frowned, reading my thoughts exactly as we watched Sau stumble away. "Make sure he's still breathing."

"He should see a doctor. I think he's dying. You think he's going to die?" I babbled, staring appalled as Sau stopped to lean on a phone pole, hunched over, and choked into his rag.

"Hell, he's mostly dead already, and he's still getting cough syrup from half the croakers in Honolulu." Billy grinned at me. "Don't worry; most important thing is, he'll live for four more hours, which is just long enough to finish this deal."

Back in the car, Billy explained what he had in mind to his still-shaken roper. "See, we've got to get both of these crumbs in possession. That complicates things. It'd be easy enough just getting Russell to give us a tin. You throw us the high sign, and we take him right then and there.

"Watch out for that truck," he continued as I turned onto King Street. The worst slums of Honolulu were off to the left: a sea of weathered wood and mango trees and rusty corrugated roofs. "That only gets us Russell, though. We want Holt, too, so we got to wait for him to come along and take their dope back. Which means we're gonna have to let him rob you, you get right down to it."

I hadn't thought of it in exactly those terms, and they didn't make the proposition any more appealing. I felt a little better when I saw that I had a very passive role. "You're mostly there as a witness," Billy said. "Sau's done this a million times. He'll have the money. He'll do all the talking. And when Holt shows up, you just sit on your hands, don't do anything to make him think you're raising up on him. No point getting dead over this thing."

I gulped and nodded.

"We'll grab him when he starts to leave with the stuff. All you have to do is stay out of the way."

"Don't worry, I will." I slowed the car as we reached the Federal Building.

"No, no. Drive on down the road a ways. I don't want you around the office till we pull this off." He stopped me in front of a diner on King Street. "You can wait here. I gotta line everybody up, fill the boss in, get everything ready. Just sit tight."

As I watched him make a U-turn and head back toward the office, I wondered—not for the first time that afternoon—just what in the hell I'd gotten myself into.

CHAPTER 4

Ala Wai Inn, Waikiki
Saturday, September 12

She locked herself in the bathroom with the bottle, sulking alone until Tommie came looking for her and knocked. "Hurry up, Thalia," he said through the thin wood panel. "We don't want to keep everyone waiting."

She didn't open the door but told him she wasn't going, didn't feel well, wasn't up to it, some other time. Next Saturday, maybe. He brushed her objections aside and said he needed her to be there. "No" would not be an acceptable answer, she thought bitterly and took a deep pull from the bottle before opening the door.

Beatrice, now sitting outside on the front steps, had neatly laid out the green silk dress Tommie had selected for the evening. Thalia snatched it off the bed and wriggled into it. The silk slid easily over her girdle and slip as she fumed and planned further objections.

She caught him in the bathroom where, still humming, he took the drink she'd brought him. "Thank you, dear," he said, smiling at her reflection in the mirror.

"Please, Tommie. I'm just not feeling up to it this evening. Maybe next week."

"Nonsense, you'll have a fine time," he said absently, angling his head to check for shaving nicks. "Everyone will be there. Two of the skippers said they'd stop by tonight. It's a chance to make a good impression."

"You should go alone, then," she said. "You'll have more time with them."

"I am *not* going without my wife," he said sharply, and slapped his hairbrush down on the sink. "That's final. Now go show our guests some hospitality."

Shoulders slumped, she retreated. Her dark mood grew darker every moment. A few minutes later, she dragged herself into the back seat of the car, sandwiched tightly between Beatrice and Genny Branson, a Navy wife. She pouted out the window as the last of the day's sunshine vanished in the west.

Thalia cheered up slightly after they stopped to let Beatrice out of the car on King Street; a short cloudburst chased the girl with heavy drops as she ran for the overhang of a nearby building. The mood didn't last, though, and by the time they turned into the dirt parking lot by the Ala Wai Canal, she had snapped at Genny, who now icily ignored her.

Saturday nights were Navy nights at the Ala Wai Inn, a second-rate nightclub perched on the edge of Waikiki and the fringe of respectability. Every Saturday, dozens of the junior officers from Pearl Harbor's submarine fleet, back from a week at sea, gathered at the Inn with their women—eating, drinking, and dancing until after midnight. It got rowdy at the Inn on Saturday nights, and local people went somewhere else.

Thalia loathed Saturday nights, loathed the Ala Wai Inn, and loathed the officers and their women, so she did what she always did: hung back as far from all of it as she could get. Even on the other days of the week she was a little aloof, a little apart, off in a place where the people from her husband's world weren't wanted. Those around her sensed it, and they usually left her alone there.

The doorman at the Ala Wai Inn got paid to know trouble when he saw it. Joe Freitas marked the trouble going in as he chatted for a moment about boxing with her husband. He felt the chill coming off the green dress before the girl in it swept through the door he held open for her.

Even though Prohibition was in full swing, booze flowed freely in the club that night—bootleg whiskey and sugar cane rum and *okolehao*, the potent local home brew that the sailors called "oke." Everybody brought a bottle or two; almost no one planned to leave sober. One of the submarine commanders had brought an entire carton; the raw and fiery oke was tempered with fruit juice provided by the club. Thalia had two bottles of her own in her little handbag and drank her share as she moved from group to group at the tables off the dance floor or the deep booths on the upper level.

Her mood brightened again for a time as she was relaxed by food and drink, by the boisterous crowd and lively music. But she got bitchy when she drank, and she'd been drinking for hours. Before long she wasn't welcome anywhere, which suited her fine. Now she only stayed in each place long enough to cut one of the women with a catty remark about her dress, or flirt with an officer in front of his wife before moving on. She never left without firing a shot at Tommie, either, who was laughing it up with his shipmates in the only booth she pointedly avoided.

It surprised no one when, late in the evening, one of the young lieutenants, drunker than most, told her what he thought of her, nor shocked anyone when she slapped his face and lurched away.

At the front door, Freitas marked her going out again, and watched her stop in the parking lot to talk with a local boy before turning toward Waikiki. He could not remember the time, although the time would be the only thing that mattered. "Was around midnight, though," he said. "Half hour before, half hour after, maybe. Band neva' quit yet, so before then."

Nobody else saw her go, nobody missed her, and when the band stopped playing at one, everyone piled into their cars and moved their party back to Manoa. Tommie, one of the last to leave, assumed she'd gotten a ride with someone else. He phoned his house from the club, but got no answer.

Half an hour later, he found himself at another officer's house, a thoroughly drunken sailor without a wife.

When he saw Thalia again, somebody had beaten all the bitchiness right out of her. By the time she finished her story, the drunk little lieutenant was stone-cold sober.

CHAPTER 5

1305 Center Street, Kaimuki
Saturday, September 12

It was a good plan, even remarkable, when you considered the fact that Billy Wells had put it all together in the span of three hours. Naturally, it started going all to pieces as soon as we got to the address that Ernest Mori had given Sau.

My part began with another meeting at the diner where I'd been drinking coffee since Billy had left. He showed up again around eight with his scabrous informer in tow and said everything was all set. He drilled me for an hour on my role and Sau's, then packed us off to Kaimuki.

Center Street launches itself up the face of an old cinder cone, a prominent reminder of the island's volcanic origins. Short but steep, the road climbs past homes built in the 1920s for the city's growing middle class. One of these, 1305, loomed over us. A wide *lanai* faced the street above a neat lawn. I parked just below a driveway that ran alongside the house to a garage almost at the back of the property.

From my uneasy perch on the side of the volcano, we had a splendid view that stretched from Diamond Head and Waikiki past the city all the way to Pearl Harbor and beyond. It was a placid and upscale setting a light year or so away from Lau Sau's usual haunts. An occasional car rolled past and some kids played under a streetlight farther down the hill, but nobody came out of the house or stopped to talk with us.

C.T. Stevenson, our Chief, and Honolulu Sheriff Pat Gleason were following Holt and Russell. Billy was covering me, and I got a little more nervous not seeing him. Sau smoked a cigarette, ignored me, and coughed out the window. I don't know if he'd done a million of them as Billy had said, but this wasn't his first time waiting on a dope deal.

Every few minutes he swigged some codeine from a brown glass bottle. It didn't seem to do much for the cough.

Time lagged and I tried making some conversation, asking first about his travels around the Pacific, then a ropy scar on one hand—the result, he said, of a shipboard accident.

"What about your nose? When did you get that?"

Sau turned to me, his dark eyes fathomless and cold. "Man fight, he bite," he said languidly. He shrugged and looked away. "Long time past."

"Bit your nose off? No shit?"

"No shit."

I contemplated this for a minute or two. "What did you do?"

Sau looked back; the headlights of a descending car were full on his deformed face. "I keel him with my knife," he rasped, as though he was describing the weather.

I gaped at him for a long moment before he turned away, giving me a good look at his abbreviated profile.

"No shit," he said to the house on Center Street.

You might be able to think of some witty response to that line, but I couldn't think of another damned thing to say after that, so we 'keeled' the time in silence and looked at the city lights spread out below our little corner of Kaimuki.

At ten o'clock, Billy strolled up along the sidewalk, just a shadow pausing at the window of our car to ask for a match. He lit his pipe and filled us in.

"We'll give 'em a little while longer. Russell got held up," he said through a cloud of smoke. "He's actually doing some real police work. Should be anytime."

"I can't see you," I told him.

"You don't have to. What matters is, I can see you. Just don't get out of the car."

Below us, the lights in the houses winked out as the island fell asleep and the wait went on. Finally, just after eleven, a black Dodge rolled slowly down the hill. The driver's face was framed pale in the window as he passed by. Brake lights flashed as he approached the movie theater on the corner at Waialae Avenue. We'd gotten the once-over from Albert Holt. My heart pounded loud enough, I thought, to be heard over Sau's coughing.

Fifteen minutes later, a Ford touring car turned into the driveway and ground toward the garage at the rear. Within moments, a stubby man I guessed was Mori appeared at the corner of the house and motioned at us to come over to him. Sau reached for the door handle.

"You heard Billy. We're not supposed to leave the car," I whispered. "We're supposed to make them come out here."

He shrugged. "Got to go."

"Hold it. That's not the plan," I exclaimed, panicking, but I was talking to his back. "That's not the plan, damn it!" I got out of the car and followed, fighting the urge to look around for Billy.

Mori led us along the side of the house to a little apartment off the garage. We found out later that his sister worked as a domestic in the house, although she had the night off because the owners were on the mainland.

The apartment, sparsely furnished but immaculate, connected to the main house by an open door, in which Bill Russell stood as we entered.

"Eh, Bill. This my friend Sau," Mori said.

Russell scrutinized us both, giving us a hard cop's appraisal. I hoped he was seeing a *yen shee* man and his white buddy.

"I know you. I see you around, downtown," he said to Sau, who nodded. With that face, he was used to being remembered.

"I live Chinatown, long time," Sau said.

"Bill Brown," Russell said, turning to me.

"Jack Lowson," I croaked.

"So, Ernest says you off a ship."

"Uh, yeah. I'm signed on to the *Empress of Canada*."

"How long you staying here?"

"We're sailing Monday."

That was it, my three lines of the agreed-upon story. Sau was supposed to back me up on it, and he pitched in on cue.

"I know him since he small kid. We on ship together before. He *yen shee* man."

Russell just grunted, counting his options, and looked me over.

"Ernest, get over here," he finally ordered. "Go get the bag."

Mori disappeared into the main house and returned with a green muslin bag. Its contents made a metallic clunking noise as he handed the bag to Sau: the welcome sound of tin on tin. Sau reached inside and withdrew a five-tael can.

These containers were shaped almost exactly like a Prince Albert tobacco can—flat, with rounded corners and a paper label. One tael is equal to one and a third ounce, so a five-tael tin held 6.66 ounces. They were always sealed, either with wax or solder, making them difficult to open, and I peered over Sau's shoulder as he struggled with the lid. The label on the tin looked worn and water-stained; the red rooster and Chinese characters were faded to a pale brown.

"Ai!" Sau slapped the tin down on the table, then pulled a folding knife from his pocket. In one quick move, he opened it, jammed the blade through the label, and punctured the metal beneath. He worked for a minute on the hole, muttering under his breath, then withdrew the blade.

A coating of brown paste clung to the flat surface of the knife. Sau raised it to what remained of his nose, sniffing, grimacing, eyeing Russell suspiciously. Flipping the knife upside down, he took a match out of his pocket. He struck it, held it under the knife, and waved it back and forth, nearer and nearer to the blackening gum, as Russell, Mori, and I expectantly awaited the test results and leaned in closer to watch.

As the opium began to sizzle, bluish fumes curled up, filling the room with the nasty smell of burning hair. Sau blew out the match, wiped the smoking blade on his trousers, drew a long, rattling breath, and whirled suddenly on Russell.

"This shit no good!" he screamed. "You try steal!" He brandished the knife blade in Russell's surprised face. "No buy! No buy! Shit!"

To this day, I don't know who in the room was most flabbergasted by this turn of events. Probably me. I had, after all, sat in while Billy briefed Sau twice on exactly what to do and how to do it. He hadn't covered this. Sau's completely uncharacteristic burst of energy and startling departure from our script left me without any of my own memorized lines to speak, but I could see the shipwreck looming and figured I better say something to try and ward it off.

"Wait a minute," I started.

"Yeah, what the hell you talking about?" Russell, about a foot taller than Sau, got over his own surprise and glared down angrily at the informant.

"No!" Now Sau whipped around and waved his blade in my face, just a couple of inches from my nose. I backed up a step or two; the little room suddenly seemed a lot smaller. "This man crook! This shit stink! He steal you!"

"Yes, you idiot," I wanted to say. "The whole reason we're here is *because* he's a crook and trying to 'steal' me." But I froze again in horror as Sau picked up the tested can and flung it back into the bag, then thrust it at Russell. The big cop showed no inclination to take it, however, and crossed his arms on his chest as Sau dropped the bag back onto the table.

Thinking I could salvage something of the deal, I reached toward the bag, then was shocked again as the agitated informer slapped my hand away.

"You come back with better hop!" he ordered Russell. "Bring good stuff! This not real Lam Kee!" He lapsed into fevered Chinese, and punctuated the one-sided argument with the flashing blade. Though nobody else in the room understood a word of his tirade, the message came through loud and clear.

I wanted to reach over and choke his scrawny neck, but my new ally, Bill Russell, took a different tack.

"Okay, okay. I'll give you a break on the price. Fifty bucks a tin. That's a good deal in this town," he said, aiming his pitch at me.

Seeing an opening, I tried to meet him halfway. "Yeah, that does sound good. He's helping us out here," I told Sau, trying desperately to make contact with those wild maroon eyes. "We're gonna save some money."

"No!" he shrieked. "Cannot sell! Cannot even smoke this shit! No pay fifty. Not worth ten dollar!" Sau's knife glittered in the light, arcing through the air between us, and sliced my fading aspirations into pieces. Venting his outrage in a crescendo of curses, he spat on the floor and, before we could respond, charged out the side door, still chattering in Cantonese.

One of the longer and more uncomfortable silences of my young life ensued as Russell, Mori, and I contemplated the empty doorway and Sau's echo fading away into the darkness.

"So what? You want this or not?" Russell finally asked, pointing at the bag on the table.

That was a good question with an easy answer. I did want it. God knows I wanted that bag and the success it represented. Right there, close enough to touch. I wanted it as fervently, as passionately, as desperately as any hophead anywhere on the planet ever wanted two pounds of opium.

But the key to success had just hiked off into the evening trailing a sulfurous cloud of Chinese curses and carrying the $400 in official funds that I needed to pick up Bill Russell's bag of dope.

"Yes," I said sorrowfully. "But he's got the money."

Russell shrugged, and gestured Mori toward the door.

Mori obediently collected the bag. My eyes followed him as he carried my ambitions out toward their car. Russell punched the button on the light switch, leaving only the porch lamp illuminating the little room

I was so reluctant to leave. But the lights were out and it was over, and with nothing left to do, I moped dejectedly out the door.

Russell and Mori passed me in reverse on the driveway as I reached the sidewalk. The cop accelerated away in a fierce clashing of gears, slowed almost to a stop by a car parked near the corner, then sped up to take the turn. As he disappeared, the parked car started and bore down on me with headlamps flaring.

I knew it was Albert Holt, but I'll never be able to swear to it because the driver's face was below mine and shadowed by the bill of his cap. I could see one thing clearly, though; the polished brass of a police cap badge glistened for a moment in the light from the street lamp as the car cruised past, inches away. Then I stood alone in the road, mourning Billy's plan, knowing I should have saved it, when its author ambled out of the shadows between two houses, towing Sau by the collar. "Come on," he said, shoving Sau at the back door. "We got to catch up with C.T. and Gleason. They're following Holt."

We piled into the car. Billy ignored the Chinese informer's protests. "You shut up now," he told the still-agitated Sau. "I heard enough from you already. What the hell happened back there?" he asked me.

I described the fiasco on Center Street, and emphasized Sau's abrupt deviation from Billy's plan. "There wasn't anything I could do," I concluded, hoping he'd agree.

He didn't say anything; he just looked back at Sau and shook his head.

"We'll try Holt's place first. Russell probably went back to his beat."

"I'm sorry, Billy,"

"Don't sweat it, hoss." He started working on his pipe. "You're gonna find out, these things never, *ever* go on time or according to plan. No reason why yours should be the first."

When we got to Lukepane Street, we eased past the little bungalow Billy said was Holt's place. The black Dodge I'd seen twice before that night sat in the driveway.

"There's C.T.," Billy said. I stopped just beyond a cluster of men, and got out with Billy to face the boss.

"You stay here, understand?" Billy told Sau, who nodded.

The small circle of detectives that included our chief and Sheriff Gleason parted silently to admit us. While Billy didn't seem upset about the fact that his scheme had turned completely to shit, Stevenson and the sheriff weren't too happy about it. Their moods didn't improve as I told the story again.

"Goddamn it, Billy, you said he could handle this thing," Stevenson said, glaring at me. "Sounds to me like he shot it all to hell."

My heart sank further. This was my very first encounter with my new boss. I clearly hadn't made a good first impression, and he was letting me know in front of an interested audience.

"No, I think we're still okay. Let's see what we got," Billy said, turning to me. "Did you see the dope?"

"Yeah. I saw the cans. They're in a cloth bag in the car. Or were."

"Did you see Sau get the hop out?"

"He tested it right in front of me. That's what set him off."

"Russell. Did he make the offer to sell?"

"Not to start with, but then he offered to lower the price to fifty. But he," I pointed at the car with the informer in the back seat, "wasn't having any of it."

"See? We still got them," Billy told Stevenson. "Sau told me it was opium, just real bad stuff. Jack saw it, and heard the offer to sell. That's enough."

"Not Holt, though," Stevenson countered.

"We saw him at the scene," Billy argued. "And followed him here. I say we grab him, squeeze him, do the same to the other two, and see if we can find the stuff. One of 'em is bound to turn. Mori will; he's already snitching for Vice."

Nobody seemed too pleased about our limited options, but at this point, nobody had a better plan. One of the detectives, a wiry man in a pearl-gray fedora, watched me with piercing dark eyes that never left my face, then sniffed and looked away.

"Sheriff?" Stevenson prompted.

Gleason wanted it over. "Let's go," he said firmly.

The three of them, accompanied by the other detectives, went to yank Holt out of his house while I took Sau back to the office. We had a long, silent ride, and didn't get back until early Sunday morning.

CHAPTER 6

2850 Kahawai Street
Sunday, September 13

"No, please, Tommie. Don't call. I'll be all right," Thalia begged, grasping at his shirt as he turned to use the telephone on the table by the door. "It doesn't hurt that much anymore. I'm sure the doctor can't help."

Tommie, his face ashen and numb now—not from drink, but shocked to the marrow—looked at her, incredulous. "But we have to tell someone," he said. "There has to be a report." He dialed the operator, and asked for the police. Thalia retreated to the bedroom, closed the door behind her, and flung herself onto the bed. The pain in her jaw stabbed at her.

When the first police officers arrived, slouching into the living room, their hats in their hands, asking about an assault and battery, Tommie quickly set them straight. His wife had been battered, all right, but she had also been raped, he said. Something had to be done.

One of the detectives asked for the phone as the other tried to get a coherent statement from Tommie, who started to babble. His control slipped, feeling the effects of six hours of heavy drinking, and nothing sounding right.

Maybe they should talk directly with the victim, the detective said gently, as the other came back from the telephone.

Notebooks in hand, the two detectives stood over Thalia as she haltingly related the story for the second time. There had been a car, and four men. She had seen no faces, but they were Hawaiians, she was sure. The car might have been a Ford or possibly a Dodge, dark brown or black. It didn't run well, and the canvas roof flapped as if it had been torn. She couldn't remember any more. No, she hadn't seen the license plate on the car. "It was too dark," she said.

Was she certain about the men being Hawaiian? Newcomers frequently had trouble with the Islands' racial mix, lumping everyone not white into the "native" or "Hawaiian" category. She had been around, she said, and she knew the difference. "They were Hawaiian."

More police came, and Thalia told the story a third time, and then a fourth, now to a lieutenant in a pearl-gray fedora whose dark eyes followed Thalia and Tommie even as he gave instructions to his men. A patrol car, its radio turned up and blaring, pulled into the crowded front yard.

Jerry Branson, one of Tommie's shipmates, drunk and disheveled, leered out of the back window. No, Branson couldn't be involved, Tommie wearily told the lieutenant. "You heard my wife. You need to be looking for four Hawaiians," he said. Jerry had been with him for the entire night.

Branson, still clowning, left the police car and joined a growing crowd of Navy men and their wives who were all talking among themselves in a tight little circle in the street as they watched the police confer in the living room inside the open front door.

"We're going to the hospital," the lieutenant said to Tommie. "You two ride with me."

"I don't want to go," Thalia whined. "Don't make me."

"We have to go," Tommie insisted. "We have to help the police catch these monsters."

"I don't care. I'm not leaving," she wailed, her voice climbing. But Tommie hung a blanket over her shoulders and pulled her, still protesting, to the lead vehicle in a procession of police and Navy cars that stretched for two blocks down East Manoa Road.

Emergency Hospital, Miller Street
Sunday, September 13

At the Emergency Hospital, a nurse whisked Thalia into an examining room next to the entrance. "The doctor will be here in a moment," the nurse said, helping her out of her clothes and giving her a gown to wear. She did not want to be left alone, so she held her jaw and called for Tommie, who came in a moment later.

More Navy men and their wives had come down, carloads of people from the party, most of them drunk and still celebrating. She could hear the buzz of conversation outside the louvered glass window, male and female voices, talking about her, she knew. Although they kept their tones low, she could hear the excitement, the titillation, and the room spun around her.

"I can't do it, Tommie," she pleaded. "It was too dark. I can't remember anything."

"You're still in shock. You'll remember more later. You have to try."

"But what if the doctor can't… What if he doesn't believe me?" she said.

Tommie's jaw dropped. "What do you mean? Of course he'll believe you."

Her eyes slid away from his, filling with tears that she hid by staring at the floor. She didn't look up when the doctor, a harried-looking Chinese man in a white coat, came into the room and was surprised to see Tommie.

"I'm sorry, you'll have to wait in the hall, I'm afraid," the doctor said, holding the door open.

"I'll be right outside, darling." Tommie turned away.

"I'm Doctor Liu," the doctor said as Tommie left, and held out his hand. "I know you've had a rough time." He pointed at the cuts and bruises on her face. "That looks like it hurts. We'll take care of that, and I'll try to make the rest of this as easy as possible, okay?"

Thalia nodded.

"Do you have any questions before we get started? I'll probably have quite a few myself."

She didn't look up at him, but kicked one heel against the leg of the examining table. "How can you tell? I mean, how can you know if someone…had sex?" she asked.

"Sure. Good question. It can be hard to tell for someone who's married, and especially if they've borne a child. Do you have any children?"

"We lost the baby. I miscarried. In March."

"I'm sorry. Well, I'll look for injuries, of course, but for traces of semen, too. The assault, there was more than one person involved, the detective said."

"Four," Thalia muttered to the floor.

"They'll have probably left some trace. Unless you showered or douched afterward. That would make it more difficult."

Thalia looked up sharply. "I did take a shower when I got home," she quickly agreed. "And I douched. Twice. I didn't want… I didn't know…"

"That's a very common reaction. Very normal for girls in your situation. We'll just have to do the best we can. Could you lie down on your back?"

When the examination was over, Tommie came back in, and he had news. The police had found suspects, had already identified the car that her attackers were driving. He had the license number, he said, and gave it to her. She could hear the radio in the police car parked outside broadcasting the same number; the dispatcher was telling police officers to be on the lookout for the car and those in it, four men suspected of being involved in an assault on a woman. When the men were caught, the police would want her to identify them, Tommie told her.

"But I can't," she protested. "I've told you already, I couldn't see their faces."

"Maybe you'll know them by their voices, then," he persisted. "Just try."

"I don't want to!" she exclaimed, starting to cry. "I just want to forget all about it."

Tommie set his jaw and shook his head. "It's too late for that," he said firmly, and left the room to look for the doctor.

She sat on the table and wept as the nurse came in with a syringe full of morphine for the pain in her face.

In the corridor outside, Dr. Liu met with Tommie. One of the detectives stepped closer to listen. "Her jaw's broken on the left side," the doctor explained. "She'll have to be x-rayed and the jaw wired. She has some other bruising, but I don't think anything else is broken, although a couple of teeth are loose. She won't need stitching for any of the cuts."

"What about the other thing. The assault," Tommie demanded.

"Rape?" the doctor clarified, then shrugged. "It's possible. There's a couple of bruises, minor, on her legs. She's a married woman, and she said she miscarried recently. She could have been assaulted and not show signs of it, and she bathed afterward." He shook his head. "If there was any evidence of sexual activity, that probably eliminated it.

"But…" The doctor looked Tommie in the eye. "I can tell you for certain that somebody hit her in the face pretty hard, and the worst of it came from a ring." Tommie glanced down at his hands and saw the heavy blue and gold Naval Academy class ring on his right ring finger. "Like that one," the doctor added, his brown eyes emotionless.

2850 Kahawai Street
Sunday, September 13

Doctors made house calls in those days, and in this house, the doctor was puzzled. Commander John Porter watched his patient cross the room to the ringing telephone, then pick it up and talk animatedly with the caller, obviously another Navy wife.

She hung up the phone and turned to him, smiling brightly. "She's going to come by with a basket. I've had five calls already this morning," she said. "Tommie's captain and his wife are coming over, and the squadron commander phoned."

Porter saw her flop onto the bed, then grimace as the vibration rippled through her broken jaw.

"I hope you're going to give me something for the pain," she said. "My face hurts. Whatever they gave me at the hospital last night made me feel all fuzzy and warm, but it wore off too quickly. I've only slept for an hour, but I had the best dream."

Porter, who felt like he might be dreaming himself, told the girl who claimed to have been beaten and gang-raped less than eight hours earlier, to lie face up on the bed, and began his examination. Twenty minutes later, he piled the last of his things into the black bag, snapped it shut, and left a written prescription and vial of tablets on the shelf next to the bed. She rubbed the spots on her shoulder where he had injected the morphine. "I'm going to call Queen's Hospital later today," he told her. "I think you should be admitted for the injuries to your jaw. I'll call you this afternoon to let you know the details."

"That's nice," Thalia said dreamily. "I can't wait. Will you do something about my face? I hope there's something for the pain."

Porter squinted at her. "Maybe I'd better speak to Tommie and let him fill you in," he said slowly. "I've given you some tablets and a prescription, and you had the injections. You'll need to see another man about your jaw. And Doctor Askins at Pearl. He's a dentist. You're probably going to lose one or two teeth."

"Oh, yes," she murmured, tilting her head to look at the pills and the paper. "Another man," she said. "That will be fine. I'm feeling sleepy now. I think I'll have a nap."

Porter shook his head, picked up his bag, opened the door, and found Tommie standing outside. He gave the little lieutenant a brief summary of his findings. "Are you all right, son? You look all in."

"I'll be okay, sir," Tommie assured him. "I haven't slept since…"

"Of course. Well, Mrs. Massie seems to be holding up. Her spirits seem quite…bright. I gave her some morphine. Odd. The first injection didn't seem to have any effect, so I gave her a second. I think that relieved the pain. She should be able to sleep now. I've left some medication and prescriptions for more. That should handle it."

"Thank God." Tommie drew a shaking hand across his forehead. "But the police are coming down this afternoon. I'll have to wake her. They want her to identify the men who did this to her." His face haggard, he turned to Porter. "I just want it to be normal again. That probably can't happen."

"It may take some time," the doctor said.

"Sir. Is she…damaged? I mean, from the assault. The rape?" Tommie asked, his voice almost a whisper.

Porter shook his head. "No, I don't see any kind of injuries like that. When was the miscarriage again?"

"In March. We lost the baby in March."

"Right. Not that long ago. She should be fine."

"I'm worried about children. We want to try again."

"I don't see any reason why not. She's been knocked around a bit, but she's young. She'll heal."

"Thank you, doctor." Tommie shook Porter's hand, and turned with him toward the front door. "I'm going to try and get a little sleep before the police get here. Before it all starts up again."

2850 Kahawai Street
Sunday, September 13

Soaring on morphine's wings, Thalia sailed out of a cloud into bright sunshine. She arced past cotton candy columns in pastel pink on a whisper of wind. Ahead of her, just above the tops of the clouds, a tiny golden object danced and sparkled in the sunlight. She hurried after it, but a voice tugged at her, and the despised words dragged her back toward the gray earth below her clouds.

"Darling. Sweetheart. Angel, I need you to wake up." She felt the pressure on her arm pulling her down, calling her back to the other world.

Her flight slowed, and she sank out of the dream. One final golden spark flashed just out of reach as the darkness closed in. The words grated on her, each one a blow to her fractured jaw.

"Please, darling," he spoke again, and she heard herself moan in despair.

Back in the room, she saw Tommie's face above her. Concern wrinkled his young forehead as sunshine filled the room.

She smiled, although pain throbbed and nausea rose in her when she tried to swallow. He touched her cheek where the bruising flushed purple. Then he sat next to her on the bed, stroking her face and holding her hand for several minutes while she climbed back to consciousness.

"How long have I been asleep?" she asked, looking around the room. Sunlight poured through the open windows.

"Only a couple of hours. I'm sorry, but the police are here. They've brought the men who…" He couldn't finish.

"Attacked me," she said, and saw him flinch. "They've caught someone else?" She sounded shocked. Then the last of the morphine mist drifted away, and she recalled last night's trip from the hospital to the police station. They'd asked her questions and more questions; she'd had to tell her story yet again before stern-faced detectives who had jotted down copious notes. She remembered they'd brought in a local boy, a rather short young Japanese man wearing a leather jacket. His face was a blur in her memory, as was whatever she'd said when the detectives had brought him in.

She glanced toward the closed door and then back at Tommie. "And you're sure they're the right ones?"

It was an odd question, he would remember afterward, but for Tommie Massie, whose world had been turned upside down and emptied out overnight, all he had for her was reassurance. He patted her hand gently and let the question pass. "They seem very certain. The police, I mean. They've caught four already; they're still looking for the last one."

"Four of them," she repeated slowly, trying to remember how many people she'd told Tommie and the police were in the car.

Now Tommie looked at the closed door and dropped his voice. "You said they were all in the car together. Do you remember the license number? They may ask again."

"What? No. I'm sorry, Tommie. I… My head."

"That's all right. I remember it." He recited the number broadcast to the police at the hospital hours earlier, but she still hung back.

"Must I look at them, then? Again, I mean? It was very dark. Out there, where it happened."

"I told them, but they want you to try."

"My face hurts terribly. I need some more medicine."

"In a few minutes, dearest. I'll make sure of it. Doctor Porter left some pills."

He helped her to rise, though she swayed and almost fell against him; her head spun and the nausea flowed in waves. He helped her to dress in a Hawaiian muumuu, long-sleeved and floor-length, he found in the closet. With it, he covered every inch of her he could. She leaned on his arm, and reluctantly turned with him to the door.

Seven people waited in the little living room, and four more were on the porch just outside. Tired-looking detectives in rumpled suits stepped aside to leave four men—boys, really—standing, literally, she would giggle later, on the carpet in the center of the room. One of them, big, dark and Hawaiian, looked curiously at her as the others studied the scuffed work shoes they shuffled on her rug.

She let Tommie lead her to a chair he had moved into a corner. He stood beside her, one hand on her shoulder. The last of her clouds had fled now; the pain throbbed, nudging her fully alert. They had darkened the room, pulling shut the curtains, recreating the scene she had described.

One of the detectives—she recognized him as the captain in charge who had taken her statement at the police station the night before—stepped to her chair and spoke softly with a Scottish burr. "Take your time, and be certain, miss," he said. "Ask anything you like."

She leaned to one side to look around him, all four boys staring at her now.

"My glasses, where are they?"

Tommie handed them to her, and she held them to her eyes, critically examining the boys as an entomologist might scrutinize some foreign species of bug. She saw four local men, all out of their teens and all from working-class homes in Palama, on the rough western edge of Honolulu. She did not know their names, of course, but the detectives remarked later that she seemed oddly at ease in the presence of these four strangers standing there in the middle of her home. The same men, she told them, who had gang-raped her only twelve hours earlier.

"Do they call you 'Bull'?" she asked, pointing the glasses at the biggest, who gazed at her in confusion.

"Huh?" he asked, and looked for help to one of the detectives. The man only shrugged.

"Bull," she said more confidently. "One of the others called you Bull."

It was a gesture she remembered for the rest of her life, one small movement that changed everything for her. She raised her arm, later thinking it might have belonged to someone else, seeing her hand in clear focus, the finger extended like the barrel of a rifle, leveled at the blurry form at the other end of the room.

"Yes. Yes, he's the one," she said, and a thrill ran through her as raw fear swept away the boy's confusion. "He hit me. And the other thing. He did it. I remember now."

Holding the glasses to her eyes, she saw the others gaping at their friend—saw wonder and confusion there, too, but no fear, yet, for the shorter Japanese boy who was shaking his head in disbelief.

She had a vague recollection of him from the captain's office, hours before. They had brought him into the room at the police station, stood him in front of her, challenged him to look at her face, to see what he had done. Her hand came up again, and the finger stopped in the middle of his chest. "And him. I remember his jacket. He drove the car."

"No!" The boy gaped at her, disbelieving. "No, you can't. You're crazy, lady!"

But it was as if someone had suddenly yanked open a curtain, the light shining, and she knew now that she could, and she nodded. "I'm quite certain. It's all very clear. Oh, yes."

She rose and reached for her husband's arm as he glared at the four boys. "I'm tired now, Tommie. I'm going to bed. And I need my medicine."

"What about the other two, miss?" the Scottish captain asked.

"What about them? They were there, weren't they? I told you what they did. What they all did."

At the door she turned back and watched the detectives chivying the four toward the front door. All of them were protesting; the short Japanese lad was twisting his head around to stare at her, his mouth slack with disbelief. It hurt her jaw to do it, but she smiled anyway. Not counting the time she spent in her dreams, for the first time in months—maybe years—Thalia Massie was full of warmth, bathing in a glow that cut through all the pain and bitterness.

She climbed back into her bed, lay back on the stacked pillows, and smiled up at the ceiling. They'd listened to her this time.

She thought again about her dream, and about the fear on the boys' faces. She closed her eyes, and stretched out her hand. The treasure was close enough now to touch, even without the morphine.

CHAPTER 7

Federal Building, Room 213
Monday, September 14

They collared Holt after midnight at his door and led him to the car in handcuffs. His wife clutched at him and wailed. He wasn't impressed, and although they worked on him for an hour, he didn't say anything except that he wanted a lawyer.

They gave up on Holt, and the Sheriff had the police dispatcher call Russell, who was still on duty, over to the Federal Building. The Sheriff started by taking his badge and showing him Holt's, which was already on the table.

Billy told him Holt had already squealed—just a little white lie—and Russell gave them the whole scam. He took them to his house on Waiola Street where they had 61 tins stashed, all in the same terrible shape. Some had no labels at all, while the paper on the rest was water-soaked and barely legible. Ten of them were in a green muslin bag, and one of those had a hole the exact shape of Sau's pocketknife in it.

Altogether, we'd bagged over twenty-five pounds of smoking opium, a decent haul for 1931. The chemist at the Territorial Board of Health tested the tins, and confirmed Sau's appraisal. It was opium, just not very good. "This shit stink," ultimately proved to be a fairly accurate description.

Russell made a full statement detailing their past escapades and gave a complete account of that evening's events. He certainly made our case a lot easier, vindicating Billy's resolve to arrest them and salvaging that shipwreck I hadn't been experienced or sharp enough to avoid.

Before Holt and Russell got their day in court, though, Billy had to clean up some loose ends. This meant dealing with George Soon, whose raid had been the first step on the path to the two crooked cops. Soon's hearing was scheduled for Monday morning, and Billy said he wanted me to see how the process worked.

"First time in court?" Billy asked with a smile as we walked across to the Territorial Courthouse on Monday morning.

I nodded, and took in the swarm of people behind the statue of King Kamehameha I in front of the courthouse. "There's an awful lot of people here."

"Monday. Busiest day of the week. Everybody who got arrested since Friday has to be here Monday morning." Billy lit his pipe and waded into the crowd, shaking hands with police officers, attorneys, and just about everybody else he ran into. I tagged along, looking for Kam, who was supposed to be waiting for us at the courtroom.

When I finally saw him, leaning against the wall next to the door, he waved and started over, making his way through a group of Navy men in white uniforms filing inside.

"Billy, I gotta run. Some stuff came up."

"What is it? What are all these Navy people here for?"

"That's it. The rape thing. Chief wants us to go interview some of the boys' friends in Kalihi, see if they heard any bragging."

"What rape thing? Who got raped?" Billy demanded.

"You never heard?"

"Hell no, I've been busy. I was wondering where you've been."

"Some Navy lady. Says five local boys took her down to the beach, gangbanged her Saturday night. We picked them up yesterday."

"Holy smokes. No wonder it's so packed."

"Yeah. They're pretty upset. So, can you take the hearing on Soon?"

Billy frowned. "Sure, but that means Jack's got to give your testimony."

Kam clapped me on the shoulder, a gentle blow that knocked me into a Navy lieutenant. "No problem, then. Brother can handle it."

Kam thanked us and hurried off. Billy shook his head. "That explains why we only had the Sheriff and a couple of lieutenants to help us last night. Everybody else was busy on this other deal. Okay, you clear on what you're gonna do?"

I was not at all clear, and it must have showed. "Um. You want me to testify for Kam?"

"Yeah. It's simple. This is just a hearing to see if there was probable cause to arrest Soon and hold him. Hearsay's admissible. You just tell the judge you saw Sau and Akana going into Soon's place, and Kam told you he recognized them both."

"That's it?"

"Nothing to it. Not even any cross-exam. Take you five minutes."

"Okay. I can do that."

"Good. Here's my report from the other night. Make sure you've got the times right. That's all there is to it."

While I was thinking this over, Billy turned to let the prosecuting attorney know about the change of plans, bumping into a Navy man.

"Excuse me," he said. "Oh, Lieutenant Butler…Commander, I guess it is now. I heard you got promoted. Congratulations. You got one of your boys on the docket this morning?"

The commander took his offered hand. "Billy. No, we're down here for the rape case. It's a Navy wife."

"I just heard."

"That's her husband over there." Butler indicated a little lieutenant surrounded by four or five other young officers. "The one who looks like he hasn't slept in a week."

"His wife all right?" Billy asked.

Butler grimaced. "I don't know. She was banged up pretty badly."

"I guess the cops got the ones who did it, huh? That was fast work."

"Hmmm. Very efficient. We'll see, I suppose."

"Yeah. Hey, Jack, let me introduce you. Lieutenant Commander Carl Butler…Jack Mather, our new man. The commander's second-in-command with the shore patrol here in town. Not for long, though. I guess the Navy'll be shipping you out pretty soon, then? You got any idea where?"

I stood and shook hands with Butler.

"Sea duty," Butler said. "A year or two on shore, especially someplace as nice as Hawaii, the Navy wants you back on a ship. I hope it's bigger than my last one. That gunboat wasn't much bigger than a bathtub but at least the Yangtze counted as the sea. I won't be leaving right away, though. This mess," he gestured at the crowd of Navy men starting to file into the courtroom, "is going to cause an uproar. It already has out at Pearl. The admiral's really upset."

"Well, we don't want the brass mad. That's never good for anybody," Billy said, motioning for me to follow the two of them into court.

Our case was the first one up. Billy testified about the arrest and then it was my turn on the stand. Like he'd said, it didn't take long. After the clerk swore me in, the prosecutor asked what happened the night we raided George Soon.

"Yes sir, we were waiting on the roof next door, Inspector Kam and I. We hadn't been there very long when I saw three people come out of the apartment. Two men and a woman. A few minutes later, two men came up the stairs and went in. The Inspector told me that one of them was Sammy Akana, and the other one was Lau Sau. He said they were both opium addicts."

The judge asked me if Kam had been right about the two men's identities, and I said he had been. He asked me to point out George Soon, which I did, and that was it.

Soon got released on bail and the clerk called another case, leaving me to suppose there wasn't much to this job. This false sense of confidence lasted until the preliminary hearing for Holt and Russell, and then it vanished forever in a half-day grilling by two determined defense attorneys, while waves of hostility radiated off the two cops and their supporters.

CHAPTER 8

2850 Kahawai Street
Monday, September 14

On Monday morning, Tommie again nudged Thalia awake, this time after a full night's sleep for both of them. When she'd gathered enough consciousness to understand him, he explained that he had to go down to the courthouse. "There's a hearing for those five hoodlums," he said. "I need to be there."

"That's fine," she nodded. "Can you stop and fill Doctor Porter's prescription for me on the way?" She pointed to the paper on the side table.

He tucked the prescription in his pocket and told her the doctor was making arrangements for her to check in at Queen's Hospital, probably the next day. He would call, Tommie assured her just as the phone rang in the hallway. "That may be him now."

"You'd better go," she urged. "Send Beatrice in, please, Tommie. I need to tell her what to do while I'm gone."

He left the room and spoke briefly with his submarine's commander. When he hung up, he found Bea Nakamura in the kitchen.

"Beatrice, could you see what Mrs. Massie wants? I'm going down to town. I should be back by lunchtime."

When her maid came into the room, Thalia nodded shortly. "Get me a glass of water, please, Beatrice," she ordered, the words only slightly slurred.

She waited until the girl returned to open the bottle of white tablets, then shook one into her hand and swallowed it with a gulp of water.

"Good," she said. "I'm going to go into the hospital tomorrow, and the doctor thinks they may keep me for a few days. When I get back, I'm not going to be able to do much around the house. I'll still be under a doctor's care. If I need something, I expect you to come quickly and to do as you're told. Do you understand me?"

"Yes, missus."

Thalia leaned forward, her teeth clenched, her tone cold, each word a little slap. "You'd better not forget your place again, girl. I don't want to have to tell Lieutenant Massie that we need a better Jap because this one didn't work out." She glanced toward the living room, and heard his car start in the driveway. "There's a big depression now. And you'll never work in another officer's house again if I tell them you're no good." She leaned back against the pillows, speaking brightly in a chirpy imitation of the local pidgin English. "You no likee me do that, do you?"

Beatrice shook her head, and stared at the floor through hot tears. She squeezed her eyes tightly shut and one drop fell, landing with an inky little splash on her faded black shoe.

Thalia smiled. "No. No likee. You may go now, Beatrice."

CHAPTER 9

Federal Building, Room 213
Tuesday, September 15

"Why are you here?"

I'd been asking myself the same question for almost a week now, but it sure sounded worse coming from across District Supervisor Clarence T. Stevenson's desk. And he didn't have an answer, either.

"I mean, I've been pestering the commisioner for more people; we're short four men. And this is what he sends me? A goddamn bookkeeper?"

Stevenson, a big, rangy lawyer born in Missouri and raised in California, had been a Treasury agent since 1919 and served all over the country. When he got upset, the Ozarks came back strong into his voice. I could hear them plainly now.

"What am I gonna do with you? According to this..." He slapped my personnel file, which was open on his desk. "You're fresh out of college. Never been a peace officer, no pharmacy training, no law school. I'm trying to add this up, but all the numbers keep coming out zero."

"I'm willing to learn. I..." I began.

"No! Whoever it was hired you sent you down here to do one thing and by God, that's what you're gonna do. I don't care if they did give you a gun and a badge, all you're gonna need is a pencil and one of those damned green eyeshades. I hope you brought one with you, 'cause we sure as hell don't have any laying around."

"I'll do the best I can."

"You bet you will. I don't want any more screw-ups. You just get on those records and if, by some miracle, you actually manage to trap the White Friend, you sing out and let a real agent know." He closed the personnel file with a bang, and tossed it into the pile of other papers that teetered on his desktop. "Get to it," he growled. "I'm going out."

Knowing precisely where I stood, I retreated to my desk. From his corner by the window, Billy stopped his laborious typing to throw me a quick wink. I'd had only one report to write, a short chronicle of the Center Street disaster. He had evidence to process—arrest reports, statements, and affidavits—so he'd be up until midnight or later.

This was not unusual; I came to find out that Billy seldom left work before ten or eleven, and sometimes worked straight through to the following morning. "There's always something to do," he'd say. Today, I wasn't helping with questions about the White Friend.

"No, no, ask away," he told me. "Talking to you'll take my mind off this bullshit paperwork."

I wanted to get an idea about where my best starting point would be, where in the files the answers might be hiding. "So when did this opium hui get started?"

"Oh, man." Billy looked up at the ceiling. "About eighty years ago."

"Eighty... *What?*"

"Eighty years. That's how long these guys or somebody like 'em's been running opium down here. This particular bunch—the hui—got started in the late '20s, probably around '28, and they just beat us to death, bringing in opium by the crate."

"What happened? How did you finally catch them?"

"Luck. Oh, we knew they were out there. Word kept coming in from the birds, plus we were up to our asses in Lam Kee hop for about four years. Every time we turned around, we were banging on the red rooster. Between us and Customs, we got pretty close a couple times early on, but never could put it all together until last year."

"So, who were they?"

"They were all Chinese, of course. And the source was in Macao. The Portuguese run a legal opium monopoly in Macao, and Lam Kee's their brand. The two ringleaders on this end were a couple of businessmen, big in Chinatown, Chin Sheu and William Lee. Lee was the biggest shareholder. That's how a hui works; everybody buys shares in the load, and they get back that percentage of the profits. It spreads the risk around so nobody takes too big a bath if something bad happens."

"Like the load gets seized."

"Exactly. There were ten shareholders. Lee's number one, but Chin Sheu had a good-sized piece, and he's the one with the import-export business here in town they're using as a front, so he's a key player. He's got a business down on Pauahi Street, the Yee Lung Tai Company—imports from China, Hong Kong, and Macao. Chinese food, herbs, dried fruit. Legitimate stuff, but it makes a good cover for an opium shipment."

Billy got up from his report forms and stretched, then walked over to my desk and hefted one of the boxes from the floor to the desktop.

"We got about five boxes on this deal—some ours, some from Customs. Even Internal Revenue took a crack at them. There's more in the cabinet, but this is the one with the case reports. You want to, you can go through it, see if anything gets you excited."

Already excited, I opened the box and found it filled with brown folders—ranks of silent soldiers waiting to give their reports.

The story began a year before in a most unlikely place: a box of dried fruit. In 1930, you got to Hawaii like I had, by steamship. One of the shipping lines servicing Honolulu that year was the Dollar Line, whose steamer *President Madison* arrived at Pier 7 on the next to last day in August.

What caught the Customs inspector's eye in the consignment of dried fruit off the *Madison* was not the commodity itself, but the paperwork. Of the sixty-nine crates in the shipment, twelve were consigned to the Yee Lung Tai Company.

That one business should get twelve crates was not especially noteworthy; what was unusual was the numbers—none of which were in sequence—specifically identifying twelve boxes. If all sixty-nine were identical in size and content, the inspector wondered, why did Mr. Chin Sheu, the manager of Yee Lung Tai, want those particular twelve?

While a Chinese teamster waited to collect the shipment, the inspector went to find out. He broke open a crate and dug into one of the large canisters of fruit. A moment later, he held up a tin of Lam Kee hop, then yelled for help as the teamster dropped his handcart and headed for the door.

The first crate held 275 tins of opium. Help arrived to empty the remaining eleven wooden boxes of a total of 3,339 tins. The entire shipment contained an astonishing 1,391 pounds of opium. As far as I know, this was the largest opium seizure ever in Hawaii—or anywhere else in America, for that matter.

I stopped to calculate the value of the haul at the going rate of $70 per tin, then leaned back in my chair and softly whistled.

Billy looked up from his paperwork.

"It was worth $234,000," I said.

"Told you. That's some serious money," he agreed.

Customs referred the case to the U.S Attorney, and then disaster struck; all four of the people indicted won acquittal in a jury trial.

"I thought they had them stone cold," I protested. "Chin's name was right there on the shipment, and the teamster tried to run when they found the opium."

"Nah, you never want to bet on what a jury's gonna do," he shrugged. "This bunch had their doubts about whether Chin knew there was dope in the boxes."

"What about the teamster? He sure acted like he knew."

"They chalked it up to nerves. He said he got scared when all those white people were staring at him." Billy held up a hand to stifle my protest. "I know. But they had a good lawyer. Bill Heen. Part Chinese, former judge, very smart."

"I'll bet Customs was fit to be tied."

"Three quarters of a ton of opium and nobody to pin it on? That's a bet you'd win," he chuckled.

"But we didn't just give up."

"Hell, no. Chin might have been out of it, but we knew he was just the tip of that iceberg." He shoved his papers aside and stood up. "Enough of this shit for a while. Let's get something to eat."

"Okay, but one thing, Billy. If Chin beat the rap, why couldn't he just go right back to peddling? I mean, his organization's still there, and the White Friend."

"This is a smart bunch, no doubt about it. They moved a lot of hop in here, who knows how many shipments. We just got that one off the *Madison*. And they're smart enough to know better than to trust somebody we're watching. They cut Chin off cold. That's the end of that hui, and Chin's career in the dope business too."

Pauahi Street
Thursday, September 24

"So Chin's out," I said as we walked down King Street. "But the rest of the hui's still out there. There should still be some of the Lam Kee opium on the street."

"Nope. You need to keep reading. We burned those guys, top to bottom. Nailed everybody from the source in Macao to the runners here in town. Got the accountant, got Lee, got all but one."

"The White Friend."

"That's him. Reason you're here. The key to the whole scheme, and we've got no clues about who he is."

"We must know something."

"We know he's white. There was that one guy who talked about seeing a uniform. But almost all the Customs and Immigration boys are white. Some of the guards on the piers. All the ships' officers and most of the crews that come in here, for that matter."

"Who actually knew him? I mean, there must've been somebody in the hui who dealt with him directly."

"Who knew him? That's the second big question, all right. Only one man we know of knew. Lee, but he's off doing eleven years in Atlanta and won't say. So, if you can figure it out, you get to be a big hero."

I still very much wanted to be a big hero, so I sifted the information I had so far as we wove through the lunchtime crowd on Hotel Street, working our way into Chinatown. On the busy sidewalks we paused in front of this business or that restaurant, where Billy explained how they and their owners fit into Honolulu's opium market, giving me a guided tour of an underworld I had never known existed.

When we got back to the office that afternoon, I had a head full of information and a better idea of how the dope business really worked. I started by flipping through my notepad to a fresh page and wrote "White Friend" in neat little letters across the top.

If my bookkeeping experience had taught me anything, it was that a pile of records would, if properly parsed, lead to a positive conclusion, an absolute and unequivocal bottom line. Not this pile, however. At the end of that day, my pad bore exactly two lines. At the end of the month, they would still be there, all alone.

Trying to find the man who Billy said "beat us real bad" meant navigating my way through a sea of unfamiliar names and events now years in the past, all described on forms from three different Treasury agencies. Statements translated from Cantonese told of successful opium shipments and treachery among the conspirators. Witnesses disagreed on dates or amounts. Shipping manifests led to dummy companies and false fronts. Nobody who was asked could or would supply the name of the white man who had somehow helped import tons of opium into Honolulu.

As the days wore on, I focused on the comforting financial records in the files. These islands of familiarity possessed a reassuring certitude the other evidence could not possibly provide.

Billy and Stevenson had gotten the actual books of the hui itself, brought in by one of the conspirators. They'd subpoenaed more evidence from the local banks. Using them together, I followed in their path, tracing the profits of the conspiracy to banks in Honolulu and Hong Kong, and to the pockets of men as far away as Macao.

None of it, however, pointed at anybody's white friend. Frustrated, lost, and sure I'd missed something important, I asked Billy for some help one afternoon near the end of September.

"I've got some questions about the Chinese records," I told him, and pulled out some of the ledgers.

"What about them?"

"I've been all through them. I mean, I understand them; they're very complete. But these things, they're really incriminating."

"So?"

"So why would they keep evidence like that? It seems so stupid."

Billy laughed. "You're an accountant, right?"

"I guess, yeah." Stevenson had made himself clear that this wasn't necessarily a good thing. I found myself hoping Billy didn't feel the same way.

"What's the whole point of accounting? Not to lose anything, right? Good accountant, he makes his books come out down to the penny. Banks, businesses, they can't afford to lose a nickel or nobody would ever trust them again."

"Yeah, but that's the banks. What they're doing is all legit."

"The same thing holds for the crooks. Even more so. Look, if you get into a dispute with the bank over some money you think they lost, you're going to get a lawyer and take them to court, right?"

"Sure."

"Not an opium smuggler. These boys, if they get in some pissing match over who owes who, or who paid who, one of 'em's liable to take a hatchet in the forehead. So they all keep records—the ones that can write, anyway."

He had a point, and you didn't have to be an accountant to appreciate the special need for accuracy in a situation where your life depended on it.

"Okay, that makes sense," I said. "And I'm not complaining. Their books are really helpful."

"Yeah, losing somebody else's money's a capital crime for these guys. It's in one of the oaths they take."

"Oaths?"

"Thirty-six of 'em. The Triad societies all have the same ones. They can't cheat each other, and they're supposed to keep things secret. Stuff like that. Break the rules, and you're killed with 'five thunderbolts' or a 'myriad of swords.'"

"The opium hui people were Triad, you think?" I had read about the secret societies whose members dominated gambling, prostitution, and above all, the opium trade in the Chinese community.

"Absolutely. Triads run the show from here to Macao. Top to bottom."

I knew from the reports that Billy had gotten Chin to cooperate; his statements were in my files. "But Chin talked," I pointed out. "If he was Triad too, he must've been breaking one of the oaths."

Billy leaned back in his chair, recalling the case that had taken him across the Pacific. "Yeah. You'd think so. But revenge must be more powerful than fear sometimes. Here's Chin, who's just beat the rap on the biggest case in history, and you'd think he'd be all happy. Everybody's sitting pretty.

"Only it didn't work out that way for Chin. Look at it from his perspective: he's lost the money he had in the shipment, and his buddies have cut him out of the dope business for good. Thanks to the trial, everybody in Honolulu thinks he's a kingpin opium peddler, but he isn't even that anymore." Billy puffed for a minute on the pipe, and watched the smoke eddy up to the ceiling.

"So," he went on, "he spends four months in jail, his regular business is about ruined, and he's got all these bills for his lawyer. He might not look it, but he's a wreck. And he's real pissed off at those other guys because they—Lee mostly—didn't help him. And now Chin's got to face all that disgrace, the criminal charges, all by himself. And that stigma didn't go away when he got acquitted. Very big loss of face, you know."

I nodded, understanding.

"One of those Triad oaths says a member has to pay the lawyer's fees, got to support the family of a brother who gets arrested. Don't do that and you get the 'death from five thunderbolts,' whatever the hell that is," Billy shrugged. "But Lee didn't do shit, and all the thunderbolts land on Chin. Meanwhile, ol' Lee's sitting pretty, got the connections to put the next load together, and he's still got the White Friend to help out. Chin loses every way you slice it."

The phone rang. Billy took it and jotted a couple of notes before turning back to me.

"Now Chin wants revenge, and he knows just who to see to get it. I get the call, go see him and his wife, Alice, who's even more pissed at Lee than he is. First thing he does, he hands over all the books the hui kept. Turns out he's the treasurer for the bunch, so he knows a lot more than he originally let on." He laughed. "Now I got the key player, all that dope, and these books, which are an absolute gold mine. My cup runneth over."

My copies of the hui records confirmed Billy's opinion of their importance. They were simply devastating, recording the dates of shipments, amounts of opium imported, money spent, and profits allocated. The names of the conspirators were all listed, along with their income from the shares they held.

"But there's nothing in there you could use to identify the White Friend," I said.

"That's true," Billy admitted as he leaned back, hands behind his head, still relishing the victory. "The books showed where the money was paid out—the $53,000—but even Chin didn't know who the cash actually went to; Lee kept that secret. Lee's not talking. Back to the starting line."

"Dead ends," I said.

"Yep. Ran out of leads, ran out of time, passed this stuff off to the tax boys and now you. Still, we did pretty good. I sure would like to find that white sonofabitch, though. Especially if he's a Customs man." He ratcheted an evidence form into the typewriter. "I think he's gone, though."

"I hope not," I said. "I'd like to do something to make Mr. Stevenson happy."

"He's not a bad man to work for," Billy shrugged. "But he'd like to get out of here, get back to the mainland. A little closer to the power."

"He doesn't think much of me."

"Get the White Friend for him. Everybody from the Commissioner on down wants to nail that bastard. You nab the White Friend, it's a big feather in C.T.'s cap. He'll be your friend for life."

I thought about the police department's reaction to Holt's and Russell's arrest, and my well-known role in it. I'd gotten the cold shoulder and worse since the day the two crooked cops had gotten pinched. "I could use a friend. The whole Honolulu police force hates me."

Billy laughed. "Don't sell yourself short. The boys on the Vice squad couldn't be happier. They'd probably vote for you for mayor."

I had my doubts, but went back to the records with renewed purpose. And when, a little after one o'clock, we turned the lights off and called it a night, I was tired, but comfortably back in a place I understood. A snug corner of the world where my neatly penciled numbers fit precisely into columns that perfectly divided one fact from another. Where a mistake could be rubbed out in a moment with an eraser, and did not mean an encounter with a walking dead man's knife blade.

For the moment, at least, I was safely out of the whirlwind of Billy Wells's opium war.

CHAPTER 10

2850 Kahawai Street
Friday, September 25

He was going to be an admiral one day. He'd been telling people that for years, even before he left Kentucky for the Naval Academy. He, Lieutenant Thomas H. Massie, was going to fly planes, command ships, marry well, and have three or four children—Navy brats who would look up to him when he became famous.

In the end, though, Tommie got none of it but the fame, and that he'd have been better off without.

As September dragged to its conclusion, he was Thalia's nurse. The doctors had wired her broken jaw shut; he and Beatrice fixed all of her food so she could take it on a spoon or drink it through a straw. She had even started using the straw in her medicine bottles, and the engineering officer in him fretted that she couldn't possibly measure a proper dose. She never seemed to take too much, though, and the empty bottles piled up in a box under the kitchen sink.

Sometimes they went together to one of the doctors' offices, or to pick up more of her medicine. But even after she got back from the hospital she slept a lot, not getting out of bed until after noon every day, while Beatrice flitted through the house, cleaning silently, going to the store and walking the dog.

When Thalia was awake, she had little to do but read and nag at the maid over this trifle or that. Tommie had given her a small hand bell to ring when she wanted something, and he or Beatrice answered its call twenty times every day, bringing soup, pudding, water, or her medicine, day and night. After three days of that, all his friends told him he looked worse than she did.

Whenever she slept, he stayed in the room with her, reading a book or a *Time* magazine from a stack piled on the floor by her bed. He kept a pair of wire cutters at hand in case she vomited into the wire gag. Except when he answered the bell, he avoided her when she was awake. She thought she knew why, and she waited for two weeks after that night to find out for certain.

That Friday when she stirred, he rose quietly to go, rolling his magazine in his hands.

"Have they confessed yet?" she asked. Her teeth might have been mechanically clenched, but her mouth worked fine; the cuts had healed and her speech was clear. He had no trouble making out her words although he would say, years afterward, that he never really understood her.

"I'm sorry, darling, what?"

"Those boys. The ones who raped me. Have they confessed?"

He shook his head. "No. I talked with the Attorney General yesterday. They're still in jail, but they haven't admitted anything."

She watched him in his discomfort, and her blue eyes glittered. "I wonder why? I thought they were proud of what they did."

"Don't think about it, angel. It only distresses you."

"I think about it all the time. I can't forget. I even dream about it. Those five, climbing on top of me, one after another, rutting on me like… like wild animals."

A ragged sigh was torn from his chest, and he stood motionless at the foot of her bed. She went on as if she hadn't noticed. "Do you think they're talking about it down at the jail? I do. I can almost hear them sometimes, telling all their colored friends about the innocent white girl they ruined forever. I imagine the vulgar details will be all over Honolulu by now. All the darkies in town, knowing about me, about the things only you and I were supposed to share."

"Darling…"

She sat upright in the bed. "I swear, Tommie," she pleaded. "I tried to fight, tried to save myself, I did. But they were so big and so strong. Like black jungle animals, feeding on my body."

Tommie was rigid and staring now, and drained of all color; he might have been in the throes of a seizure. His mouth worked, but no words came out.

"You weren't there, of course," she said forgivingly, easing herself back onto the pillow. "You were back at the party with your friends, and I was all alone." She picked at the edge of her blanket, her eyes downcast and hooded. "I tried thinking of you when they were on top of me. It was easier with the two Jap boys—they're small, like you. But the others, with their jungle smells and their big, dark muscles; big black bucks, that's how I think of them. So different from you. So much…bigger, and stronger."

There was a tearing sound, and another that might have been a man being strangled, and Tommie turned, blindly fleeing the chamber.

Not long after her surgery, she'd discovered that by humming certain notes, she could create pleasing vibrations in the wires holding her jaw in place. Now, purring a little Hawaiian tune, she climbed out from under her blanket, and knelt on the foot of the bed.

Where Tommie had been a moment before, the magazine lay twisted into a grotesque shape, torn almost in two. Still humming happily, she eased herself back under the covers. She thought she might give it five minutes, then ring for him again.

CHAPTER 11

Canal Cafe, Waikiki
Friday, September 25

"If you're going to be a snitch," Billy said, "you've got to have something to spill *and* a reason to spill it. We'll give George three to five good reasons."

When things settled down after those first hectic days, Billy went back to George Soon and gave him some good reasons why he wanted to be a stool pigeon—"three to five" being the number of years he wouldn't have to spend in Leavenworth if he played ball. George made the right decision, and a couple of weeks after the raid, Billy took me out with him to meet our newest informer. But it was a rocky beginning.

The plain fact was that at his level of the drug trade, George Soon didn't know all that much. Billy summed it up disgustedly, "This boy is gonna need a goddamn stepladder to get up to street level."

George knew enough to throw Kam a few dens, an oke cooker or two, and some neighborhood speakeasies. He also gave up a friend who'd been pimping his eleven- and twelve-year old daughters. Kam's own girls were roughly that age. With blood in his eyes, he pronounced Soon no longer completely worthless, and added that he wouldn't try to catch him again for at least one full month.

We met George Soon at the Canal Cafe, a restaurant about a block from the Ala Wai Inn in Waikiki. Billy did the questioning while I took notes and tried to keep up with the strange names the two of them tossed about.

"Let's start with Sammy Akana," Billy said, wincing as Soon polluted some perfectly good green tea with four or five teaspoons of sugar.

Like most addicts, Soon had a mad sweet tooth. Also like most serious pipers, he had few real teeth left. He smiled ingratiatingly at us, baring two snaggled front teeth seemingly placed at random in his mouth. "I get three tin from him, not even one week ago. The one you folks get was from him, too. You folks gonna pinch him again?"

"We'll see. He ever say where he was getting his stuff from?"

"I think maybe Los Angeles. Couple year back, he working on a ship? Cops grab him up there. He get friends there, too."

"You know who he's selling to, besides you?"

Soon considered this question over his tea. "One Chinaman from Kauai, I think, maybe. Four or five from here. Akana get one good line, plenty buyers." Soon named some names. "Was dry for a long time, but now he get plenty."

"Anybody else dealing? Someplace you can go for a tin?"

"Joe Kubey get sometimes. He no trust me, but."

"We just indicted him again. He probably doesn't trust anybody right now." Billy grimaced. "But if you find out he's got any for sure, let me know."

"People say get plenty hop in town right now."

"What about some dens? You know any going?"

Soon slurped his tea and smacked his lips with obvious satisfaction. "I know couple joints still running. I tell Kam. They floating places all over."

The public holds a popular image, spread mostly by dumb-ass novelists or newspapermen who had never been in one, of an opium den as an elaborate subterranean hideout with rows of luxurious beds, incense, and hanging lanterns, all idyllic and sensual. Don't believe everything you read. I certainly never saw anything like the lavish dens described in the dime novels.

The joints we hit mostly looked like George Soon's: squalid little sepulchres tucked behind businesses, above shops, or off tenement hallways. They were invariably small, fetid, and filthy. The proprietors sealed the doors and windows against the escape of any fumes that might cause the cops to come sniffing around. This reduced air circulation to nothing. They were badly lit, though this seemed to be the smokers' preference, and the operators invested very little in furnishings or other comforts.

In the average Chinatown den, the hopheads smoked off the same pipe as consumptives and lepers, or anybody else who had the price of a *yen pock*. TB took a heavy toll, and the flu epidemic in 1918 cut through them like a scythe. Any romantic illusions you might have cherished about the exotic allure of opium vanished pretty damned quick in the face of a working den's rank reality.

In Honolulu, those working dens still clustered in Chinatown and some of the hard-case neighborhoods nearby. Being a den operator himself, Soon had full access to the goings-on at this level of the traffic. He told Billy about some of the places and their keepers, all of whom were Chinese and all well-known police characters, while I recorded the names, places, and associations.

Billy finally brought the subject back to Sammy Akana, Soon's connection for the opium we'd recovered. "You think you could get another tin from him?"

"Sure. He sell me. I gonna need seventy dollar, but…"

"I'll give you the money, that ain't a problem. Better yet, if you can find out when he's dropping off to his other customers, we can bag him and the buyers. Then we won't have to spend anything."

"Like the Kauai one? He tell me when that one come down."

"Okay. Yeah, you find out when the guy on Kauai's picking up, and we'll take 'em both off. We do it right, they'll never know it was you."

"I try find out."

"Let me know by tomorrow, okay? 'Cause I'm going to Hilo for a couple days."

"Sure." George nodded enthusiastically and bared those two choppers again.

"What about croakers? You know any script doctors?" The main purpose of Billy's trip was to check on doctors and pharmacies on the Big Island.

"Down Hilo way, supposed to be one haole doctor. He usually good for some M."

"Morphine, huh?" Billy said. "You know who he is?"

Soon examined the restaurant's ceiling. "I get his name for you. Up here, get that new Korean doc, Kim, downtown. Union Street. He give a script, you get a good line."

We talked for a few more minutes, all of us enjoying the food, but the meat of the conference had been eaten.

"Rick! Hey!" Billy suddenly called, waving to a well-dressed man who had just gotten up from another booth and was headed outside. He tossed some bills on the table. "Those two are for you, George. You folks finish up. I gotta talk to this guy." He left the restaurant, and stepped onto the street corner. I could still see him through the plate glass window, but I guessed he wasn't coming back before we were ready to leave.

"What about haoles? You know any white people involved with opium?" My mission was fresh in my mind, so I was thinking of the big Chinese opium syndicate and their mysterious White Friend.

"Now and then get some haoles go in the joints. Short timers." Soon poured himself some more tea, then reached for the sugar bowl. "Sailors, that kind. Mostly, they chase the dragon a couple times and they outta there."

He was describing smokers, which was not what I had in mind. "No, I'm talking about somebody big, somebody with money."

He noisily lapped up some sugared tea and pondered it. "Get that one *haole* girl. Her boyfriend always get cash," he said hopefully. I guessed he thought the new boy might be good for another buck. A line on the White Friend would be worth more than a dollar, but this didn't sound promising.

"Who is she?"

"Oh, man. I don't even know her name. But she come up to my place plenty times."

"Is she a prostitute?" Most of Honolulu's working girls were white, and quite a few were opium users.

"Nah, respectable lady, *yen shee quoy*, but."

The term he used in this oxymoron meant "opium devil," generally reserved for serious, long-time dope fiends—confirmed addicts like George Soon himself.

"A 'respectable' yen shee quoy? How's that possible?"

"Got the ring." He pointed to the finger a wedding band would be on. "Got a car. Plenty cash. Oh, yeah, she can do five, ten pills a night, easy. Pretty cute gal. Likes her hop, that one."

"When was the last time you saw her?"

"I dunno. Before you folks get me. Plus, too, you don't believe me, ask Sammy Akana. He know her good."

"Was she up there the night we arrested you? With Akana and another man?"

"Could be. Her boyfriend brung her around before. Sammy, too."

"I think I saw her that night. That was her boyfriend, huh? Is he a white man?"

"Shit, yeah."

"Was he smoking, the time you saw him?"

Soon shook his head. "Nah. Just her doing it. He look like a cop to me. I never trust him. I keep one eye on him the whole time, but he just watch her."

A cop. Great. That would be all I needed, to catch another Honolulu cop, this one hanging around an opium den. That would seal it with the department, but I didn't think the White Friend was a Honolulu police officer and he definitely wasn't a haole woman, however respectable. I told Soon we were done for now and watched him leave on nervous junkie legs, already anticipating his next bowl, with two bucks in his pocket to crank-start the pipe dream.

Billy was in a good mood in the car. "Rick Biven and I were in France together. Driving ambulances. Signed up with a bunch of other local boys and we all got shipped out together." He started the now-familiar process of getting his briar going as I drove.

"That was a helluva thing. They tell you you're supposed to be over there, saving the world, ending all wars or some noble bullshit. You know what it all boils down to? Trying to find a dry place to sleep and keep from getting blown up. 'Course we had the ambulances, so staying dry wasn't too big a deal."

There was a long pause as we both watched the city roll by. Billy was thinking about a long-ago war in a faraway place, and I was focused on one closer to home.

"Do yourself a favor, hoss," he said at last. "You get a chance to go to war? Skip it. It ain't all it's cracked up to be."

"Yeah, I'll remember that," I promised, and promptly forgot. "Hey, Billy, listen to what George just told me." I ran down Soon's story about the respectable haole girl, her opium habit, and the white boyfriend who'd taken her to George's den.

"It's possible," he mused. "All kinds of people get the yen." He puffed contentedly on the pipe, confident of the imperfection of human nature that guaranteed us lifetime employment.

"George said her boyfriend looked like a cop."

"Hey, could be he's doing it, too. Wouldn't be the first time that happened, either. Had some agents go that way. I knew a couple of Marines in China, picked up the habit in Shanghai and brought it home with them, and there were doughboys who came back hooked on morphine. God bless 'em. All kinds of people get the yen," he repeated.

"Don't you think we should check this girl out?"

Billy looked surprised. "Why? You catch her, all you got is another smoker."

"That's right, she's a dope fiend."

"They're a dime a dozen. The Vice boys get twenty or thirty a month, most of 'em repeaters. I'm amazed they ain't got her yet, if she's really doing it. Anyway, first time, no judge is gonna do anything to her."

"We could talk to her. If she's as respectable as George says, she's sure got a hell of a lot to lose. And there's Sammy Akana. George said he knew her, too."

"I'm more interested in him, but we'll probably get him through George."

"I was just thinking, what if the guy taking her to the den is the White Friend? What if it's her husband?"

Billy looked at me, pipe smoke drifting toward the window. "That'd be kind of a long shot, wouldn't it?"

I thought about the records piled all over my desk, none of which had yielded a single clue. "I haven't got much else, to tell you the truth."

"Hmmm," he said through the smoke. "The White Friend. Who the hell is this guy?"

Federal Building, Room 213
Tuesday, September 29

I spent most of Saturday and all of Monday checking out the information George Soon had given us at the café. Like most of the names George dropped, Sammy Akana already had his own card in our filing cabinet and more. A folder full of reports from our Los Angeles office described Honolulu resident Samuel M. Akana, a ship's steward on the *SS Golden Star*, who had been pinched going into L.A. with 170 tins of opium in 1929. This had earned him a twelve-month stretch in a federal penitentiary and another entry on a rap sheet already crowded with previous arrests in Honolulu. Interestingly, he'd been arrested with another crewmember, an assistant purser named Donald Haig. A British subject from Hong Kong, Haig had somehow managed to avoid conviction in the case, leaving Akana to take the fall alone.

The photo from the Los Angeles collar showed two sorrowful-looking characters dressed in their white uniforms, standing next to a desk piled high with five-tael opium tins. Even in the grainy black-and-white picture, you could clearly see the rooster labels on the tins.

And the red chicken had come home to Honolulu to roost. A worried Inspector Kam had called the office on Monday afternoon to let us know his Vice squad had picked up a couple of Lam Kee hop tins on Saturday, and ten more that morning.

"The load must've come in," he said on the phone. "Every yen shee man in Honolulu's talking about it."

Stevenson canceled Billy's trip to Hilo so they could follow up the leads the informants were feeding us. He didn't need any help from his new agent, however.

"What are you working on these days?" he asked, not getting too close to the stacks of files on my desk; they were a paper contagion he made a point of avoiding.

"I've got the bank records for everybody who worked for Customs and Immigration in 1929 and '30," I replied.

"Found anything yet?"

"No sir. At least, nobody living way above their means. They don't get paid that much; it would probably show."

"Waste of time," he sniffed. "Forget that crap. Get me a list of all the arrivals from the Far East for the last two weeks. Maybe we can figure out which ship all this shit came in on. Track it back from there."

This took about fifteen minutes, and toward the end of the day I asked Stevenson if I could take the picture of Haig and Akana over to the Hotel Street souvenir shop where George Soon was nominally employed, keeping his probation officer happy. "I'll do it on my way home. Haig's white. Maybe he's the same one that was at the den that night."

"You get those shipping schedules yet?"

"Yes sir." I got my notes off the desk. "The *President Lincoln* got in on the tenth from Tokyo, the *Taiyo Maru* on the twelfth. Those were the only liners this month. They both started in Hong Kong, and stopped in Shanghai and Yokohama on the way. A cargo ship, *SS Hanover*, stopped here last Sunday. She was coming from Hong Kong. The only other one was an army transport, the *Meigs*. She got into Pearl on Monday, coming from Manila and Shanghai before that."

"So all of them started out in Hong Kong?"

"Except for the army ship."

"Yeah." Stevenson thought about it for a minute. "It'd be a huge pain in the ass," he said finally. "But what else have you got going? Here's what I want you to do. First thing tomorrow, go down to Customs, get all the records for all the shipments on those three ships, and bring them back here. Then check those against all the companies we got in your boxes there. Maybe there'll be a match." He stood up, looking satisfied. "That should keep you busy for a month or two."

"Yes, sir. What about the picture?"

"Sure." He waved at me like he was brushing away a particularly annoying insect. "Show the picture. How can you mess that up?"

I didn't know it then, but the correct answer was, "You could get pushed in front of a bus."

King Street and Nuuanu Avenue
Tuesday, September 29

At the corner of King and Nuuanu, I waited in a crush of other pedestrians to cross busy King Street, which was alive with traffic in the afternoon rush hour. The hand hit me in the small of the back, a hard shove that carried me off the curb and into the lane of traffic. I almost fell, but caught just enough of my balance to stumble forward. Those two long staggers saved my life. A green city bus, brakes screaming and tires smoking, shuddered past just inches from my left shoulder. The driver's eyes were wide above the "HRT" diamond and the big silver bumper.

I finally lost my balance, and fell to one knee on the center line as the riveted metal side of the bus ground to a halt next to me. As his passengers picked themselves up off the floor, the driver leaned out his window and peered down at the front tire, obviously expecting to see what was left of me protruding from under his bus.

When he looked back and saw me climbing to my feet, he worked his mouth without sound for a few seconds before babbling in a high-pitched and incoherent mixture of curses and questions that boiled down to, "What in the hell do you think you're doing?"

I had no satisfactory answer, so I walked shakily to the other side of the street past the drivers who stopped and stared, and turned back toward the office.

Billy and Stevenson were still there, wrapping up the day's work, when I pushed through the door.

"You're back pretty fast," Billy said. "What'd he say? We get lucky?" Then he squinted, checking out my torn pants and the look somebody has on their face five minutes after they've had a too-close encounter with mass transit.

"What the hell happened to you?"

Stevenson looked up sharply from behind his own pile of paperwork, silently taking in my shaky explanation. I concluded with the observation that I hadn't seen the person who'd tried to kill me.

"I swear to God, you are the biggest screw-up I've ever seen, and that's saying a bit," Stevenson marveled. "I send you downtown to show somebody a goddamn picture and you almost get yourself run over by a bus."

"Somebody pushed me. I'm telling you. I felt it. I can still feel it."

"Right. We've had a real problem with that sort of shit lately. I've been reading all about it in the Honolulu papers. 'Wave of Bookkeeper Murders Continues.'" He gave a short bark that might have been a laugh, stood up, and turned to Billy. "Talk to him. Explain why he ain't important enough to waste energy on trying to kill him."

Billy hadn't said anything during the boss's rant. He looked at me and shrugged, but Stevenson wasn't finished until the sentence had been pronounced, and now he delivered it.

"No more picture shows. No more roping. Just you and your paper palace. And the best part is, unless some assassin can figure out how to get a city bus up here to the second floor, you should be as safe as if you were in church." He grinned at Billy and headed home.

When the door closed behind him, I spun to face Billy, who held up both hands. "No need. If you say it happened, then it did. You got any idea why somebody would want to pull a stunt like that? That'd be the big question."

I'd been thinking about it in my half-stunned walk back. "It's got to be the cops. They hate me for Holt and Russell. I haven't done anything else since I've been here except go through this paper."

"Whoa, now. Don't be saying that to C.T., or anybody else for that matter. Did you see anybody you recognized?"

"No. I had my back to the crowd. There were lots of people waiting to cross. And after, the bus was between me and the sidewalk. It could've been anybody." Just hearing myself, I understood how foolish I sounded. "Ah, Billy..."

"Never mind. I'll go down there and talk to some of the cops. Have Kam feel them out. Maybe it's my fault. Maybe I misjudged this thing. They're a tight bunch. Half of 'em are related to each other."

I hung my head, and picked at the hole in the knee of my trousers.

"You just go home now. I got some stuff to wrap up. And Jack?"

I looked up. He wasn't smiling. "We're gonna be up to our asses in Lam Kee. I need you to catch this bastard." He jerked his thumb at the White Friend's boxes. "You be careful crossing the street."

CHAPTER 12

2850 Kahawai Street
Thursday, October 15

It had been Tommie's idea to bring Grace to Hawaii, and he did it over Thalia's objections. Thalia didn't hate her mother, exactly; she'd just never found any good use for her, and the feeling was mutual. Grace Fortescue hadn't been around much while her daughters were growing up. There had always been some cause or another that kept her too busy to raise the three girls.

Their father had showed even less interest in his daughters and stayed away from all of them, so the girls had grown up free and wild, either at a family estate on Long Island or the mansion in Washington, D.C. Unburdened by any effective adult supervision, Thalia had been driving the family car at age twelve, driving it drunk at fourteen, and had earned a thorough, extensive, and first-hand knowledge of sex by the time she'd married at sixteen.

That marriage in Washington's National Cathedral and a move five thousand miles away had taken Grace more or less permanently out of Thalia's picture, which was okay with both of them, since it had freed Grace for her crusades and left Thalia equally free to do just what she wanted. Tommie's telegram changed all that, and two weeks later, Grace charged into town trailing four carts piled with luggage and her youngest daughter, Helene.

Grace was a prominent member of the Washington and Long Island social scenes, so she always did things properly—like releasing a proper announcement to the local press before the ship docked. It let Honolulu know that Grace Hubbard Bell Fortescue, of the Washington, D.C., Hubbards and the Alexander Graham Bell Bells, wife of Granville

Fortescue, cousin and Rough Rider confidante of Theodore Roosevelt, arrived Tuesday aboard the *SS Malolo* to visit her daughter Thalia, wife of U.S. Navy Lieutenant Thomas H. Massie.

Grace came at the proper time, too, because Tommie had reached the end of his rope. Thalia pouted for days after he sent the telegram, and even before that she barely spoke to him other than to make some new request. He needed help and Grace didn't disappoint; she arrived on the Matson liner a month after the assault.

With Grace in charge, Tommie could return to his submarine and his naval duties, gratefully leaving someone else to answer Thalia's little bell. Grace threw that in the trash the second time she heard it. She'd campaigned once for physical education in women's colleges, and bluntly told Thalia she would recover more quickly if she got up and about. And did more work around the house.

Thalia despaired for a day, but it only took her another twenty-four hours to come up with a use for her mother after all. It started in the kitchen with a conversation at noon—normally breakfast time for Thalia—one that began with another nagging from Grace about the late hour and the condition of the house.

"I'm just not feeling well this morning, Mother."

"I shouldn't wonder. Lazing about in bed until all hours."

"No," Thalia said, laying her head on the table. "These last few days, I've been nauseous every morning. It goes away later, though."

A vast stillness penetrated every corner of the kitchen, the two girls and their mother locked for a moment in a frozen tableau. "Have you ever heard of a pregnant silence?" Thalia laughingly told an acquaintance later.

"My God," Grace finally breathed. "Is it possible?"

"Is what possible?" Thalia raised up and asked innocently.

The rest of the day was a whirl of doctors' visits and examinations, of appointments made and whispered conferences between Grace and various others. Thalia was shunted aside as Grace took command, but she observed all of these interactions quietly and carefully. She knew her mother: Once Grace got good and wound up and ready to go, once she'd worked herself into a really proper lather, she would need only the sound of the starting gun to launch her on her latest crusade.

Thalia listened most of the afternoon for her cue, and when she was sure she'd heard it, she pulled the trigger.

"Mother," she said in the car on the way back to Manoa. "If I'm pregnant…"

"It will be taken care of, dear."

"I'm so glad. I can't bear the thought of one of those, those…things growing inside me."

"A D&C is a routine procedure, dear. There's no risk, and it would end any pregnancy. You don't have to worry."

"But that's not all. I worry about the others, too."

"What others, Thalia? What are you talking about?"

"Oh, Mother, can't you see? Those creatures ruined me. I can never be the same. It's too late for me, but what about all the other white girls? All the Navy women are alone when their men are at sea. There are hundreds of us here. Thousands, maybe. And now that those beasts have a taste for white meat…"

There was a deadly silence in the Massie car as it trundled up Punahou Street toward Manoa. Grace was momentarily speechless; Helene kept looking back and forth between the two in the front seat.

"Well, no white woman is safe," Thalia shrugged. "They can ravage anyone they choose. Who will protect us, Mother?" she finished on a plaintive note, putting as much doubt and fear in it as she could, hoping she'd read the signs correctly.

"You're not to give it another thought, Thalia," Grace vowed, her jaw set and her blue eyes shining. "Mommy's here."

CHAPTER 13

Hotel Street
Tuesday, November 10

All of October passed and some of November, too, and I didn't come close to catching the White Friend or anybody else. Most of the time I had the office to myself; Billy and Stevenson spent their days tracking the red rooster that now seemed to be everywhere.

In late October, Stevenson had captured the ringleaders of a group smuggling opium from Honolulu to Kauai by nabbing a trunk full of Lam Kee hop at the ferry pier. He'd taken the steamer over to Kauai to wrap up the loose ends, once more leaving Billy in charge of the office and me.

The piles of shipping manifests and bills of lading dwindled, along with my hope of ever finding the man behind our troubles.

One Tuesday morning I reluctantly told Billy the well was dry. "I don't think anything's going to come of any of this stuff," I said.

"Yeah, C.T. figured. But you never know."

"Did you ever show Akana's picture to George Soon?" I asked.

"Nope, I never did. The only thing worthwhile he had was Akana, and he said a couple of days after your bus deal that Sammy'd left for the mainland. I didn't waste any more time on George after that."

"Would you mind if I took it over there?"

"Sure, go see him. I haven't been by there lately. Only…"

"I know. I'll look both ways."

I found Soon at the pretend job he held to satisfy his probation officer. The shop, which catered to servicemen and thrill-seeking tourists, was a hole-in-the-wall sandwiched between a couple of bars. Soon's cousin/employer waved him to the front as soon as I walked in.

I laid the photograph down on a glass case that held a collection of postcards, all of Polynesian or Asian girls wearing grass skirts and flower leis and nothing else.

"Sammy Akana," George said immediately, picking up the picture. "Hoo, hoo, he don't look too happy, yeah?" He flashed both front teeth in a misery-loves-company sneer. "You guys catch him already?"

"No, this is from before. I wanted to ask you if this guy here…" I pointed to Donald Haig. "Was he the haole man in your place the night we got you?"

He didn't hesitate. "Nah. I never seen that one before. He get arrested with Sammy?"

"This is from the time in Los Angeles."

"Yeah, I told you I heard about that one before. Sammy end up in some bad place, some jail island. He all the time cold."

"McNeil Island," I interjected. "In Washington. He got a year."

"Whatever," he shrugged. "Too long. I thought you was here about the other one," he said, handing the picture back.

"What other one?"

"The girl I told you about. The haole yen shee quoy."

"No. But what about her?"

"She stay in the papers."

"She got arrested?"

"Nah, nah. She the one say those boys rape her."

This tidbit, casually delivered, hit me like a fist, and the first picture that came into my mind was that of the worn-out looking naval officer at the Territorial Courthouse that Monday in September. Stories about the crime filled the local papers every day, and the information that the little lieutenant's wife was something less than the model of purity and innocence that the reporters portrayed came as shock. The trial was scheduled to start shortly and, judging from the lurid and breathless reporting, all five of the hoodlums were headed for a long spell in Oahu Prison.

"Wait a minute. You're saying the Ala Moana victim is a dope fiend?"

"Ala Moana? I guess, yeah." He looked puzzled. "I told you, she get the yen."

"This can't be real. How is that possible?"

"Whatever. You can believe 'em or not, but I know it's her. My cousin…" He jerked his thumb at the back of the store. "He knows one of the boys they arrest."

I was still having a hard time grasping the concept, but I pushed her aside for later. "What about Akana? Have you seen him lately?"

"Nah. Billy told me, call if I seen him, but I never. He ain't been around practically since you folks catch me. I hear…" He leaned in conspiratorially. "He go up to L.A. Probably knew you was coming. I ain't seen her since around then, either."

"Didn't you say Akana knew this girl?"

"For sure. He the one brung her and her boyfriend around the first time."

"I thought you said she was married. The girl who got raped is married to a Navy man."

"Could be her husband, I dunno."

"The one that looked like a cop."

"Yeah. Or could be an Army-Navy guy. Something like that."

When I left the shop, Donald Haig was off the hook for the time being. Sammy Akana was still missing. And I had a couple of questions about a respectable lady in an opium den.

Police Headquarters
Wednesday, November 11

The answer to one question was Thalia Hubbard Massie. After a few hours in the library and a couple of phone calls, I knew a little about this woman whose story had turned Hawaii on its ear. Thalia was just twenty years old, married to a Pearl Harbor submariner, and she lived with her husband, Thomas, at 2850 Kahawai Street in Manoa, less than a mile from my parents' home. Nothing in the newspapers even hinted at any opium connection to the "refined" and "upright" Mrs. Massie.

By midnight, I had gone as far as I could go without talking to someone. Since it was too late for that, I went home, going out of my way to cruise past Thalia Massie's little cottage. The houses on Kahawai Street slept peacefully under a light rain as I rolled by 2850. In my imagination it looked deserted and vaguely sinister.

I woke up thinking about Soon's story. The thing *sounded* right to me, but I couldn't figure out how to prove it. I also had to ask whether I should even be trying. I was fairly certain that Stevenson and Billy were ultimately going to tell me to pass the information off to the Honolulu police.

But they weren't around this morning. Stevenson was still on Kauai, and Billy was out in the country, checking information about a peddler on the other side of the island. He planned to leave for Hilo the next day on the trip he'd postponed in September, and wouldn't be back in town for a week. I was uncomfortably on my own, and one other thing bothered me on the way to the office: the nagging thought that this rape case was not only bigger than a couple of dirty cops and an opium den—it was much hotter, too.

Heat practically radiated from the two big local papers, since both spoke loudly for the haole business interests who ran them and everything else in Honolulu. The Navy, they reminded everyone frequently, with hundreds of other dependent wives in the Territory, wanted swift justice. Translated, this meant conviction and imprisonment, if not death, for the men Thalia Massie had accused. Both papers competed to describe how high the "lust-sodden beasts" should be hanged.

Local politicians facing tremendous pressure passed it right on down to the cops investigating the case. Everyone had an interest, and everyone had an opinion. All things considered, you had better believe I was thinking hard about sticking my nose into that meat grinder.

I dithered alone with these thoughts for a couple of hours that morning, fretting about the various possibilities and their probable outcomes. I kept coming back to the cold fact that George Soon was an informer, and I was obligated to verify his credibility in the event we wanted to use him to make some dope cases. So far, everything else he'd told us checked out, and that just left the rape victim and no other good reasons to stall.

The Honolulu police had just moved back into their renovated station on Merchant Street, five or six blocks from the Federal Building. The work hadn't been finished when I opened the door marked "Detectives" at the top of the stairs. I found a big room full of scarred wooden desks and telephone lines draped from the ceiling, empty except for a wiry man in a dark blue suit seated at a desk in the far corner, looking every bit as tough as his reputation. A pearl-gray fedora sat on the desk by his left hand.

Detective Lieutenant John Jardine was already a fixture in Honolulu in 1931. He ran the night shift and had been there to arrest Albert Holt. He was a brooding, silent presence taking everything in as he stood in the background that night, watching from under that fedora while C.T. and Sheriff Gleason led the charge.

I came to know Jardine fairly well over the next couple of years, but I never got over the feeling that his dark brown eyes could spear you like a bug on a pin. He spotted me right off and followed my approach without any sign of welcome or even recognition.

I offered my hand. "I'm Jack Mather from the Bureau of Narcotics."

He considered the extended hand, then took it briefly. "The secret agent Billy used for Holt and Russell. Punahou School. Folks live in Manoa. I remember. You got some nerve, coming up here." He said the last in the same tone you might use to answer a stranger's request for the time.

For reasons of my own, I hadn't really advertised my local ties, though Kam obviously knew about them. Detective Jardine must have done some checking of his own, and found a place for me in his mental card file. He didn't seem exactly overjoyed to see me again.

"Look, about those two, I just did what they told me. My job, I mean."

"You apologizing, Punahou?"

"Er, no. Not exactly."

"Good. No need. They had it coming, dumb bastards. Crooks like that, they make all policemen look bad. I might not've handled it the same way, but your way worked." He gestured to a chair. "What can the Honolulu police do for you today, Punahou?"

I had already decided, in the infinite ignorance of my youth, that I was going to try to keep as much as possible about my informant and his information a secret from the Honolulu cops. I hadn't counted on trying to pull this off against somebody as astute as Jardine, but I was in too deep to quit, so I bulled ahead.

"I'm doing some follow-up on a guy named Sammy Akana. I was wondering whether you had any information about prior criminal activity or whatever."

"Prior criminal activity. Like, his rap sheet?" He leaned back, and the chair groaned skeptically.

"No, we've got that. I was thinking more of associations. People he might be buying from or selling to."

Jardine looked at me for what seemed like forever. "That's Inspector Kam. He handles Vice," he finally said, reluctantly stating the obvious.

"Right. Sure. I did talk to him, uh, about Akana."

Jardine didn't say anything. I was starting to sweat.

"So I guess I should wait for Kam to come in, huh?"

"That would probably be best." Jardine folded his hands on his desk and waited. "You want me to have the dispatcher tell him to come in the next time he calls?" he finally asked.

"No, no. If he doesn't come back in ten or fifteen minutes, I'll just get together with him later."

Jardine grunted, and reached for the folder he'd been reading when I came in. The ceiling fans hummed and his chair creaked in the quiet as

I tried to think of some way to work this debacle of a conversation back around to my original question, still unasked.

As we sat in silence, Jardine reading and me stewing, a young Chinese officer in plainclothes came into the room through a side door. He took a seat at a desk against the wall, and began examining a pile of photographs with a magnifying glass.

Swell, I thought, that's what this little talk needs: a witness.

"I guess you're getting ready for the big trial next week." This was the best I could come up with.

Jardine looked up from his file. "You got something you wanna ask me about the Ala Moana case, Punahou?"

"No, not really. I heard you folks had it wrapped up tight."

"Tight enough. They're good for it, those five."

"Are any of them into hop?"

He thought that one over carefully without ever taking his dark eyes off my face. "Nah, that never came up. We talked to almost everybody they know. We'd likely have heard."

"What about the victim. Are there rumors about her?"

Jardine nodded and set down his file, as though this was the question he had been anticipating all afternoon. "That she's a dope fiend? I heard that. I heard a lot of other stuff, too. Whole buncha people in this town, they think the boys are getting blamed for something they never did. They think maybe this girl's hiding something."

He leaned back in his chair, and the wood protested again. "Let's see. I heard she was screwing a beach boy. People are saying her husband caught her with some other Navy man, the same one we picked up that night by her house. They say her husband broke her jaw. I heard the other Navy boy broke it. I hear a lotta things. Sammy Akana's name even came up. People talk. But you know what, Punahou? You don't want to believe everything you hear."

He delivered the last part with emphasis, and came forward in the creaky chair. I had the very distinct feeling that his little caveat was more than simply good advice for a rookie investigator. Maybe it was a warning to somebody thinking about poaching on John Jardine's territory.

"You're right about that. Well, I'm going to head back. Let Inspector Kam know I stopped by, will you?"

"Sure. But let me ask you something now, Punahou. You look like a haole, and you're from an old-time haole family. You go to the big haole school, go to a mainland college. Got a federal job with other haoles, father works for Walter Dillingham. Right?"

"I guess so."

"So how come you're poking around this thing when every other haole on the island doesn't want anything but those boys' asses?"

"I told you, I don't care about it, one way or the other."

He gave me one last long, penetrating look. "Yeah, maybe. And maybe you're not as haole as you look."

He picked up his file again, and I left with as much dignity as I could. The little Chinese cop ignored his photos to watch me go.

Okay, I thought as I escaped down the stairs, I made a total ass of myself, and I don't know a damn thing more than when I started.

I'd gotten one thing, though. I *was* thinking about poaching in Jardine's territory, and I'd been warned.

CHAPTER 14

Federal Building, Room 213
Thursday November 12

That had been an utter disaster. Although I had, in all probability, persuaded one of Honolulu's best detectives that I was a meddling idiot, I was no closer to catching Thalia Massie in an opium den. Worse, a widening circle of people was aware of my interest, and I had an eight o'clock appointment to make it even wider.

My meeting was with Will Moore, the Assistant U.S. Attorney on the Holt and Russell trial, on the docket for the end of November. The Justice Department offices were one floor up, overlooking the Territorial Courthouse next door. Come Monday, Moore could look out his window on the participants in the Ala Moana rape trial—ranks of police, witnesses, jurors, and lawyers, and maybe a young lady who my informer said was a dope fiend.

Moore arrived early and stayed late, like most of the agents who brought cases to him. He'd been in the office for a couple of years and worked his way up to what passed for the big leagues in Honolulu by handling the opium hui prosecution for Billy the year before.

"Hey, Jack. What can I do for you?"

"I've got an informer problem I need some help on."

Moore appeared suddenly concerned. "Not that guy from the Holt and Russell thing? Billy was worried about him."

"No, no, Sau's okay, as far as I know. It's another one. This one has something that might tie into a major crime. It's opium related, sort of, but I'm just not sure how to handle it."

"Who has jurisdiction? Not Treasury?"

"No. Honolulu. It's not even Federal."

"We can help them out if you think the information's worth it. I know we've done it before. What's the crime?"

I hesitated a moment. "It's the Ala Moana case. The stoolie says the witness—the victim—is an opium smoker. He's seen her in a den." The words seemed to float across the room, and landed on Moore's desk with an almost audible impact.

He looked surprised, then picked up a pencil and twirled it in his fingers without speaking. "You'd better give me the details," he suggested, and pulled a notepad to the center of the desk.

"That's just it. There aren't any details." I ran down the essentials of Soon's statement, leaving out his name and how he had come to be a stool pigeon. This didn't take long.

Moore listened attentively, took notes, and asked a couple of questions. When he put the pencil down, I thought he was going to chew me out for going off half-cocked or give me grief for listening to wild tales. But what he finally said was, "Sandy! Hey, come in here a minute, will you?"

I twisted around in my chair and saw the United States Attorney back into the open doorway. Sanford Ballard Dole Wood had held the top Federal law enforcement post in Hawaii for several years. He was about 30 years old and a fellow Punahou alum. He had a pleasant round face, and carried a few extra pounds. Easy to get along with, too; most of the agents in the building liked Sandy, who was named after the man who had led the revolution against the Hawaiian monarchy and been the Hawaiian Republic's first president.

This morning, Wood's reading glasses were propped on his forehead, and a cup of coffee was balanced precariously on some law books he'd been carrying to his office down the hall. He gave me a big grin and a handshake after he got rid of the drink and the books. The grin didn't last too long after Moore started recapping my problem. Wood's mood traveled quickly to thoughtful, then somber.

"How reliable is this person?"

"I don't know, Sandy. I just started talking to him a couple days ago. Everything's checked out so far."

"You're not saying you've been investigating the Ala Moana case?" He looked horrified by that possibility.

"No. I mean I've tried to verify all of the opium information he had. I don't even know if I should be asking about the Ala Moana thing."

"You shouldn't. It isn't our jurisdiction. We don't want to do anything to mess up the Territory's case."

"I'm not trying to mess up their case. I just want to corroborate my informer, like the manual says. It's not his fault their witness has a problem."

"Whoa, now, slow down." Wood shook his head. "We're getting way ahead of ourselves here. We don't *know* that they've got a problem. We only know some individual of uncertain reliability says their witness *might* be questionable." He held this out like it was a hat he was trying on for size.

"I talked to Lieutenant Jardine. He seems pretty sure they've got the guilty parties. I don't see why it would make a difference whether she smokes hop or not. If they raped her, then they raped her. What does the opium thing have to do with it?"

Wood buried his face in his hands, rubbed his eyes, then asked in a muffled voice if I had told Jardine about the informer. I told him I hadn't said anything about a source; I'd just pretended to be interested in their case.

"That cagey sonofabitch," Wood said vehemently. "He probably guessed anyway. Got eyes like a goddamn cobra." He'd obviously had past dealings with Detective Jardine.

"So what should I do, Sandy?" This was the bottom line, my reason for coming. If nothing else, I wanted to be able to tell Stevenson that I had referred the question to the U.S. Attorney and followed his advice.

Wood settled in to argue his case. "Look, it's possible that the informant is just full of bull or doesn't really know anything. He could just be making it up, passing along some gossip, or trying to buy a favor with us.

"Or he could be trying to help out the defendants. He could be spreading this disgusting rumor to taint the jury pool or cause dissension in the prosecution. We know the police are divided on the case already. There's talk some of them are actively helping the defense.

"He could also be telling the truth—as he knows it. But I'm telling you right now, I've met Mrs. Massie, and I don't believe it for a minute. Her mother came from New York to be with her for the trial, and she's a fine woman. You know they're related to Alexander Graham Bell?"

I shook my head.

"Well, they are. He's Mrs. Massie's great-uncle. And her husband Tommie's solid. A naval officer and a truly decent man." Wood shook his head vigorously. "I was there when she was interviewed at the police station. She told a very convincing story, kept her cool the whole time. I wouldn't hesitate to use her as a witness."

"You don't think the stoolie's playing straight with us?"

"No, I don't. Of that, I'm sure. I know this girl, and there is no way she would ever go somewhere like an opium den. It's simply not possible."

He sat on the corner of Moore's desk and gave me his closing argument. "Jack, her reputation is what makes this whole case so compelling. She *is* a lady. She *was* terribly abused. She is a completely innocent victim. We both know there are no innocent victims in an opium den. Therefore, she cannot possibly be a person who goes to opium dens. The Territory has some physical evidence—tire tracks and such—but the key to their whole case is this lady and her eyewitness identification. Anything, anything at all that tarnishes that witness is going to be very damaging, maybe fatal for the prosecution."

I heard a big, maybe huge, logical flaw in this argument, and thought this over as they waited for my reaction. "Okay. I guess I can see some of it. What I don't understand, though, was why me? If he was going to drop this little bomb on somebody as part of some big secret plan, why would he pick me? Why not Billy? Or Mr. Stevenson? And why wait until it's almost time for the trial? That part doesn't make sense."

Wood smiled faintly. "Yes, that's pretty obvious, I think. The defense attorneys want to spread this gossip to somebody they thought might be…receptive. They know you're new in the job and they know your family; they might have thought you would be that person when Billy or C.T. wouldn't."

"My family? I don't understand."

He got up again and walked over to the window overlooking the Territorial Courthouse. "Putting it bluntly, C.T. is white, and you're not." He held up his hand to stop me. "I know. We don't see things that way in Hawaii, but this case has changed a lot of attitudes. Things are different now."

I could feel myself flushing; heat prickled my neck under a collar too tight. "So my grandmother is half-Hawaiian, which makes me…"

"It makes you a Federal law enforcement officer who's too smart and too honest to fall for that kind of trap. Jack, we've got a victim who's white and five defendants who aren't. Most of the Navy men here are from the South, and they don't see a dime's worth of difference between our people and their Negroes. Those five would be dead right now if we were in Alabama, but we're not, and it's up to us to make sure we get justice for this young lady in our courts, not in a hanging tree. You'd agree with that, wouldn't you?"

"Sure, but…"

"Those people, the Navy, they don't believe we're going to deliver that justice, Jack, because they already see everything through the prism of race. They look at us and they see Sheriff Gleason, who's part-Hawaiian,

Jimmy Gilliland, the County Attorney, who's part-Hawaiian. All the detectives on the case except John McIntosh are Hawaiian or part-Hawaiian. Because of their prism, they think all those people will be loyal to their race, that they won't try to get justice for a white woman.

"If we're ever going to achieve statehood, we have to prove our system works as well as any other state's. We need the Navy's support, and once those five are safely locked away for twenty years in Oahu Prison, no one—not the Navy, not Congress—no one will be able to say that Hawaii's system failed."

There was an even bigger logical flaw in this argument, but I didn't point it out. Instead, I took it back to the office with me to stew over for another time.

Wood collected his things. "Thanks for letting us know. We're not going to do anything to confirm this stuff, and as long as none of it can be confirmed, Honolulu can do whatever they have to. No Federal interference or involvement."

Moore and I looked at each other as Wood walked out, whistling down the hallway. Moore shrugged—apologetically, I thought. "He's got a lot more invested in this case than people realize," he said quietly.

I must have looked surprised; on the face of it, the federal government had no stake whatsoever in the Ala Moana case. In fact, Wood had just said so.

Moore continued speaking in low, confidential tones. "There's tremendous political pressure out there. So far, at least, it's pretty well contained. But if Griffith Wight loses this case, Congress could federalize the whole Territory. They could declare martial law and make Admiral Stirling the military governor, or appoint some commission picked in Washington."

He didn't have to add that this was a nightmare scenario for the Big Five and Hawaii's haole elite. Martial law or commission rule meant a complete loss of control, the assumption of their carefully hoarded power by outsiders who might not place the elite's interests first. Some extremely important people in Hawaii—the same ones who had gotten Sanford Ballard Dole Wood his job—had gone to a lot of trouble to steal that power in the first place, and would pull every string possible to keep from losing it.

I had some other stuff to stew over back at the office. Sandy Wood and John Jardine might not agree on much of anything, but they had one thing in common. They both seemed to think that John H. Mather might not be the person they'd thought he was two days earlier.

CHAPTER 15

1141 1st Avenue, Kaimuki
Thursday, November 12

I had no trouble finding the address Kam had given when he'd called my office that afternoon; the grandly named 1st Avenue was only two blocks long. Kam's home would one day lie in the shadow of Honolulu's elevated freeway, but in 1931 the area was a quiet backwater of new homes and neighborhood stores.

Kam's wife met me at the front door with a smile. For someone who had borne thirteen children, most of whom were still at home, she looked remarkably unstressed and energetic. I followed her to the dining room, where Kam sat in what was obviously his accustomed place at the head of a long table. On his right, with his back to me, was another man, much smaller than Kam, dressed in the brown suit that served as the Honolulu Police Department Detective Bureau's semi-official uniform.

As I rounded the table, I recognized him at once.

"Agent Mather. This is Samuel Lau of the Honolulu police." Kam rose to make his formal introduction. Lau followed suit, but watched me warily.

"Samuel's my wife's cousin," Kam confided. "He's family."

"I remember you from the detective bureau. You were there when I was talking to Jardine," I said.

"Yeah, that was me." He was obviously uncomfortable, maybe remembering my performance.

"I guess I sounded pretty stupid, huh?" I laughed.

He smiled thinly. "Jardine had you down pat."

"I hear he's pretty good at that."

"Yeah. So is he right about you being hapa haole? You don't look it."

It had taken me all afternoon to wind down from my meeting with Sandy Wood and Will Moore, hours of growing doubts about who I was and how I was perceived. On a day when I had reluctantly confronted an ugly reality, not just about Hawaii, but about me, this was an area I really did not want to revisit.

"My grandmother is half-Hawaiian."

But Samuel Lau didn't seem especially interested. "So, true then. Hmmm. What do you know about the Ala Moana thing?"

"What I read in the paper. I know the victim's name. It sounds like you folks got a pretty good case."

Lau snorted, disgusted, though whether at the prosecution's case or me I couldn't tell. "They got shit," he said, answering that question.

"The papers say…" I started.

"The papers talk for the haoles. They don't know the real facts."

"What facts?"

Lau looked to Kam, who nodded, giving me his seal of approval.

"If that's all you know about the case, they got nothing to fear from you," he said, sounding puzzled. "They're all worried for nothing."

Somebody was afraid of me? This came as a shock. I'd thought my performance in Jardine's office might have inspired a lot of emotions, but fear wasn't one of them.

"Who's 'they?'"

"Jardine, McIntosh, Wight. He called 'em right after you left. And the ones behind it."

"Behind the prosecution?"

"Behind the damn screw job," he said scornfully. "That's what's happening. It's nothing but a screw job by the haoles. They know that *wahine* was never raped. They know those boys couldn't have done it, but they're gonna shove it right in the locals' faces, just 'cause they're Hawaiian and Chinese and Japanese." He sounded pretty bitter, and if what he was saying was true, I could understand why.

"Look, I don't know anything about a screw job. I'd like to know what happened, but I'm sure as hell not gonna interfere with anything the prosecutor's doing. I only want to find out some things about the victim."

"Dope things?" he asked.

"Yeah. Do you know anything about that?"

"Massie? No." He shook his head. "I heard what Jardine told you, so maybe somebody did say she was a dope fiend, but nobody never told me that."

Kam spoke up. "Sam, you give Jack the whole story, let him make up his own mind. Jack, you listen. Maybe there's something you can use."

Lau rested both arms on the table and began his story.

"I'm just a clerk, technically. I ain't a policeman. I want to be, someday. For now, you gotta know, I'm at the bottom. Somebody says, 'sweep up,' I go for a broom.

"I got one main job at the station—photographer. They call it 'Identification Officer,' but it's just taking the mug shots, developing them. Sometimes, too, they let me go to the scene and take the pictures there, mostly 'cause I know the equipment.

"I work days, so I wasn't on when all the stuff happened that night, but I found out most of it later. Can't help hearing; everybody in the station's talking about it. Still, most of this is secondhand, okay?"

I shrugged.

"So, it's real early on Sunday morning, September 13. You gotta remember that this is Saturday night. You know what that's like at the station."

I knew from the papers that Thalia Massie had gone to a Navy party at the Ala Wai Inn. I also knew about Saturday evening, the biggest night of the week for the Honolulu police. What with soldiers, sailors, and everybody else out for a night on the town, the police station hummed until the early hours of Sunday mornings. Saturday nights were jammed with more arrests, more injuries to care for, more drunk drivers, and more traffic incidents than all the other nights combined.

"Around one o'clock," Lau went on, "this big fat Hawaiian lady, Mrs. Peeples, comes into the station all hot, says these boys almost run into her car over by Liliha. They stop, she stops, and she's yelling, 'Why don't you look where you're going?' or something, and then this big Hawaiian gets out of the other car and cracks her a couple times.

"She ain't really hurt, but she's pissed, wanting them arrested, so she gets their license plate, tells her husband, some barber, 'Drive me to the police station.' She gets there, she raises hell till the receiving desk lieutenant puts out a bulletin for the patrolmen to find the car and pick it up. And Jardine's back from your thing on Holt and Russell, so the desk man calls upstairs and lets him know.

"Shoot, this is nothing for a Saturday; fights happen all the time. But now another call comes in. This is from a Navy man in Manoa who's saying his wife was assaulted by four Hawaiians. Not raped. 'Assaulted.' You know the difference?"

"I guess."

"Okay, so the lieutenant calls Jardine back and tells him about the new case. The two of them, they talk, and they're thinking, what if the Hawaiian lady and the Navy wife get the same suspects?

"Jardine sends some detectives up to Manoa to talk to the Navy wife. Little while later, one of 'em calls in and says the haole lady wasn't assaulted, she was raped by four or five Hawaiians. Now Jardine is all shook and tells the lieutenant to find the car and the people who were in it as fast as possible. Then he leaves for Manoa.

"The thing to remember is, it's only like two o'clock, maybe a little after, and already some pretty big wigs get their minds made up that the Peeples lady and the Massie girl are connected. You saw Jardine. He ain't wrong very often, and if he thinks he's right, he's going ahead, full speed. Right or wrong, you better stay out of the way."

I could believe this, based on my admittedly limited experience with Lieutenant Jardine. "But you don't think he's right," I murmured.

"No, no, no. Me? I don't *know* one way or the other. Maybe he is, but I think a detective gotta keep an open mind, you know what I mean?" he asked Kam, who just shrugged, not committing himself on a possible breach by a fellow detective.

"Now things is really heating up. They ain't panicking yet, but they're getting close. Bad enough they call McIntosh in from his house."

According to the newspapers, Captain John N. McIntosh, the Honolulu Police Department's Chief of Detectives, was the key man in the Ala Moana investigation. Because he was Kam's boss and our link to the department brass, I'd met McIntosh on my introductory rounds. He was a former colonial police officer in South Africa and New Zealand who'd come to Hawaii as a plantation overseer before going back to police work. Our meeting had been short and chilly. Given the potentially explosive nature of the case, it wasn't surprising to hear that he'd been called in on a Sunday morning.

"Captain gets in, he takes over. First thing he does, he gets reports from everybody. By this time, they've found the car they're looking for and brought it down to the station with this kid, Horace Ida, who was driving it. McIntosh starts putting the picture together, and he sends Benton and Bond out to the old quarantine station where the wahine is saying the rape happened. You know Benton?"

I shook my head.

"Claude," he drawled sarcastically. "He's a patrolman, drives one of the radio cars. Wants to be a detective." He rolled his eyes and sniffed.

"Claude goes out, finds tire tracks, finds some stuff the wahine dropped. Beads and shit. He leaves Bond out there to guard the place, goes running back to the station to tell McIntosh. Kiss his ass.

"Meantime, Mac is talking to the first guy they found, Ida. He was driving his sister's car, a Ford Phaeton, a year or so old, so used but in good shape. You seen it?"

"No."

"I've been in it. It runs good, nothing wrong with the body or the top. That's important." He jabbed a finger at me to emphasize the point.

"Okay."

"At the station, Ida's lying to McIntosh about where he was and what he was doing in the car, which is really dumb, because Mac ain't stupid, and he's getting more reports every minute. By now he knows for sure Ida's lying. He just doesn't know why.

"Jardine's already got the Navy wife at the Emergency Hospital. She's told three different detectives the same exact story, which is she's walking along on Ena Road and this car pulls up and stops. Might be a Ford, might be a Dodge, she can't tell. Two guys jump out, grab her, start hitting her, and throw her in the back seat. There's two more guys in the front seat.

"They drive her to the old quarantine station, take her out and rape her a bunch of times, then drive off. She gets picked up by some haoles, who take her home. She tells the detectives it was dark, she cannot see anybody real good, and she never sees a license plate on the car. She also says the four guys were Hawaiian, but she never really seen their faces, but maybe she can identify 'em by their voices. And the only name she heard was 'Bull.' You know what is 'Bull?'"

I did. It was the Honolulu equivalent of "buddy" or "pal," and absolutely useless for identification purposes.

"All she remembers about the car was it sounded old, running rough, and the top might have been torn or something, because it was flapping in the wind as they were driving."

He stopped, pointing again to me. "You remember what I said about Ida's car?"

"It was in good shape."

"Yeah. I was in it two days later, and it was cherry—real nice car."

"That's a pretty big discrepancy."

"Not the only thing, though." Lau practically spit in disgust. "She starts out talking about *four* boys, all Hawaiians, but when they catch the guys, they got five—two Hawaiians, two Japanese, and one Chinese.

And they're not in some old wreck, they're in a nice car with no torn top, and it runs fine."

"Almost nothing matches," I said. "How in the hell did they come to identify these five?"

"Because once the wahine gets to the hospital, she starts remembering all kinds of new stuff. Now she remembers the license plate number, 58-805. So she get the license plate right, or close, anyway. Only one number off; theirs is 58-895. Good enough, except right outside the window at the hospital, you got the squad car parked with the radio going, and the dispatcher is shooting out calls every five minutes on Ida's car. The wahine, she can't miss the number coming over the radio, and even if she miss 'em, by this time you got like ten Navy people standing around right next to the car. Pretty soon, like magic, she get the license number."

"Maybe. Maybe she just remembered it."

"No chance," he said, dismissing me with a wave. "She's all in pain, the doctor giving her dope, and you know witnesses, their memory get worse, not better, time goes by."

I ducked my head to hide a grin at the clerk giving the Inspector and the Federal agent detective wisdom, but I did know, even in my limited experience, that he was right about witness memories.

He continued, "Now it's getting to be morning time. Ida finally tells McIntosh the names of the other guys in his car, says he only lied 'cause he didn't want his friend to get in trouble for knocking down the Peeples lady. He still saying he don't know anything about the haole wahine. Chief sends some dicks out to Palama to pick up the other four—Joe Kahahawai, Henry Chang, Ben Ahakuelo, and David Takai."

I knew these names, of course. By November, everyone in town did. Thalia Massie might not have been identified, but the newspapers weren't shy about printing the names of her assailants, their addresses, and police mug shots.

"Meanwhile, Jardine takes the haole wahine from the hospital, and when she gets to the station, McIntosh brings Ida in and says, 'Is this one of the guys who rape you?' She goes, 'Yeah,' which is enough for McIntosh. If Ida did it, then the other four did it, too."

He paused for a moment, thinking on the Chief of Detective's actions that night, seemingly puzzled. "That's not like him," he finally said. "All jumping to conclusions."

I didn't say anything, remembering that I, too, had concluded, based on my reading of the local papers, that the boys were guilty.

Lau shook himself. "Anyway, Monday morning, I come in. McIntosh tells me, 'Go back with Claude to the old quarantine station, take some pictures of the tire tracks there.' I get my camera and stuff, and I go with Benton. He says, 'Let's take Ida's car, we can compare, take pictures of both. And hey, let's take Ida along, too. We'll show him the tracks, he'll see they match, and we'll get the confession.'" Lau shook his head, frowning at the memory. "We're both gonna be heroes," he said sadly, sighing. "I ain't no detective, but it sounds okay, so we go. He's above me anyway, so I can't just say 'no.'

"We get there, he drives right out into the place by the cement slab. We're in Ida's car now. We get outta the car, and there's some tracks on the ground, lots of tracks. Some is ours, we just drove up, and some is from before. Only thing is, you look, you can't tell which is which. They're all the same.

"Benton, he's all confused, too. He says, 'I don't remember seeing this many before.' I tell him, 'No shit, we just made half of 'em.' 'No, no, seems like way more than on Sunday,' he tells me. What a mess." Lau stared at the tabletop.

"Finally, he tells me, hell with it, just take the picture of these, side by side. I'm looking at him, and I say, 'I can't take that picture. If I do, come time for court, I gotta say, you coulda made the tracks just now.' He says, 'You gotta take the pictures.' I say, 'How come?' and he says 'Because Mac wants 'em, that's how come.'

"Hey, I might just be a pissant clerk, but I know this is wrong, and I tell him, 'Fine, but court time? I'm gonna say you could've made both sets.'" Lau's voice climbed, defiant.

You've heard people talk about inscrutable Orientals? Not police clerk Samuel K. Lau. Pain and disappointment twisted his features. It had cost him plenty, maybe every dream he'd ever had, to stand up to that police officer who claimed to be speaking for the Chief of Detectives. Sitting there, you could see in his face that he knew the price.

"What's Ida saying while all this is going on?"

Lau shook himself out of it. "Oh, he's saying he don't know how the tracks got there, either, 'cause he never drove the car there before."

"But you said some of the tracks were there before you got there?"

"Yeah, I'm gonna get to that. So, they was still doing the investigation while we was out. By then, they had four of the boys in the lockup, all of 'em but Takai. They never get him until later that day. Mac and them took the four they had out to her house in Manoa on Sunday afternoon, and she sort of picked out three more. She was solid about Kahahawai and Ida, but wasn't sure about Chang and Ahakueleo, and later on she couldn't pick Takai at all. But they was all in the same car, so you ask McIntosh and Jardine, they was all guilty."

"They took them to her house?"

"Yep. Just brought 'em inside, say, 'This is them, yeah?' and leave."

That seemed pretty strange, too. Not just the failure to use a lineup, mixing some other people to make things a challenge, but taking the suspects into the victim's house. I would think a lot of rape victims would say anything just to get these threatening strangers out of her home.

"How can Jardine be so sure, then? I mean, how do they know they haven't got the wrong boys?" I asked.

"Bull," Lau frowned, unwittingly addressing me with the name Thalia Massie said her attackers used. "There ain't no right ones, 'cause this lady was never raped. Her clothes, I took the pictures of 'em, they're perfect. Shit, my wife's clothes is messier than these. No way five guys is gonna do what she said they did and leave her clothes in good shape like that. They ain't torn, they ain't ripped. Get some blood on 'em, mostly up around the neck, but not a whole lot, considering."

"What about, uh, other kind of stains?"

"Sex? Nah. The doctors didn't find anything and when they looked at the girl's clothes, they only found something they said 'might've been.' But could've been beer or macaroni salad. And there wasn't nothing on the boys, either. They was all still wearing the same underwear and stuff when they got picked up that morning. Plus, too, she get no injuries, except for her jaw is broke. Nothing to show she been raped. Uh uh. Somebody cracked her, all right, but not like she said. Whatever. I know for sure it wasn't those five."

"You seem pretty certain."

"I got photos, bull. That's what I do, take pictures. I got evidence, says no possible way those five did the rape."

"Pictures of the clothes?"

"Not just them."

"I thought you said you didn't take pictures of the tire tracks."

"I never did, but that don't matter, 'cause remember I said there were tracks already there? We wasn't the first ones to drive the car back there."

"What do you mean?"

"McIntosh. He came down Sunday to Ala Moana. He was driving Ida's car, and he drove it all over the quarantine place."

"McIntosh? You're kidding."

"Nope. He was there. Plenty other guys in the department seen him."

Horace Ida's car had certainly been getting a workout, making at least two trips down to the crime scene after the fact. Its tire tracks must have carpeted the whole area.

"So what? You gonna look into this anymore?" he asked.

"I don't know," I admitted. "This stuff is way over my head."

"If you do, I'll tell you what. All this shit? It's good, but the times is the most important thing. You can remember that?"

"The times?"

"Yeah. The times everything happened: when the wahine left the club, when they supposed to have snatched her, when the boys left the dance, when they almost hit the Peeples lady. All the times together."

"Okay, I'll keep it in mind."

"Good, 'cause once you see the times, you know them five couldn't do it."

Having said what he came to say, Samuel Lau got up, thanked Kam for having him over, and headed out into the night without another word to me.

Kam and I sat for a few moments, listening to the sounds of his family readying themselves for bed. A boy of about fourteen came through the room, all long limbs and big feet that promised to someday fill out to his father's size. "Joey," Kam said, motioning him over. "You all pau with your homework?" The boy nodded. "This is Mr. Mather. Tell him what you're gonna do when you get older."

"Gonna be a policeman, like Pop," he said, parroting the answer he'd been rehearsing for years. Kam smiled wanly as the boy went out the front door.

"Ahhh," he sighed. "They're killing us here. This thing, this trial, it's gonna tear the department apart." His broad shoulders slumped as, head down, he spoke of the gaping wound in his police force.

"Good men think the boys are guilty, they'll cross the line, do anything to prove it. Other ones think the boys are innocent, they'll cross over to help them. I been here twenty-some years, I can't tell who's who anymore." He sighed again, maybe thinking about a son who wanted to follow in his father's footsteps, and the tangled thicket where those tracks led. "You better watch your ass, Jack. There's so much pressure on, people are getting crazy."

"I'm starting to see that."

"One more thing you should know. The Tuesday after this all happened, McIntosh gets called to a meeting at Walter Dillingham's office. He's got, like, twenty businessmen there, along with the big dogs from the Navy. Called in Gleason and Jimmy Gilliland, the County Attorney, too.

"Dillingham took over the whole prosecution, right there. He's gonna pay for lawyers to help out, got up a $5,000 reward for information. Gilliland and Gleason and McIntosh all tell him they thought they had the right guys locked up. Right then, they're in cement. There's no way they could even look at any other suspects."

"Walter Dillingham," I murmured, thinking that the kind of pressure applied by the most powerful man in the islands would be measured in tons per square inch. And he was my father's boss. "That's not good."

Kam rolled his eyes. "No kidding. McIntosh knows we're not ready for trial. I think he knows now the boys didn't do it, but by the time he figured it out, it was too late. I've been trying to keep myself out of this mess, but the whole thing is just slopping over on everybody."

We sat for another minute or two, both of us knowing nothing was going to be resolved this night. "Come on, I'll see you out," he finally sighed.

I stood to leave and noticed a small shrine: a tray, a block of wood with Chinese characters in gold, and a bowl all sitting atop a table in the corner of the living room. Brightly colored joss papers lay next to the altar. I walked to it.

"My wife, she burns the joss on special occasions," Kam smiled.

"She doesn't think thirteen kids brings the family enough luck, huh?"

"You can offer them for other people, too."

Some of the papers were folded in the shape of small boats. I picked one up. The gilded characters gleamed.

"When it's burned, the ship carries the prayer directly to heaven," Kam explained.

"Maybe somebody better burn some for the Ala Moana boys," I suggested. "It sounds like they need all the luck they can get. Maybe the department, too."

Kam grunted, and doubt was heavy in the sound. "I think it's going to take more than joss to fix this thing."

I said goodbye and walked to my car. On the seat lay the pale rectangle of a manila envelope. Inside were twenty photographic prints, very professionally done, each depicting a different page of neat handwriting, easily read, even in the poor lighting of Kam's driveway. The top sheet began: "Statement of Thalia H. Massie made to John N. McIntosh at the Detective Bureau at 3:30 a.m. on September 13."

CHAPTER 16

2670 Hillside Avenue, Manoa Valley
Friday, November 13

The problem smoldered all the next day. I was alone in the office with the telephone and the records of the opium hui, but my thoughts kept drifting away from the White Friend's blank silhouette to the more corporeal contents of Samuel Lau's manila envelope. Yet they held none of the reassurance I expected from a sheaf of papers. There was no comfort here, no order or precision. They could not be placed into balance by making an adjustment or made to reconcile by correcting a figure. They just sputtered away all day like a slow-burning fuse, and that evening there they were, still smoking.

I took out the photographs and re-read each of the notebook pages. The entries in John McIntosh's pin-neat handwriting documented not only Thalia Massie's statement, but other aspects of the case as well. As far as I could tell, the notebook chronicled the entire record of the first forty-eight hours of the investigation. All of the detectives working that first night and the next day had reported directly to McIntosh, who'd dutifully recorded the information they brought him in his book.

I guessed these papers had enough ammunition to blow some big holes in the prosecution's case, but the defense would never see it. This all took place long before court decisions forced the government to hand over copies of any statements made by witnesses in criminal cases, so it was obvious to me what Lau hoped I would do.

He wanted me to give the papers—or at least the information in them—to the defense. He didn't want to do it himself; Lau might only be a clerk, but he knew that such an act would certainly carry the seeds of his own destruction and possibly those of his department, too.

But I was an outsider. If pressed, the defense attorneys could say that the documents came from someone outside the department, possibly taking some of the heat off Lau. And if anyone asked him on the witness stand, he could honestly say he hadn't actually handed them to anybody.

I didn't think this was going to work. After all, McIntosh would immediately recognize his own notes if they turned up in the hands of the opposition. And he was a good enough detective to be able to remember who in his own Detective Bureau not only had access to his office, but was also a photographer.

Ultimately, though, that was Lau's problem. I had enough of my own to worry about. The biggest was whether or not to go to the defense attorneys with the information in the first place. Given my shaky relationship with C.T. Stevenson, who'd be happy to fire me, and an even shakier one with the Honolulu police, one of whom I was pretty sure had tried to push me under a bus, I had to wonder why I should do Samuel Lau or the defense attorneys any favors.

One of attorneys I barely knew. William Heen, Hawaii's first part-Chinese judge and a Territorial senator, had gotten Chin Sheu off in the *President Madison* case, so he was no slouch. He'd represented Albert Holt and given me a good grilling in our hearing, but he seemed good-natured and mellow out of court, although my contact with him had been minimal.

William B. Pittman, however, was a completely different story. We had been much closer for years. Mr. and Mrs. Pittman—Bill and Bertha—had a home on Hillside Avenue, directly downhill from my parents' house on Terrace Drive. Our backyard overlooked the Pittmans' and in my school days when I'd been hurrying to get to the Japanese store on East Manoa Road, I'd shaved two blocks off the trip by cutting through their yard to come out on Hillside.

Another tie, this one a secret I've never disclosed to this day, bound us. Bill Pittman's brother Key served as the senior senator from Nevada and was President Pro Tem of the United States Senate; he was a man with a lot of clout. This was why, when I went looking for a job with the federal government, I wrote to my neighbor down the hill, who called his brother across the ocean.

I'm sure my boss suspected I'd used political connections to get my government position; that sort of thing happened a lot. The fact that many others, perhaps even Stevenson himself, had done the same did nothing for my conscience.

The guilty feeling that I hadn't actually earned my job faded slowly over the years, but politics and favors being what they are, I had to assume in 1931 that I owed Key Pittman and his brother Bill at least one favor in return.

So at eight o'clock that night, after Mr. and Mrs. Pittman had finished dinner, I clambered down into their backyard, feeling like a kid again and carrying a manila envelope full of problems. Mrs. Pittman answered the door and recognized me immediately, even though it had been a while since I had been by.

"Johnny! Come in, sugar. It's so good to see you again." The wide, grandmotherly lady gave me a hug.

"Bill! Come out here. Johnny Mather's come by to see us."

Mr. Pittman came into the room carrying the *Star Bulletin* in one hand, reading glasses in the other, and an equally big smile on his face. He was a large man, getting a bit paunchy, and older than I remembered. He wore a toupee, though not with any enthusiasm or confidence in the deception. It was always my impression that the rug served less as a sop to his own vanity than a device to humor his wife.

"Well, well. A Treasury man. I heard you were back. Bill Heen said he ran into you at Federal Court." He spoke softly with the southern drawl of his native Mississippi.

"Nice to see you again, sir. Yes, we had a case with Judge Heen."

"I hardly knew who to root for in that one," he said with a grin.

"It was a good case. He didn't have much chance."

He laughed. "You're not here to gloat about that, I suppose."

"Actually, sir, I've got some business we need to talk about."

"Official business! The Treasury Department never sleeps, eh? Betty, could you excuse us, let us get this official business out of the way?"

"Oh, of course, you men talk. But Johnny, before you go, I want you to tell me about your mother and how she's doing. I see your grandmother at meetings, but I haven't talked to your mother in ages."

I agreed and waited until she left the room.

"First of all, I wanted to thank you for helping me out with the job and all. Talking to your brother, I mean. I've been intending to come by."

He waved this off. "It's nothing, nothing. Nice to have someone responsible in that position. Key knew you were a good man for the job, or he wouldn't have lifted a finger, believe me."

"Yes, sir. But I have to thank you anyway. Now, I've got a case I want to talk to you about."

He frowned. "I don't have any narcotics matters at the moment. I don't much care for them, to tell the truth."

"No sir, it's not a dope case. I understand you're representing two of the defendants in the Ala Moana rape trial."

His puzzlement turned to concern. "You're not getting into that snake pit, I hope. I haven't had any indication my clients were involved in the drug trade."

"It isn't that. I can't really say what information I have on the narcotics end. We're still working on it, but I don't think it relates to any of the five boys."

"You've certainly got my attention."

"Are you aware that there are some people on the police force who don't think the boys are getting a fair shake?"

Bill Pittman laughed heartily, "Now there's an understatement. Yes, son. Half the police department, at least, is actively pulling for the defense in this trial. It's the damnedest thing I've seen in thirty-some years of legal practice."

"Do you know why they're taking sides like that?"

"They've all got their own reasons, a lot of it political. Whatever, it's completely split the department into pieces."

"It's not just political, though. There're some who don't think the boys are guilty."

"And rightly so. They aren't guilty. I told you I wasn't taking opium cases? The main reason is, everybody you and Sandy Wood bring to court are guilty as all-get-out. Like those policemen. My end of things, the motions, the trial, the legal end, it's just a game to see whether you people did your job right. That sort of exercise simply doesn't interest me anymore. And I wouldn't have taken this case, either, if I thought for a minute that the boys were guilty. They're innocent, and I don't believe that Griff Wight is going to be able to prove otherwise."

"I started out thinking they did it," I confessed. "I guess I was believing what I read in the papers. But some people talked to me, and now I'm taking a different view."

"That's all well and good, John, but I still don't see what this has to do with you. You've got no dog in this fight; why jump in where you're bound to get bit?"

"I've got an interest. An informer, that's all I can tell you."

Pittman looked thoughtful and even more concerned. "Hmmm. All right, I certainly respect your need to keep your sources confidential, but how can I help you?"

"I'm in a jam here, Mr. Pittman. I'm supposed to be on the prosecution's side of the fence, even in a case that doesn't involve me. But I've come by some information I think helps the defense, and I don't know whether I should give it to you or not."

He nodded slowly. "I don't mind telling you, we've already gotten quite a bit from certain people who were close to the investigation. We might have the same information you do."

"Maybe, but I think I'm the only one who has this. It may be important, but I don't know enough about the case to be able to tell."

"And you're not sure what you should do with it."

This was the crux of my dilemma. "I feel like I should give it to you, but I also feel like I'm stabbing the people on my side in the back."

Pittman got up and walked to the big window at the front of the house. The lights of Manoa spread out below him. "Your side," he mused. "This case is a nightmare for Hawaii in so many ways. If I look up the valley, I can see the roof of that woman's house. Do you know that?"

I nodded. I had noticed the same thing from my own window. "Yes, sir."

He shook his head and turned back to me. "I cannot, for the life of me, understand why that woman is lying the way she has been. If a jury accepts her story, five boys will go to prison for a long, long time for something they did not do.

"I'm sure you've heard the talk about imposing the death penalty for rape. Some idiot actually proposed making it retroactive for this case, never mind it would be totally unconstitutional and all of it because of this twenty-year-old girl's fabulous tale. Did you read about the Salem witch trials in that awful school of yours down the road?"

I smiled. He'd been teasing me about Punahou for years, although he'd always stopped to give me a lift if he saw me walking down Manoa Road toward school in the morning. "Yes, sir. It was part of American History class."

"It should be Current Events. Because here in Hawaii, that's just what's happening. We are actually going to try these five young men solely on the word of one girl who can't tell a Japanese from a Hawaiian or one make of car from another. She says she was raped, so the police, the prosecutor, the Navy, the Big Five, everybody who's anybody lines up behind her to crucify five innocent young men. Now *that* is a crime."

"Who are you representing in the case?"

"I've got Joe Kahahawai and Horace Ida."

"And she's positively identified your clients?"

"Both of mine, she has. She wasn't as clear on a couple of the others, but they were all in Horace's car, so they're going to hang together or not at all."

"But the prosecutor has more than that," I said, knowing that if what Samuel Lau said was true, he didn't.

"No, son, they don't. That much we do know, thanks to those in the police department who, for whatever reason, also find this entire affair offensive. Oh, Wight says they have eyewitnesses, tire tracks, even some medical evidence, but that's nonsense." He banished this fantasy with a wave of his hand. "The fact is, it's just the girl. It always has been. Now, if what you've got in that envelope sheds some light on why that girl is saying what she is, I would be most pleased to see it. Because I simply do not understand how or why one human being could do this to another."

I handed him the packet. He gave me a last chance to change my mind, then opened the envelope and began to read. A minute or two later he stopped and re-read one of the pages. He rose slowly, holding the papers, walked back to the window, read again as he stood there.

When he was finished, he carefully placed the photographs back in the envelope. "I'm not going to ask you how you got these, of course," he said. "I'd like to talk to Judge Heen and my clients before I say anything else to you about this." Then he evidently thought otherwise because he waved the papers at the window and addressed the steep mountain walls that enclosed our valley home.

"I want so much for this to all be about Thalia Massie. I want to believe she brought all this evil with her, and when she goes, it will go with her, and good riddance. Now, I just don't know. I can understand how the Navy would protect one of its own, even going beyond the pale because she's theirs.

"But the others, are they willing to sell their souls because she's white? Are they really willing to destroy five lives for the sake of some twisted concept of honor?"

"I don't know," I confessed, not sure if he was really asking me the questions. "What others?"

He went on, not hearing my interruption. "When we're young, you know, we're filled with all sorts of illusions: we'll live forever, we'll make great discoveries, we'll right the world's wrongs. As we grow, our outlook changes. All our imaginings translate to a more practical plane.

"When you're young in a place like Mississippi, they infuse you with another set of illusions, darker ones, that some people are better and that everyone else, all the others in the entire world, are less. Much less, in fact. They're just inferior.

"William Heen, inferior. Can you imagine such a thing?" He turned toward me, amazement and disgust written on the lined face that seemed to grow older as he spoke. "He is a better lawyer, a better public servant, a better man than I in every respect. Yet he and I could not sit together in a restaurant in Vicksburg. We could not stay in the same hotel."

He thrust a thick finger at me, making a point as if in closing arguments. "*Those* are the illusions we should leave behind. But we grow older, not wiser, and one generation to the next, we draw this evil along with us, even as it stinks and molders, even as we cast the noble in us aside."

I could see now that he wasn't talking to me. Perhaps he planned to use these words in the trial, or maybe he was trying to warn everyone of the snake coiled behind the Ala Moana case. He faced back to the window and gazed out at the darkness and beautiful Manoa beyond. I had to strain to hear the soft words, bitter and sad, of an old man chastising himself for revealing an embarrassing weakness.

"And I. I cherished the illusion, foolish old dodderer that I am—that somehow, I had left all that behind. I believed Hawaii was a place where, if race mattered, it mattered less. That this was one place where the delusions of superiority and inferiority could be exchanged for something better. Now this. This comes along, and another mirage—another dream—vanishes."

He stood in the silence for a minute, his shoulders sagging, then turned and started, seeing me without recognition, wondering for a moment how I had gotten into his reverie. Then he recovered. "Ah, the maundering of an old fool," he said sheepishly. "What you must think."

"Mr. Pittman…"

"Are you free tomorrow, John?" he asked abruptly.

"Yes sir, I was planning to go into the office for a couple of hours in the morning."

"Fine, fine. Can you meet me at Judge Heen's office? It's in the Hawaiian Trust Building, Room 204. About eleven?"

"Sure. I guess that would be okay. I'm not joining the defense team, am I?"

He laughed again. "I'd be glad to have you, but no. I would like to introduce you to someone, and he'll be there. I'm sure Judge Heen will be happy to see you again, too."

So, ten minutes later I was out on Hillside Avenue, walking home in the dark, with time to think about what kinds of dreams I might have when I got to be Bill Pittman's age—and whether any of them would be worth keeping.

CHAPTER 17

Hawaiian Trust Building, Room 204
Saturday, November 14

That was the longest night of my life. Lines between right and wrong seem so much more cleanly drawn when you're young. The path of justice seems so much more clearly defined. And your conscience bitches and moans at you interminably in the wee, small hours.

My carping conscience assured me that sneaking around in the middle of the night, delivering photographs of the prosecution's secrets to a defense attorney, fell most resoundingly on the "wrong" side of the line. The clandestine nature of my meeting with Samuel Lau and the talk with Mr. Pittman reinforced the distinctly treasonous feel to the whole enterprise.

Those dragging hours after midnight provided plenty of time for doubts and the inevitable second thoughts that come to someone who is too late in considering consequences. Thoughts, for instance, that some in the fractured police force, maybe the same ones who hated me already, wouldn't look too kindly on activity that seemed designed solely to sabotage their investigation. Or that prosecutors like Sandy Wood or Griffith Wight would remember the saboteur next time he came in with a case. Or that Clarence T. Stevenson would want to know what any of this had to do with a pile of papers on his junior agent's desk.

Even the most sinister imaginings of 3:00 a.m. usually brighten up in the light of day, but my mood was not much improved as I clumped along the short distance from our office to the Hawaiian Trust Building.

Honolulu, fair and cheerful, bustled that Saturday morning. Shoppers crowded the markets and big department stores downtown. More people strolled up from the waterfront and the train station, so I wove my way along sidewalks thronged with soldiers on leave and sailors on liberty from Pearl Harbor, who mingled with local folks in from the country and tourists visiting Chinatown and Iolani Palace. In my tired imagination, they shied away from the traitor in their midst, barely concealing their distaste and suspicion behind their warm smiles and soft expressions.

Judge Heen's secretary, a young and attractive haole lady, asked me to wait while she got Mr. Pittman out of his meeting. "They're expecting you," she said brightly.

"There you are!" Pittman exclaimed as he emerged from a room off the main hallway in the office. With him was the smaller Chinese lawyer who had saved Chin Sheu. Judge William Heen smiled warmly and invited me inside.

"I'm glad you could come in this morning. Thank you, Eva," he said to the secretary, who took her place at a desk by the door. The sound of typing followed us down the hallway to Judge Heen's office.

"As you've probably guessed, we're getting our last-minute preparations done in the Ala Moana case." Heen motioned us to chairs facing his desk.

"We—that is, Bill and I—would like to thank you for bringing the matter of those notes to our attention," he said, taking his own seat. I could see the manila envelope on the desk.

"I'm hoping I did the right thing, Judge."

"Oh, I'm quite certain of that. But then, I would be expected to say something of that sort, given my position in the case."

"We knew this posed something of a moral dilemma for you, John," Pittman interjected. "That was why I asked you to come down this morning. Judge Heen and I agreed that we would, of course, protect your identity. Wild horses couldn't drag your name out of our mouths, so I don't think Griff Wight will be able to."

"But that's only the legal side of it," Heen cautioned. "Bill said you were the kind of young man who would be more anxious about the ethical question. You'd be asking yourself, 'Is this right?' You've done us a favor. I think you deserve to be confident on that score, too."

I'll admit I was curious about how *that* could be accomplished. I must have looked doubtful, because Pittman laughed. "Don't worry, we'll do our part," he said. "I'm going to do something no good lawyer would ever do. I'm going to instruct my clients to tell you their story, no holds barred. You listen, and if you hear something that convinces you they're guilty, you can walk out clean. We'll give you back these photographs, and we won't make any mention of them at the trial."

"It sounds like you're kind of going out on a limb with this."

Pittman smiled. "No, Judge Heen and I have absolute confidence that our clients are innocent." Heen nodded his agreement, but I noticed he wasn't offering up his own clients for a little chat.

"In the moral sense, you're the one who's out on the limb. We realize that, but we want you to see the right and wrong of this for yourself," Pittman explained. "And we're not being completely altruistic here. We have to believe that whoever fed you this very valuable information feels strongly enough about the case to feed us some more."

I considered the offer for a moment, knowing it represented a clear choice between wading out or getting in much deeper. What the hell, I thought, it couldn't hurt to listen.

Joe Kahahawai and Horace Ida, known to his friends as "Shorty," were sitting together in a cluttered little room down the hall. I sized up Bill Pittman's clients as he made the introductions.

Joe Kahahawai was a big man in his mid-twenties, dark-skinned and well built. I could easily envision him in the boxing ring or the football field, the only places he'd ever received any notice before Thalia Massie pointed her finger at him. He had attended St. Louis, a Catholic high school, distinguishing himself mostly on the football field, and drifted from job to job after leaving school.

Horace Ida was, as his nickname implied, slight though fairly solidly built. His dark eyes followed me closely and were filled with caution.

Both of them had grown up in Palama, an area in which the police weren't always welcomed with open arms. A certain reserve, if not outright suspicion, toward the law could be expected, particularly from two people who'd been at the blunt end of the justice system for several months.

It was Ida who spoke first. "Agent? You're a lawyer for the Federals?"

"No, I enforce the narcotics laws. Opium and other drugs."

"So, you're like a cop."

"I guess. More like a cop than a lawyer, anyway."

You could tell Kahahawai had no interest in opium whatsoever, and not much use for cops. Ida, more wary, was trying to make the connection. What was this Federal man doing here at his lawyer's office?

"And what? They think we're doing opium now? We're some kind of dope fiends?" Ida demanded, a note of defiance in his voice.

This brought Kahahawai's interest back. "Who's been sayin' that? I never have nothing to do with that stuff."

"Nobody. I've never heard anybody say that about you. Any of you. I'm just a friend of Mr. Pittman. He thought I might be able to help, I guess."

"Help how?" Ida cocked his head, skeptical.

"I don't know, really. But I'd like to start by hearing your side of the story."

"Ahh," Ida waved his hand. "We told this thing so many goddamn times already. To the cops, the lawyers, hell, anybody who ask. The other cops never believe us, how come you gonna?"

"Maybe I won't. Mr. Pittman's pretty sure I will, though."

Ida studied me, calculating his risk, measuring the pressures of his instincts against the advice of his lawyer. He looked at Kahahawai, who shrugged, and both stared at the floor. "It was that goddamned car," he began.

Ida told how he'd returned from the mainland only a couple of weeks earlier, how he'd begged his sister for the use of her almost-new '29 Ford so he could cruise the old neighborhood in style that Saturday night and reconnect with old friends.

Chance encounters at various nightspots had drawn different people into Ida's car, and he'd chauffeured them from party to party, reveling in the attention. With Benny Ahakuelo and David Takai, he'd wound up at a luau on School Street, where the invited guests had passed them free beer over the fence.

Another excursion, this time to the dance at Waikiki Park across town, and back to the luau where Ida had encountered Joe and Henry Chang, also mooching free beer, for the first time in the evening. With their welcome almost worn out, Ida had mentioned the dance at the amusement park.

"I said, 'Shoot, let's check 'em out,'" Joe put in. "Those folks at the luau was runnin' out of beer, anyway."

Ida guessed that the five got back to the amusement park at around 11:30 p.m. He was vague because, "None of us get enough money for one watch." He gave a short, bitter laugh, knowing now how important time was about to become.

The dance had ended at midnight, so they'd had barely enough time to crash this party. They'd found nothing of particular interest, so all five had assembled in the parking area on Ena Road. "Remember, now," he told me, "this is the only time all night we're all together."

Kahahawai nodded solemnly. "They try to say we're like some gang. We go hunting for this wahine or something. Bull! That was the only time in our whole lives when we was all together, just us five alone. The first time, after that dance."

That comment provoked some questions. How likely was it, for example, that five young men, brought together because one of them happened to have a car, would jump into a major crime? It wasn't like these five were bosom buddies. A couple barely knew the others. And now here they were, at the exit of the amusement park, just yards from where Thalia Massie was abducted, all five together for the first time in the evening. If they did it, it looked like a spur of the moment kind of thing, to say the least.

As they piled into the Ford, they saw another group of partygoers leaving. Since they knew at least two of the people, they followed this car back toward town, exchanging good-natured insults along the way. In front of the Art Academy on Beretania Street, they even stopped long enough to get matches, hopping from one car to the other.

If what he was saying was true, they had gone in almost exactly the opposite direction from Thalia Massie and the beach road. What was more, they had a second car full of witnesses who could, and presumably would, testify to that fact.

With their evening nearing its end, and ruin approaching the intersection from another direction, Ida slowed down. He paused between shortened sentences as if he could somehow push back that fateful moment, wrung his hands, and pain twisted his face.

"And then you went back to the luau," I prompted.

They only stayed for a few minutes and talked to a couple of friends. They found no more beer, but racked up more alibi witnesses. Then Ida dropped off Ahakuelo and Chang and turned toward King Street.

Kahahawai picked up the story and told of the near miss with the Peeples's car, the woman's challenge, and the escalation.

"I crack her one time, and she kind of fell. Not that hard, 'cause she right back up, grabbing me like this." He demonstrated with both hands on his throat. "She one big wahine. They pull us apart, and we go to my house. She go to the cops." He said this last with a mixture of hurt and amazement, as though he couldn't understand why an obviously unreasonable woman, knocked down by a much younger, bigger, stronger man, would feel compelled to report the incident to the police. "I stay pretty drunk," he added, which was beyond a doubt the understatement of the day, and a fitting end to the story.

Both of them sat, contemplating a future now totally based upon the prosaic set of circumstances just related. Their story certainly had the ring of truth, and they had described at least twenty other people who could account for their whereabouts almost minute by minute throughout the evening. I assumed Heen and Pittman had these witnesses all lined up.

Not only did opportunity appear to be lacking, but the motive looked absent, too. Joe Kahahawai had followed friends around town, hunting and often enough finding free beer. Horace Ida was mostly interested in showing off in his sister's car. The others seemed more like kids out cruising, drifting from party to party on a Saturday night, than predators stalking a potential rape victim.

"Let's talk about you two for a while," I suggested, wanting a better feel for the people the newspapers were calling "lust-sodden beasts."

Joe Kahahawai took over the conversation. You could tell he was proud of his strength. He would talk about boxing or football for as long as you wanted. He'd been a boxing heavyweight, though without any apparent skill, and he was all enthusiasm and very raw power. Co-defendant Benny Ahakuelo, another heavyweight, had enough talent to be picked to represent the Territory at the 1931 AAU matches in New York. Joe could handle himself in local amateur bouts and street brawls with sailors or other local kids, where there was plenty of opportunity for that type of practice and little chance for refinement of any latent skills.

He was actually better known for his ability at barefoot football, a uniquely Hawaiian institution that drew large crowds every weekend to games around town. The league play was well-organized, featuring the same sort of unrefined power, speed, and elemental violence characterizing Joe's boxing career. Here, he and Ahakuelo were more evenly matched, and both of their names appeared regularly in the newspapers on the Sundays following the games.

He'd been in trouble before. A year or so earlier, after doing some drinking after a game, he'd gotten involved in a dispute that had escalated into a first-degree robbery charge. After a hung jury, he had pleaded guilty to the lesser crime of assault and battery. The episode had cost him thirty days in the county lockup.

He didn't regard this experience as anything too terrible; he certainly hadn't been traumatized or even, it appeared, very inconvenienced by his short stay in jail. He wasn't anxious to go back in because of Thalia Massie's rape complaint, though.

I'm no expert, even now, but Joe didn't seem the rapist type, although he was definitely much more likely to act on impulse than any sort of calculated deliberation. And I was seeing him sober. Who knew what he was like when he was drunk?

He seemed like the original "go along" kind of guy, so he might have gone along that night if the others had formed a plan or acted equally impulsively. Had Ida and the others led Joe into this mess?

What "type" was he? I have to confess that Joe Kahahawai did fit some of the stereotypes assigned to Hawaiians over the years. He was easygoing, fully prepared to take life as it came, whether it offered riches or relative poverty. He would work hard if he saw a reason to do so, though his interests were limited. He was without prospects or ambition, so there was no frustration in his life—and before Thalia Massie, not a hell of a lot of stress.

We talked for a while longer. I kept trying to get a feel for these two men, one a little older and one a little younger than me, both of whom were in a serious fix. When I thought the picture was clearer, I thanked them and went back to Judge Heen's office, where I found Pittman and his co-counsel continuing their conference. Both of them wore expectant expressions as I came into the room.

"What they're saying sounds true. I've got a couple of questions, though."

"Ask away. If we can answer without violating a confidence, we will," Pittman promised.

"Okay. What time did the dance stop at the Waikiki Park?"

Bill Pittman looked at Judge Heen and smiled. "Midnight, or five minutes either side. It was supposed to stop a few minutes before, but it ran a little over, according to the manager."

"And what time was it when Kahahawai hit Mrs. Peeples?"

"The police are saying 12:37 a.m. She got to the station about five minutes later."

This gave the boys less than forty-five minutes to collect Thalia Massie, drive her to the old quarantine station, rape her at least five times, and then drive almost to Kalihi. And along the way, be seen by people in a car, people at a luau, and who knew who else.

Samuel Lau's warning about the "times" made sense.

"You know, I read her statement to McIntosh." I pointed to the envelope on the desk. "She said in there she left the party at the Ala Wai Inn between twelve-thirty and one o'clock."

Bill Pittman spoke calmly, quietly, but with steel supporting his words. "She made that statement less than four hours after the alleged attack. According to this…" He tapped the envelope. "She would have been walking on Ena Road at 12:37 a.m., exactly the time our clients were five miles away in Palama.

"Based on that statement, the police should have been looking for someone driving a rough-running black Ford or Dodge with a torn top. Our clients were driving a brown—light brown—Ford in perfect condition. Based on the statement, the police should have been looking for four Hawaiians, not two Hawaiians, two Japanese, and one Chinese-Hawaiian.

"If you take Thalia Massie at her word of Sunday morning, September 13, our clients should never have been arrested."

"Why were they?"

"Ah, that is why your action last night is morally correct. That is why I subjected you to my ramblings about race. The answer, I'm afraid, is that the police—no, that isn't fair. Many, even most, of the police don't like this any more than we do. Let's just say that some people need a conviction. And unless we stop them, the ones they convict are going to be five innocent men."

"In order to get their conviction," Judge Heen interjected, "they've had to change some facts. Mrs. Massie had to revise her story to make it a better fit for our clients. She's now saying she left the party around 11:30 p.m. They don't know we have the information about the earlier statement, of course." He indicated the photographs of McIntosh's report.

It couldn't have been any clearer. Just like Samuel Lau said, it was a frame-up all the way. These two lawyers were only confirming what I had already come to believe.

The envelope lay on the desk, silently waiting for my decision. So, I told them most of the rest. About tire tracks and a clerk who wanted to be a detective. About orders to take pictures of "evidence" just manufactured on the spot. About a Chief of Detectives driving the suspect's vehicle around the crime scene, making sure there were plenty of matching tire tracks to be photographed. And finally, about a secret meeting of the Chamber of Commerce and the Navy.

Some of it they knew; some they probably suspected. All of it added up to one conclusion: Powerful people were out to nail five kids from Palama, by hook or by crook. But then, they already knew that part.

What they didn't know, and I didn't tell them, was why I was there in the first place. Thalia Massie's opium problem, if any, would remain my little secret until I figured out what to do about it.

290 Kamakela Lane, Palama
Saturday, November 14

As a favor to Bill Pittman, I took one of the five home that afternoon. Joe Kahahawai's house was on a little lane that doesn't exist anymore in lower Palama. It was a mean part of town, though not the meanest by a long shot. His mother, Esther Anito, came to the door and stood, looking out at yet another police car containing her son. She was a short, chunky woman, pure Hawaiian, who wore a red-flowered muumuu and a quizzical expression.

Joe's parents were divorced. His mother, who had remarried a Filipino man, did laundry and took in ironing, helping to support a family that still included Joe, who wasn't working. He'd had some offers from sympathetic (mostly non-white) employers who felt he and the others were getting a raw deal, but Joe was waiting to see what else turned up.

"You like come in?" he asked me.

"That's okay, I've got to get back to the office."

Joe shrugged. "Whatever." He climbed out of the car, then leaned back through the open window.

"I never did nothing to that wahine," he said. "Why you think she say that stuff?" Meaning, "You're a haole like Thalia—what makes her tick?"

I, of course, no more knew Thalia Massie than I did Charlie Chaplin. I could only manage, "I don't know, Joe."

"You think I going back to jail?"

"What does Mr. Pittman say?"

Joe looked out through the windshield toward the corrugated roofs of Hell's Half-Acre. "He says no chance, but I ain't so sure."

I wasn't so sure either, and hesitated long enough for Joe to get that message. He nodded, and regarded me evenly. "That's what I figger, too." He stood up, then slapped a big hand down on the door. "Well, I been there before."

Joe Kahahawai turned toward his little house where his mother stood smiling now in the doorway. She pushed open the screen door and welcomed her boy home.

CHAPTER 18

Federal Building, Room 213
Monday, November 16

"What in God's name are you doing with this Massie thing?" C.T. Stevenson was back from Kauai and steaming.

"I don't know. I'm trying to develop an informer, I guess."

"No, no, no. Billy already told me that. I had to spend extra to phone down to Hilo to talk to him. He stuck up for you, by the way. I didn't ask what you were *trying* to do. I asked what you're *doing*."

Stevenson got up from his desk and, head down, started walking back and forth behind it. This pacing was something he said helped him relax and think better. Watching him made everybody else nervous, especially when he was towing the telephone around to and fro over the desktop, threatening the pile of reports, notepads, envelopes, and assorted government paperwork heaped seemingly at random.

"Since I got home last night, I've had calls from Sandy Wood, John McIntosh, Harry Hewitt, and Griff Wight. I even got one from some jake called Weeber who's representing the Chamber of Commerce—which means Walter Dillingham—and a Captain Wortman from Pearl Harbor. That's not a bad morning's work: the U.S. Attorney, the Chief of Detectives, the Attorney General, and the U.S.-by-God-Navy. In fact, the only people who haven't called me yet have been the governor, Commissioner Anslinger and, oh yeah, you." He stopped long enough to glare at me.

"I haven't gotten very far on it. I wrote up what I've done up to now, and I was going to fill you and Billy in when you came back."

"Well, I'm back. And you've gotten exactly as far as you're gonna get on this little number, sonny boy. What the hell were you thinking?"

I sat mute, aware that there wasn't much I could say to improve things. The phone rang. He didn't answer it, just looked at me with raised eyebrows as if to say, "Who is it now?" He sat back down when it stopped ringing, and picked up where he'd left off.

"You like it here?"

"Sure. I mean, it's my home and all."

"Ha! It ain't gonna be for long. There's lots worse places we can send you. Detroit or St. Paul—someplace where, winter comes, you gotta drink antifreeze just so you can take a leak. I don't know how you got this job, but you sure don't have to do it here. I'm gonna get on the wire to Washington, see if I can't get you shipped off someplace where the sun don't shine six months a year."

I slumped in my chair, feeling the current that had carried me away from shore into waters way over my head now pushing me toward exile in disgrace.

"Yeah, I thought you could stay out of our hair and run out the string on the White Friend, but I see now I was wrong. Now I gotta scramble around to find something official for you to do that's got nothing to do with informers or real police work, and that something is inspections."

I had been around just long enough to know that this was a sentence to purgatory.

"Do you think you can handle that without getting half of Honolulu pissed off and calling me up?"

"Yes, sir. I'll do a good job."

"I don't give a shit whether you do a good job or not. Just stay the hell out of trouble until I can get rid of you."

"Okay, I understand. No problem."

"Good. Here's a copy of the regulations." He pushed a paper pamphlet across the desk at me. "Read up on it and make me a list of the doctors and druggists here in town you're planning to inspect. Stay away from any of the ones Billy's got flagged. No point spooking his game. I figure that trial's gonna run about two, maybe three weeks. Say, a day or two for each one, so you'll need about ten places. Better make it fifteen. By that time we'll know what Mr. Anslinger's gonna do with you."

The phone rang again. This time he answered, giving me on opportunity to slip away with my pamphlet and what was left of my butt. When I looked back, he was up and wearing out the path behind the desk again.

Benson Smith Drug Store, 99 South King Street
Thursday, November 19

I came across the prescription accidentally, six hours into my fifth inspection of the week. Although I can't say the work was especially hard, it was hot, dusty, and boring with, under the circumstances, more than just a touch of pointlessness.

An inspection was essentially a paper pursuit, a task better suited for an accountant than a cop, so I fit in all right. When you got right down to it, there wasn't much difference between going through bank records and going through pharmacy files, except banks always keep things neater.

Benson Smith, the biggest and busiest pharmacy in Honolulu, also had the most records; doctors' prescriptions were kept in chronological order in boxes. I decided right away to work on 1931, mostly because those scripts were relatively dust-free and still fairly easy to read, which was an important consideration since doctors aren't exactly known for their penmanship. You try going through five or six thousand prescriptions, some written in Latin, all in handwriting that looks like some little kid was trying to write cursive for the first time. After six hours, you'll be seeing double or even triple, at least.

The way to get through it is to focus only on one line, looking for a combination of letters, like "a-i-n-e," or "m-o-r." This quickly eliminates most of the prescriptions. The process gets automatic enough that your mind, at least, can wander off to the beach even though your ass is still on a box in the storeroom.

So, with my fingers moving as fast as they could go and my thoughts in Waikiki, it was a bloody miracle that I saw the script at all. Somehow it registered, and I flipped backward for a closer look. The script wasn't written for morphine or cocaine. It was for a narcotic, though; laudanum, an ancient but effective mixture of alcohol and opium. Very popular with romantic poets like Coleridge and women addicts around the turn of the century. Junkies loved it. If you just wanted to get blasted, laudanum would do very nicely, thanks.

But it wasn't the drug that had caught my eye; it was the patient's name: Thalia Massie. She had gotten four ounces of laudanum on October 10, just a month before.

Two blocks down the street, the Ala Moana trial was well underway. The daily papers kept me up to date on developments. Jury selection ended on Tuesday, with the Territory's first witness—the same Thalia Massie—taking the stand on Wednesday morning.

The *Advertiser* reported that she looked pale and gaunt, "her body bent and wracked with anguish, her voice trembling at times with emotion and fatigue," which had sounded to me like one of my books' description of a junkie in withdrawal. On second thought, though, the prescription I was holding might mean she hadn't had to kick her habit. Maybe she'd just gotten herself a new connection, one with M.D. after his name.

I held onto the prescription for maybe five minutes, thinking about my next move. This lady had already caused me no small measure of grief and was probably going to get me transferred, if not fired outright. I had never even seen her, but I still wasn't sure I wanted to tangle with her again. And she did have plenty of legitimate medical reasons for getting narcotics—her jaw had been broken and even if she hadn't really been gang-raped, *something* painful had happened to her.

Still, that drug was an odd choice. I knew from my reading that morphine was a better alternative; the dose was easier to control, and the effect was much more predictable. Doctors prescribed morphine for broken jaws and laudanum for chronic, long-term pain. When it had been legal to do so, they had prescribed it to maintain narcotic addiction.

So I was kicking myself already as I started back at the beginning of the year. This time I was looking for a different combination of letters as I paged through the scripts. This time, I was looking for M-a-s-s-i-e.

When the store closed at six, I had twenty-seven prescriptions with her name on them, going back to April 9, a full five months before Thalia Massie had or hadn't gotten raped.

Federal Building, Room 213
Thursday, November 19

A Honolulu policeman I didn't know was sitting in my chair when I got back to the office that night. He started to get up, but I just waved him off. "Make yourself at home; I'm not staying," I said, going to the registrant file cabinet. Billy and Kam were huddled together at Billy's desk and there were the usual raid tools lying around, so I guessed they were all going out after a den. McKeague waved from behind his newspaper at Stevenson's desk.

"How's things down at the pharmacy? All the scripts still there?" Billy smiled, letting me know he didn't mean it in a nasty way.

"Yeah, yeah. Go ahead, I got it coming."

"It won't be forever, and hey, it might do you some good."

I had no response to that. "How'd you do in Hilo?"

"Got a couple of tins of Lam Kee, and a line into that one doctor. He looks pretty good."

"Score one for George Soon, then, huh?"

Billy threw me a warning look, and I decided to talk to him later when we were alone. I retrieved the typed list of the registrants in Honolulu, pulled the two pages of drugstores from the file, and slammed the drawer. The list went in my briefcase with Thalia's prescriptions.

"You boys have a good night. I wish I was going along." I grabbed my hat off the rack and started for the door.

"Maybe we can call you for the next one, Jack," Billy said.

"Sure. Assuming I'm still in Hawaii."

I'd reached the stairwell when Billy caught up with me.

"You should have waited till I came back, hoss," he said.

"Hell, Billy, all I did was read a few newspaper articles and go see Jardine."

"That was plenty, as it turns out."

"I know that now."

He laughed. "They do say experience is something you get right after you really, really need it."

"Not having any sure cost me."

"What's the list for?"

"Just trying to decide who gets to spend a fun day with me tomorrow."

"C.T. took some grief over this."

I turned to face him. "What would you have done, Billy? I mean, the informer comes in and tells us something, we're supposed to check it out, right? That's what the book says."

"Right. But there's ways, and there's ways. Everybody's so goddamn touchy over this rape thing, you have to anticipate there's gonna be a hubbub. Hubbub isn't something you ever need with an informer."

"He's your bird. What are you going to do about this?"

"You mean the Ala Moana stuff? Nothing. We passed the info along to the police. We didn't identify the source, but Kam knows." Wells looked pensive. "I don't know if he'd tell McIntosh, though. You know, they got a split over this case in the department."

I knew this all too well, but I just shrugged. "I guess that's not our problem, either."

"No. And we're going to keep it that way."

"But what if it's true, Billy? That's what I wanted to tell Sandy Wood. If it's true, it isn't good enough to just say, oh well, we can't corroborate it, and let it lie. If it's true, their witness is a goddamn junkie. Who knows if she could even see straight that night? She could have been so blasted on hop, she couldn't tell if the Marx Brothers raped her." Considering how much laudanum she'd gotten, this possibility no longer seemed so wild.

"It's still not our problem."

"No. It isn't. But you know whose problem it is? Those five boys who go back to court tomorrow morning, that's who. Who maybe didn't do what some dope fiend says they did. You know what, Billy? I'm glad it's not my problem, 'cause I sure don't want their little dilemma on my conscience."

Billy shook his head and laughed shortly. "Boy, you are gonna get yourself in all sorts of hot water. Probably already in over your head. Are you sure it's worth it?"

"I don't know what it's worth. I just wanted to do what was right."

"Yeah," he sighed, looking back toward the office. "We all started out saying that. Like I said, there's ways and there's ways. You just go on home. Make your list. I'll do what I can with C.T."

"I hope it does some good."

"Go on, then. I'll see you tomorrow." He turned and went back to the office. I watched him go, and then followed his orders.

CHAPTER 19

2663 Terrace Drive, Manoa Valley
Thursday, November 19

Tantalus, one of the mountain peaks that enfold Manoa in a wide green embrace, begins in a gentle rise from the valley floor. Halfway to the back of the valley, Terrace Drive hugs this slope, a narrow plateau flanked by large houses like my parents' home, which cling to the hillside before it grows impossibly steep.

From my window, all of Manoa spread out before me—a panorama stretching from high mountain walls softened with lush vegetation down to Waikiki and the blue Pacific beyond. Bill Pittman had commented that you could easily see the dark roof and tall chimney of Thalia Massie's house from the window, if you knew where to look. As I went through the papers and prescription records I had moved up to the house, I was more and more certain that I knew exactly where to look.

There were about twenty drugstores in Honolulu, but I concentrated on seven larger pharmacies located between downtown and Waikiki, places where I figured Mrs. Massie would be most comfortable.

C.T. seemed very pleased at the pace of the inspections, although he definitely wouldn't have been so happy if he'd known what I was looking for. It took eight days to hit all seven stores—a couple I'd already visited once before—and I hit pay dirt in five of them. I came back with a grand total of sixty-four prescriptions written by four different doctors and a dentist. Thalia Massie wasn't the only person in Honolulu getting laudanum, by a long shot; I found Lau Sau's name on a few scripts, too. But Thalia was the best customer at these places. Her tally looked like this:

BENSON SMITH (DOWNTOWN)	DR. O'DAY	27 PRESCRIPTIONS
BENSON SMITH (S. BERETANIA)	DR. WITHINGTON	9 PRESCRIPTIONS
CITY DRUG COMPANY	DR. PORTER	8 PRESCRIPTIONS
PEOPLE'S DRUG	DR. KIM	15 PRESCRIPTIONS
BLACKSHEAR'S DRUG COMPANY	DR. ASKINS	5 PRESCRIPTIONS

This added up to 396 ounces of laudanum, or just over three gallons, and knocked me back a bit. At forty-five grains per fluid ounce, three gallons of laudanum contained almost three pounds of opium, a very impressive amount even over an eight-month period. Hell, if you get right down to it, three gallons was a lot of ninety-proof alcohol. Not only did Thalia Massie have some good opium connections, but in the middle of Prohibition she also had one of the better lines for hooch.

And I could see how she kept her little secret. By taking scripts from each doctor to a different pharmacy, she gave each druggist only a piece of the whole picture. I still needed to know what she'd told the doctors to get them to prescribe the medication for her, though. This made a difference, because getting opium for a legitimate medical need was no problem, but lying to get it was a crime.

I was also pretty sure the prescriptions didn't tell the whole story. Lots of doctors kept stocks of narcotics on hand to give directly to their patients. Thalia could have gotten even more opium in that way, but I would have to go to the doctors' offices to find out.

I added two names to my inspection schedule, and left it on C.T.'s desk on Friday night. Billy had already flagged Kim, so I couldn't approach him yet. John Porter and the dentist, Robert Askins, posed another problem. Both were Navy doctors at Pearl Harbor. I knew if I showed up with questions, they would probably buck the hot potato up the chain of command, which would then roll it right back down onto C.T. I wanted to have plenty of ammunition in the bag when the calls started.

Dr. Paul Withington was one of the physicians who had treated Thalia after the assault. All of his prescriptions were written after September 13. Since he was a likely witness in the Ala Moana case and maybe a friend of the victim's family, I put him second in the batting order.

This left Chris O'Day. He was the first to prescribe for Thalia, and he'd written the most prescriptions. Although these dated back all the way to April, the volume got much heavier after September 13. He didn't have any overt connection to the trial, so I put him at the top of my list.

Across the street, the trial dragged on. The prosecution finally rested, but their case had been badly shaken by a procession of witnesses who failed to corroborate Thalia's rape claim. The tire track evidence had been thoroughly discredited on cross-examination; McIntosh had no answer for why he drove the car down to the quarantine station and then wanted pictures taken of the tracks he left.

Even friendly witnesses, like the doctors who had examined Thalia on the morning of the assault, left the stand without helping her case. Doctor Porter said that although he hadn't seen any signs of forced sex, he couldn't prove it hadn't happened as Thalia testified. Bill Pittman asked Doctor Liu if Thalia had looked to him like someone who'd just been violently assaulted six or seven times by five large men. "I wondered about that," the doctor admitted. "Except for the injuries to her face, she was as neat as a new pin." But she had taken a shower before she saw him, he added lamely.

If Thalia's supporters provided little comfort, those who testified for the defense drew public scorn. Samuel Lau and several other police officers were bitterly branded as traitors by Griffith Wight. More than ever, the split in the police department lay like an open sore for the public to see.

All in all, it was an excellent time to be a pharmacy inspector, even one with a hidden agenda.

Federal Building, Room 213
Monday, December 7

"Hung jury!" The city responded by going onto a low boil. The papers said the Ala Moana jury was divided along racial lines, seven to five for conviction, forcing Judge Steadman to declare a mistrial on Sunday afternoon. Tensions soared on Monday as the haoles fumed and the Navy made threatening noises. Supporters of Joe Kahahawai, Horace Ida, and the others celebrated, but the prosecutor promised a retrial.

At Pearl Harbor, Admiral Yates Stirling fulminated about local justice, and talked of keeping the fleet away from Honolulu during its winter exercises. This was tantamount to an admission by the Navy that its ships and crews weren't safe in an American port. The insult meant Honolulu would lose the business of 20,000 sailors—and hundreds of Navy wives who normally came with the fleet for a romantic Hawaiian visit.

Local merchants, horrified at the prospect of losing an estimated $6 million in business, demanded action from their politicians.

Scores of Navy wives who feared that the mistrial signaled an open season on white women bought guns and ammunition; Sheriff Gleason spent most of Monday at his desk signing pistol permits. It was starting to dawn on everyone that Thalia Massie's problem had become everybody's predicament.

The Ala Moana trial's inconclusive end muddied my status in the office. C.T. couldn't decide what to do with me. There had been no response from Washington and the White Friend's case files were still waiting, so he was ready to "give you back your green eyeshade," at least until he got back from a trial in San Francisco. Much to his surprise, I offered to complete my inspection list.

He regarded me with narrowed eyes. "Let me see if I got this straight. You're *volunteering* to finish off on your inspections?"

"Sure. I've only got three or four doctors left on the list. That shouldn't take more than a couple of days. I found a few people who've been seeing more than one doctor, getting scripts for morphine and opium. I'll talk to the doctors and see what they say." This was perfectly true, as far as it went. "I left a list on your desk."

As Billy busied himself at the evidence locker, staying out of the way, Stevenson contemplated this unexpected, possibly unprecedented, enthusiasm for drudgery by drumming his fingers on the desk while his mental wheels turned.

"All right," he said at last. "I don't know why this is making me all twitchy, but I expect I'm fixin' to find out. You go finish those doctors, and then I'm gonna have you go through all those boxes and see if there's anything on this Sammy Akana character Billy was telling me about. See if anything got missed."

I had already done this, so I didn't object. "No problem. You got the names of those doctors?"

He stirred the drift of paper on his desk. "In here somewhere." The ringing phone prevented him from delving any deeper in the pile.

I grabbed my case folder from my desk and caught Billy's wink as I headed for the door. I, too, was fixin' to find out.

CHAPTER 20

2850 Kahawai Street
Monday, December 7

Thalia found the United States Navy a crashing bore. Early in Tommie's Hawaii assignment, he'd taken her on a visit to his new submarine. Everything about it—and this included the crew—was, in her opinion, slimy, smelly, and stupid. She'd fed him her disdain for weeks afterward.

One aspect of the tour, though, had left a different, though equally powerful, impression. This one, she'd kept to herself.

In the submarine's control room, Tommie had proudly displayed the dials, switches, wheels, and levers the men used to move and fight their ship. One of these was a large gauge with a white face and black and red lettering. Tommie had explained that this instrument measured a boat's operating depth. The red numbers represented a concept she found utterly fascinating.

She didn't understand the physics; her interests lay in other areas. But the outcome was certainly clear enough. The deeper one of those boats went, the more force was applied by the water outside. At some point, this pressure would become so great that the hull would collapse, flattening the boat and everything in it in an instant of cataclysmic violence. The submariners had a name for this silent but deadly point in the ocean. They called it "crush depth."

Engineers had calculated the exact level at which this catastrophe would take place, Tommie had assured her, mistaking her interest for concern. The captain was careful never to exceed, or even approach, the red numbers on the gauge. He'd patted her hand, a gesture she detested. She needn't worry.

Thalia wasn't worried, but the men were. She heard it under their bluster and their bravado. Oh, they cherished each other and their Navy. They kept their faith in the institution that sent them down into the cold Pacific waters and, most of the time, brought them back up. But the young lieutenants and their women all understood that mistakes happened. Engineers could be wrong. A lapse by a crewman, a faulty repair or a bad weld, some forgotten little nothing—any of these could push them and their boat together to a place from which there was no return—all the way to crush depth.

The Navy had sent Tommie to sea for most of the trial, so he'd missed all of the testimony. His submarine had returned to Pearl just in time for him to hear the jury deadlock. He was in court that day, where he watched the defendants celebrating with their lawyers, heard the prosecutor's weak assurances of better luck next time, and instantly sank into a hopeless melancholy before going home to give Thalia the news. He drank himself insensible that evening and fell asleep in the living room.

When he awoke on Monday morning, depressed and hung over, Thalia was ready to plumb the depths.

She didn't leave her room right away, though; she was content to let Grace drive Tommie lower into despair's black pit. She listened at the door from time to time as Grace inveighed for an hour against the "black savages" now threatening every white woman in Honolulu.

When she heard her mother on the living room telephone, Thalia finally emerged.

Tommie sat slumped at the kitchen table, and he turned weary eyes to her as she entered.

"I heard Mother. She's right. This will only encourage the beasts," she said.

He hid his face in his hands, shutting out the room and its occupants. "I don't know what else to do. It will never end. The juries here will never convict their own. The courts don't work."

Thalia stood at his chair. "'*I don't know what else to do,*'" she sneered. "You're pathetic. What kind of man lets this happen to his wife and doesn't do anything about it? You weren't even here during the trial, so I had to face them alone all over again. I thought you loved me." She pivoted, strode quickly to the bedroom door, and slammed it shut without looking back.

She was awake when he came to her that night, so she heard the door open and saw his shadow cross the moonlit patch to her bed. As he pulled back the sheet, she asked him what in the hell he thought he was doing, which stopped him dead.

"I—I wanted to show you I loved you. I wanted to tell you that hadn't changed," he stammered.

"*Nothing changed?*" she shrilled into his shocked face. "You must be joking. The man I married wouldn't let this happen. What have you done but get drunk and go out on your precious boat? And leave me here alone while the animals laugh at me. Then you say you love me? How can I believe it? A real man would prove it to me."

When he had crept back out the door toward the guest room, Thalia hopped up and went to her dresser. She drew the cork on a brown glass bottle and inhaled the delicious tang of the laudanum. She took a deep pull and thought, as she waited for the opium to warm her, about what a man looked like when he reached crush depth.

CHAPTER 21

Dillingham Transportation Building, Room 405
Wednesday, December 9

Paul Withington and I didn't meet; it was more like a collision, although I think we parted with an understanding. I had gotten some additional ammo from Dr. O'Day, whose precisely kept records showed he'd prescribed a total of 142 ounces of laudanum for Thalia since April 9, and directly dispensed another forty-eight ounces to her in the same period. Her total was getting grander all the time.

O'Day reacted with shock and a deep sense of self-preservation; he didn't want to take the fall for something a drug addict patient might have done. Thalia, he said, never told him she was getting laudanum from more than one physician. The fraud case looked better and better.

Dr. Withington, who had a larger role in Thalia's life, was just as prickly and defensive as I'd thought he would be. The inspection started out routinely. I found several discrepancies, none of which were important enough to cause any problems for the doctor, but he did not want to discuss Thalia Massie.

"I have a privileged, confidential relationship with Mrs. Massie and her husband, and I am not going to discuss her case with a policeman."

Although there was enough acid in his words to etch his pronouncement on metal, I thought I might have something to neutralize it. "Yes, sir, I understand, but I don't want any privileged information from you. I know there are some things you can't discuss, but we need to find out what's going on with this drug addict—why she's gotten almost four gallons of laudanum since April and who's responsible for that happening."

"Four gallons? That's absurd." He was red-faced and actually spluttering.

I put my chart and all the prescriptions on the desk, inviting him to give me his professional opinion. Following C.T.'s instructions, I left Dr. Kim's name out of the picture, but it was clear enough without it. Dr. Withington looked like somebody had just told him his mother was earning extra money whoring down in Chinatown. As he read the chart and leafed through the other prescriptions, his mouth opened and closed several times in the mute and staring expression you see on a moray eel, though without the menace.

A considerably changed man finally broke the stunned silence. "This is unbelievable," he said. "I can't understand it." He gaped at me, appealing for help, for some clarification that would somehow sweep the mess away.

I shrugged. "Don't look at me. I was hoping *you* could explain it."

"I can't. My God. She's getting…"

"I added it up. It's between three and four ounces a day."

"Incredible. She's just a little thing. I don't know how she can possibly stand the dose."

"She's a junkie. Eight months, she's got a high tolerance built up."

Withington looked shocked all over again, started to deny it but ultimately said nothing, calculated, then finally conceded the truth. His features were suddenly cast in hurt and disappointment.

"I've got to ask you, doc. Were you aware of the scripts from the other doctors?"

"No. Of course not! There's no way I would have allowed this to go on for five minutes if I'd known. John Porter. Amazing. Chris O'Day. How did she keep it from us?"

"For starters, she took your prescriptions to one pharmacy, Porter's to another, and O'Day's to a third. You doctors weren't talking to each other, and the druggists weren't talking to anybody. She slipped through the cracks. She's not the only junkie in town doing it. I found three more just in the week I was checking pharmacies."

"I wish you wouldn't call her that."

"Junkie? Okay. But we're going to have to call her an addict, aren't we?"

He contemplated that question for a moment, thinking about the ramifications. "She's been through so much. And her husband, I'm really concerned about him."

"You think he's getting some of this stuff?"

He started to say no, but stopped himself. Ten minutes ago, he would probably have ordered me out of his office just for making the suggestion.

Now, with the harmony of his world jarred, he was prepared to consider any possibility.

"No," he said finally. "Thinking back now, I have seen indications that Mrs. Massie—Thalia—was seeking drugs. Damn it. I should have paid more attention; the signs were there. I haven't seen anything like that with Tommie." He shook his head sadly. "This is such a tragedy. You know about the assault?"

"Yes. I know she had a medical need for narcotics." I offered him a bone that, to his credit, he rejected.

"Not to this extent. And certainly not in this underhanded fashion." Clearly wounded, Withington was seeing Thalia Massie in a whole different light, maybe my light.

"Is there any reason you can think of why she would need to get this amount of opium from five different doctors?"

"No. That's not the way to go about it. And this is plainly excessive. I'm just so disappointed in her."

"Why? Because she lied to you?"

"I thought I had really established a good relationship with Thalia and Tommie. He's been under tremendous strain. Rape cases are so stressful for everyone. Even if there aren't physical scars, the damage is often permanent. I don't know if their marriage will survive, and now this."

"Her addiction is going to be a problem. The regulations say she can't be treated the same way."

"Treated? Hah! She's gotten the last prescription she'll be getting from me. And I doubt any of the others will want to continue seeing her. No one likes being played for a fool." Then he seemed to reconsider. "She does have real problems, beyond those caused by the assault. There's no doubt she needs medical care. All the lies, though…so sad."

He looked so crushed, I actually felt sorry for him. "Don't feel too bad, Doc. She pulled the same thing on four other doctors and who knows how many druggists. Lots of lies."

"I'll give John Porter a call. We discuss her treatment fairly often," he said. "I'm sure she lied to him as well." He sighed, and then a strange expression flew across his face. It was the look of a person who, having been suddenly confronted by a particularly dark and frightening reality, caught just a glimpse of something much more terrifying in the shadows beyond.

"She's lied. Dear God," he whispered. "She's lied."

CHAPTER 22

Dillingham Transportation Building, Room 405
Thursday, December 10

I got the call from Paul Withington on Thursday morning. He sounded subdued and tired, like someone who might not have had a lot of sleep the night before. But he wanted to talk, and asked if I could walk over to his office.

When I got there, he didn't want to discuss opium at all. Through the window, I watched two tugboats muscling a steamship into its berth at Pier 7 across Ala Moana, and waited for him to get to the point.

"Are you familiar with a condition called pre-eclampsia?"

"Can't say I am. What is it?"

"It's a woman's problem associated with pregnancy, sometimes with miscarriage. Hemorrhages—bleeding—in the liver and kidneys cause nitrogenous wastes to be retained in the bloodstream. Will this mean anything to you?"

"Probably not."

"Well, it can be dangerous, very dangerous. In the advanced stage, eclampsia could even be fatal if not treated properly." He swiveled in his chair and followed my gaze out the window. "In one of these cases, someone might have symptoms such as weight gain, elevated blood pressure, and small secondary retinal hemorrhages—essentially bleeding inside the eyes. Are you following me?"

"I guess so. Is this eclampsia something painful? Would you need narcotics to treat it?"

"*Pre*-eclampsia. No, no. It isn't painful. It's the effect on the eyes that might be important. The bleeding might cause blurred or faded vision, perhaps patches of blindness, even after the pregnancy."

"You wouldn't need opium for that, either."

Withington turned back, regarded me steadily, and spoke carefully. "No, you wouldn't. But that still isn't the real problem."

He was waiting for me, but my mind was focused elsewhere—on what four gallons of laudanum might do.

"Visual acuity—the ability to see things—might be drastically reduced," he finally continued. "Especially at night, particularly if that person had weak eyes already. Someone with that condition would have trouble seeing in the dark. She would probably have difficulty, even in daylight, recognizing objects or people."

I finally got it. He hadn't called me to help with my fraud case on Thalia. He had never mentioned any names, and certainly not that of the patient who had grifted him—and four other doctors—out of enough laudanum to keep five junkies happy. He had just talked about a condition I had never heard of, and 'someone' with already weak eyes who'd had this pre-eclampsia thing. 'Someone' who might have gained some weight as a result; opium users tend to lose weight, so they are thinner than non-users. 'Someone' who could have trouble seeing, and who might even effectively be as blind as a bat.

All this made me ask myself how 'someone' with this condition could identify five boys or read a license plate in a dark corner of Honolulu like the beach road that night.

Dr. Withington, who had been inspecting me from across the polished surface of his desk, had apparently been thinking the same thing himself since he'd met the real Thalia Massie for the first time yesterday.

And he wanted to do something about it.

"I called John Porter out at Pearl, as I mentioned yesterday. He understands the situation. We've agreed that he'll be the only one who prescribes any narcotics from here on out. He'll talk to Bob Askins, the dentist. I assume Chris O'Day will be cutting her off, too?"

"Yeah," I agreed. "He was pretty rattled. Didn't know about either of you."

"And there was another physician…"

"We're taking care of him, too."

"All right. Dr. Porter's busy today, but he can see you tomorrow—wants to see you tomorrow. Make sure we're all singing off the same page of the hymnal."

"I appreciate it, Doc."

U.S. Naval Hospital, Pearl Harbor
Friday, December 11

The rhetoric was still hot and tempers were hotter on Thursday. Stocks of firearms in Honolulu sporting goods stores were almost exhausted.

Rumors spread through the military that the Ala Moana boys and their friends planned revenge on Navy women. Bill Pittman ridiculed that notion; the boys were still on bail, and the last thing on earth they needed was more trouble with the Navy.

I noticed he wasn't laughing, though.

"Business as usual" seemed to be the order of the day at Pearl Harbor. At that time, only some submarines and minesweepers were homeported there, but all the minesweepers had left for maneuvers with their crews, leaving a lot of nervous wives back in Honolulu.

By Friday morning, those wives—most of whom lived off base—were sequestered at home with their new guns and plenty of ammo.

The base itself was quiet when I arrived at the dispensary to see Dr. John Porter, who treated the Navy wives for their gynecological needs. Porter was tall and competent, with the courtly manner of a Virginia gentleman. He gave me one of the nicest brush-offs I've ever received.

Efficient Navy nurses and equally methodical corpsmen in white staffed the clinic, massaging the military's usually stifling records system. These people had more forms and paperwork than we did, and every transaction was documented in triplicate. I wasn't surprised that their narcotic records were perfect. They showed that an additional thirty-two ounces of laudanum had been dispensed directly to Mrs. Thalia Massie on the orders of Dr. John Porter.

He had no problem confirming the dispensing records and his prescriptions, saying he'd already discussed the matter with Withington. No, he continued, he didn't think the amount he'd prescribed was out of line, given her obvious need. But he acknowledged that the grand total was clearly excessive.

When I asked whether he had noticed any sign of dependence, he considered carefully, then observed that she had received a particularly large dose of morphine on the morning following the assault. "You undoubtedly recognized that from your examination of the records," he said generously.

Actually, it was the first time I had noticed.

He said he had been called out to the Massie home on the morning of Sunday, September 13. After an examination, in which he had concluded she was hysterical and might have a broken jaw, he had injected her with morphine. When the first injection had not taken effect, he had administered a second. Both doses were noted in the narcotic log.

"She was already tolerating narcotics when she got hit…"

He smiled ruefully and nodded. "That would be my conclusion, yes."

This was as far as he would go, however, in discussing his patient.

"Well, she's been getting these drugs—a lot of them—by fraud. She can't keep doing that," I told him.

"Of course not. I hardly think she needs to resort to fraud. Her injuries—physical and psychological—are real enough," he said mildly.

"Yes, sir," I agreed. "But that only provides justification for one physician to treat her. She can't repeat the process with every doctor in town."

He smiled again. "I understand completely. Dr. Withington and I are in total agreement, and so is Dr. Askins down the hall. They'll refer her to me, and I'll be the only one prescribing for her—assuming, of course, that she still has a legitimate need. I'm sure we can resolve this matter in Mrs. Massie's best interests. And I especially want to thank you for bringing it to my attention."

He rose and showed me the door. "I'll send a corpsman along with you, just to make sure you get off base without difficulty."

"Thanks, but I can find my way."

"I'm certain you can. But there's been some trouble here at Pearl. Liberty may be canceled this weekend."

This was the first I had heard of any problems on the base itself. Up to now, it had all been in town. "What sort of trouble?"

"A note was sent to the Petty Officers Mess at the sub base this morning," he reluctantly admitted. "It said something to the effect of, 'We have raped your women and we'll get some more.' It was signed, 'Kalihi Gang.'"

"Kalihi Gang? I've never heard of it."

"Yes, a childish prank. It's obviously a hoax, but some of the men are already very upset, particularly those from my section of the country." He grimaced. "Mess halls are wonderful breeding grounds for gossip and rumor. Some of the things that have been said about Mrs. Massie have been quite incredible. The Navy will close ranks behind her against any…" He paused for the right word. "…let's say 'aspersion' that might be cast."

Maybe it was the military setting, or all the order and discipline of the hospital, but unlike the beginning of my meeting with Dr. Withington, I was staying right in step with this likable and temperate Southerner. He'd made himself clear as a ship's bell: the Navy wouldn't take too kindly to any innuendo directed at Thalia Massie, such as the suggestion that she was a dope fiend and an opium eater.

That raised a disturbing question. "Besides Dr. Askins," I asked, "do you have to report any of this up your chain of command?"

Again he smiled. "Mrs. Massie is a civilian dependent. She isn't under Navy discipline. She's just a patient, and I don't disclose patient confidences unless the patient authorizes me to do so. I made an exception for you, for obvious reasons; it's the law. But I don't believe Mrs. Massie wants anyone else to hear anything about what we've discussed here today. Do you?"

No, I was pretty sure of one thing: Thalia didn't want any of this getting out.

CHAPTER 23

2850 Kahawai Street
Sunday, December 13

It had taken Tommie almost a week to put it together since all the sailors had been confined to their duties until Saturday. But there had been no shortage of willing—even eager—volunteers at Pearl Harbor.

This time Thalia welcomed him into her bed, listened breathlessly to his description of the events at the Pali, and thrilled to the story of Horace Ida's torture.

"The men were wonderful," he told her, although Ida hadn't confessed. "But we made him pay."

She made him repeat it, asking again how they'd used their belts. When she closed her eyes, she could imagine the scene taking place in the headlights. She could see the boy groveling in the circle of angry sailors as leather and brass and hate had rained down.

Ida's failure to admit his guilt puzzled Tommie. "We beat the hell out of him," he admitted. "You should have seen it. His back was all torn up and when a belt hit him, the blood went everywhere. It even got on the car's window. I didn't think anyone could take that kind of punishment."

"He's a Jap," she sneered. "They don't have feelings like normal people." Even when you're whipping them bloody, she thought, you can't know what an Oriental feels.

"They probably shouldn't have tried one of the Japanese kids first. They may be too cunning," she added, sounding like an authority. "The colored ones, the Hawaiians, they're simpler. The ones named Benny and Joe would have been easier. They're bigger, but dumb."

"We took the first one we saw," he said. They had only been hunting for a few minutes when he'd spotted Ida on the street corner. "The men grabbed him right away."

"Anyway, it doesn't matter if he didn't confess," she reassured him. "We know what he did, and you made him suffer. What matters is, you did it for me. Tell me again."

When she had heard enough to be able to replay the scene in her head, seeing it as clearly as if someone played it for her as a movie, she pressed him for the details of his own involvement. "Where did you kick him? In the face? In the balls?"

But he hadn't actually kicked anyone. He'd stayed in the car, out of sight, watching through the window as the others worked.

"Oh," she sighed, the word a pregnant midpoint in a long silence. "When you said 'we,' I thought you…"

"Ida knows me," he pointed out. "He's seen me here and in court. I couldn't take the chance."

He'd done what an officer should—planned, directed, motivated. And when he and Jones had gotten the mob in a proper frenzy, he had led them to the target and pounced. That was how it worked in the submarines, too: The officers decided when and how the torpedoes should be fired, and told the enlisted men to fire them.

Thalia listened to him breathing and considered this, wondering if it was enough. "Maybe he's dead," she suggested. "If they're dead, you don't have to worry about them coming back and saying things about you. Maybe just beating them isn't enough." She couldn't see his face in the darkness but felt the excitement.

She reached for him and found him ready. His lips moved, but the words were lost in the rush of her power. "You do love me," she sighed.

CHAPTER 24

Damon Building, Room 321-D
Monday, December 14

Horace Ida looked like hell, and Bill Pittman looked worse when I walked over to his office on Monday morning to find out if the rumors about Ida were true. Judging from his appearance, I'd heard right about the kidnapping.

A welter of cuts and bruises in a riot of reds, blues, and purples covered Shorty's face. One eye was swollen partly shut.

He managed a weak grin when he saw me. Pittman, though, wasn't smiling. He hovered over his little Japanese client, and his own expression was a mixture of anger and grief.

"Holy smokes!" I marveled. "You look like somebody ran over you with a bus."

"Wait, wait. You ain't seen nothing yet." Ida stood and gingerly removed his shirt. They'd bandaged him up in the hospital, but swellings and welts were still visible. I didn't even want to think about what might be under the white cloth.

"I'm having a photographer come over. We're going to get some pictures," Pittman said tightly.

"The cops get some already," Ida shrugged. He worked the shirt back on, moving stiffly and wincing at the effort.

"Why aren't you still in the hospital?" I demanded.

He shrugged. "They like to keep me, but they can't do nothing. Just give me some pills."

"John, I simply cannot believe this could happen here," Pittman said, almost pleading. "We knew it was risky. There've been plenty of threats, but this…"

"It cuts both ways," I said. "The Navy's been complaining about those threats to the wives. Everybody's scared."

"I keep wondering how much of a spark it's going to take to set this place off. This might have been it."

"I don't think so. Folks are upset, but there doesn't seem to be any big backlash yet."

"These people put up with so much," Pittman sighed.

"How's Joe doing?" I asked.

"Scared. Mad. Confused."

"So's everybody else."

"He's supposed to be coming in this morning. I don't mind telling you, I'm worried. This isn't just about Joe and Shorty anymore. I've gotten threats here at the office, for God's sake." Pittman reached for his phone. "I'm going to see about some protection for these boys."

I turned to Ida, who was slumped in his chair. "What happened out there?"

"You always coming around, asking questions." He sat up, trying to get comfortable. "The cops already been here twice. I told them what those assholes do."

"I'd like to hear it."

He winced, looking beaten in more ways than one, then sighed a long "Ahhh."

"Saturday night, I was just standing in front of this place on Kukui Street, talking to my friend, and I see this car. Get five, maybe six haole guys inside. I seen this one I know, he's Navy. Might've been him yells, 'Hey, that's one,' and some jump out. I tried to run but they grab me, throw me in the car. Man, I stay plenty scared. I figger they gonna kill me for sure."

Ida spoke with eyes closed, replaying the scene neither of us believed he'd ever forget.

"They get another car following; they're taking me up the Pali. All the time they're saying, 'You gonna talk, we gonna make you talk.'

"One of them get a gun, and he stick it right here." He pointed at his side. "They're saying shit like, 'You gonna fly tonight, *kanaka*,' and 'We gonna send you down to join your ancestors.' Hell, I'm Japanese; I get no ancestors up the Pali."

I knew what they'd meant, though. The sheer cliffs of the Nuuanu Pali overlook the windward side of Oahu. In the 1795 battle that won him control of the island, King Kamehameha's army drove their opponents up to the Pali, then over the one-thousand-foot drop to their deaths. It was remote and lonely at night. If his captors had wanted to pitch him over the cliff, it would have been easy enough to do.

"But," he went on, "when we get up to the lookout place, get some other cars parked. They never like those people see 'em, so, they all talking about, 'What should we do?' and, 'Should we wait or what?'

"Finally, this guy says, 'Wait a minute, I'll check,' and he goes over to their other car, talks to somebody I never see, and comes back. He says, 'Hell with it, we going down,' and we drive down to the other side. Man, they stop and it's so dark." He shuddered at the memory.

"A couple of 'em pull me out of the car. I never like go, 'cause I figger, I get out, they gonna kill me. But they get plenty guys, and bam, I'm in the road.

"All of 'em start hitting me, hitting me, asking questions: 'Whose idea was it for rape the girl? Who rape her first? Who hit her in the face?'

"I'm screaming and crying, and they whipping on me with those belts. Those wide ones? Some was swinging the end with the buckle. God, that hurt." He grimaced, feeling the heavy brass buckles on the leather belts biting into his body.

"By and by, they get me down in the dirt, kicking me. That's how I get this," he added, pointing to a golf ball-sized lump in angry shades of red and black over his left eye.

"I'm crawling in the dirt and they're all around me, kicking and swinging those belts. All this time, they're saying, 'Admit you did it,' but I never did. I just act like I'm knocked out or dead and they finally said, 'Hell with 'em,' and dug out.

"Whoo, I was happy when I hear 'em get in their cars."

"How'd you get out of there?"

"I wait a while to make sure they gone, then I walk on the road. This car came up from the other way and pick me up. They take me to the police station in Kaneohe. The cops bring me to town."

Shorty hadn't had time yet to appreciate the ironies of his situation. Here you had the victim of a crime standing on a Honolulu street corner on a Saturday night, hauled into a car by unknown assailants, taken out into a remote area, brutally assaulted, then left in the road. All in all, it sounded a lot like Mrs. Massie's story.

Ida shifted himself in his chair, trying to find an unbruised spot to rest on.

"You ought to be in the hospital, Shorty," I told him. "Those guys did some real damage."

"They kick my ass for sure," he admitted ruefully. "Nothing I could do."

Ida showed no signs of outrage. His reaction, like that of the city generally, was muted, almost resigned; most people waited to see how the authorities would respond. Maybe the pain had exhausted him, but it looked to me like he didn't expect much from that quarter.

Bill Pittman did, and he vented his considerable fury in language I'd never heard him use before, demanding action from the police and prosecutor.

"Goddammit!" he yelled into his phone. "None of them are safe if you let this go by…

"…No, they're not going to surrender their bail, why should they?…

"…Does the phrase 'innocent until proven guilty' have any meaning for you?…

"…They're going to rely on you to protect them, like every other taxpaying citizen, that's what! So get on with it!" He hurled the phone into its cradle, then picked it up and slammed it back down on the first bounce.

At that moment, Joe Kahahawai came through the front door, accompanied by his father who was wearing a Honolulu bus driver's uniform.

Pittman extended his hand and hurried to them. "Mr. Kahahawai. Joe. You can't imagine how glad I am to see you. Have you had any problems?"

"No," Joe Sr. said. "He stay with my sister up by Punchbowl last night."

Joe Jr. did a double take when he saw Ida's battered face. "Ooh, bull. You look like hell," he exclaimed.

"That's what he said." Ida pointed at me.

"Those guys mess you up good." Joe, the part-time professional boxer, was impressed.

Pittman broke up Joe's examination by describing his telephone calls to various authorities that morning. He concluded by summing up the position of the Navy, the prosecutor, and the Massie family, all of whom wanted the five boys locked up "for their own protection."

"The prosecutor, Mr. Wight, is asking whether Joe and the others will voluntarily agree to withdraw their bail and remain in jail until the retrial. He says it's for your own good," he added, lifting a hand to stop Joe, Jr.'s protest. "I know, I know. And I don't agree, but I have to advise you of their proposal and let you make the call."

Joe, Jr. glanced sideways at his father. He needed to make the decision himself, but like any son, he wanted his dad's approval.

The elder Kahahawai turned his cap in his hands, then tapped it against his leg. "Why they doing this to my boy?" he asked.

"Pop…" Joe began.

Thalia and Tommie Massie, Long Island, New York, June 4, 1932

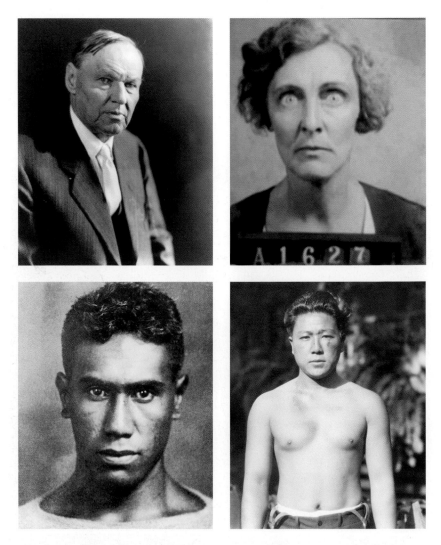

Clockwise from upper left: Clarence Darrow, Grace Fortescue (mug shot from HPD rap sheet), Horace Ida after beating, Joe Kahahawai

Billy Wells's Federal Prohibition Agent credentials, 1921

Top: Massie residence, Manoa Valley; Bottom: Ala Wai Inn, Waikiki

Top: US Federal Building, Customhouse and Courthouse, King and Richards Streets, downtown Honolulu; Bottom: Abandoned Animal Quaratine Station, Ala Moana Beach Road

Top: John Ena Road, Waikiki, including location at far left where Thalia claimed her abduction took place; Bottom: Sisters Helene Fortescue and Thalia Massie

Top: On the governor's balcony at Iolani Palace, Clarence Darrow, Grace Fortescue and Thalia Massie with Tommie Massie and fellow defendants Edward Lord and Albert "Deacon" Jones (second and third from left), sheriff Maj. Gordon Ross (fourth from left) and defense counsel George Leisure (far right); Bottom: Crowd at Merchant and Bethel Streets awaiting arrival of murder suspects, January 8, 1932

Top: Opium paraphernalia including a lamp, opium box, five-tael tin of Lam Kee hop, pipe scraper, and (foreground) Thalia Massie's opium pipe, given to the author by Billy Wells; Bottom: The USS Alton moored at Pearl Harbor

"Hush, you," Joe, Sr. said firmly. "I just like to know, what is the reason behind all of this *pilikia*."

Bill Pittman considered the question for a long minute before answering. "Mr. Kahahawai, I'll be honest with you. I think they got themselves boxed into a corner and couldn't get out. What I'm afraid of is that the only way out now is over these boys' dead bodies."

You didn't have to look any farther than Shorty Ida to believe these words could come true. The living proof winced as he touched the lump over his eye. "This is because we are Hawaiian? We got to die because this wahine say so?"

"It isn't up to her, fortunately. And Joe has a lot of support."

"Why she lie about my boy if he never do nothing to her?" Joe, Sr. demanded.

"I don't know why she's lying or who she's protecting." Pittman looked me straight in the eye. "But I know she *is* lying. And yes, they believe her because she's white and your son isn't. I don't like it, but there it is."

"Nothing personal, then?"

Pittman frowned and thought carefully. "No. No, it's nothing personal."

Joe, Sr. nodded slowly. "I no like see Joe end up like this boy," he said, gesturing at Ida. "He shouldn't suffer for something he never do."

Pittman faced his client. "Do you want to be jailed for your own protection?"

Joe, Jr. shook his head.

Pittman turned back to the telephone, and called Griffith Wight with Joe's refusal. I listened as Shorty gave Joe an abbreviated version of the kidnapping story, ending with his interview at the police station.

"What the cops said?" Joe asked when Ida finished.

"They say they gonna ask the Navy to bring in the sailors for me to look at. You know, like they did when they show us to the haole lady."

Joe considered this gravely. "But, get like, ten thousand guys out there. How you gonna pick out the ones?"

Ida snorted in disgust. "Cannot. Was dark. All I was seeing was one belt or one boot coming at me. I'll try, though."

"Just pick anybody. Tell the cops, 'That's the guy.' That's what they do to us," Joe said bitterly.

"Uh uh, brah." Ida was having none of this idea. "No way. I ain't going down to their level. We ain't like them."

Joe bristled slightly at the implication that he might resemble Ida's assailants, and then sighed. "Yeah, you right." The prizefighter clenched both fists and threw a half-hearted punch at the air. He stood for a moment, listening for the bell that would give him his chance to box the United States Navy. Then his shoulders slumped. "I like kick their ass, but…"

That prospect seemed long dead, so Shorty left with Joe and his father, and all three headed for the police station to see about protection. I waited while their attorney made one more call.

"There's going to be a retrial, John," he said when he got off. "This won't stop it. We absolutely destroyed them last time, and more than half the panel still voted to convict. I don't want to be blasphemous, but it's almost as though they want their crucifixion and they're not going to quit till they get it, one way or the other."

"The cops know they've got no case. Wight probably does, too, by now."

"They don't need a case if all they're going to do is take the boys out and hang them to the nearest tree."

"No, sir, they don't."

Bill Pittman reached over and took my hand. "John, I have to ask you. Do you know something that can stop all this?" His warm brown eyes pleaded for some reassurance.

I shook my head. "I don't think so. Not enough. Not yet."

He let go of my hand and gave it a pat. "I told you this wasn't your dogfight," he said, his voice firming. "I was wrong. This is everybody's fight now."

He was right, but we both knew I couldn't win this battle alone. And a certain Clarence T. Stevenson didn't want me fighting it at all. I knew I'd better have some cover, or the next time I communicated with Bill Pittman it would be by telegram from Buffalo or Cleveland.

I told Pittman what I knew and what I needed. He told me not to worry and, worried sick, I headed back to the office to see if anybody wanted to enlist in my army.

CHAPTER 25

Federal Building, Room 213
Monday, December 14

"We've been talking," Billy said. He and Kam were waiting when I flung open the office door. Horace Ida's kidnapping was the topic of conversation all over Honolulu, so I didn't have to ask what they'd been talking about. With Stevenson on the mainland testifying in a smuggling case, Billy was once more in charge of the office. Kam sat stoic behind the pile of papers on Stevenson's desk.

"This shit's getting completely out of hand," Billy went on. Kam nodded his agreement. "Who knows what's going to happen next?"

"Somebody's gonna get killed, that's what's gonna happen next," I said.

"We had the others at the station earlier, just to make sure nobody else got hurt," Kam said.

"That's swell, but it's too late for Ida," I responded.

Kam shrugged. "They got bail and they wanted to stay out. I don't blame them. It used to be their town."

"Yeah. Used to. Now it belongs to a bunch of thugs who're listening to fairytales from a teenage girl."

"Have you heard what the Navy boys wanted?" Billy asked.

I noticed that Billy, like everybody else in Honolulu, assumed Ida's assailants were from Pearl.

"Yeah, I think I got the whole story. I saw Ida at Bill Pittman's office. They took him out in the country and beat on the poor bastard with belts, trying to get a confession out of him. Of course, he can't do that, 'cause he's got nothing to confess. He doesn't even know this girl."

Billy and Kam both winced, appreciating how bad a fix that would be.

"So what do you want to do?" Billy asked.

"I want to nail that junkie bitch to the wall. She started this whole thing. I hate to say I told you so, but…"

"What have you got on her?" Billy's voice was calm, determined.

I gave them a short synopsis of Thalia's adventures in modern pharmacology, and a reminder of what George Soon had said about her visits to the dens.

Billy whistled. "Four gallons, that's a lot of laudanum."

"In eight or nine months? I'd say so, yeah."

"She's gonna be tough to do, hoss. All the Navy people are battening down the hatches."

"The admiral's been screaming at Gleason for protection for the wives. Saying the 'natives' are planning something to get even for Ida," Kam grumbled.

"Bates and Butler from the Shore Patrol were at the police station all morning. Rumor is, the Navy's gonna put on a hundred armed sailors to protect dependents living in town," Billy said.

"Yeah, I heard that one. I think it's true. And they're pushing for a fast retrial on the Ala Moana case," I said.

"How in the hell can we make a case on this lady with all this crap going on?" Billy said, mostly to himself.

"I've already got the damned case. That's not the problem," I said. "The problem is there's no way Sandy Wood is going to do anything to mess up the Territory's prosecution unless we've got this girl nine ways from Sunday. I don't think fraud's gonna be enough."

I thought back on my conversations with Will Moore. "It's political," he had said, with currents and undercurrents that nobody at our level would ever see. Everybody could sure feel them, though. Horace Ida certainly had. "We'd have to catch her red-handed with opium to do any good. I can't believe she's stupid enough to still be smoking," I finished.

Billy looked up sharply. "When it comes to dope, you don't ever want to overestimate a junkie's intelligence. They'll do some mighty dumb things to get a pipeful."

He and Kam looked at each other, evaluating their options, thinking about handling the hottest potato in the Pacific.

"We'll just have to scheme on her a little bit," he decided, and pulled his chair closer to my desk. "The laudanum thing's completely out?" he asked.

"Not completely, but in order to do it, we've got to go with a historical case based on the pharmacy records and the doctors' statements. Withington might be okay, but the others?"

Billy grimaced. "Doctors. They may sound solid now, but those guys always fade in court."

"It would dirty her up pretty bad, though. Maybe ruin her as a witness in the retrial."

"No. That's no good. Sandy Wood and everybody else'll be all over us if they think all we're trying to do is screw up their case." Billy started on his pipe. "No, the best thing would be if we could catch her smoking opium. Grab her in a den."

Kam seemed doubtful. "I never heard anything about her being in town at night. None of the *yen shee* people are talking about her. I've been asking, the last few days."

"What did Soon say exactly?" Billy asked me.

I told him again.

"She was going to his laydown? The one on River?" Billy looked expectantly over at Kam.

The big detective shifted his toothpick. "He ain't been back there. We've been keeping an eye out. He might be floating his joint, but no place permanent."

There was a long silence as everybody fit the known facts into their mental puzzle boards.

"What if we had George hook up with her? He could talk to her, right?" Billy said.

"He has before. But how's that gonna work? She can't find him."

"No," Billy said thoughtfully. "But *we* could find her, couldn't we?"

"Sure. I've been by her house plenty of times. We could find out where she goes, maybe follow her around."

"You wouldn't want to get caught, though," Kam cautioned. "Navy would probably shoot you."

"I doubt she'd be looking for a tail, and she doesn't know me. Plus, according to Withington, she can't see anything more than five or ten feet away."

"So we can find her," Billy continued. "That part's easy. We follow her around a while, see if she's laying down somewhere. We bang that joint and her in it, problem solved. And if she's not, we can run George into her. She's gotta go to the store or someplace public. We have George with us, have him bump into her, accidental-like, see if she remembers him."

"I dunno, Billy. Some Oriental coming up to her? Kam's right, he's liable to get lynched or something."

"Maybe. Maybe. Depends on how bad she wants a smoke," Billy countered.

"And what good's that gonna do? So she tells George she misses going to the den like she used to. Then what? It's just his word against hers. Nobody's gonna believe him over her."

"True. But what if he could set it up so she went back to the den?"

"You mean have George take her to the place?"

Billy nodded. "Sure. She's a junkie. That's the first thing to remember. And if you're a junkie, you gotta get that stuff. She wants it, but since we nailed Soon, she's got no place to go."

"Except the doctors."

"Except the doctors," Billy agreed. "But you said you shut her down there, too."

"Withington sure won't be giving her any more, or O'Day, for that matter. Porter said he'd be the only one prescribing, and I didn't talk to Kim."

"Okay, there you go. She's gonna be hurting. She can't get any smoking opium, and now her connection for laudanum's getting cut. That girl's gonna be in a mighty bad way before too long."

"She'd be present where opium was being smoked," Kam said. "And she's not military, so the Territory would have a violation."

"Right. Only if we get her that far, we ought to be able to catch her holding a tin. Then it'd be a Federal beef."

"But where's she going to get a tin? If she had some hop, she could smoke anytime. In her own house, if she wanted to."

Billy gazed through the pipe smoke at the ceiling and talked to the light fixture, seeing what it thought of his next idea. "Well, she doesn't have any, so we'll just have to see she gets some."

"Give her opium?" I asked incredulously.

"Why not? That's what Holt and Russell were doing. Maybe those two assholes were onto something. We'll steal a page out of their book and do the same thing, only legal."

Kam and I were both stunned.

"You mean we give her dope and then arrest her?"

"Sure." He was warming to this bizarre idea, though I was aghast as I pictured Commissioner Anslinger's face if he found out. Or Stevenson's, for that matter.

"She ain't gonna know it's our dope," Billy continued. "All she'll know is she's the one that's holding it when the cops show up."

"That would never stand up in court. It's entrapment." I'd practically worn out the pages on this subject in my little green manual during the Holt-Russell case. "Hell, Billy, it's a goddamn frame-up."

"Hoss, this thing is never getting anywhere near a federal courtroom," he said patiently. "And I thought the point of this was to scare her into snitching on this boyfriend of hers, whoever he is, and get her to back off the rape thing."

"It is, but…"

"But nothing. We want her to think she's a junkie who just got caught holding a tin full of hop, and that's just what she'll think. If she doesn't spill over that, we'll never get her."

"Yeah, but even if it's legal, it seems sort of…underhanded."

"Ordinarily I'd agree with you. Ordinarily I wouldn't do anything like this, and I don't ever expect to again. But look, it's not like we're forcing her to do anything. We're just baiting the hook, is all. She sees Soon, she either talks to him or she doesn't. If she bites, she either shows up at the den or she doesn't. She can stay on the side of the angels anytime she wants. It's all up to her."

The way he put it, it sounded pretty logical, even reasonable, and almost fair. Another picture swam into my mind, though—that of Albert Holt's reaction the day he got sentenced on our case, and the way his face crumpled when Judge Lymer sent him to Leavenworth for two years while his wife wept behind me in court.

"Gee, Billy, I dunno. I mean, we locked up Holt and Russell for doing practically the same thing you're talking about."

"It's close, I'll give you that," he admitted. "But we're not doing this for personal profit. We're investigating a reported violation, just like the manual says."

We schemed for another hour, trying different ideas, checking the fits, discarding them, and always coming back to Billy's original plan.

When Kam and I were finally almost comfortable with the idea of building a frame for Thalia, Billy hit us with the rest of it. "There's more. I don't think it'll be enough to just get her in the den."

"What do you mean? You just said we'd have her cold."

"Jack, Jack, this gal's a junkie. She'd make up some story or another once she had some time to think about it. She could say we drugged her and took her there." He turned to Kam. "You remember that preacher you caught in the cathouse down in Iwilei a couple years back?"

"Haole boy. Missionary family. Porking some Filipino girl, real young," Kam recalled.

"Right. What'd he say?"

"Said somebody must be out to destroy him. They slipped him a mickey and he woke up in bed with the girl."

"Exactly," Billy pointed his pipe at Kam. "We had the Chamber of Commerce and the Big Five boys down here pounding on the table. 'Where'd they get the drugs they used to make the mickey?' Came to nothing, of course; there never were any drugs. But the point is, he didn't come up with that story right away."

"No," Kam said. "He was too shook up at first to talk any kind of sense. We had him cold. It took him a day or two to come up with the drug story."

"She'll probably do the same thing or something close, and people will buy it," Billy concluded.

"Those Navy people will back her up," Kam agreed. "She says something like that, this whole place could explode."

It was an unsettling prospect, but in the current heated climate, not exactly outrageous or even unlikely.

We contemplated the possible implications of yet another Thalia Massie lie. I had to agree with Billy since I knew the lady, even indirectly. I guessed her first instinct would be to fib her way out of trouble.

"There'd be three of us, maybe more. It would be our word against hers," I tried, not even liking the sound of it myself.

Billy didn't care for it, either. "No, we can't get in a swearing contest with this girl. She's got too many friends. You learn about Pyrrhic victories in school?" he asked me.

"Yeah. Somebody wins, but everybody's dead."

"Right. I'd rather pass on that honor, thanks. And I'm not so sure we'd win, anyhow."

"So how do we get around her lying?"

"Hell, I don't know. I'm just throwing it out there. You know it's what she'll do, though."

I nodded, depressed to be closer but still so far away.

"She's gonna be real shook as soon as the cuffs come out," Kam wasn't giving up. "She'll probably be babbling like a baby. The preacher was."

"Got to get her while she's hot," Billy agreed. "Bag her red-handed, she'll be in a talking mood. Jack's right," he said. "She doesn't know the system; she'll be ripe to give everything up."

"That wouldn't be all bad," I pointed out. "If she knows the White Friend and gives him up, we'd at least have that much. We'd be able to go from there."

"Probably. But we wouldn't have her."

We all slouched in our chairs for a few minutes; we had a goal in sight, but the obstacles ahead were clearly outlined.

"Maybe we could get a court stenographer to take it down, like an affidavit," Kam suggested.

Billy jerked up. "Or record her."

"How can we do that? We've got no equipment," I said.

"No, but the Army does. I know a colonel in the Signal Corps up at Fort Shafter. He might be able to give us a hand."

"How would it work?"

"I don't know the mechanics. I've never done it. But if we could get her confession on a record, she'd be locked in. We could play it for anybody who tried to give us grief."

"Convict her with her own words," I said, liking this one.

"This," Billy pronounced, "has got some possibilities."

2850 Kahawai Street
Tuesday, December 15

The plot, as they say, thickened overnight. By Tuesday morning, we each had a parade of new ideas, as well as the usual litany of objections and doubts. We batted these around for another hour at the office before getting down to the nuts and bolts of our creation.

Everybody had something to do. Billy got on the phone to Fort Shafter and wheedled some equipment. He hung up beaming, and told us they were going to send something down by Thursday.

Kam and a couple of his boys headed out to look for George Soon, and squeeze some informants to see if anyone had heard about any haole girls coming around the Chinatown dens.

I'd be tracking Thalia, looking for an opening we could push Soon through. I grabbed a car and headed for Manoa, hoping to catch her before she left on any errands.

When I got to the house, which was already familiar to me after a dozen drive-bys, it was just after nine and all quiet in the neighborhood. Since it was only a couple hundred feet from Manoa School, the sounds of children on the playground drifted over the rooftops as I parked down the block.

Although the family car, a brown Ford, squatted in the driveway, no sign of activity showed at the house. Around eleven, another car—a powder blue Durant roadster—showed up, driven by a middle-aged woman who parked directly behind the Ford. With the driver were two other women—girls, really—moving away from me as they entered the house. Half an hour later, all three emerged, and I finally got a good look at Thalia Massie.

My field glasses showed me a short girl who was maybe a bit overweight. She wore her light brown hair cut close to her head and just off her shoulders. The sulky expression on her face and her stooped posture clearly said she didn't want to be leaving. The older woman appeared to be giving Thalia a piece of her mind, though none of the words reached me. They all squeezed into the little Durant and motored out.

I followed them into town where they stopped at the Pacific Club, one of the tonier private establishments in Honolulu. A dapper-looking gentleman met them out front and escorted them inside; evidently luncheon was planned. I parked down the street where I could see the Durant if it left, then went to find a phone to check in.

When they left the club some time later, the older woman drove into downtown and parked on Fort Street. Quickly, the two girls jumped out of the car and were gone, lost among the sidewalk strollers and shoppers. I was still trying to find a parking place when I discovered I only had the older woman in sight.

I'd learn in later years that this was a typical surveillance: screwed up before it really got started.

Since I was left with no choice, after indulging in a short and unproductive temper tantrum I stayed with the lady as she took her promenade down King Street. She moved like high society, looking haughtily at any who approached her, disdainful of all beneath her exalted status. This included everybody at her destination, which was the undistinguished Diamond-Hall store at Fort and King Streets, a place that sold mostly hardware, paint, marine supplies, and sporting goods.

Where she was buying a gun.

As I lurked stealthily in a forest of bamboo fishing poles, I pretended not to watch while this society matron picked out a nice little .32 caliber Iver Johnson snub nose, showed the salesman a pistol permit, and paid in cash. She didn't leave it in the box, either. Ignoring the hovering clerk, she loaded it up with some bullets she bought, snapped it shut with authority, and stuffed the revolver in her purse before she ever left the store.

Acutely aware that the only one packing any heat in my surveillance was my subject, I kept a much more respectful distance when I trailed her out the door. Once she reached her car again, she stood around impatiently until the two girls returned. They spoke for a moment, then split again. The younger girl accompanied the woman as Thalia Massie headed off across the Iolani Palace grounds, which gave me a chance to get close to the young lady who had caused all this commotion.

She walked alone, and wanted it that way. Her downcast, slightly bulging blue eyes patrolled the pavement for some cause for offense as her thin, tight lips and penciled eyebrows prepared a sarcastic response for use when the inevitable insult manifested itself. Her head was rolled forward and her back was bowed, so the ridge of her spine formed a chain of low hills under the gray silk dress, an aiming point for the knife that her pouting expression seemed to anticipate at any moment. I dropped back to let this cloud pass on ahead, carrying its cargo of gloom into the Territorial Library just down the block from our office.

She emerged an hour later and strolled back to the car, where she got another lecture. The older woman was still talking when they drove home and, armed to their patrician teeth, settled in for the evening.

I called Billy about the gun purchase later that afternoon and listened to him gloat about having the easier part of this investigation. He sure had the safer part. Diamond-Hall told him they'd sold the revolver to a Grace Hubbard Bell Fortescue, whose local address was a rented house on Kolowalu Street only about three blocks from the Massie home in Manoa.

"Grace Fortescue bought a gun?" Kam said the next morning. "That's Thalia's mother."

He said Mrs. Fortescue had come from the mainland after the assault to support her daughter and poke at the police. "She's a royal pain in the ass, is what," he said. "All the time going around telling everybody how we're a bunch of stupid crooks."

I asked Kam if he knew who the younger girl was.

"Sure, that's Helene. Thalia's sister. About sixteen. Came out with her mom."

Helene must have slept over on Tuesday night, because on Wednesday, she and Thalia left together in the afternoon and went shopping downtown. They didn't seem to have a care in the world, and took a late lunch at the cafe in the Alexander Young Hotel. It was particularly encouraging to see them separate for long periods of time, obviously arranging to meet later. If this turned into a pattern, Soon could easily make contact.

"Settle in for the long haul, hoss," Billy cautioned. "It may take a couple of weeks to get her down pat, and even longer to set up the meeting."

Kam's job had been to root out George Soon, which was a job made more difficult since he'd left the souvenir shop. Kam found him at his new hole off Kukui Street, on another edge of Hell's Half-Acre. He said

Soon hadn't seemed pleased to see him, which meant he was probably back at his old trade.

The three of us met him on Wednesday evening at a chop suey place in Kaimuki. He went over the story again for Billy and Kam and I didn't hear any discrepancies, which was a good sign that he was sticking to the truth, as much of it as he knew.

"Sure, Billy, I help you folks," Soon said, like he had some choice. "I help get the haole girl."

Kam also sweet-talked his sister, who ran a small *manapua* bakery on Beretania Street, into letting us use the shop as our base. It had a telephone, and Soon agreed to walk over there every morning to wait with Billy or Kam until I called with Thalia's location.

None of us wanted a repeat of Lau Sau's Center Street fiasco. Billy and Kam drilled Soon down at the shop until he could play his part in his sleep. A promise of twenty bucks if he turned the trick cheered him right up. Thalia Massie meant less than nothing to him, so the twenty dollars was like getting paid for breathing.

CHAPTER 26

Federal Building, Room 213
Thursday, December 17

Shortly after eight o'clock in the morning, before we left on our respective errands, the office door burst open and a red-faced man in a U.S. Army sergeant's uniform wrestled his handcart into our office. The military had landed, bringing with it the recording equipment Billy had finagled from his connection at Fort Shafter. I remember looking at the crate and being both relieved and astonished. Although it arrived on time and as promised, the thing was huge and inhabited a shipping container the size, shape, and weight of an icebox, as the sweating, swearing technician could attest.

Technical Sergeant Irving Schutt, a chunky man with a thick New York accent, told us to call him "Sarge," and let us unload the container while he caught his breath, then gave us the introductory lecture as we worked.

"If you gents can uncrate that Kraut sonofabitch," he panted, "we'll get started."

I opened the lid, half-expecting to find the promised German in the coffin-like case, but the overhead lights reflected instead off the face of modern technology in a box. All of us paused for a moment to admire the shining metal and polished wood.

"It's pretty big," Kam said doubtfully.

"It's bloody huge," Billy muttered.

"It's beautiful," I breathed.

"Yeah, now, this sonofabitch here," Sarge indicated the contents of the box and the object of our attention, "is a magnetic wire recorder, latest thing. We just picked it up from the limeys, who stole it from those Huns.

It's a Blattnerphone," he added unnecessarily; the name, emblazoned in oversized gold letters across the varnished wood facade of the machine, gleamed in the light.

"Even though we call it a wire recorder, it don't actually use wire," he explained, rummaging through the box and pointing to a smaller, but still sizable, container. "Lift that outta there, will ya, sonny?" he instructed me.

I picked up the indicated green metal box, or tried to; it felt like it weighed more than fifty pounds. I grunted in surprise and heaved it onto my desk.

"Heh heh," Sarge chortled. "Heavy sonofabitch, huh? Them two reels go thirty-five pounds each, but depending on how you're gonna use it, they'll give you two hours of record time. What are youse gonna be using it for?"

None of us really wanted to say, and he got that picture clearly as he watched us shuffle our feet and throw sideways glances at each other. He tried again. "Morse, voice, or music?"

"Huh?"

He smiled indulgently. "You gonna record Morse code, voice, or music?"

"Oh. Voice. Somebody talking."

"Good. 'Cause this thing don't work worth a damn on music or anything else where you need high fidelity. For that, you still got to record on disc, play it on a phonograph. 'Course, you do that, your recording time ain't for shit."

"We thought we might need an hour. That's what I told the Colonel," Billy said.

"You got it. That's why he sent two reels. For voice, you can have thirty-three minutes on each of these babies. You get twice that for Morse, because all you're recording there is the dahs and dits, and you don't need any kinda fidelity for that. We made some changes in this big bastard so we can run it at a slower speed for Morse."

"What's the quality like on speech?"

"You won't have no trouble recognizing whoever's talking. There'll be some hiss, maybe some other noise. Depends some on your source. You sirs gonna use the microphone or record off a phone line?"

"It'll have to be a microphone. I told the Colonel we needed one," Billy answered.

"Yeah, I brung one. It's in here somewheres; pretty hefty sonofabitch, too. You boys hoist that thing out of the box and set her down easy on the floor while I dig that mike out."

We gingerly lifted the Blattnerphone out of its cradle as instructed, setting it next to the desk. Out of the box, the machine was even more impressive—a now-silent monument to the future of technology. I loved it at once.

Sarge rummaged in another compartment of the box and produced a large microphone, exactly like those broadcasters used. The pedestal-mounted microphone was suspended on a web of elastic bands in a wire frame and sat almost a foot high; hiding this thing would be a trick. The technical possibilities might exist, but the practical problems were mounting.

While I studied the microphone, Billy examined the recorder. "What do you use it for?" he asked.

The sergeant turned coy. "I really ain't supposed to say, sir," he said, leaving us to imagine the top-secret applications of such a beautiful toy to our national security. I conjured up visions of enemy wireless transmissions being intercepted, and mystifying codes being decrypted with the aid of the improbably named Blattnerphone while Sergeant Schutt sat at the controls. The image wasn't entirely comforting.

"We'll hook her up and get her going, you can see what you think." Sarge set to work with the electrical leads and other wires while he continued his training lecture.

"First thing to remember: Put this big bastard someplace and leave it there. You don't wanna go moving it once you're set. It ain't designed to be shuffled around all over the goddamn place, and it's got a lot of breakable parts, tubes and shit, so if youse want it to work, plant it and leave it. Okay?"

We all nodded in unison, each thinking about where in the already cluttered office we might conceal something this ponderous.

"Second thing, believe it or not, this is one dangerous sonofabitch. Lemme show ya." He got one of the reels out of the box on my desk, and pulled out a length of shiny metal ribbon.

"The way you'll be using it, this strip or ribbon, or whatever you wanna call it, is gonna be traveling at over a yard and a half a second. That's pretty fast, and if you get your finger in there, it'll take it off—zip! Just like a razor blade. Here, feel of this."

We dutifully touched the edge of the thin silver strip, which did in fact resemble a very long and very deadly razor blade, imagined it slicing through a wayward digit, and made silent resolutions not to let the little beast too near. Unfortunately, Sarge quickly killed that determination.

"Third, you gotta set her up just right, or it ain't gonna work. That means this path here"—he pointed at a faint line on the face of the machine—"has gotta be followed exactly. Don't kink or bend the ribbon, and make damned sure it goes where it's supposta. Otherwise you're gonna get thirty-three minutes of dead air."

He levered the big platter of ribbon onto the left side of the machine, and put an empty metal reel of the same size on the right. Next, he carefully threaded the ribbon around a series of small drums and wheels, and finally brought the end to the empty reel, which he called "the take-up."

"Once you got the ribbon on the right path and it's hooked into the take-up, you're ready to switch it on. It'll take a little bit for all them tubes and shit to warm up, so turn the sonofabitch on and wait a couple of minutes before you try to record. Use the time to check your path." He did this. "And keep your fingers away from the transport."

After about a minute, he decided the machine was ready and flipped the switch marked "record." The two reels whirled into life and turned rapidly. The take-up spun like an airplane propeller, the silver ribbon obediently followed its convoluted path, and we all stood there, hands safely in our pockets, admiring the magic box.

Sarge broke the awed hush. "Well, say somethin', damn it. You're payin' for this shit."

"Is it running now? What should I say?" Billy asked.

"Just talk into the goddamn mike."

"Okay, uh. Jack and Jill went up the hill to fetch a pail of water."

"Cute, really cute. Try a test pattern. Here, lemme do it." Sarge moved the microphone so he could better address it, then pronounced some Signal Corps mantra, giving the date and a series of numbers, Ables, Bakers, and Dogs. Then, with a little fumbling and growing more comfortable with the idea that we were being recorded, we each tried talking around the microphone, speaking trivial phrases or commenting on the machine.

"That's enough o' that shit," Sarge finally pronounced, and shut off the Blattnerphone. "Now, let's see what we got."

Rewinding the tape was a chore. Sarge explained that the motor they'd installed was only designed to run in one direction. To rewind, you had to disengage the sonofabitch, then turn a hand crank until all of the tape was safely back on its original reel. If you'd recorded to the end of the ribbon, you had just under two *miles* of silver tape to rewind—a process that I will testify took time, patience, and plenty of arm strength.

Once rewound, however, the possibilities in our world expanded. All three of us grinned like idiots as we heard, for the first time in our lives, the sounds of our own voices. The recording hissed and wobbled; it wasn't hi-fi by any means. But you could clearly make out every word and, as Sarge had promised, identify the speakers with ease.

The shape and shadows of our scheme now began to emerge. Technology had provided us with the means to record Thalia's confession, though doing so without her seeing the elephant-sized equipment in our little office was a problem still to be resolved.

He knew nothing about law enforcement and we knew nothing about Blattnerphones, but Sarge was more than happy to help out with the solution to those problems. After a lengthy discussion, we eventually concealed the recorder underneath the worktable. Kam went out and bought some wood, then constructed panels around three sides, making the table look like a desk. The machine could be easily turned on and off by the person sitting behind the "desk," and if you sat in the chair we'd reserved for Mrs. Massie, you couldn't see that the area in front of you was quite literally filled with recording gear.

Fortunately, the Blattnerphone operated in near silence. You could hear a faint humming sound if you put your head right next to it which, if you valued your ear, you definitely did not want to do when the tape was running. The spinning reels sounded like an electric fan. We covered both noises with a real fan positioned behind my chair.

The microphone was a bigger dilemma, since it would have to be standing more or less right out in the open. Billy spent the rest of the day building a box consisting of a wooden frame with a thin cloth cover, which he secured in place by screwing it to the top of my new desk.

The whole arrangement was supposed to look like a cloth-covered bookend, and we shoved some volumes of the U.S. Code up against one side of it to complete the barely-plausible effect. Nobody thought it was completely successful, but we guessed it would do the trick.

Best of all, despite its dubious appearance, the device actually worked. Even after Sarge departed and his profanity faded to a blue memory, the reels turned quickly and silently, the ribbon transported itself on its devious path from one side of the machine to the other, and the sound of our voices somehow mysteriously found their way onto the metal strip. Billy, sitting in the chair Thalia would occupy, was especially clear.

You might believe that nobody would fall for this trick, but think about it. Back then, the only recordings people ever heard were gramophones—phonograph records—or the movies. And people hadn't been talking for too long in those in 1931, either. We weren't the only ones who'd never heard the sound of his own voice; if you weren't an entertainer, a radio personality, or maybe a famous athlete or politician, you never got the chance. So the idea that I might be secretly capturing her words on my Blattnerphone would have been as outrageous to Thalia Massie as space travel. We might get a short recording of Thalia telling us to pound sand, but all in all, we were betting it would work.

I left the office to go sit on our target's house in a positive mood. After two days of preparation, we were ready to rope Thalia Massie.

She wasn't ready for us, however, and the surveillance ground into the routine I would learn so well in the coming years: hours of mind-numbing boredom and minutes of frantic activity. It was, as Billy said, "the long haul."

Thalia was an easy tail; she never wore the glasses she needed in order to see more than a few feet. Her mother, though, focused her own icy blue eyes on anyone presumptuous enough to approach within her danger zone. Keeping her little gun in mind, I kept well back.

"I think I'm getting the routine down now," I told Billy on Friday morning. "She's never gone anyplace that might be a den, but she's out a lot every day. "

"What about her husband?"

"He isn't back yet. Probably today. I've seen the shore patrol come by, in uniform, with the armband, but they don't go in. I did see some other guy last night and the night before."

"Really? Thalia got something going, you think? Her boyfriend, maybe?"

"I don't know. I doubt it; she's got the other women around all the time."

"What does he look like?"

"White, short, stocky, maybe thirty. Civilian clothes, but he's got the military look."

"Maybe he's another officer. Friend of the family."

"No, I think he's a swabbie."

"Probably. He's packing some heat, then. You watch yourself. You're not just sitting out in the open, are you?"

"Nah, I talked to one of the neighbors across the way. He lets me park up next to his house, off the street. You know, it's funny. I don't see any other Navy wives coming around, nobody visiting, just the two girls and their mother. I don't think Thalia's got any friends."

"From the way you described her, I'm not surprised." He signed off.

The grind continued. I didn't see that shore patrolman or whoever he was around the house after Thursday night, but like the proverbial bad penny, he would turn up again.

Down at the bakery, Billy, Kam, and George Soon sat around playing cards and eating manapua, much to Kam's sister's distress. Billy reported in one of my Thursday phone calls that she was making vague threats against Kam who, like me, could never resist the doughy treats with their char siu pork interiors. I could sympathize; he was a big man with a hell of an appetite. By Friday, Billy said she was muttering darkly in Cantonese and wielding her cleaver with increasing enthusiasm.

"What are you going to do?" I asked, as I was concerned we might be losing our base.

Billy laughed. "Kam swears he's not worried, but George and I are moving outside to the picnic table."

"And laying off the manapua?"

"Yep. Got to figure Kam can eat enough for all three of us anyhow."

The window we were hoping for hadn't opened by Friday evening when Lieutenant Massie and some of his Navy buddies showed up after their week's cruise concluded. I stayed around until eight and then wrote the surveillance off; even if Thalia went out that night, she'd likely be going in a crowd.

CHAPTER 27

Royal Hawaiian Hotel, Waikiki
Friday, December 18

When Tommie got home, he found that plans for the evening had already been laid.

"We've been invited to dinner by the Wortmans! Isn't that exciting?" Thalia exclaimed. "And at the Royal Hawaiian, too. Mother was so thrilled."

"Captain Wortman asked us to dinner?" Tommie echoed, surprised.

"For Mother's birthday. It was last month, of course, but Captain Wortman only just found out. He and Mother talk all the time. All of us are going. Lieutenant Martin said he would escort Helene. It will be so much fun."

The Royal Hawaiian Hotel, Hawaii's most opulent, had been the Waikiki gathering place for the rich and famous since its opening in 1927. Known as "the Pink Palace of the Pacific," the hotel would play host to such luminaries as Franklin D. Roosevelt, Shirley Temple, and the Duke of Windsor, but in 1931, with the Depression limiting the number of people who could afford a month in Hawaii, it catered to very wealthy visitors and members of the local elite. On weekends, higher ranking military officers and executives from the Big Five companies met for dinner and dancing in one of the most romantic settings in the world.

This evening, the Wortman party crossed the wide lawn from Kalakaua Avenue, and the palm trees swayed like Hawaiian dancers in a gentle trade wind. Lines of electric lights, each in a round paper ball, had been strung between the trees, and tiki torches marked the walkways as guests in evening attire strolled through the velvety darkness toward the dining room that overlooked Diamond Head and Waikiki Beach.

An imposing Hawaiian maître d' escorted them to their table as the orchestra played in one corner of the big room, which was open on the side facing the ocean. While Helene and John Martin left them to walk to the water's edge, the others ordered juice they could fortify from the flasks each of them carried. The conversation flowed smoothly over topics non-threatening, and Tommie felt himself relaxing.

The mood was contagious. On her second drink, Grace pulled at Wortman's sleeve and pointed at a large Hawaiian woman who had just entered the room. The woman moved with great dignity as she stopped to greet people at other tables, and the men and women stood to speak with her. She wore a broad hat with a feathered lei band, more leis around her neck, an iridescent blue evening gown, and white gloves that extended above her elbows.

"Who is that woman? She's dressed very well to be one of the entertainers."

"Hah," Wortman laughed. "She wouldn't be amused to hear that. And her ancestors might have had your head. That's Abby. Princess Abigail Kawananakoa. She'd be the Queen of Hawaii today if people hadn't come to their senses and done away with that nonsense."

"A princess? How lovely. Could you introduce us?"

Wortman grimaced. "I don't think that would be a good idea."

"Why on earth not?"

"Because even though she doesn't have a kingdom any more, the princess takes her responsibilities to her people very seriously. If they're in trouble, she finds some way to help them. It's feudal, really—the royal duty to the little people."

"That's very admirable."

"Yes. But some of the people she helps aren't so admirable. The word is that she's paid for the defense attorneys for at least two of the Ala Moana boys—Kahahawai and Ahakuelo, they're both natives—and maybe all of them. If they've got the best lawyers money can buy, it's the princess who bought them. And people listen to her, people like native police officers and jurors. She doesn't have to command, but if Princess Abby wants something, she gets it."

"You mean…the trial."

Wortman nodded. "She wouldn't even have to say anything, but a native or a half-breed, they'd feel the pressure. Couldn't resist it. And it only takes one on a jury to get a mistrial."

Grace's eyes narrowed, and she watched as the maître d' escorted the princess to a large table overlooking the beach. Other guests, all of them haole, rose to greet her.

"Why, she's actually going to stay and eat," Grace exclaimed, looking with amazement at Wortman. "They're going to seat her."

"Sure. She has a suite here at the hotel, and her family owns just about everything west of Pearl Harbor, and a good chunk of the rest of the Territory."

"Well, I never. This would never happen in the District, I can tell you. The coloreds know their places and stay there."

"You'd be surprised," Wortman said. "She's a power in the Republican party, not just here, but nationally. The white business community walks very softly around her. Look at them, they're all but kissing her ring."

"Shocking, just shocking. This place is so confusing. It's so modern, and yet things like this remind you that they're only a few steps out of the jungle. Thank God for the Navy. They're all that's standing between civilized people and savagery."

"Why, thank you, my lady," Wortman smiled.

Thalia listened to all of this with interest, watching the woman across the room as she took her place at the head of the table. Power fascinated her now, and she studied it, monitored it, felt for its ebb and flow. She saw it in Wortman, whose gold braid and white uniform announced it to all, and in her mother, whose money paid for it. But she also sensed it in the princess who didn't need a uniform, high office, or even wealth to exert it.

She also felt the vacuum of power, the absence of it. She'd sensed it in her husband, who moved in whatever direction someone with power—usually his Navy—directed. So she waited until after dinner, after the others had gone to the dance floor and her mother left them for the ladies' room, to push him.

"If the captain is right about that woman, then what you told me is true. They'll never be convicted. Even if they confess, the jury will listen to her. The natives will look after their own."

Tommie didn't want to discuss it—not tonight, not here. "Let's talk about it another time," he pleaded as the tension that was never far away nudged at his relaxed mood. But he no longer had the power, and Thalia knew it with certainty.

"And they'll be free to ruin all the other white women the way those animals ruined me."

Tommie flinched, shrinking away, Thalia noticed, as he always did now.

"I talk to Commander Butler at least once a week about the case and protection for the wives. You know that. So does Grace. He's got men patrolling in Manoa every night now," he pleaded.

"Carl," Thalia sneered. "You've got him and his men protecting us. Someone else, doing the job you didn't. And that doesn't do anything for me. Where is the justice for me?" she demanded. "How will we get it? What are *you* going to do?"

CHAPTER 28

2850 Kahawai Street
Saturday, December 19

We started the Saturday surveillance early on the last weekend before Christmas. If Thalia wanted to pick up some presents or maybe get a script filled, this would be the day. I was at Kahawai Street by seven, and I spent the next four hours alternately baking in the hot sun and being misted by Manoa's periodic showers.

This morning, the old lady and Helene arrived at eleven. All three came back out at noon, left in Mrs. Fortescue's blue Durant, and headed for town. This time when they split up I was ready, and kept Thalia in view as she and Helene walked toward downtown on Hotel Street.

The usual crowds of shoppers thronged Honolulu's commercial center, letting me stay close. At Bishop Street they checked their watches, then split up again. Helene set off toward the ocean while Thalia kept on toward Fort Street. I thought for a minute she was going into Chinatown or to one of the drug companies where she'd gotten her prescriptions filled, but she turned up Union and went into a building near the corner.

I recognized the address. James Kim, the other doctor who'd been prescribing for Thalia, had his office on the third floor. He was a new doctor in town, and had already popped up in Billy's scope on an informant's tip. A second informer, our own George Soon, had mentioned Kim as a possible source of morphine. That was two strikes, and if you came to Billy's attention in that context, it was time to leave town before you drew the third. Kim didn't, and Billy got him a couple of years later.

While Thalia was inside, I found a telephone and called the bakery, which was only a few blocks away. Kam got the phone from his sister.

"Kam, I think she's upstairs at Kim's office on Union, getting a paper. If we're not there, go to People's Drug. That's where she gets his scripts filled."

"Right. We're on the way." He hung up.

I waited where I could see the entrance to Kim's building and hopped from one foot to the other as the minutes ticked by. If Thalia left before Soon got there, I would have no choice but to follow her and hope they'd catch us at the drugstore.

Fortunately, Kam rolled up and parked on the sidewalk. Soon, who'd been thoroughly briefed and was wound up and ready to go, bolted from the car like a racehorse coming out of the gate. He half-ran with me over to the building foyer where we waited for Mrs. Massie to return.

George stood by the door while I hung back in the corner, looking at the tenant list posted on the wall. Footsteps sounded in the stairwell and Thalia emerged into the lobby, walking as she usually did with her head down and a slip of paper in her hand.

Soon stepped right in front of her, partly blocking her way outside.

"Missy," he said. "Missy, I know you."

Her eyes wide and white, Thalia shied away from him like a pony who's seen a snake.

"Excuse me?" she stammered, looking past him to the doorway. She started easing her way sideways, circling toward the street.

"I know you from before, you remember?"

"Before? I'm sure you must have made a mistake."

"You come by my place. River Street."

Thalia stopped edging toward the door and stood still, measuring the threat posed by inoffensive George Soon.

He bobbed his head, grinning. "You remember, yeah?"

"I don't… Have I met you before?" she asked warily.

"I say my name, 'George,' and…"—he lowered his voice dramatically and glanced over at me—"…sell you half-rooster." He made the shape of an opium tin with his hands.

He hadn't mentioned selling anything to Thalia before, but this is typical of informants. What they don't want you to know, they don't tell you. Of course, those are usually the things you most need to hear about.

I was getting nervous about the way he kept looking at me; it wouldn't be long before Thalia, already suspicious and obviously keyed for flight, would catch on, so I left them alone and passed them on the way out the door.

As I brushed past, Thalia rummaged in her purse for a pair of glasses that she lifted to her eyes, then peered through them at Soon. "Yes," she said, "I do remember you, George."

From across the street, the three of us could see our informant and his intended victim in close conversation. Moments later, both of them came out onto the sidewalk. Thalia turned toward Hotel and Nuuanu, where People's Drug waited with its gallon jugs of laudanum behind the counter. Soon walked in the opposite direction. All of us followed him; as Billy said, if she'd taken the bait, we'd be seeing her again. And if not, well, we'd be needing a new scheme.

George met us by the Catholic cathedral at the top of Fort Street with good news.

"She coming tonight." He shook his head sadly. "Cute girl. *Yen shee quoy*, but."

I had to agree; if she'd decided to come to our den, she truly was an opium fiend.

1119 Nuuanu Avenue
Saturday, December 19

Billy's other job, besides arranging for the Blattnerphone, had been to set up the opium den trap. It was magnificent. He'd secured a one-room walk-up on Nuuanu Avenue. George would operate the den, and I would keep an eye on him.

"She'll be more comfortable if she sees a white man there," Billy noted. Then he grinned at me. "You're younger, and you've got that hop head look," he kidded.

"Thanks, I guess."

"You just make like you're getting ready for a smoke, then give us the high sign."

Our communication system—makeshift, like everything else in this operation—consisted of a string running through a hole in the floor to the bakery below. One end was looped to my wrist. If I got a pull from below, it meant Thalia was on her way up. After she got there, one jerk from me would bring the cavalry.

Dim yellow light from the two oil lanterns washed over the room, aging the dirty wallpaper. The same lamps threw flickering shadows of handheld pipes and figures hunched over guttering flames. With the window closed, no breeze stirred the air that was so stale and thick, you felt you could drown in it.

The opium normally found in a five-tael tin, a brownish mass with a unique spicy scent and the consistency of cold molasses, must be prepared for smoking. This is usually the job of the den operator, known in the trade as the chef, who works while the smokers consume their pills. George prepared several of the yen pock opium balls, and then we waited for Thalia's witching hour to arrive.

I felt the string attached to my wrist jerk twice, the signal Thalia had been spotted. I told Soon, who immediately began to heat one of the yen pocks. Fragrant opium smoke filled the already-heady room with additional atmosphere.

Three hesitant taps sounded on the door, and Soon scuttled to answer. Thalia Massie, dressed in a dark brown dress and carrying a cloth purse and wooden box, peered intently into the room. I lay off to one side, my face partly hidden by the lamp and the pipe I held over it.

"Come in, missy, come in," Soon murmured, bobbing his head and bowing obsequiously.

Thalia lingered a moment in the doorway, doe-eyed and jumpy, straining those weak eyes through a pair of spectacles she held to her face, piercing smoke and shadow, absorbing me, the lamps and the paraphernalia spread out in the room. Thick tendrils of opium smoke drifted past her into the hallway. Making up her mind, she stepped inside, and Soon closed the door behind her.

George, the fawning host, showed her to the second bed across the room. She took a seat on the bare pine, opened her wooden box, and extracted an opium pipe from its cloth-lined interior. Even from ten feet away, I could see that this was no ordinary pipe; its almost luminous quality spoke of wealth and luxury.

Most pipes were about twenty-two inches in length and consisted of a plain bamboo stem topped by a metal saddle about two-thirds of the way from the mouthpiece. A ceramic bowl, or *young dow*, fit into the saddle. Some of the pipes used by wealthy smokers were made of bone, jade, or ivory, and were often elaborately carved or embellished with scrimshaw. This one was exquisitely sculpted from ivory to resemble a stalk of bamboo.

Most dens provided smokers with the pipe and one or more bowls, but Thalia had brought her own gear, and needed no help in preparing it for smoking.

She got her own bowl from the wooden box, and the *gee* rag, a cloth disk about two inches across, used as a gasket. Once she fit the *gee* rag across the pewter saddle on top of the pipe, she slipped the bowl into its place. Then she settled onto her side and waited for George Soon to fetch the first pill. Eager anticipation lit her face.

This was all done without a word. In many dens, the white smoker would speak no Chinese and the chef would speak no English. All, however, were in perfect harmony with the universal language of the opium fiend.

George carried a yen pock from the cooking lamp to me, took my pipe, and transferred the hot pill to the bowl. All I needed to do now was to hold it in the flame of my smaller lamp, and watch Thalia as the spectacle unfolded.

Her lamp was already lit and trimmed, and her slender fingers were dancing anxiously along the stem of the pipe. Her wedding ring flashed in the flickering light. Her gestures were those of a flutist practicing the notes in her mind before the concert begins. The sonata, though only Thalia Massie heard it, played clearly in the pale blue eyes tracking George Soon's every move.

When he turned to her with the tray of smoking paraphernalia, she quickly inventoried every item, and her eyes widened when she saw the can of Lam Kee hop in the center.

"You have money, yes?" George wheedled.

"Yes." That was the first word Thalia spoke in the den.

"Twenty dollar, one half-can." Soon picked up the can and plunked it back down onto the tray before Thalia's worshipful eyes. "Only one half-full," he said. "You like?"

Thalia nodded yes, fumbled at her purse, then passed him the money.

"I fix you one *toy* for now," Soon said, and palmed the twenty dollar bill.

Opening the tin, he used a hook-shaped scraper—the same *yen shee ngow* that Billy used on his tobacco pipe—to extract a small amount of the molasses-like smoking opium, then transferred it to the smaller container known as a *yet toy* or simply a toy. The small round box held about an ounce of opium, a quantity two people could consume in an evening.

Soon left the tin with Thalia, took the toy to his lamp, and fell into the expert moves of the opium chef he'd been for so many years. First, he took up a yen hock, a rod shaped like a knitting needle, and captured a small amount of opium on the tip. He held this to the flame and heated it, never letting the opium get close enough to burn. By twirling the yen hock in his fingers to keep the opium in place, he let the heat remove the moisture and allow the pill to form. He returned occasionally to the toy to gather more opium onto the growing ball on the yen hock. As he worked, he mimicked the huffing sound of a smoker. Thalia, lost in rapt concentration, matched his breathing.

Properly prepared, a yen pock is the size and shape of a kernel of corn. George, who had plenty of practice, could produce five yen pocks in ten minutes, all perfectly sculpted and completely uniform.

When the *yen pock* pill was at last formed, Soon nodded to Thalia, who held the bowl of her pipe closer to her own lamp's flame and heated it to receive the pill. Her hands caressed the pipe more intensely, stroking its smoothness as she followed the progress of Soon's preparations.

Before receiving the yen pock, she spirited the opium tin from the tray and eased it into the purse she snapped shut with her free hand. Then she shifted her position again, stretching more fully on the bed and raising one knee.

Soon crossed to her, and crouched with the pill impaled on the needle. She offered the pipe up to him, and steadied it as he placed the kernel of gum directly over the tiny hole on the top of the bowl. When he withdrew the needle, he created a miniature tunnel in the pill, one that would allow the pipe to draw as the opium was smoked.

When he was sure the *yen pock* was in place, Soon backed away.

Thalia inverted the pipe again, and suspended the pill in the heat from the lamp. It hissed and popped as she drew on the pipe in a long, consuming breath. Her blue eyes focused on the pill and the dream world beyond it; her entire body seemed to vibrate as she drew in the gray smoke.

Remembering my responsibilities, I pulled on the string, and felt the line go slack as Billy dropped it to head upstairs. Seconds later, the door crashed open, ruined by Kam's huge shoulder. He and Billy burst into the room with Billy yelling, "Police! You're all under arrest!"

Nobody moved. Thalia, frozen in shock, gripped her pipe and didn't notice the opium flare as it touched the live flame. I set down my own pipe and blew out the lamp. "She's got some in her purse," I said. I got up, walked to her, and took the pipe from her numbed fingers. "I don't know who you are, lady," I told her. "But you picked the wrong night to chase the dragon."

"Lam Kee opium," Billy said, trying to sound surprised. "About three ounces. That's Federal weight."

"You're under arrest for violation of the Federal narcotic law," I told her. She fell back onto the opium bed, dazed.

"Let's get everybody out of here," Billy said, and began collecting his paraphernalia on the trays. Kam made a show of handcuffing George Soon: another special effect for Thalia's benefit.

"Thalia Massie," Billy said, reading aloud from an envelope he'd taken from the brown purse. "Damn, I know that name from someplace."

We headed downstairs. Billy and I took Thalia and our evidence, leaving Kam to follow separately. As I was putting her in the back of our car, I got a moment to talk to Billy. "Man, you guys got there fast. I think she only got one drag," I whispered.

"That's probably enough. She doesn't look too happy right now, that's for sure."

"I guess that's good, huh?"

"You bet," Billy said. "We'll go to work on her in the car."

We needed to turn this girl quickly; she couldn't stay away from home for too long before the search parties would be out looking for her. That can of opium she'd put in her purse made for a powerful incentive; we were both hopeful.

"Thalia, listen to me," I said as I climbed behind the wheel. "We've been trying to get the chef's supplier for a couple of months now. If you help us, we can help you. Do you understand?"

"No. What's going to happen to me?"

"We're going to our office at the Federal Building. Everybody gets booked down there. It's a good place to talk."

"You've got to let me go. I'm not supposed to be here."

I shook my head. "No chance. The problem is, we caught you with the opium in your purse. We've got you and the chef cold."

"But what can I do?"

"Hey, we trade smokers for peddlers all the time. We want your help."

"And if I help you, you'll let me go?"

"If it's good information, you can be home this evening."

"And nobody will know what happened?"

"We won't say anything, will we Billy?"

"Nope. Got to protect our sources."

She considered the offer. "I'll do whatever I have to do, only nobody can know about tonight," she said finally.

"You have to give us something good."

She mulled that one over. "Yes, I'll do it."

As the car rolled into the courtyard, I could see Billy's broad smile in my mirror.

CHAPTER 29

Federal Building, Room 213
Saturday, December 19

I left Billy and Kam with Thalia, bounded up the marble steps to the second floor, and galloped down the corridor to our office, key in hand. Inside, I turned on the lights and found the Army recorder's warm-up switch. When I flipped it on, I heard the faint hum as the machine awoke. We knew from practice that it would take a minute or two for the tubes and the other mysteries in its interior to groan to life, but the next step would be simple: just reach down and turn the knob to "record."

Billy and Kam brought Thalia in, and parked her in the chair in front of the concealed microphone. It was time to see if Billy's scheme would work.

I sat down and peered over the books and the concealed microphone to where Thalia hunched dejectedly, staring down at her cuffed hands.

"Thalia, you said you wanted to cooperate with us…"

"It's just that the whole story is so…degrading. I'm embarrassed to tell it," she confessed, hanging her head.

"Would you feel more comfortable if you just spoke with one of us?" This was part of our plan, too. "One on one, she might think, 'I can just deny everything later,' but then we'll tell her we've got the tape," Billy had said.

Thalia went for it. "Could I?"

"Sure. Of course, Mr. Wells and Mr. Kam will have to be right outside the door. They'll stay there in case you try to attack me or anything."

She smiled wanly. "All right. I think I'd feel better just talking to you."

"We want you to be comfortable. Billy, could you take off the cuffs? I think Thalia's going to be okay. Right?"

She nodded.

As Billy moved in front of her with the handcuff key, I bent down and turned the recorder on. From now on, every word spoken would be going onto the wire spool.

When the reels started turning, I nodded to Billy. *All set.*

He and Kam grabbed a few chairs and headed for the door. "We'll be right outside the door, hoss."

"Thanks, Billy. I think we're gonna get along just fine."

"Yeah. You sing out if you need anything." The door closed behind them.

Thalia Massie liked to talk. I let her, while I kept an eye on the spinning reels under the desk. She told me how she'd gotten started smoking, and was taken down to her first den by a Navy friend of her husband. We hit a snag, though, when she wouldn't give up the name of the guy she called "Tommie's friend."

"I just want to wait for a few minutes," she said. "He scares me quite a lot, to tell the truth."

"Keep her talking," Billy had told me. "You can always come back to the hard parts." So I pressed on. She said this man knew "Sammy," had introduced her to other Chinese men, and had taken her to another den besides George Soon's. She spoke flatly, calmly relating her experiences, though she bit down on "Tommie's friend" every time.

She didn't have any scruples about the man she knew only as Sammy. She readily admitted he'd been the one who had met her that night at the Ala Wai Inn, one of the four men who'd *really* taken her for the ride that ended on the beach road.

Her personality might have left a lot to be desired, but I found her bright and articulate enough. I did a lot of interviews after this one, and it flowed along easier than most. I could feel the undercurrent of condescension in her words, though. She didn't like sitting there, talking to this grubby little policeman, but she would if she must.

"That's okay," Billy said later. "Folks who think they're better than you usually want to prove it by telling you why." And Thalia incriminated the hell out of herself in the process, recording a dark and disturbing engraving of herself, her marriage, and a man who might be the White Friend on that silent silver ribbon.

As the thirty-three-minute witching hour drew near, I could tell we were going to need to change reels. It was a process that, in practice sessions, never took less than five minutes. Fortunately, Thalia responded positively to a suggested break.

While Billy escorted Thalia to the restroom at the far end of the building, I sweated out the reel change under the desk and filled Kam in on the progress so far, knowing he'd pass it along to Billy.

Kam didn't seem surprised to hear that Tommie's friend was a Navy man, and we were both relieved that it wasn't a policeman as Soon had first suggested. "That'd be all we need," he said. He was most interested in the two places Thalia said she'd gone with Tommie's friend—another den in Chinatown and a private home—and gave me some questions to ask her to try to identify the Chinese people she'd met.

When Billy came down the hall, whistling a warning, Kam was already standing in the doorway, giving him the "safe" sign. The reels on the Blattnerphone flashed in the shadows under the desk.

I closed the door and was alone again with Thalia. I intended to get some additional background and ask Kam's questions, but we spoke first about her visits to all those doctors and about all that laudanum.

Then Thalia wanted to talk about something else. She took a long drag on her cigarette. "Do you know DeQuincey, Jack?" she asked, and the smoke escaped from her painted lips in short puffs.

"No." My mind was elsewhere. "Is he another Navy man?"

Her look was a withering cross between pity and scorn. "No, Jack, he's a dead author who wrote about opium. Thomas DeQuincey?"

Then it clicked. "*Confessions of an English Opium Eater.* Yeah, I've heard of him. So?"

"Yes. Did you know that his drug—the opium he wrote about—was laudanum?"

"I think I heard that."

"I'd read him before. He was a great comfort, afterward. He reassured me I wasn't the only one who'd had my experiences. He wrote about his opium dreams, but I couldn't have imagined what he meant until I started smoking."

Where in the hell was this going? I started thinking about how to get her back on track, but she was on a roll.

"I've told you so much already," she continued. "Do you want to hear what the opium was like?"

"I'll listen to whatever you've got to say."

"You're sweet," she murmured, not meaning it.

She leaned back, suddenly age twenty going on fifty, wreathed in the cigarette smoke that drifted above her head, and looked up at the fancies swirling there. "It's a fabulous world, so different from this one—and infinitely better, if you're a person like me. The faces that join you there are all somehow kind, benign, not like the ones you see here." She looked distastefully at our little office and its only other occupant. "I don't suppose you would know what I mean."

"Probably not. I've never smoked any dope."

"Dope." She flinched. "That's such a cruel word for it. So ugly and shabby. Something as wondrous as opium should have a better name. DeQuincey called it 'just, subtle, and mighty opium.' He said it was a panacea. Do you know what that means?"

"I have a college education, Mrs. Massie."

"Yes." She laughed shortly. "Well, you don't learn about things like opium in college. It was a discovery for me, a revelation, as though I was the first person setting foot on the most heavenly island in the world. I had beautiful, haunting dreams the first few months I was smoking. I flew and floated through warm peach-colored mists, drifted in the wind with the birds. I could visit castles in the sky. Soft cloud palaces filled with light and music and kindness.

"For me, opium was like…like a master tuning fork that aligned everything to one divine, harmonious pitch. As if you were wearing rose-tinted glasses, only for all of your senses. Everything is luminous, and everything is shaded in the same…sublime, that's the word, sublime way.

"Most people I've spoken with, they say their dreams leave them when they wake. They barely remember having them, much less what the dream was about. It's lost to them forever. Is it like that for you?"

"I guess," I said, not wanting me or my dreams discussed on the Blattnerphone.

"I was like that before opium, so I suppose we're normal, you and I. But after opium, every dream was vivid and memorable, and even after I woke up, I could recall it perfectly—almost reach out and touch it, because it was so real.

"And the colors, the sensations. Everything so exciting and vibrant. I felt more alive, more genuine when I was in my opium dreams."

Her face suddenly darkened, as when a cloud passes across the sun, and her blithe reverie flew into cold shadow. Her eyes dropped from the ceiling, and she gazed directly at me for the first time since she'd started talking.

"DeQuincey warned me about the other sort of opium dreams, the ones that ravish you in the night and horrify you in the daylight, but I didn't believe it. The world I'd found for myself was too perfect to admit the kinds of things he wrote about." She took a long pull on the cigarette, and exhaled the smoke in a thin, sharp stream.

"He had his own dreams, of course. Everyone's unique. He dreaded Orientals—he called them 'Malays'—but his obsession was crocodiles. Hideous, grinning crocodiles giving him 'cancerous kisses.' He wrote that, you know. Can you imagine anything more horrid? I couldn't, not then. Later, though…"

She shuddered, visibly shaken by something hovering in the haze of cigarette smoke above her, and tried a curt laugh, one utterly without hope that it could dispel the apparition.

"I knew it must have been something in his own soul, some flaw that allowed him to think such terrible thoughts. It couldn't be the opium; it was impossible for the opium *I* knew to hide something so awful.

"I am a special person," she said unconvincingly. "I knew nothing inside *me* would ever allow a crocodile into my dreams.

"Then the crows came," she whispered. "I don't know why it was crows. I've tried to think why. I'm sure there's a very good explanation."

She bound herself with her arms, an unavailing hug, then looked directly at me. Those remote blue eyes implored me, crying for an answer, and I felt the oddest chill. It was as though the cold, dark mist at the center of a cloud suddenly flowed around me, eddying as if stirred by some fluttering wing, and then dissipated in the silence that followed. What remained was the sure and certain knowledge that I had nothing for her.

She looked away, knowing it, too, then continued talking to herself in a voice reedy and hopeless. "The crows are my crocodile. I can fly again, only sometimes the crows are there with me." She uttered the last words in a voice as sharp and shivery as shattering crystal.

I tried again to turn the conversation from terror to relevance. "Did you smoke that night at the Ala Wai Inn?"

She shook her head decisively and brought herself back. "No. I hadn't the opportunity. Tommie was at home that Saturday. I couldn't get away. Perhaps I *am* spoiled. People do say that. I didn't get what I wanted that night."

"Some of the witnesses said you looked drunk."

"I do drink, but alcohol alone makes me sappy and silly. I get all girlish. Or bitchy. I had too much to drink that night, and ended up slapping Ralph Stogsdall. That never would have happened if I'd been smoking opium."

"But you drank some laudanum that night."

"Yes, I had some in my purse, maybe a few ounces. I went outside the inn and finished it in the parking lot. That was when I saw Sammy again."

She still sat in the chair, but I could see she'd gone off somewhere again, this time remembering what must have been one of the worst nights of her young life.

"I stood there for a few minutes, then walked toward the amusement park. By that time, I was feeling much better. My troubles all dropped away as I walked. That's what opium does. That's what it did for me that night. The evening was suddenly warm and serene. All of the bad feelings seemed bearable.

"I hadn't wanted to go to the party. I was upset at being forced. I didn't care to be around all those boring Navy people. But a little laudanum, my panacea, and all that faded away."

"You were under the influence when you were walking on Ena Road."

"Yes, I was 'under the influence,'" she mimicked, rocking her shoulders from side to side in time with the words. "And thank God. The experience was bad enough even with my medicine to help me. It would have been unendurable without opium.

"I wasn't intoxicated, though. It would have taken more than I had to get there, and I wouldn't have been walking anywhere." She paused for a moment, reflecting. "That's why opium is smoked lying down, I think. You need the chance to be quiet and still. You can take flight—your mind is moving, even though your body's at rest.

"When I smoked, all of a sudden I could call up all the visions and images of my childhood. I could recall old incidents when I was a girl, and places—especially Long Island at my grandfather's house—just will them back and live them again. And everything would be just as it was, only somehow brighter and clearer…because I was outside, looking back at it, I suppose. All of that came right out of the smoke," she added, remembering it, marveling at it, craving it.

"Children can do that. Everything is so real to their imaginations. But we lose that when we grow up unless we have opium to bring it back. Do you know how people say, when they're near death, their life passes before them, that they live it all over again in a flash of time?"

"Sure."

"I could summon those same visions with opium, but I had no control over them. They came to me whether I wanted them or not, only they seemed to take forever. The opium slows down the time and makes everything expand. All your emotions and everything physical seem larger and longer."

She paused and smirked suggestively at me. "That's a good thing if you're a man, I suppose. But oh, then you wake up to reality."

"You're talking about sex, I suppose."

"Sex and opium. It is a wonder. For men, as I said, it's all a dream. The opium gives them the desire, poor dears, but cages the ability. Somebody wrote that, and it's true. For women, for me, it was…exalted. I could get aroused just hearing the pill cooking. Do you know how you start salivating when you hear bacon cooking? That man, Pavlov, talked about it."

"Yeah. With the dogs and the dinner bell." I shifted uncomfortably in my chair, willing myself not to look under the table where the Blattnerphone spooled faithfully on, capturing Thalia's ever-more intimate confession.

"Yes. That's how it was with me and opium and sex. Just the sound and the smell of it was enough to excite me."

She pondered that thought for a moment, then turned away from it with a clouded frown. "But you have to buy a ticket for the flight. I had to pay and pay."

"What? To buy the opium?"

"No, not that," she said impatiently. "There were awful, gloomy feelings of depression. The worst sort of disturbing emotions. I can barely stand to think about them, even now. I've never told anyone about them before. It was like the sensation of slowly falling, going down, sinking so far that you have this terrible suspicion… no, you *know* you can never, ever come back. You'll just keep falling into a worse and worse place. Hell, you think, would be an improvement, would be upward progress. What's below Hell? I don't know, but I've been there, and I know it's barren and sunless and cold." She no longer looked at me; her eyes were focused on something far away, something ghastly and coming closer. "I thought about suicide a lot," she said in a small voice. "I'm thinking about it now."

"You're not going to do that," I said, alarmed at the prospect.

"No," she agreed, shaking her head decisively. "No, because there's the chance I'm going to get some opium tonight. I'll live for that chance. I've got some at home. A big brown bottle. Several, in fact. My redeemers."

She looked defiantly at me. "You can take my pipe, but I can get another. And I can see a doctor and get more laudanum. I will get what I want," she insisted.

I recalled the soft swirl of cool air currents in the little office. "Can't wait to get back to those crows, eh?" I deliberately picked the image that seemed to bother her most.

She jerked as if I'd slapped her, then stood beside her chair and leaned forward over the table. "You're being cruel. Taunting me with the crows. But you don't know them, or you wouldn't say anything. I'll tell you.

Maybe they'll visit *your* dreams. First there's the one, then they multiply and swarm." She straightened, lowered her voice, and took a step back toward the wall. "Before you can even breathe, there are more crows, then dozens and dozens of them, shining perfectly black and repulsive. Each one has a yellow beak, flaming red eyes, and a pink mouth that opens to swallow you." Her hands drifted across her face. "You wouldn't like these crows."

"Sit down. I don't like any crows. I don't know anybody who does."

She moved back to the chair and sat heavily. "They terrify me. Crows peck your eyes. I read that in a book. The library across the street there has it. Isn't that lovely? They're an omen of death. The Greeks thought crows were sent to collect people's souls when they died." Her voice brightened for a moment as she dodged away from whatever horror stalked her, and then despaired as it caught up. "The book said crows eat carrion, and peck out the softest parts of a dead animal's body."

"That might have been more than you needed to learn." And lots more than I wanted to hear.

"Carrion." She shuddered and protected her face with her long, slender fingers, seeing something—maybe herself—in the darkness. "Oh, God."

Shaking herself free of the recollection, she breathed, harsh and ragged. "The Chinese girl in the den had hair the same color as a crow's feathers. That shiny black, almost blue color? When we smoked together, I would bury my face in her hair. She smelled of almonds, and her mouth was wet and pink. I often wondered if maybe that's where the image came from.

"But it doesn't matter," she added, realizing that logic was irrelevant to her crisis. "I can't escape the crows, no matter how rational I try to be when I'm not smoking. They come and cover my face with their black feathers all fluttering, and oh, their beaks come down on my eyes. I can't feel anything; I only see black." Her voice climbed an octave, lunging toward madness. "Then their mouths open for my soul." She covered her face with her hands, once again shutting out me, the room, and the dreadful pipe dream she evoked.

I twisted in my chair, sharing—if only for a few uncomfortable seconds—her awful imaginings. Then, for a single evanescent moment, one so fleeting I can still pretend it was never there at all, Thalia Massie presented me with another vision—of a scared and lonely teenager, five thousand miles from home. Of a girl with no real friend in all the world except an inflexible chemical master who issued the commands for her debasement from the bowl of an ivory pipe.

Everyone confronts evil with a different face. Some are fearful, some brave and resolute, some kind and caring, and some a mirror image of the corruption itself. On December 19, I wore indifference and shoved that instant aside, promising to revisit but never, never returning.

"You're right," I said casually. "I wouldn't want those birds after me. So why don't you just stop? It doesn't sound like a very good experience. All that horror and death."

She shook her head, and her soft brown hair rippled as she expelled the vision. "Oh, la. How you talk. Give it up? Even if I could, I wouldn't want to. I've got the chance of flying in the sunlight. The wonderful sex. My memory times. I can't give it up."

"You aren't getting any more opium from those doctors, I'm gonna see to that. And I don't think the den will have you after tonight."

"I shall have to find some way," she said primly. "Or I'll be ill soon enough, throwing up all over your lovely furniture and being sick on your floor. You won't want that, Jack. You're going to let me go home to my laudanum and my dreams, however terrible they might be."

"Thalia, you are a sick person. Seriously, you need to get some medical help, and I'm not talking about the kind of doctor who'll just give you some more laudanum."

"An alienist, you mean," she scoffed. "How is he going to analyze these dreams? How is he going to help me leave something I don't care to leave?"

"You're not ready to quit taking opium?"

"Of course not. I want some right now. Let me smoke some pills, Jack. You have that tin right there, and my pipe. I'll do it naked, and you can watch me. You can do more than watch, if you want."

She stood quickly and slid the straps of her dress off her shoulders. The silk fell forward, exposing a white undergarment…a slip, I suppose. She started working on that, and I knew I had better do something quick.

"What are you doing?" I protested to the Blattnerphone. "Behave yourself, Thalia! Billy! Gimme a hand here."

The door opened a beat later, and Billy and Kam strode into the room. Thalia fell back into her seat, covered her breasts, and turned away from us so she could slip the straps back over her shoulders. I gave her a few seconds to compose herself, and everybody pretended they hadn't seen or done anything.

"Uh, I think we've finished with the basic story," I stammered, badly flustered.

"Let's wrap this up Monday, then," Billy said. "We'll have more time, and you look pretty worn out." I knew he was thinking of the second spool even though his words were directed at Thalia.

"I am very tired. Are you really going to let me go tonight?" she asked the floor.

"You said you want to cooperate, and I'm sure you'll keep your word, right?"

"Yes, I want to help you."

"That's what we want, too. We'll work together, all right?"

"All right. I want to get home."

You bet she was hot to get home; she'd start in on the shakes any time now. None of us wanted to be around when that crisis began.

"We'll drive you to your car."

Billy and Kam escorted Thalia out of the office while I reached down and shut off the Blattnerphone, and silently celebrated. The whole scheme had actually worked, I gloated. We had leads that, on Monday, would take us closer to a white man who wore a uniform and who was connected to Chinatown opium peddlers—and to Sammy Akana—a perfect description of the White Friend.

Better yet, Thalia Massie had been corrupted as a witness about as thoroughly as anyone could hope. The Ala Moana boys were off the hook.

Elated, I snapped off the lights, remembered Holt and Russell, and thought how much better this deal had turned out.

In our haste to leave, I forgot an important detail—one that would circle back and bite us in the ass before we knew it was even there.

CHAPTER 30

Federal Building, Room 305
Monday, December 21

"Uh oh," Billy fretted when the summons came bright and early Monday morning. "Why does Sandy want to see you?"

"I don't know. Maybe he wants to talk about a case."

"He didn't say?"

"No. Just asked me to come up."

"What time are we supposed to see Thalia?"

"Ten. She's coming down at ten."

"This is not good," Billy muttered. He was quite right, as usual.

As I analyzed Sandy Wood's brief call, I concluded that I was in trouble and that, also as usual, it probably involved Thalia Massie. Wood had sounded edgy and harried, and as I trudged upstairs I inventoried my evidence, though I already doubted it would make a difference.

Conversation spilled out of the U.S. Attorney's office into the hall: one voice strident, Wood's quieter, placating. Sandy had quite a crowd this morning. There was a regular party going on in his office, and I was the last invited guest to arrive. Nine sets of eyes shifted to me as I stopped in the doorway and tapped lightly on the frame. None of them had even a hint of warmth or kindness in them as they followed me into the room.

Wood introduced me first to the man covered in gold braid who'd stopped talking when I knocked. Admiral Yates Stirling didn't stand or offer to shake hands; instead he held me off with a cold glare. Charles Weeber, a representative of the Chamber of Commerce, acknowledged me with a small wave, but the others all sat stonily as Wood went through their names.

I had seen the short, intense young man in civilian clothes at the courthouse once before. Now, leaning forward on the edge of his chair, Tommie Massie practically vibrated with tension. His mother-in-law, Grace Fortescue, someone I felt I almost knew personally, sat at his elbow. The broad-shouldered officer next to her wore a hostile expression with his Navy captain's uniform. He was, I learned, Ward Wortman, the commander of the submarine base at Pearl Harbor and Tommie Massie's ranking superior. I'd seen the other Navy man at the courthouse, too, but Carl Butler from the Shore Patrol just nodded to me. Will Moore and a local attorney, Montgomery Winn, rounded out the posse.

"Jack, thanks for coming up," Wood finally said, and showed me a vacant chair in the crowded office.

I tried to sound casual and slightly quizzical, as though I didn't know what was happening. "What's going on?"

"What's going on," Stirling snapped, "is that you are harassing the wife of one of my officers, and I want it stopped. Immediately!" His voice started in a bellow and ended in a roar. Stirling's already ruddy complexion contrasted sharply with the white and gold of his uniform and seemed to color more deeply every minute.

My heart sank. We hadn't told anyone about Saturday evening's events, so this must have come from Thalia. She'd turned herself around over the weekend, resulting in this assembly who were lined up, looking for blood.

Wood looked like a man trying to juggle a hand grenade with the pin already pulled. "These gentlemen and Mrs. Fortescue are concerned that the federal government may have been…misled by elements in the police force into taking a position that could interfere with a Territorial prosecution. I assured them we would never knowingly do anything like that."

Apparently this was the extent of the support I could expect from Sandy Wood. I wasn't evil or corrupt, merely stupid.

The admiral, however, was having none of Wood's sophistry. "Oh, come now. This is an obvious attempt to subvert the retrial of the Ala Moana case by destroying Mrs. Massie's reputation. I don't think blackmail is too strong a word."

The other seven heads swiveled to me, waiting for the return volley, as though we were the main attraction at a tennis match. Though I was already fairly confident that nothing I said would make any difference to this bunch, I still had to say something. "Blackmail? With what?" Getting ready to tell them about a girl in an opium den.

"Mrs. Massie says you talked with her about her use of the prescription medications she requires for the aftereffects of this terrible incident." Wood threw himself back into the growing conflict. "She said you threatened to use your information to discredit her in the retrial of those hoodlums."

"That's it?" Wondering what, or even if, she had told them about the rest of it. "That's all she said?"

"Isn't that enough?" Stirling shouted. "My God, man! This poor woman has suffered unbearably, endured pain beyond what most strong men could stand. If she needs the assistance of medications legitimately prescribed by a physician, who are you to say otherwise?"

"There's evidence of criminal activity…" I began and looked at Wood, trying to bypass the antagonism focused on me like a heat lamp.

"This office would never accept that type of case. We wouldn't prosecute anyone else, and we certainly aren't contemplating a prosecution of Mrs. Massie." Wood might have been looking at Monty Winn, the Massie's family attorney, but he was talking to me. "I will advise the District Supervisor, Mr. Stevenson, of our decision."

I opened my mouth to respond, but thought better of it even before Wood intercepted me.

"That's my final word, Jack. We don't act on gossip or rumor. This office cannot be a party to a witch hunt orchestrated by people who want to destroy this lady's reputation."

Everybody looked fairly mollified except Wortman and Tommie, who were both obviously steaming. Mrs. Fortescue didn't look too happy, either, and bored holes in me with her ice-blue eyes. She probably had her little gun in her purse and was itching to use it.

"If that's your decision, I guess I'll have to go along with it. I'll talk it over with the boss."

Winn spoke before Sandy could respond. "Just so we're clear, I'm Mrs. Massie's attorney, and I'm telling you that she does not want to speak with you or answer any further questions. If you attempt to contact her without my consent, we will take legal action against you and the federal government. I think that covers it, doesn't it, Sandy?"

"Absolutely." Wood, now standing, wanted the pin back in the grenade. "Since there will be no prosecution, there will be no need for any further contact. I don't think that will be a problem."

"We'll be putting additional security—armed security—on Mrs. Massie's house," Stirling said. "With orders to shoot if necessary."

"We've already had a shore patrolman stationed in the neighborhood," Butler said, though I already knew, this, having seen the uniform from time to time while I was staking out Thalia. "There are three other officers living within a block or two. But we'll post one there full time to make sure there's no… threat."

That was it. Thalia was bulletproof. Even if I spilled all the evidence I had, Sandy would never take the case. And, except for the wire recording of her confession, there wasn't much of a case to begin with. She'd frequented an opium den, but that was a violation of the Territory's law, not ours. She'd admitted possession of smoking opium, but that was hardly a matter Wood wanted to take to court, particularly under the circumstances. The only real crime, since you couldn't count our little setup, was possession of the laudanum she'd gotten from the doctors—and Wood had just shot that case down in flames.

A bugle sounded in my ear. *Time to retreat.*

"All right. I've got the picture. No contact," I said to Winn, ignoring the admiral who appeared ready to sound off again. "If that's all, I'll head back downstairs."

"No. That isn't 'all.'"

Yates Stirling might have been finished with Sandy, but he and Grace Fortescue hadn't even started on me. Between them, they gave me the longest two minutes of my entire life.

"I predicted this disaster," Stirling said, talking to Wood but looking at me. "All of this race mixing everyone here is so proud of, and what is the result? A police force filled with crooked coloreds and half-breed natives, most of them protecting their hoodlum cousins. You even let mixed-bloods on your juries, and then you're surprised when they won't convict their own kind. It's not a surprise; familiarity between the races breeds contempt!"

"It obviously bred something else," Grace said, curling her lip as she eyed me up and down.

"Yes," Stirling nodded. "I was disgusted to see that when I first arrived. White men—prominent white men, mind you—surrounded by their half-breed children, some of them darker than mulattos, but some like this one here. All of them thinking they're our equals. That's exactly the kind of thinking that creates false expectations for both races, and it destroys the superior-subordinate relationship." Stirling rapped on Wood's desktop for emphasis while his own subordinates, Wortman and Massie, nodded their agreement.

Grace wasn't interested in the admiral's broad generalizations, however. She was aiming her salvos at a target closer to home.

"I understand the term they use here in Hawaii, hapa haole, means half-white. They don't even distinguish by degree."

"Don't they call them quadroons, Mother?" Tommie Massie interjected.

"That would be someone with a quarter part of black blood, dear. His father, I suppose. But he," she sneered in my direction, "doesn't even have the excuse of that much taint. I believe the correct term for his kind is 'octoroon.'"

"The correct term is 'mongrel,'" Stirling growled.

Grace went on, her eyes blazing, "Oh, one would think that the superiority of the white blood would overcome the inferior eventually. But sadly…" She used her dove-gray gloves to brush away an imaginary spot on her handbag while she measured me for the knife. "It never happens. Farmers have a saying, you know. It's rather coarse, but you'll forgive me. 'The least bit of manure in the milk ruins the whole pail.'"

Sandy Wood and Will Moore had enough decency to look appalled, but not enough to say anything to stop her. Everybody else just sat there, watching the slaughter.

Thankfully, she was almost done.

"Hawaii is so lovely—it's just tragic that it should be spoiled this way. Now the half-caste scum has oozed so far from their proper place that they're even allowed to be teachers and engineers. And a decent person can't know anymore, just by looking…" Here, she paused for a few long beats, and kept her icy gaze fixed on my face. "…that there is a nigger in the room."

Over the years, I've thought of many things I wish I had said—should have said—to Yates Stirling and Grace Fortescue. In my dreams, it doesn't hurt. In my dreams, I'm witty and cutting, and nonchalant in dismissing their vicious bigotry. At the time though, I could no more have spoken than flown out the window and up to the moon. My face burning and almost blind from rage and humiliation, I stumbled through the door and down the marble hallway.

I didn't go back to the office, and I have no idea to this day how I got home. I must have walked the four miles, because my car was still at the Federal Building the next morning when I needed it to get back to work.

2663 Terrace Drive
Tuesday, December 22

My grandmother might have retired from teaching, but she wasn't dead yet, as she was fond of telling everyone. When I got downstairs the next morning, Grandma had already made breakfast and was getting ready for one of her meetings, this one at the YWCA around the corner from our office. I asked if I could catch a ride downtown with her.

My father looked up from the paper. "We didn't see much of you last night. I didn't even know you were home."

"I wasn't feeling well."

"Hmmm. Your name came up at work. That have anything to do with it?"

This could not be good news. "I don't know. Maybe."

"Walter Dillingham's man, Chuck Weeber, came out to the office. He mentioned he'd seen you earlier."

Swell. It looked like yesterday's misery had bubbled over to today. And onto my father. I was starting to doubt that would ever end. "Yeah. I met him and a bunch of other people yesterday. What did he want?"

"Officially or unofficially?"

"Both, I guess."

"Officially, he wanted to know how construction was going on the ammo bunkers. Unofficially, he wanted to let me know he was interested in what you were up to. Since I don't know, I couldn't help him."

"I'll bet that made him happy."

"He didn't seem too bothered. He was more concerned with making sure I knew I worked for Mr. Dillingham." He laughed. "Like I could forget. That man Weeber used to be a sergeant major in the coast artillery. He's about as subtle as a sixteen-inch gun."

"Oh, Dad. I'm really sorry. I never meant to cause any problems for the family."

"Don't worry about it." He got up and tossed his napkin onto the table. "They need me a lot more than I need them. We'll be okay."

Now I had something else to worry about, and I fretted in Grandma's car, trying not to think about Stevenson's reaction. The pressure wave was obviously spreading outward from Thalia's bombshell, and if it had reached Pearl Harbor, it must have already arrived at our office door.

"So, Pono, a bad day yesterday." Grandma steered her Buick out of Manoa and looped through the quiet streets toward Punchbowl crater.

"The worst. You haven't called me that for a long time."

"You were little. Sixth grade, I think, when you decided Jack sounded better. It's all right. Your parents choose your name. Your nickname is one of those things you should get to choose."

"I guess I'm not surprised you heard about my day," I sighed.

"You hear everything eventually, Pono. We live on an island. Everybody knows everybody else, knows where they came from, where they live. People know your family, your friends, where you went to school. That's Hawaii, and Hawaiians know each others' families going back a thousand years, because where you came from is part of who you are."

"It's a good thing somebody knows, then, because I don't have any idea who I am anymore."

"You thought you were haole, and just found out otherwise? That's a shock, all right."

"It never used to be like this, Grandma. Nobody cared if you or Dad were part-Hawaiian, much less me."

"Oh, Pono," she sighed. "It always mattered to some people. Hawaiians have been dealing with that for a hundred and fifty years. You think because you call yourself Jack and play sports with Walter Dillingham's sons and the other mission boys, you were one of them?"

"Our ancestors were missionaries, too."

"And they're all buried together in the same graveyard behind Kawaiahao Church, Hawaiians and missionaries both. But it still mattered, so the haoles are in one corner and the Hawaiians are in the others."

"Well, it doesn't matter to me."

"No? That's good. That's the way it should be." She smiled. "What makes someone special is what a person does, not who his parents were, whether they were Hawaiian or came from Connecticut. Do you remember what *hoʻopono* means?"

Of course I did. I'd been reminded often when I was little—usually by Grandma. "To do right. To find justice," I recited.

She nodded. "Are you doing right, Pono?"

"What do you mean?"

"This trial, with the haole girl. You're getting mixed up in it. Is it for the right reason? Is it hoʻopono?"

"I'm trying. But how do you know anything about it?"

"I talk to Bertha Pittman. She's going to be at the meeting this morning. We think we know what's right, too. Some of the ladies raise money to pay the lawyers. Some talk to their husbands about jobs for the boys. We do what we can to make things right."

"It can get you in trouble. It's got me in plenty. Maybe Dad, too."

She laughed, just like my father had. "I'm not dead yet, but I'm too old to worry about trouble from people like little Walter Dillingham. He was a know-it-all in ninth grade and he still is."

She turned the car onto King Street, and the Federal Building slid into view. "Besides, if doing right was easy or cheap, everybody would do it. Then how special would it be?"

CHAPTER 31

Federal Building, Room 213
Tuesday, December 22

I didn't feel very special. I felt more like a kicked dog going upstairs that morning. Not only had my case, my career, and maybe my life turned completely to shit, I got to the office knowing it was all my fault.

If only I'd told Thalia that night about the recording. Shown her the Blattnerphone before she left the office. Let her know there wouldn't be any sliding out of this one. If only I'd gotten the damned name from her. But I hadn't done either, and those mistakes meant all that work went right down the toilet.

Now I had a statement and an opium pipe. The latter, though quite beautiful, was useless as evidence. Unfortunately, without Thalia, the same went for the statement. She'd left us with some good leads, but moving ahead now meant leaving Thalia Massie behind.

I can't say I was terribly disappointed. She'd cost me plenty already, and all the bills hadn't even started to come due.

First things first, and that meant squaring up with the boss. Or almost squaring. Since we didn't officially have a den, we didn't have a Blattnerphone, either. The rest of it was, Billy said, "the truth, the *hole* truth, and nothing but the truth. Just make damn sure," he drilled me like one of his informers, "you remember where the hole in the story goes."

I remembered: Soon told us that morning that the white lady would be coming to the den later the same evening, which was true. We saw her go in and found her in possession of the opium, which was also true. We managed to get her confession, along with some good leads to some other yen shee men before it all blew up. All true as far as it went.

Stevenson, who'd gotten back from San Francisco on Monday evening, listened attentively, smiled at the right parts, frowned at some others, and agreed wholeheartedly when I concluded that things could have gone much better.

"Yep. I'd say you took a real cowshit bath on this little number," he cheerfully confirmed when I'd finished. "I'm surprised Commissioner Anslinger hasn't been on the wire already. Probably be a cable this afternoon tellin' me to ship your ass out to Billings or Buffalo or some damned place." He sounded awfully pleased at the prospect.

"I got close, though. She was right there."

"Yeah? Then how come we don't have the bastard's name? How come you didn't seal the deal on this lady?"

Billy spoke up. "It's my fault. I told him not to push her too hard on the first go-round. But you know, boss, it isn't too bad. We did get the girl cold. And Jack covered every base on the laudanum thing. If we came out of this with nothing more than a good line on the White Friend, we're way ahead in the game."

Stevenson looked skeptical. "And you think you got him?"

"I think we're close." Billy ticked off the clues Thalia had given us, stressing that we hadn't even begun to check any of them out. "And the best part is, Jack actually saw this guy once."

"What?"

"Yeah," I said. "She told me she was at George Soon's den the night we hit it. I remember she came out of the place with Akana and another man just as we were setting up. She said Tommie's friend was the other man."

"What did he look like?" Stevenson's interest now was apparent.

"I only saw him from behind. Dark hair, maybe five-eight, solid build. He could've been Navy. He was definitely white."

"If this guy who took her around to the dens is the Friend, we're closer than we ever have been before," Billy pointed out. "Getting him would make Washington pretty happy."

Stevenson considered this. "You got some pretty fair leads there," he conceded. "Something could come of it, after all. A Navy boy. We never thought of that one, but that would explain why we never had any luck before." He reflected on the implications of going after one of Admiral Stirling's officers, and looked at me. "Did you mention him to Wood or those other folks?"

"No, sir. I thought maybe the Admiral would've strung me up."

"Humph. He'd have to get in line. God, I want that sonofabitch so bad, though." He pulled a pad of cable forms out of the pile on top of his desk. "All this crap would almost be worth it, to slap the cuffs on that bastard."

"Be a dream come true, after two years," Billy agreed.

Stevenson looked back and forth between us, and then came to a decision. He tossed the cable forms back onto the pile and told Billy, "I got to be crazy, but see if you two can identify this Chinaman she's talking about. Make me a list of the leads you think are worth following up from this statement.

"And sit on his ass," he ordered Billy, pointing at me. "He don't blow his nose unless you're holding the hanky."

"Sure, boss." Billy turned to me with a wide grin, and it began to dawn on me that I might have dodged one large-caliber Navy bullet. Maybe things were starting to turn around.

Federal Building, Room 213
Wednesday, December 23

"Okay," Billy exclaimed, rubbing his hands together like he was sitting down to a good meal. "Let's see how everything we know stacks up."

I pulled out my file that summarized the evidence on the White Friend. The other files on Sammy Akana and Thalia Massie were already out and open.

"Start with Sammy. When did he get nicked in L.A.?"

By this time, I had Akana's file almost memorized. "February 23, 1929. He was a steward on the *SS Golden Star*, coming from Shanghai via Kobe, Yokohama, and Honolulu."

"Shanghai? Not Hong Kong?"

"No. I already checked."

"That's weird," Billy frowned. "Lam Kee's strictly a Macao brand. It all comes from there and Hong Kong."

"Akana had a hundred and seventy tins of it when he got to L.A. Maybe he picked it up here."

"Maybe. It was probably part of that load the hui ran that same month. I remember right, the books show they got a load in February and the White Friend got paid at that same time."

"Yeah. He got $28,000 on February 15th." I had those books memorized, too.

"Shanghai. That could be important. So, we got Sammy and the White Friend both here in February '29, same time a load comes in. What else puts them together?"

"Thalia said Tommie's friend was a Navy officer, and he introduced her to Sammy. They went to the dens together, and they were waiting to talk to her the night she got kidnapped."

"And George Soon backs her up."

"He says Sammy brought her to his place the first time," I nodded, "and she had a white man with her. I didn't show Akana's mug shot to Thalia, but George says that's the guy."

"We got any candidates for who the Navy boy is?"

"I started out thinking it could be her husband, but he's at sea a lot. Practically every weekday and sometimes longer, and George said she'd come to his place during the week. Plus, she told me Tommie didn't have any idea she was having an affair with his buddy.

"The only other names I've got are Jerry Branson and Ralph Stogsdall. Branson's the one the cops picked up that night by her house. He and Stogsdall were both at the party at the Ala Wai Inn—but they don't fit because they weren't even stationed here in '29."

"These guys come and go," Billy shrugged. "Two or three years here, and they're off to California or Virginia or someplace."

"That could help narrow it down if we find out who was here from that first shipment in late '28 through September. Might still be a couple thousand men, though."

"Not that many probably. The way she met him, he's most likely an officer. There aren't nearly as many of those."

I brightened a little. "And Thalia told us he had shore duty, so he's definitely not on a sub."

"There you go. They've got big staffs, though—all the supply and medical people. Marines. Signals." Billy thought a moment, then decided, "Still can't be that many."

"Can we get a list of the ones who've been here the whole time?"

"I'll call Dick Bates at the shore patrol. He's only been here a year or so, but he can probably get us the names of the ones who went back further."

"If we get anything, I can run it against the hui files. If we could get pictures, we could show George Soon," I said, the possibilities expanding.

"I'll ask. We just never thought about Navy boys, but we're on the right track." Billy sat back and puffed contentedly on his pipe. "We just got to keep looking. Something will turn up."

"I wish I'd gotten the name out of her," I said, voicing the regret I kicked myself with a hundred times a day.

"Water under the bridge. No matter; we get our hands on Sammy, he'll tell us what we need to know."

But then the pot boiled over, and we had no time to look too hard for the elusive Mr. Akana for a while.

CHAPTER 32

Federal Building, Room 213
Monday, January 4, 1932

"I'll sure be glad when this is all over," Kam groaned, and collapsed onto a chair in front of Billy's desk.

"Don't get too comfortable; we're ready to go." Billy snapped a magazine into the Thompson he'd spent an hour cleaning. "Any word on Lyman?"

"Nah. We spent most of last night looking out by Moanalua. That's the last place anybody saw him." Kam heaved himself to his feet as Billy and Stevenson moved toward the door. Each man held a machine gun under his arm.

The new year began with another rape and a manhunt. Every cop in town but me was looking for the rapist, an escaped burglar from Oahu Prison named Lui Kaikapu. He and convicted murderer Daniel Lyman had walked away from O.P. on New Year's Eve, then split up, and each had taken a separate but equally malicious path.

Kaikapu had stolen a car and visited with some friends on New Year's Day before returning to his original trade. On January 2nd, he'd broken into a home on Wilhelmina Rise, east of downtown. Jimmy O'Dowda, who was a few classes ahead of me at Punahou, had left for work, but his wife had been home. Kaikapu had beaten her badly, tied her up, and raped her before stealing some items and leaving. One of the things taken was Jimmy's evening attire, a dinner jacket that fit well enough that Kaikapu had worn it for the rest of the day.

Word of these new crimes flashed over the city, and Kam called early on Saturday to say he'd be busy until Kaikapu fell. The sheriff needed every man on the force to take him, dead or alive.

For the terrified residents of Honolulu who flocked down to stores like Diamond-Hall and bought out their remaining stocks of guns, dead sounded just fine.

And dead should have been easy. Kaikapu, still wearing his tuxedo, went downtown for a shave and a haircut, then wandered over to the police station to check on the progress of the manhunt. When a patrolman asked why he was dressed so well, he responded that he was a waiter. This apparently satisfied the officer's curiosity, and he let Kaikapu amble off unmolested—leaving a mortified police department in his wake.

"I hope he wasn't counting on that promotion to detective," Billy snorted, shaking his head.

Now terror turned to outrage. Admiral Stirling, who'd been yelling for months about the incompetence of the local authorities, swept into town demanding more protection for his men and their women. He wanted a couple of other things, too, including an immediate retrial of the Ala Moana boys. Allowing Thalia Massie's assailants to remain free on bail was a slap in her face.

While the governor was at it, Stirling said, he could reorganize the prosecutor's office and the police department so this sort of thing didn't happen again. To drive home his point, the admiral noted that the battle fleet was due at Pearl in February, and if he didn't see some changes, he was going to cancel shore leave for all twenty thousand sailors due to the "unsafe conditions" in Honolulu.

This threat hit the papers like a bomb. With businessmen clamoring and politicians scrambling, the police force's reputation was at stake. They redoubled their efforts. All of the Federal people were told to help with the search. The White Friend was all but forgotten as Stevenson and Billy hooked up with the Vice squad each morning and joined the hunt.

The police grabbed Kaikapu late on January 2nd, still in his stolen car and Jimmy O'Dowda's evening jacket. Now the focus turned to the murderer Lyman, and things promptly went downhill.

"I didn't think it could get any worse," Kam said one morning as he waited for Billy and C.T. "You heard?"

The night before, officers searching for Lyman had mistaken some poor Filipino deckhand off the Army transport *Meigs*, just arrived from Shanghai and Manila, for their quarry, and shot him to death before he could correct the false impression.

"Yeah. It's in the morning paper already," I said.

"Maybe the admiral's got a point," he admitted. "We're not looking too good right now."

Lyman would not be caught. With people jumping (and occasionally shooting) at every new sound, with the newspapers practically hysterical over every new sighting, and with the cops chasing (and occasionally shooting) the wrong people everywhere, the perception of ineptitude, if not corruption, was unavoidable.

For people like Admiral Stirling, Daniel Lyman was living proof that the Hawaiian justice system he held in such contempt was truly and irrevocably defective. It couldn't arrest the right people, couldn't convict them when they were arrested, and couldn't keep them in prison when the prosecution somehow managed to stumble into a guilty verdict.

Everybody had gotten quite used to hearing this from the admiral and others. What Lyman and Kaikapu had changed was the response. This time, people were actually listening. Thalia's earthquake had rattled the local power structure, but the Lyman and Kaikapu aftershocks pushed it to the breaking point.

The police department was sitting right smack on the fault line, so it was the first thing to fall. A hastily called special legislative session passed a law making rape a capital crime. Two other statutes yanked the police department out from under the elected sheriff and made the public prosecutor independent of the elected county attorney.

The reporters gave Governor Lawrence Judd's next move plenty of coverage when he persuaded Major Gordon C. Ross of the Hawaii National Guard—and a troubleshooter for the Big Five—to return as head of the Territorial police to lead the hunt for Lyman. Ross had made headlines before. He was best known for breaking a sugar workers' strike some years back on the island of Kauai. Troubleshooter Ross had settled the labor dispute by the simple expedient of shooting some of the trouble, and several had died. Ross was single-minded, military, and white, so he fully satisfied all of Admiral Stirling's job qualifications.

It took a few days, but the major got his act together. He set up his headquarters in the barracks behind Iolani Palace, and brought with him some boys from the National Guard plus volunteers from the American Legion. Four or five Prohibition agents represented the federal government on the task force, and Billy and Stevenson eventually returned to their regular duties.

All of this commotion occupied the front pages of every newspaper published in January's first week. The only bright spot in this miasma of bad news was that the wheels of justice ground Lui Kaikapu to mush in record time. After confessing to his various crimes and sparing Honolulu another divisive trial, Kaikapu found himself back at Oahu

Prison. The elapsed time between the rape and his life sentence was less than thirty-six hours.

It wasn't much; Lyman was still uncaught, the Ala Moana boys were still unconvicted, and the admiral was still growling about shore leave. But it was a start.

Everyone in Honolulu and people as far away as Washington, D.C., waited to see what would happen next.

CHAPTER 33

King and River Streets
Thursday, January 7

"You 'member me? I help you with the cops?" The unmistakable gravel voice of former stool pigeon Lau Sau came clearly through the telephone receiver. I cringed as he confirmed the ID with one of those wet, growling coughs that hacked up bad memories of an interminable evening on Center Street.

"Yeah, Sau. I remember you. What's happening?"

"I hear you looking for Sammy Akana. That so?"

I sat up sharply in my chair. Billy and Stevenson were still out searching for Lyman while I answered the phone and worked on the missing pieces of Thalia's puzzle. The most important, Sammy Akana, had so far proved to be a very elusive customer. "You know Akana?" I asked, holding my breath hoping it was going to be that easy.

"I seen him, down Chinatown. I know where he stay."

Hallelujah! "Where?"

"I cannot say. I show you."

"Okay, where are you?"

"By and by you come Shige's *bo lau*, you know, at King Street by River?"

"Bo lau?"

"Pool hall. Bo lau. Next door in lane. I meet you."

"Okay. Shige's Pool Hall. I'll come over."

"No bring other *sikh dai*; other people know them."

I looked at my watch. It was only four o'clock. Broad daylight on King Street. It shouldn't be a problem, even going alone. "Okay. No other detectives. I'm leaving now."

The phone clicked and I wrote out a short note to Billy, letting him know where I'd gone and who I was meeting. I wasn't looking forward to seeing the tubercular Sau with his "keeling" knife blade again, but a lead on Sammy Akana was worth the trouble. Those two would hang in the same circle, know the same connections, and share the same patch.

I was halfway out the door before I remembered Billy's admonition. "You carry that thing until somebody catches Lyman. Who knows? You might be the one to run into him, get a chance to be a hero." So I headed back to my desk, took the government's .38 out of my drawer, and tucked it into my waistband. Just in case the opportunity for heroics arose.

After I parked the car half a block from the corner at King and River Streets, I eyed the area warily. Two blocks down, the green water of Honolulu Harbor glittered in the afternoon sunshine. Nuuanu Stream rolled sluggishly toward its meeting with the harbor. Bits of rubbish eddied in the current. Across the stream, strollers crossed the grass of Aala Park toward the railroad station and the pineapple cannery in Iwilei. This was a neighborhood of hard edges, and to confirm that appraisal, I saw a cluster of corner boys loitering at the intersection that was my immediate destination. Heads were bent together over a magazine one was holding; they hadn't seen me yet.

Corner boys had kept the police busy for fifty years on the streets of Chinatown. They were toughs and rowdies who engaged in a variety of petty crimes and frequently challenged servicemen and the police, who rousted them, moved them, and fought them when necessary.

At one point in the '20s, HPD had organized Jardine and some other cops into a special squad armed with blacksnake whips to take back the corners once and for all. They drove the boys off, but the squad only lasted a few months until one of the officers whipped the wrong kid. The squad disbanded, and the corner boys returned to their old haunts—one of which was outside Shige's Pool Hall at King and River.

They noticed me when I neared their corner; sideways glances were exchanged as the group shifted and spread out slightly. Then one of them turned toward me, and I realized that I knew him. Joe Kahahawai's sullen gaze flashed into sudden recognition, followed by a wide smile. He shook himself out of the group and crossed to meet me.

"Joe, what's news?"

The other boys drifted back together and passed a cigarette. The pages of their magazine fluttered in the breeze.

Joe met me in the street. "You working down here?" he asked.

"Yeah. Got some people to see."

"Bad place. Good for the dope, though."

"Yeah, that's what I hear."

"You can give me a ride back to my house after?"

"Sure. Let me just find this guy, and I'll come back over here and get you."

"Shoot, thanks." Joe grinned broadly. "I see you, then."

I walked toward the narrow passageway on the Diamond Head side of the pool hall, but didn't see Sau anywhere. By standing in the opening, I could see a wall at the far end of the alley, probably the back of the building that faced Hotel Street, one block north. In between, rows of laundry hung in several levels and filled the passage—multihued Hawaiian prints higher up, white sheets and checkered tablecloths lower down. Trade winds, channeled by the brick walls on either side, threw the cloth into vibrant, colorful motion—a sea of flowered muumuus and loud shirts dancing on the breeze. The laundry created a festive island of bright colors and clean smells, but I didn't see Sau.

"Cop!" The voice seemed to come from a flimsy-looking stairway that climbed the wall on the pool hall side of the passage. I ducked under a tablecloth and around what looked like a set of ladies' bloomers.

"Here. I stay up here." Sau's head emerged from a doorway at the top of the stairs; he peered between some flapping shirts. I moved a few paces deeper into the textile jungle to get a better look and called to him to come down. Instead, he stepped back inside and was replaced in an instant by two younger Chinese men in black jackets. They quickly dropped down the steps and disappeared into the fabric, but not before I saw each of them holding something in his hand. Gun? Knife? I couldn't tell, but I knew it was time to get back out onto King Street before I found out the hard way.

I quickly backed up, pulled out the .38, and aimed it in the general direction of the two black jackets that were now hidden behind walls of billowing cloth. Rapid Chinese from two loud voices came from behind the screen of damp linen.

I ducked low, peered underneath, and saw a set of legs moving to the right, so I pivoted back toward the safety of the street. A wet bedsheet tangled the revolver. I clawed past it, and pointed my gun toward the shouting behind me. Why were they yelling? They were standing right next to each other…

And what was that other voice?

I got a bad feeling, and crouched low again to check it out. This time I looked the other way, up toward the alley entrance. About fifteen feet away, another Chinese face—this one capped with a black bowler—grinned at me. He had one gold tooth in his smile, and a cleaver in his right hand. Even as I watched, he waved it at a fourth set of legs that moved toward me from behind another sheet, and spoke urgently in Chinese.

Swiftly I crabbed sideways to the wall. Rough brick grated against my shoulders as I aimed the .38 at the waving sheet, waiting for the figure to emerge, and still tried to keep one eye on the end of the passage where more trouble was approaching.

Bursts of Chinese now came at me from both sides. They had a real advantage—thanks to Gold Tooth, they knew right where I was and could coordinate their attack without me knowing when or how it would be coming. The gun wasn't much help; I might get one of them, but if they timed it right, the others would be all over me. And if they had guns, they just needed to maneuver around so they wouldn't shoot each other and let me have it.

Shit, shit, shit! I wrestled with disbelief as the voices got closer. I was running out of time and options.

I made a quick decision: Drop down and plug Gold Tooth, then try for the first set of legs I saw. Even if I missed, maybe the gun would scare them off.

I bent low and looked where I thought Gold Tooth had been a moment before. He'd moved closer to my wall and was now staring back at me, looking cocky, saying something in Chinese to his unseen companion. I twisted toward him and brought the muzzle of the .38 around. Alarm flashed across his face, and he jumped sideways behind a trash bin. The cleaver sparked against the pavement.

Behind him, a fifth set of legs—this one in blue denim—closed the distance down the alley. Damn. The odds were getting longer by the minute!

I could only hope Gold Tooth would be too busy to spot for the rest of the pack and ran in a crouch over to the other side of the alley. Wet clothing slapped me on the back like cold hands, and I kept flinching away from a blade falling on my neck. Jesus Christ, I thought. They're going to find me dead under somebody's goddamn petticoat.

Time for another peek and maybe a shot at Gold Tooth. He must have seen me move. I could hear him shouting directions; he was now maybe just a row or two of laundry away. His buddies, who weren't saying anything, probably weren't much farther off.

I dropped to one knee and bent even lower, then sighted in on the trashcan where Gold Tooth was sheltering. We looked directly into each other's eyes—mine over the sights of the Smith as I took up slack in the trigger.

Then his eyes rolled to the right in shocked surprise, and the whites shone brightly under the shadow of his hat. He started to crank his body around, but something hard drove down into his neck, and his face slammed forward into the pavement. The black bowler popped off his head and rolled under the swaying laundry almost to my feet.

Behind his prostrate form, the denim pants stepped to the right. What the hell was going on?

I didn't have much time to think about it. When I stood again, I caught motion to my left, along the wall. A tablecloth jerked up and a short Chinese, queue flying, came at me with what looked like a sword raised high in his fist. It caught for the barest instant in a pair of trousers, buying me a moment, but not enough time to aim or shoot.

Adrenaline pumped as I brought the Smith down hard, trying for his head and connecting with a solid clang. The impact jolted my whole arm, pain shooting like raw flame down through my shoulder, but he dropped as if he'd been pole-axed. His knife sailed in a glittering arc above us, bounced off the opposite wall, and fell with a metallic clatter.

Only the denim pants stood between me and Hotel Street, but the two on the other side were closing. I spun as one of the black jackets charged hard out of the hanging laundry, cleaver raised. I yanked the gun up, got the front sight on his chest, and pulled the trigger. He flinched and his face contorted as he felt the bullet coming…but nothing happened. I squeezed harder, squeezed until my finger went chalky…but the trigger would not go back. I realized I was screaming with him.

Black Jacket swerved to his right and angled behind some bright Hawaiian prints. It was a tougher shot, but he still kept coming. He'd covered half of the distance between us when his feet ran right out from under him. A heavy, wet smacking sound was followed by the sharp crack of his head hitting the pavement. The denim pants stood over the body just as the second black jacket, shrieking incoherently, flung someone's bed linens aside and rushed toward me along the alley wall.

I swung the revolver at him, mashing the trigger as hard as I could, but *still* nothing happened except that he braked to a sudden stop maybe four feet away and stood frozen, wide-eyed, in front of the gun.

"Hey," a voice called. Black Jacket number two looked uncertainly toward the sound. Joe Kahahawai stepped from behind some clothing and closed the distance to my confused assailant in two quick steps, then landed a crushing right fist to the middle of Black Jacket's surprised face. Blood splashed from his ruined nose. He only stood for another moment before a second punch to the temple drove him into the brick wall on the opposite side of the passageway, then down.

Kahahawai stood, breathing hard, over the remains of his bout. Then he took careful aim and booted the groaning black jacket solidly in the midsection. The man's body jumped a couple of inches off the pavement.

I slumped to the ground, physically drained, holding the useless revolver across my lap.

"You like I stomp these assholes for you?" Joe asked as if he was taking my dinner order.

It was an appealing offer, but I thought we'd better get out of there before we found out how many more Chinese hatchet men were hiding in the shadows.

"No, let's go. These boys might have friends. I'll call the cops. But wait a minute. I've got to get my breath back."

"Whatever," he shrugged, and gave the one I had pistol-whipped a parting kick in the head. "Shut up," he said, and the man's faint moans finally stopped.

From my seated position leaning against one wall, I could see under all of the laundry to both ends of the alley. Cars flashed past the opening, but no other people stood in the passage. Laughing voices and the scent of Chinese food drifted out of a door I hadn't noticed before in the brick wall. Whatever had just happened was over.

I climbed to my feet, still feeling plenty shaky. "Man, you saved my ass," I told Joe as we reached the alley mouth. "Those guys had me for sure."

"I seen 'em follow you inside, and I figger, I'll go see what's doing. You catch that one's hat go flyin'?" Joe looked back at the scene of his triumph, and his smile lit up the alley. "I crack him so good, I can still feel 'em." He held up his right fist and examined it. "Rabbit-punched that chickenshit. Could've killed him, probably."

"Hey, I got no problem with that," I said. "I think that's what they were planning for me."

"And that other one, the one had the square knife? I broke his nose for sure. Right jab." He demonstrated the successful stroke, and followed it with a left hook at the shadows. "Pow! Pow! Four guys," he bubbled. "I gotta tell Benny. We whip four guys with knives."

"You whipped 'em, man. I didn't do shit."

"Yeah?" He sounded pleased, and I was more than happy to give him all the credit for getting me out of the alley in one piece.

"C'mon. Let's get out of here. I'll take you home."

"You ain't gonna meet nobody?"

"The hell with that. I met all the people I need to for today."

We walked to the car. My legs were wobbly from the adrenaline overdose as I looked vainly for a patrolman. Joe stopped once at the corner to describe the fight to the boys. They didn't seem especially interested. He was still gloating over his victory when he climbed into the car with me.

"Thanks, bull," he said when I pulled up to his house. "That was some fun. Good thing you never shoot 'em. Otherwise we never get the chance to lick 'em."

"Brother, you don't know. I tried like hell to shoot those sons of bitches. The damn gun wouldn't fire."

"More better this way. Those chickenshits went *down*, boom, boom!" He wrung my hand as if I'd just given him a trophy and climbed out of the car. "I'm gonna remember this my whole life."

"Me too, Joe. I should be thanking you. You saved my ass back there."

The grin vanished in an instant, and he leaned back through the open door. "Lemme ask you something. Mr. Pittman, he said you part-Hawaiian. That right?"

"I guess so, yeah. Not a very big part."

He reached over and tapped the center of my chest with one big finger. "This part here ain't very big. Big enough, maybe, if that's the Hawaiian part."

Federal Building, Room 213
Friday, January 8

The eighth of January started really badly—and got steadily worse.

"That was a close call," Billy said the next morning. "Must be doing something right, 'cause we have these guys trying to kill us."

"That's one way to look at it, I guess. I'll tell you what—they'd have had me if it wasn't for Kahahawai." I shivered just thinking how the cleaver had sparked as Gold Tooth's blade had flashed against the pavement.

"Now the question is, what's the story on Sau?" Billy rubbed his temples and leaned over Sau's informant file.

"Why do you think he did it?" I said.

"I dunno. Could be he was forced. Or they could've just bought him. He'd go cheap. One way or another, he pissed backwards on us."

"Do you really think he knew what was going on?"

"Oh, he knew, all right. The cops find anybody when they got there?"

"Nah. They were all gone, and Sau, too."

"Too bad. Can you identify any of them?"

"The one with the gold tooth, for sure. It was real distinctive. I'm not ever gonna forget *that* asshole," I muttered grimly. "The other ones, I don't know. One of 'em's got a broken nose and I'll bet one's got a fractured skull, too."

"Let me see that gun again."

I got the revolver out of the drawer. The trigger guard had done its job nicely. When I'd brought the gun down on my attacker, all the impact had fallen directly on that narrow strip of steel. Whatever it had hit—undoubtedly the steel lining of his bowler hat, the trademark of the Chinese hatchet man—had been hard enough to mash the metal right up against the bottom of the trigger. No amount of pulling would make the weapon fire.

Billy fingered the bent metal. "You must have really nailed that guy."

"He went down hard. My arm's still sore. Plus Joe kicked the stuffing out of him." I asked the question on top of my list. "You think the White Friend set this up?"

"He probably knows we're looking at him, and we know he's got some Chinese pals, so I'd say he's the logical suspect. He's serious if he's sending the *boo how doy* after you. I don't know how we're gonna prove it, of course."

That led to my second question. "Say, Billy, if they were willing to come after me, what do you think they're going to do about Akana?"

"Kill him, probably. Unless we can get there first."

"Nobody's seen him, so maybe they already got him."

"Could be. But we have to keep looking, just in case."

"And now we need to find Sau, too."

"Yeah. I got some serious questions for that sonofabitch." Billy looked grim. "Assuming he's still breathing, of course."

He reached over to pick up the ringing phone. "Guy wants to talk to you," he said, glancing quizzically at me, and kept the phone to his ear when I picked up my extension.

"Hello?"

"You open your mail yet today?"

"What? Who is this?"

"You'll figure it out. Did you open your mail?" It was the voice of a white man, muffled but with a trace of a southern accent.

"No, we haven't."

"There's a package there from a friend of yours. It's something he wanted you to have."

"What are you talking about?"

"Just open it up. And if you're smart, you'll stop sticking *your* nose into other people's business."

The phone clicked before I could tell him that was my job description.

We hung up, and I went looking for the morning mail. Sure enough, there was a small package postmarked the day before and correctly addressed to Narcotic Agent Jack Mather.

"I don't know what this is about," I told Billy. "Why did he want us to check the mail?"

"What did he sound like to you?"

"Like a Southerner talking through a handkerchief."

"Yeah, that's what I thought, too," Billy agreed.

He crowded in close as I unwrapped the package. Inside I found a jeweler's box filled with newspaper—and something else. I unfolded it carefully, and spread out the paper to uncover a brown object crusted with dried blood.

"What the hell?" Billy demanded, recoiling.

"It's the rest of Sau's nose," I gasped, feeling sick. "Jesus. They killed him."

"Close it up. Oh, damn." Billy backed away from the package, sat down shakily at his desk, and swiveled away to look out the window into the morning sunshine.

I folded the paper back and covered all that probably remained of our one-time informant. "What are we gonna do about this, Billy? I mean, we can't have people go around killing our stoolies."

Billy was still breathing heavily, struggling for composure. He wrenched himself around. "We'll probably have to let the police deal with it. You want to get technical, Sau wasn't a government witness anymore, or even a registered informer."

"I can't believe this. I mean, I saw the guy yesterday, for God's sake. And now he's dead."

"How do you think I feel? I told Will Moore not to put him in the window. But we got no time for that." Billy pulled a notepad closer and started jotting with a shaky hand. "First thing we need to do, and right quick, is get in touch with George Soon."

"Soon? How come?"

"'Cause if this *is* all about the White Friend and the Chinese, they know who set up the deal with Thalia. If they're going around killing informers, George's probably moved right to the head of the line."

My blood ran cold. "Right. I'll call up Kam. He found him pretty quick last time."

"No, we better go over there and talk to him, make sure he's watching his own ass. While we're there, we'll put in a word to the cops to look out for Sau. We're gonna have to talk to McIntosh about this nose thing, let him know somebody might've iced Sau. And we have *got* to get our hands on Sammy Akana." He underlined a point on the pad. "He's the key to this deal, and they know we're looking for him. If we don't find him, they may just pull his plug to be sure he won't say anything. They could've already, which might explain why we aren't having any luck."

"Shit, Billy. This is getting worse and worse."

"We're a step or two behind is the problem. We need to find some way to get ahead of these bastards."

"Finding Sammy might get us there."

"Yeah, well, hold that thought." He stood up and reached for his hat. "We don't need any more distractions."

But the bad news day wasn't over yet.

CHAPTER 34

Police Headquarters
Friday, January 8

"What the hell's going on now, you think?" Billy and I pressed up against the stairwell wall that led to Kam's second-floor office at police headquarters, as a group of officers clattered down past us. This gaggle, wearing worried expressions with their usual brown suits, included Chief of Detectives McIntosh and Lono McCallum, one of his senior men.

"Something's up," Billy answered as we finished the climb. "Maybe they got Lyman."

"Or they killed another sailor." I didn't say this too loudly.

A cluster of plainclothes officers in shirtsleeves huddled in the squad room corner where a speaker relayed the police dispatcher's calls to the radio cars. Kam's broad back filled the middle of the group, and he turned as we walked up.

"Somebody snatched Joe Kahahawai," he said in answer to our unspoken question. "Right off King Street in front of your office."

"You're kidding!" I could see from his expression that it was no joke. "Holy smokes."

"When did it happen?" Billy demanded.

"Not even an hour ago."

I had an awful thought. A quick glance at Billy confirmed that he had the same one. Somebody had just collected some fast payback for Joe's bout in the alley.

I choked the question out, and held my breath for the response. "Who was it, do they know?"

"We got a description. A haole male. At least one. They're in a dark-colored car, maybe a Buick."

A haole male. My heart dropped another couple of feet; maybe the White Friend had taken matters into his own hands. Sau's nose and those hatchet men in the alley told us he would take extreme steps to protect himself and his operation. If what Thalia had told me was true, he'd also had a little practice snatching people off the street.

"We got a witness over there, says he saw the whole thing." Kam pointed to a desk in the corner where a short Hawaiian kid in a long-sleeved silk shirt sat talking animatedly to a detective. Lieutenant Jardine perched like a falcon on the adjacent desk, taking in the witness's statement. He'd seen us come in, though, and eyed me without emotion before turning away and chewing on a blue fountain pen.

"Who's the kid?" Billy asked.

"Joe's cousin. He went with him to the probation office this morning. Saw the kidnappers up close."

"And he says it was a white man? Not Chinese? You're sure?" I asked.

"No, he's pretty firm on that." Kam frowned.

"Where were McIntosh and the others going?" Billy asked.

"Over to the palace. The Attorney General's got some theory."

"Yeah? Like what?"

"Like the goddamn Navy did it," Kam said, waving his big arms. "Same as Ida. Those bastards are going to make this place worse than Chicago before they're done."

We measured that conjecture against the evidence. I hoped it made more sense than the nagging thought that I might have gotten Joe Kahahawai kidnapped. Or worse.

"Maybe they just want to try for a confession, like with Ida. Could be they're gonna thump on him a little and kick him loose," Kam suggested hopefully. The scratchy voice of the dispatcher re-broadcasting the suspects' descriptions filled the silence that followed this comment.

"If it is the Navy, if that's what this is all about, they're gonna be real pissed off when he doesn't confess," Billy said.

"Do you think they're going to kill him?"

"I don't know, hoss," Billy frowned. "But nothing would surprise me anymore."

"What about the White Friend?"

He thought about it. "Not him. Not personally, anyway. He could've got somebody else to do it for him, though." He looked sympathetically at me. "It's a possibility."

The door banged open, and a patrolman rushed in. Jardine left the witness to meet the officer halfway across the room and talked to him for a moment in low tones, then pushed him back toward the hallway. A moment later, he threaded his way between the desks to where we stood.

"What are you two doing here?" he asked flatly, his black eyes obsidian-hard and fixed on me.

Billy fielded the query. "We were gonna hook up with Kam and go looking for somebody, but it seems like you folks are sort of busy."

Jardine laughed, a short cough purged of any humor. "We're looking for somebody, too. A couple of 'em, in fact. You wouldn't happen to have any ideas, would you?"

Billy and I glanced at each other.

"For instance, you don't think somebody's getting even for Kahahawai saving somebody's butt down in Chinatown?" He cocked his head to one side, and smiled thinly at our surprise. "I told you, Punahou, I hear all kinds of things."

Billy spoke for me. "Not if these somebodys are haole, I don't think."

Jardine nodded tightly. "You're probably right."

"Lieutenant," a voice came from the officers in the corner. "Something's happening."

Jardine walked over to the speaker, and the group parted to admit him. We followed him.

"Three and eight are in pursuit," one of the detectives informed us. "A Buick, dark blue, curtains down, won't stop. They're on Waialae Road, headed out toward Koko Head."

"They can't get it to stop?"

The detective shook his head. "I guess not. They've fired at it already."

"Jesus Christ!" Jardine exploded, flinging his pen at the wall. "Who's out there?"

"Harbottle and Kekua and one of the radio cars."

"Well, I hope to hell they didn't shoot Kahahawai. I don't know how we'd explain that one." He stood thinking for a minute, and then hooked one of the detectives by the shirtfront. "Get a couple of cars. Take three or four men in each one. Grab some uniforms from downstairs. Go out that way. This could get real bad."

"How we gonna find 'em?"

"Hey, there's only one road out there...they got to be on it somewhere. If you get all the way around to Waimanalo and don't see 'em, call in. Maybe we'll know more. Get going."

Jardine turned back to us and shook his head. "We might get Kahahawai back if our own people don't kill him first."

"You think it's the Navy? In that car?" I asked.

The lieutenant shrugged. "We'll see."

"If you heard about Chinatown, you know I owe this guy."

"Yeah," Jardine said. "I think we better hope it ain't those people. Whatever. We'll figure out what happened."

"Folks in town are going to be upset when they hear about this," Billy said.

"Gleason's calling in another watch, in case there's riots. We'll have fifty more men on the streets in an hour." Jardine's mouth was set in a tight line.

The possibility of rioting no longer seemed very farfetched. All the events of the past three months, and the constant drumbeat of criticism from Admiral Stirling and others, was forcing everyone to look at each other in a way that was no longer comfortable. The Lyman and Kaikapu fiasco, so fresh in everyone's minds, served as a reminder that old ways and attitudes had vanished in Honolulu, probably forever.

If we needed any further notice that things had changed, it was provided by the arrival of a scared-looking Horace Ida, who was hustled into the room by a pair of patrolmen.

"Take him down to the lockup," Jardine waved to the cops. "We're bringing in the Ala Moana boys for their own protection," he told us. "I think we got all four already. He's the last."

All four. Just that morning, there had been five Ala Moana defendants. Now the fifth was in the wind, maybe sitting scared in the back of a car full of kidnappers, being chased and shot at by the police. And maybe he was already dead.

"One way or another…" Jardine looked at me hard. "You stay the hell out of it this time. This is our case."

He went looking for his pen, then took up his usual place at his corner desk and started the process of managing a major criminal investigation. Since he hadn't thrown us out, we joined the other detectives at the speaker, listening as new developments came in, speculating pointlessly about cause and effect.

The barely controlled chaos in the squad room swelled, phones rang, Jardine barked instructions, messengers came and went. Off-duty officers responding to the Sheriff's call hurried in for assignments. The radio speaker was an island of calm in the turmoil around us. Every five minutes or so, the dispatcher re-broadcast the same descriptions and tried to reach the pursuit. Only silence came back from Oahu's wild and remote eastern reaches. I stood to one side, watching the action and chewing my fingernails.

Finally, shortly after eleven, the radio operator canceled the lookout for Joe Kahahawai and the mystery car. The race had ended above Hanauma Bay. In the level tones the dispatcher might have used to read a sports score, he gave us the facts: one car stopped, three people arrested, Joseph Kahahawai, Jr. found. He was dead.

News that Joe had been shot was received with a murmur of low groans from the detectives and a volley of profanity from Jardine's corner. Stunned, I turned away from the speaker. Not even twenty-four hours earlier, I had seen two men—one trying to kill me, another one trying to save me—and now both were dead and gone forever. The notion that I had gotten both of them killed in one day chattered in the background as I slumped into a chair at a vacant desk.

Across the room, Joe's cousin, pale and bewildered, stood, staring wide-eyed at us, pleading, "What's happening, what's happening?" as his interviewer tugged at his sleeve. One of the detectives crossed over to pass the bad tidings.

"Kam!" Jardine gestured the inspector over.

He returned a moment later. "I got to go. Jardine wants me to find Joe's mother, bring her in. She's gonna have to make the ID."

"Oh, man," I sighed, picturing the little woman standing at her screen door, watching another police car roll up to her house. This one would be bringing a mother's nightmare. "Oh, man."

"We'll go downstairs with you," Billy said. "Nothing we can do up here."

"Yeah, that's right," Kam said. "I don't think the lieutenant wants you around, anyway."

We trailed along behind the big detective and emerged together into the bright sunshine. Kam solemnly shook our hands, and went off with another officer toward Palama.

Loose knots of people gathered on the sidewalk fronting the station: police officers, Navy shore patrolmen, and civilians, all of them buzzing with the news from within. Henry McKeague and two or three other Vice officers stood next to a car at the curb. He waved for us to come over. "You heard, huh?" he said.

"Yeah. We were just upstairs."

For a few moments we were the center of attention—carriers of the latest information from inside. Interest quickly shifted to others who bore newer tales, and we listened with the rest. Favorite bits of rumor emerged from the gabble and were tried out, repeated, accepted, believed.

"He was shot."

"…hanged him."

"…cut off his nuts before they killed him."

"It was Navy guys that did it."

"They got three of the husband's buddies."

"You got to toss out ninety-five percent of this crap," Billy said. "Nobody here really knows anything."

McKeague agreed. "I hope most of it's bullshit. Just that he's dead is bad enough."

Through the cloud of spurious nonsense, a few facts did emerge even before the arresting officers returned.

The story began directly in front of the Federal Building. At about the time I arrived at work, Joe and his cousin were meandering up King Street toward the Territorial Courthouse next door. All of the Ala Moana defendants were required to see a probation officer twice each week. Friday was one of Joe's days, and he was late, as usual.

This morning, Joe, who—also as usual—had no money for cab or bus fare, asked his cousin, Eddie Ulii, to accompany him on the two-mile walk downtown. Ulii, the distraught-looking kid in the Detective Bureau, saw the whole thing unfold, and one of the first things he noticed as they approached the courthouse was a haole woman watching them from across King Street.

While Ulii waited on a bench outside, Joe checked in. Three or four minutes later, he emerged, joined his cousin, and strolled out into the warm morning on King Street before turning toward home. The alert Ulii once again saw the woman, this time in conversation with a man. Nonplussed, he commented about this to Big Joe who, thanks to his recently acquired notoriety, was more blasé about being pointed at. "To hell with her," he told his cousin.

A minute or two later, as they passed in front of the Federal Building, a dark blue Buick pulled over to the curb in front of them. Inside, a white man dressed as a chauffeur, wearing cap and goggles, waited as a second man—a short "military-kind guy," in Ulii's words—approached Kahahawai and said, "Major Ross wants to see you." He gave Joe a hand-printed paper, which the police later recovered.

Joe didn't notice the misspelling of "Territorial," wasn't concerned with the crudely printed nature of an "official" paper, and did not examine the gold seal. He didn't question the appearance of this fatuous newspaper clipping, and if he read or even looked at anything on the paper, it was most likely the name of Major Gordon Ross.

The major, of course, was serving at the time as High Sheriff and highly-publicized head manhunter in the Daniel Lyman affair, and when Joe saw that name and heard from the kidnappers that the major wanted to see him, he got into the car. He wasn't without some reservations, because he told his cousin to hop on and accompany him. Ulii tried to comply and stepped onto the car's running board, but the kidnappers had no need for a witness and told him to wait there; they would return shortly, they said. The car carrying Joe Kahahawai sped off, leaving his cousin in its exhaust fumes—wondering what was going on, remembering Horace Ida, and suspecting the worst.

Ulii went back to the courthouse and sought out Joe's probation officer, who immediately called the police. It took some time to sort things out; Ross denied summoning Kahahawai and called Attorney General Hewitt, saying he thought Big Joe had been kidnapped.

The Attorney General, remembering Horace Ida's all-too recent experience and concerned that the lid might be coming off, called on the police to intensify the search, and also called the Shore Patrol to let them know there might be more trouble brewing. He also feared that the four remaining Ala Moana defendants might be targets, too, and took the prudent measure of asking the Honolulu police to pick them up.

Thanks to Ulii, the police had an excellent description of the kidnappers and their car. That description, which I'd heard repeated at least twenty times on the speaker in the Detective Bureau, went out to all patrolmen, though only a few of the cars had radios. Everybody else either heard it from the radio cars or got the news when they phoned in to the station.

At the foot of Manoa Valley, officers George Harbottle and Robert Kekua, who had just gotten the word, were idling in their patrol car when they saw a dark Buick, side curtains drawn, roar past. They couldn't see the occupants, but everything else fit, so they gave chase as the Buick turned east toward Koko Head and the remote cove Elvis Presley would make famous in *Blue Hawaii*.

McKeague came over to let us know the show was almost over. "They're dropping him at the Emergency Hospital and bringing the ones they caught down here."

"The hospital? Why there? He's dead, isn't he?"

"Oh, yeah. But that's where the coroner is."

"Here they come," somebody said.

TERITORIAL POLICE

MAJOR ROSS, COMMANDING

SUMMONS TO APPEAR

Kahahawai - Joe

Life Is a Mysterious and Exciting Affair, and Anything Can Be a Thrill if You Know How to Look for It and What to Do With Opportunity When It Comes

A police car, siren wailing, came blazing down King Street from the direction of the hospital, followed by the paddy wagon and several other cars. The procession stopped in front of the station where perhaps a hundred of us now stood; the siren moaned down to a pregnant silence. A number of officers climbed from the vehicles, along with a reporter from the *Honolulu Advertiser* with the scoop of his life. Harbottle, the detective who had made the arrests, walked over to us. The crowd of his fellow officers parted for him to accept the back pats and attaboys of his peers.

The atmosphere in front of the station resembled the sidelines of a football game after the winning quarterback trots off the field. I craned my neck toward the paddy wagon between ranks of broad shoulders, and waited with the rest to see if Joe Kahahawai's killers would have the faces of evil or just that of some scared sailor. I had my fingers crossed that I wouldn't see some Chinese guy in a black jacket or his White Friend.

Police Headquarters
Friday, January 8

The first man out, hands cuffed in front of him, was a stocky, obviously military type. Harbottle gestured to him. "Edward Lord. He's a sailor at the sub base."

"Ah, it's Navy, all right," I told Billy with relief. "And he looks a little shook up."

"He should be." Billy said. "Murder One's the only crime in Hawaii where the Territory's got jurisdiction over military people. Killing Kahahawai's a hanging offense."

All of the exuberance was sucked right out of the crowd like a receding wave when the next two people emerged from the truck. Looking back, it seems to me as though everything in Honolulu stopped for a moment—traffic, commerce, even time paused as they climbed down onto the pavement.

I recognized them, but didn't believe. I saw, but couldn't accept, and staggered as the island lurched beneath us...

Because the people who had killed Joe Kahahawai and gone for a drive with his body in their car were Tommie Massie and Grace Fortescue.

Billy and I stared as officers escorted them into the station, then turned to each other, unable or unwilling to speak.

"I was thinking we'd see more Navy, but..." I said, finally.

"I wasn't expecting that," he finished for me.

"Do you suppose she shot him with that gun I saw her buying?"

"Don't ask me, hoss. I swear to God, I don't know anything anymore."

With the main event over, the crowd began to disperse. Small swirls of people talked in low mutters, but without anger, just astonishment. We stayed for a while longer, listening to Harbottle tell everybody how he'd chased the car for miles along the narrow road that balanced between lava fields and the sea. "Like they had somewhere to hide," he laughed. "That old lady, trying to outrun two police cars and a motorcycle."

He described his finding of Joe's body. "We come up next to 'em, and I yell at her to pull over. She finally stops up above Hanauma Bay. I go over to the car and badge 'em, make 'em all get out. Then I see this bundle, like a rolled-up carpet or a blanket or something. White, on the floor of the back seat. I pull on it, and this damned foot sticks out. Man, I wasn't ready for that."

Finally he decided he ought to go tell his story to Jardine, so he went inside the station. But more cars came down from Manoa a few minutes later bringing another Navy man—this one found at the Massie home.

"Hey, wait a minute." I nudged Billy. "I know that one, too!"

"Who is he?"

"I don't know his name, but that's the Shore Patrol-looking guy who was hanging around Thalia's house when I was staked out there last month. Remember? We thought he might be a bodyguard or something?"

Billy looked him over as the police crowded around him on the steps. "Yeah? He looks drunk. I wonder what his part is in this circus."

"He's for sure tied in with Thalia and the rest of them. Do you think the cops know? Should I tell somebody?"

"They probably know, but we can say something to Jardine later on." He looked up toward King Street. "Speaking of Thalia, where do you suppose she is, with her mother and her husband both locked up for murder?"

Cops coming out of the station told us that the last man, who they identified as Seaman Albert O. Jones, had been found with a pistol magazine, a spent .32 caliber cartridge, and the fake summons used to sucker Joe Kahahawai into the kidnappers' car. They answered Billy's question by saying Thalia and Helene had been at the house, too, although the police hadn't arrested either of them. "They're coming down, though," one said.

When it became apparent that not much else was going to happen that afternoon, we walked back to the office to explain things to our boss, and speculated about whether any law enforcement officers anywhere ever had a tighter murder case.

"I doubt it," Billy said. "Lots of dumb crooks out there, but this bunch may have set a record."

In the Honolulu jail, the surviving Ala Moana defendants shared a cell down the hall from their friend's killers. Outside, the city was tense but relatively quiet.

Although word of Joe's death spread quickly through Honolulu, there were no riots, no disturbances to validate the governor's or his Attorney General's fears.

The Navy sealed up Pearl Harbor and cancelled liberty for its sailors as Honolulu police, the Shore Patrol, and Major Ross's "specials" prowled the streets. All of them gradually relaxed as it became evident that there had been enough killing for one day.

And they only knew the half of it.

Federal Building, Room 213
Saturday, January 9

The arrest of Tommie Massie and Grace Fortescue did not come as such a great surprise to some others as it had been to me. In fact, they had been suspects almost as soon as Joe's probation officer had dialed the phone.

I got Harry Hewitt's side of the story a couple of years later, after he'd left office to go into private practice. We sat together on a hard wooden bench outside Federal Court while he sipped some coffee from a flask and told me about the morning he took that phone call from Gordon Ross.

"You had to know Tommie Massie, and I did. That boy had been calling my office two or three times a week for two months and coming down, asking questions, bothering us about the retrial." Hewitt unscrewed the lid to his coffee container. "The little lieutenant and his mommy-in-law," he mused. "Did you know Grace?"

"Not so as I could talk to her." But I could still see the set of her jaw as she loaded her .32 in the Diamond-Hall store, and hear her hate in Sandy Wood's office.

He snorted. "Nobody, and I mean *nobody* could talk to that lady. She could sure talk to you, though," he continued. "Anyway, between Grace and Tommie, we must have spoken a couple dozen times before the killing, so when Ross called me, I thought about the two of them right away. They'd asked before about forcing a confession out of the Ala Moana boys. I told them to forget it, but as soon as I heard Kahahawai was missing, the first thing I thought was, 'Where's Tommie?' I never figured Grace for it, though." He shook his head, still amazed after three or four years.

"So I called up to the Massie's house in Manoa, and Helene said Tommie wasn't there. Then I call Grace's, and some man answered. It must have been Jones. When I asked for Grace, he told me she couldn't be disturbed until two. I remember thinking, 'What the hell?' because by two in the afternoon on a normal day, let me tell you, Grace Fortescue had been on the phone to half of Honolulu.

"Then I asked who I was talking to, and he said *he* was Tommie. I knew damned well whoever was on the phone wasn't Tommie. That boy'd been such a pain, I knew Tommie Massie's voice as well as I knew my own wife's. Right then, I knew we had trouble."

So, on the day of the kidnapping, burning with the suspicion that something bad was happening and it involved the Massie clan, Hewitt rounded up the highest-ranking posse in Hawaiian history and rode out for Manoa.

Griffith Wight and the clutch of officers that had elbowed past Billy and me in the stairwell had joined the Attorney General, plus McIntosh and a few others. They'd moved fast, almost fast enough—but they'd been too late to save the big Hawaiian.

Sometime that morning, one of his kidnappers had put a .32 bullet into Joe's left lung. He'd taken a while to die, but he hadn't bled all over Mrs. Fortescue's rented home—just discreetly in a couple of places. While the cops and their high-ranking legal advisors had moved with remarkable speed and arrived at the murder house within ninety minutes of the abduction, the kidnappers had been fractionally more efficient. Joe was already gone, stripped naked, dunked in the bathtub, wrapped in a sheet, and thrown on the floor of the rented Buick. The watch he'd finally acquired had stopped forever at 9:45 a.m.

"If I live to be a hundred, I am never going to get over that damn watch," Hewitt told me. "It probably stopped when they put him in the bathtub, so he was already dead, but I look at it, and I know we must have just missed them. Ten or fifteen minutes at the most. We got there a couple minutes after ten. If they'd dilly-dallied a little while longer, we'd have got them all there at the house."

But the killers and their victim were gone, and Hewitt's rescue party had decamped for the Massie home on nearby Kahawai Street. There they'd found Thalia and Helene in the company of a drunken sailor, the same Albert O. "Deacon" Jones who in December had been assigned as the family's watchman.

"Jones, that idiot," Hewitt continued. "He celebrates his part in this whole show by getting drunk at Thalia's house. When we get there, he's already plastered and it's not even eleven yet."

"Maybe that was why he still had the evidence on him," I suggested.

Hewitt laughed. "He made it easy for us. Drunk. Smart-mouthing the police officers. No explanation for what he's doing there alone with the two girls. McIntosh and McCallum haul his ass down to the station and find the pistol magazine and that stupid phony summons-looking thing." He shook his head in disbelief. "*And* he's got the spent .32 shell in his goddamn watch pocket. Like he was saving it for some kind of souvenir."

With the suspects in custody and the evidence piling up, the posse went back to town and got a search warrant for Grace's place. That evening, Honolulu police officers, including Samuel Lau with his camera, returned with the warrant to Kolowalu Street, expecting to find the murder scene.

Their search produced bloodstains, a next-door neighbor who'd heard a shot that morning, and an abundance of other evidence, all of which convinced both attorneys and police that—this time at least—they most definitely had the right people locked up down at headquarters.

By the end of January 9, the case was shaping up nicely.

Federal Building, Room 213
Tuesday, February 12

Talk about getting a bad rap. The press, especially the yellowed sort that thrives on sensational controversies such as this, descended on us *en masse* following Joe's murder. The New York Times sent a correspondent, as did its rival, the New York American. The Hearst news group, anticipating a captivating trial, sent both reporters and columnists. Once they were established in Honolulu, the whole bunch immediately began sending back reams of lurid copy, some of which was occasionally accurate.

These stories portrayed Hawaii as something less than the tropical paradise that our tourism promoters advertised. Of course, the incidence of rape featured prominently, with the breathless implication that women, particularly white ones, were susceptible to attack merely by stepping from the ship to the pier.

Here's a typical example: A *New York American* report quoted the Navy as saying that forty rapes had occurred in the previous year. It continued:

"The situation in Hawaii is deplorable. It is an unsafe place for white women outside the small cities and towns. The roads go through jungles, and in these remote places bands of degenerate natives lie in wait for white women driving by."

We haven't got a jungle on our island, and none of us recognized this Hawaii as our home. And we hadn't had anything like forty rapes in the Territory in the past year either.

Scrambling hard to contain the damage, especially to the formerly promising tourist industry, the governor came up with a more accurate set of figures that listed a grand total of two rapes and eleven attempts in all of 1931 and the first week of January 1932. One of those two rape victims was Dorothy O'Dowda; the other, of course, was Thalia Massie.

Unfortunately, though the governor's report was widely, almost frantically distributed—and even presented to Congress—the mainland press ignored the cold facts in favor of the much more titillating image of "degenerate natives" leaping out of nonexistent jungle trees to ravish unsuspecting (but now well-armed) white women.

On the legal front, the press's distorted lens focused not on Joe's killing and the lynching of a legal innocent but on the Ala Moana mistrial. The *American*, in its typically unbiased fashion, described the outcome of the case:

"The perpetrators of this crime against pure womanhood, against society and against civilization, were freed on bail after a disagreement of a jury of their kind."

Ordinarily, seeing Thalia described as a representative of "pure womanhood" might have triggered some to laugh hysterically, but this sort of story bred a whole different sort of hysteria on the mainland. Its effects still lingered and festered in Hawaii twenty-five years later.

The local papers joined their mainland counterparts in happily noting the continuing embarrassment of Daniel Lyman. Not even the whip hand of Gordon Ross was enough to bring down the elusive fugitive. "Self-defense" shootings of other people, however, were up. An Army lieutenant with a .45 bagged a prowler near his house on the North Shore, and a physician used a .32 revolver to pot a burglar fleeing from his Honolulu home.

Lyman stayed busy fanning the flames. In early February, he accosted a couple near the airport, tied up the young man with fishing line, and then raped his companion before disappearing again.

Down at police headquarters, Walter Dillingham tucked his man, Charles Weeber, into the chief's chair. Weeber immediately went on a tear "weeding out crooks and incompetents." Those who had testified for the defense in the rape trial, including Police Identification Officer Samuel Lau, were the first to get weeded.

Honolulu's turmoil continued on into March. Claiming that "conditions" were still too unsafe to permit liberty, the Pacific battle fleet and its twenty thousand sailors skipped Honolulu for the first time in a decade. A smug Admiral Stirling, having defied Walter Dillingham's pleas and ensured the financial ruin of numerous small businesses, continued to press for the retrial of the Ala Moana case.

Before that happened, though, Honolulu's first appointed prosecutor had a murder to try. He'd get a trial by fire. In March, the city buzzed with news of the latest twist in a case already tangled beyond belief. The man whom the press called "the Attorney for the Damned," the great Clarence Darrow, was coming to represent Joe's killers.

CHAPTER 35

Federal Building, Room 213
Spring 1932

Almost getting killed comes with some side benefits, though in my case, they only accrued after the second attempt. The most pleasant was a startling attitude change on the part of Clarence T. Stevenson toward his newest agent. After he'd listened to the story of the Battle Under the Bloomers, learned of Lau Sau's grisly demise, and heard from Billy and me about the voice on the telephone, Stevenson took a whole new tone.

"You know, we might just make a narcotic agent out of you yet," he said.

This transformation was sparked, in part, by a letter from the Commissioner of Narcotics that instructed us to "pursue every investigative option against the so-called 'White Friend' as a matter of the highest priority." Commissioner Anslinger made a point of saying that he hoped my contribution would be "especially important." I made a mental note to visit my neighbor and ask him to thank his brother in Washington.

Ironically, the letter came too late, because by that time C.T. Stevenson had developed a massive and intractable animosity toward the man he referred to ever after as "that Navy bastard."

"Killing informers. Trying to carve up Treasury Agents. We are *not* gonna take this lying down," he said, banging on the desk for emphasis. "Folks get the idea they can go around killing our people, pretty soon everybody'll be doing it. I want that sonofabitch. You two find out who that Navy bastard is and bring his ass in."

C.T. was scheduled to return to the mainland in February for a thirty-day home leave, but he told us he would take extra time to "ride the circuit" of the federal penitentiaries in Atlanta, Leavenworth, and

McNeil Island. "We got Chinese from the opium hui in all three places. I'll take all of the new information we've got, and see if any of his old pals are ready to give him up.

"But while I'm gone," he told Billy, "you teach Mather the ropes. I want that polecat's hide on the wall," he said, pointing to a spot above his desk. "Right there."

The Navy helped out. A messenger dropped off a list of about ninety officers who'd been stationed in the Islands for shore duty from mid-1929 through September 1931. Only thirty or so overlapped the whole period.

Richard Bates, the Shore Patrol commander, had arrived in June 1930, the same week Captain Ward Wortman had landed. Bates's exec, Carlton Butler, had come only a few months earlier. Admiral Stirling, who would have been my favorite suspect, had been here less than a year when the rape was reported.

I went through every name, matching them all up with the index from the hui files, then went through the whole file again just to be sure. Got nothing. And none of the names identified in the newspapers as Tommie's friends or witnesses in the case came up, either.

I called Bates at Shore Patrol and told him we needed a list of all the officers, this one including those on the subs and minesweepers. He said he'd have Butler do it. When that one finally showed up, it contained almost 500 names.

I knew the White Friend was in there somewhere, but I was starting to think we'd never make the connection.

Our best lead, Sammy Akana, was still missing. More than one informer had told Billy that Akana had left for Los Angeles back in September, and we had our L.A. office hunting. "Getting to be a whole bunch of folks looking for him," Billy commented. "Between us, the White Friend, and the triad boys, somebody ought to turn him up. Dead or alive."

But nobody did. Junkies on the streets of Honolulu talked hopefully of another big shipment on the way, and the supply of Lam Kee hop dwindled as—once again—the White Friend's trail faded into the shadows.

Honolulu
Monday, April 4

The circus came to town the first week in April. The *SS Malolo* carried the ringmaster, Clarence Darrow, and his entourage. The great attorney traveled light, bringing with him his wife, Ruby, New York lawyer George Leisure, and Leisure's wife. Oh, and about fifty reporters and assorted hangers-on who also got off Matson's luxury liner, all expecting another one of those Scopes Monkey Trial spectacles.

Darrow wasn't doing this show for nothing; word had spread that he was getting $40,000 to defend Joe Kahahawai's killers. That was a lot of money in the middle of a worldwide depression.

"This ought to be choice. I'm dying to hear the $40,000 explanation for why his clients were driving around town with a dead body in their car," I told Billy, who sighed a long "Ahhh," and gazed out the window into the sunshine.

Darrow would be earning every penny. The Honolulu Police Department, whose reputation was in tatters after Lyman and the Ala Moana fiasco, pulled out every stop on this one. In the days and weeks following the killing, they collected an impressive array of evidence. Except for the murder weapon, which never turned up, almost every base had been covered.

They even got some help from Grace Fortescue who, much to Darrow's distress, shot her mouth off to the *New York Times*. She all but admitted her role in the killing—she called it a "murder"—and said she wasn't especially sorry about Joe's death, but only that it hadn't gone better than it did. "We blundered dreadfully," she said, referring to their handling of their victim after they shot him.

This startling admission occurred aboard the *USS Alton*, a barracks ship anchored in Pearl Harbor. Nobody had known what to do with the four accused murderers after their arrest. The sheriff definitely didn't want them in his jail, the Navy didn't want them in any jail, and nobody thought it was safe for them to run around the city. When the admiral suggested keeping them "in custody" on the *Alton*, the Territory jumped on it with both feet.

Captain Ward Wortman served as the defendants' official custodian. A seventy-foot-long wooden walkway isolated their prison from the shore. Sentries manned the shoreside end of the pier, checking everyone for the special pass required to reach the ship. Darrow made sure no more reporters got passes.

Thalia moved out to the base, where she also spoke to the *Times* reporter. "I'm not anxious to go into court and tell this story all over again, but I have talked it over with my mother and my husband, and we have agreed that it is my duty to try and secure justice," she said.

"Little goddamn late for that," I muttered, flinging the papers across the office.

If Clarence Darrow thought he could come to Hawaii and roll easily over the opposition on the strength of his oratory and his reputation, he had another think coming. He hadn't met John Kelley, for one, and he had never seen or even imagined anything like a Honolulu jury pool.

Kelley, the bulldog who had defended William Russell in our opium case, accepted the appointment as Prosecuting Attorney for Honolulu after a special legislative session in January created the office. He was the first man to hold the job, and he was acutely aware of the implications of his first and biggest case.

Kelley looked like an Irish monk, with a fringe of thin red hair encircling a bald spot that periodically seemed to be struggling to match the hue of its fiery perimeter. During the Massie trial, this was most of the time. Kelley was loaded for big game—smart, aggressive, and completely unafraid of the aging lion who had wandered up on Hawaii's shores chasing a $40,000 fee.

Darrow's second problem would vex him from the first day of the trial. He knew the racial background of Honolulu and understood it to be an issue in the case, but seemed determined to hold it at arm's length.

"I've come to heal old wounds, not to make new ones. I have no intentions of carrying on a crusade for the white people of Hawaii," he said before he went off to dinner with a bunch of other white people at Walter Dillingham's Diamond Head estate.

Jury selection lasted a week; Kelley and his deputy, Barry Ulrich, searched for a panel that could stand up to the intense outside pressures they anticipated. It didn't look like they were trying to find a specific "type," but they weren't shy about taking non-white jurors.

In the other corner, Darrow and Leisure were joined by Montgomery Winn, the lawyer who had read me off in Sandy Wood's office. Winn, who was well established in town, apparently saw the threat and advised his Chicago colleague to load up on whites. Darrow was confident of his oratorical skills and his appeal to the common man, and did not seem to want the advice.

Billy, whose long experience with local jurors made him something of an expert, puzzled over the defense's game plan. He summed it up this way: "I think the old boy's been trying to get colored people on his juries and keep white people off for so long, he just can't believe it's supposed to work the other way around this time."

The final result pleased John Kelley. Seven of the men seated were white, three were Hawaiian or part-Hawaiian, and two were Chinese. Several of the men worked for Big Five companies. Walter Dillingham told the press he thought the jury was exceptionally qualified.

Darrow complained to his reporter pals that he couldn't read the Oriental minds he faced in the courtroom. For someone who was counting on connecting with those minds by oral communication, it was an ominous beginning.

Things immediately got worse when John Kelley went to work. His opening statement centered on two large boxes next to his chair. These contained the prosecution's trial exhibits. The jury, the spectators, and the entire nation beyond would watch, as the days went by, for the next item Kelley conjured from his magic boxes.

Kelley told the jurors that only Joe Kahahawai and his kidnappers could say who fired the fatal shot. Joe was dead, and the kidnappers weren't talking. He would use circumstantial evidence—the items in the boxes and more—to speak for Joe, and to prove that the kidnappers were the only ones who had the motive, the opportunity, and the means to do the crime. He promised a precise, logical presentation of the facts, then delivered exactly that.

Darrow put off his opening statement, keeping everyone guessing about how he planned to respond to the prosecution's overwhelming case.

In the evenings, we scoured the town for Sammy Akana and went through bank records or trolled Chinatown asking about a Chinese man with a gold tooth. Daytimes, Billy and I used Kam's connections with the court bailiff to hold us a seat. I planned to catch some of the prosecution's case and wanted to be there when Tommie and Thalia testified.

We saw little of Thalia, but her mother remembered me. She routinely delivered what we in Honolulu call the "stink eye." I ignored the disgust radiating from her, and told myself I was staying as a (probably futile) reminder to her daughter that if she decided not to stick to the truth, someone who knew better would be listening.

Territorial Courthouse
Monday, April 11

On April 11, the onslaught began. Like a winter storm, Kelley brought wave after wave of evidence crashing onto the defendants. He started with Edward Ulii, Joe's cousin, and the last friendly face Joe ever saw.

Ulii described their walk to the courthouse, and the haole woman who had pointed at them as they left. "That's her," he said, reversing roles with the kidnapper and pointing at Grace Fortescue. "She's the one."

Darrow let Ulii go without much fuss, giving everybody the impression he was conceding the involvement of Grace and the others in the kidnapping.

Detective John Cluney followed Ulii to the stand and testified to seeing Joe's dead body in the dark blue Buick and the three suspects who were taken from the car.

Curiously, Darrow didn't seem very interested in what Cluney or the other officers had seen or done; he wanted to know how Tommie had acted. Cluney said he and the others were quiet, rigid, and sober, pretty much how he'd expect three people nabbed by the police with a murder victim on the floor of their car to act.

George Harbottle got to tell his story again and was asked by Kelley to identify Grace Fortescue. He got up and walked across the hushed courtroom to where she sat quiet, rigid, and sober, and touched her on the shoulder. The haughty society matron flinched at the contact.

Patrolman Percy Bond had something for Darrow. He'd arrived late at the scene and approached Harbottle to offer his congratulations, saying, "Good work, kid." Tommie Massie, who'd been standing next to the detective, responded by glancing over, smiling, and clasping his hands as if he were congratulating himself. When Bond had looked surprised, Massie had said, "Weren't you speaking to me?" Bond had shaken his head no.

Next followed a neighbor living next door to the rented Fortescue house, who testified to hearing a shot on the morning of the kidnapping.

Then Kelley began the parade of physical evidence—a methodical march of facts Darrow scarcely questioned. From the boxes came a newspaper photograph of Joe Kahahawai taken from Grace Fortescue's handbag. The .32 caliber bullet taken from Joe's body. A spent .32 cartridge found in Albert "Deacon" Jones's watch pocket. A box of .32 caliber bullets found in Jones's locker at the Armed Forces YMCA.

The rope used to bind Joe's bed linen shroud contained a distinctive purple thread that was matched to an identical piece retrieved from under some furniture in Grace Fortescue's house. Kelley established that this rope was used in only one place on the island—the sub base at Pearl Harbor.

A bloody towel was recovered; the blood type matched Joe's. Printing on the towel read "U.S.N." The sheet used to wrap the body matched others from Grace's house. More bloodstains had been found there.

Darrow accepted all of this with an eerie and detached passivity, almost as though he was a spectator in the proceedings. He occasionally tussled with Kelley, but witnesses who had been wringing their hands in the hallway, dreading cross-examination by the greatest attorney of his time, escaped from the stand unchallenged. Their elation was virtually the only emotion in a courthouse spellbound by the relentless procession of fact.

Kelley's final witness changed all of that.

Going back to his boxes for the last time, Kelley reached deep and withdrew a set of plain clothing from his box: a man's shirt, a pair of blue denim pants, and some underwear. He then called for Esther Anito to take the stand.

Darrow left his own seat to position himself between Mrs. Anito and the witness box, and addressed the court as she waited behind him. "We will concede anything this witness has to say," he told the judge. "We will stipulate to her testimony that she is the mother of Joe Kahahawai, that she saw him when he left that morning... Anything."

Kelley, who was standing by his own chair, spoke for the victim's mother. "There are two mothers in this courtroom. One is a defendant, and the other has no defense. Her son is dead. We think both should be permitted to testify."

Judge Davis agreed. Darrow stepped aside, and allowed the grieving lady to pass with quiet dignity.

She began in a low, moaning voice filled with tears, almost a controlled wail; her anguish was evident in every gesture. "I saw him that morning," she answered Kelley. "These are his clothes. He was wearing them when he left."

When she was given a button the police had found under the bathtub in Grace's house, Mrs. Anito sobbed and identified it as one from his undershorts. "I sewed this button on the shorts."

"When did you last see Joe?"

"I saw him when the police call me. They take me to the funeral parlor. I saw Joseph there. They asked me, 'Is that your son?' I say, 'Yes.'"

She stopped, and her low voice was halted by her tears. Several wept with her in the silence.

"No further questions," Kelley said quietly.

When asked if he had any questions, Clarence Darrow just shook his head. He wanted Joe Kahahawai's mother out of sight as quickly as possible.

"The prosecution rests, your honor." Kelley sat down.

Territorial Courthouse
Wednesday, April 13

Judge Davis gave the jury the rest of the day off as spectators made fevered plans for the defense case's opening the following morning. Everybody expected Darrow would call Lieutenant Thomas H. Massie, and the old lawyer did not disappoint.

After introducing his client to the jury and establishing that Massie had been living in Hawaii for two years, Darrow turned to the heart of the matter. "Do you remember an incident last September, going to a dance...?"

"I could never forget it." Massie's voice held just a note of pain, almost despair. "We, my wife Thalia and I, went to the Ala Wai Inn with two other officers. Mrs. Massie didn't care about going at first—but she finally agreed."

This was as far as Tommie got for a while as Kelley rose slowly and stepped out in front of his table. "I don't intend to interrupt with a lot of objections," he told Judge Davis. "But I feel at this point we are entitled to know the relevance of this testimony." He was quite sure that Darrow planned an insanity defense, so he sparred with his elusive opponent down on the particulars. Why was Darrow, who had strenuously avoided any mention of the Ala Moana case up till now, raising it with his very first witness?

Darrow said that insanity would be an issue for "the one who fired the gun," but then turned coy on the actual shooter, saying only of Tommie that, "his hand held the gun."

Kelley recognized that Darrow was being deliberately vague, and fumed as Darrow continued with the questioning. "What happened next?"

"It was late. The music had stopped, and it was time to go. I went looking for my wife, but no one remembered seeing her. I was concerned, and thought perhaps she had gotten a ride to Lieutenant Rigby's house with one of the other couples. Jerry Branson and I drove up to the Rigbys's, but Mrs. Massie wasn't there—hadn't been there. I couldn't understand it. I called our house to see if she'd gone directly home, and she answered the phone."

He paused as an actor does, allowing the tension to build, pacing his story. The courtroom was completely hushed. "She said, 'Come home, something awful has happened.' I couldn't imagine. I thought perhaps there'd been an accident. I went directly home. As I ran up the steps, I could hear her crying. She ran to the doorway and collapsed in my arms. There was blood coming from her nose, her lips were bruised and bleeding, and there was a large bruise on her cheek. I thought at first a truck had run over her." He dropped his head into his hands and covered his face.

The haole women in the front rows sat spellbound, almost enraptured at this description of their heroine's suffering. Admiral Stirling and others in the gallery leaned forward in their seats, poised for the next disclosure. Darrow had moved discreetly to one side, allowing the entire courtroom to focus on his young client's pain.

Massie seemed almost ready to break down. When his voice dropped, the spectators pressed in to hear.

"I asked her what had happened. She didn't want to tell me. She was sobbing, saying it was too terrible. Finally, she told me four men had dragged her into a car, beaten her, taken her to a place, and…and…ravished her." He looked up; the memory of Thalia's tale was clearly written on his face. "I said, 'Oh, my God! No!'" The *haole* women gave a collective gasp as the reporters scribbled feverishly. One or two spectators murmured, "No, no," and drew a scowl from Judge Davis.

Massie paused, looking—it seemed to me—at his mother-in-law. "She said, over and over, 'Why didn't they just kill me? Oh, I wish they had killed me.'" His voice trembled, then halted as he made another dramatic pause for the words to reach everyone.

He recounted how Thalia had identified Joe as one of her assailants that Sunday at their home. "The four *people*," he said in a voice full of bitterness, "were brought to our house. She said, 'They are the ones.' Then she called me to her side and said, 'Please, darling, don't let there be any doubt in your mind, because you know what it means. Don't you know if there was any doubt in my mind, I could never draw an easy breath?'"

Massie delivered this last with a note of defiance, daring Kelley to challenge his wife's credibility as so many others, myself included, had done. But Kelley did not object to the testimony. He knew that McIntosh and the other cops who were at the viewing would testify that Thalia had been vague on at least two of the four, although she'd picked out Joe Kahahawai that morning at her house.

Now Massie's testimony began to bore in on the dead man. Darrow's questions were narrowly focused on Joe's role in the assault, painting the big Hawaiian not just as a participant, but as a principal.

"I asked which one beat her mostly. She said that there were two that beat her. One was Chang and one was Kahahawai, but Kahahawai had beaten her more than anyone. She said when Kahahawai assaulted her, she prayed for mercy and he answered by hitting her in the jaw."

Massie wept as he told of the injury to her jaw, the surgery that was required, and the pain she had suffered. Others in the gallery were weeping with him, although the jurors looked fairly unmoved.

Right on Darrow's cue, he returned to Joe. "One night she woke up screaming, 'Don't let them get me!' I comforted her. I told her there was no one there but me, but she said, 'Yes, Kahahawai was here!'"

It was an eerie moment, hearing Massie invoking the spirit of a person now dead.

Joe's face that day in the alley came to me in a flash of recollection. Surely it appeared to others there who knew him. But was there, I wondered, any room among the crows and crocodiles and visions of hell in Thalia Massie's dreams for the face of a man she had never really met?

Darrow asked about Thalia's other medical conditions, leading Massie to still another lie. "Did you know she was pregnant?"

"There couldn't be any doubt about it," Tommie said, hanging his head. Thalia had been seen by both Dr. Porter and Dr. Withington, who had performed a dilation and curettage operation on her a month after the alleged rape. Tommie insisted that procedure had terminated Thalia's pregnancy. He also said he couldn't have been the father; there had been no intimacy between them in the weeks before the rape or in the month following.

Kelley scribbled busily on his legal pad.

Nearing the end of Tommie's first day on the stand, Darrow's direction seemed clear. He had laid all of the groundwork for Tommie's "honor defense." Joe had raped his wife, beaten her, and made her pregnant. Tommie, the outraged husband, had avenged the crime, perhaps in a fit of insane fury.

Tommie, I thought, wasn't being shy about stretching the truth. Knowing Thalia, she would be even worse.

During every break, Darrow made a trip to the men's room on the second floor; he was an elderly man with a bladder that had just turned seventy-five. I thought this might be the best opportunity to catch him alone. During the first recess, he was surrounded by the usual crowd of sycophants and attorneys, but during the second break I stayed long enough to have a brief moment alone with him.

"Mr. Darrow," I said after identifying myself, "I need to speak with you concerning a witness."

Darrow finished drying his hands. "Is it something we can discuss now? I have to be back in court shortly."

"It may take a few minutes, and I'd prefer to keep it confidential."

He considered for a moment, then gave me a room number at the Alexander Young Hotel and a time that afternoon. I thanked him as Leisure and Barry Ulrich came into the room.

CHAPTER 36

Alexander Young Hotel
Thursday, April 14

The Alexander Young, one of Honolulu's oldest hotels, occupied a city block in the heart of downtown within easy walking distance of the courthouse. Darrow had turned down free lodging at the far more luxurious Royal Hawaiian on Waikiki Beach. Being downtown allowed him, as he put it, to feel "the heartbeat of the people." Of course, most of the people staying at the Young in April 1932 were mainland reporters.

He ignored the credentials I presented, offered his hand, and motioned me into the room. It was a working space littered with an assortment of papers and files. After sweeping a folder from a chair, he gestured for me to sit and then collapsed onto a loveseat. None of the aura of confidence he projected in court surrounded him here. Up close, he seemed just a diminished and weak old man.

"Thank you for seeing me, sir."

"Not at all, young man, although I can't imagine how I might be of service to you."

"I know you're busy. I'll try not to take too much of your time."

"Narcotics, eh? I must confess my curiosity is aroused. My views on the prohibition law are well known; I've been speaking publicly about them for years. I suppose I must extend them to the laws you enforce, on the theory that one stimulant is as good or evil as another. I have my preferences, of course, and I am ever hopeful that the government will once again allow me to indulge those preferences, however foolish, unmolested by their despotic edict."

He was known to practice what he preached, at least as far as the Volstead Act was concerned. Quite a few of the reporters shared their evenings in discussions with Darrow and his wife with local bootleg on the agenda, unconstrained by any government edict, although Mrs. Darrow was supposed to be more "despotic" on that score.

"I'm not a Prohibition Agent."

"No. A police officer, then, a species with whom I have had occasional dealings. Sometimes even pleasant ones." He smiled to let me know he wasn't trying to be mean. "Now, how can I help with your narcotics matter?"

"To be honest, Mr. Darrow, this doesn't directly involve narcotics."

His eyebrows rose as he leaned forward, waiting.

"We have some information that there may be a problem with Thalia Massie's testimony in the Ala Moana case. There's a question—a serious question—about her credibility. I felt I should bring it to your attention before you called her as a witness in your case."

"You felt? May I take it, then, that this is not an officially sanctioned visit? Something made at the behest of Mr. Kelley?" He did not seem distressed or even concerned at my news, and his aging face never lost its placid but curious expression.

"I don't work for Kelley. I haven't said anything about it to the police or the prosecutor yet. I guess I was planning to see what your reaction would be."

"I see. Well, my reaction, if that is what is called for, is that Thalia is a young girl, and I have often found young girls to be incredible, occasionally incredibly so. In any case, she is not the issue in this trial, and will not become the issue."

"Then you don't think you'll be calling her as a witness to testify about the rape case?"

"Son, I have just spent two days arguing with Mr. Kelley about the extent to which I may or may not delve into the Ala Moana case's past history. If you have been in court—and you have been, because I've seen you there—then you know that he has prevented Lieutenant Massie from testifying about his wife's rape. I fought the same losing battle with other witnesses, and now that I have been confined like some dangerous circus animal to a cage in the corner of this courtroom, I must find some other way to defend my clients' interests, taking into account these restrictions. Judge Davis has ruled that the Ala Moana case will not be retried in this trial, and it shall not.

"The defense in this case is quite simple. Mr. Kelley has already discerned its outline, and has made his preparations accordingly, so I need not be reticent in discussing it with you. Lieutenant Massie has testified that he took the victim to Mrs. Fortescue's for the purpose of extracting a confession—a confession he believed would bring justice for the woman he loved. He had no desire, no plan, no design, and above all, no intent to kill. That, too, is his testimony.

"Yet the native died. Regrettable. Deeply regrettable. But his death was unavoidable, the unintended consequences of a scheme to find the truth of Mrs. Massie's claim. It was as though he was struck by lightning, erased from this earth by a single fatal stroke from above. When he spoke the words admitting his guilt, he became the lightning rod, and the means of his own destruction."

"Wait a minute. That's just my point. Why would Joe admit something he didn't do?"

"But that is not the testimony in this case. It is Lieutenant Massie's testimony that he *did* hear the words. Those are the facts as this jury knows them."

"But they're not 'facts' if Thalia Massie lied about them."

"But you see, young sir, that thanks to Mr. Kelley, I cannot ask Mrs. Massie about her trauma. I am limited to asking what she *told* her husband. Therefore, if she is called, you may be certain that she will be permitted only to describe what she told Lieutenant Massie, although that description may be, of necessity, somewhat graphic."

"But she lied about that!" I persisted.

"Did she? You seem quite certain of that, but suppose she did. That fact would undoubtedly be an issue at a retrial of the Ala Moana case, but it has no relevance now. What is relevant here is what she told her husband. He believed her totally, implicitly, whether that belief was well-founded or utterly misplaced. And he acted—not because her story was true, but because of his love for, and his belief, his abiding faith, in her."

I was pretty sure at this point that I knew Thalia Massie considerably better than did Clarence Darrow. I was dead certain that unless her husband was a complete sap, he had less than an "abiding faith" in this woman.

"I'm sorry," I said. "I just can't see the logic in this. You're saying it doesn't matter that Thalia made up this story and sold it to everyone, including her husband, who killed somebody because of it."

"The killing part hasn't been established yet, but of course it matters. It matters a great deal. To the victim and his poor mother, most of all. But it does not matter in this trial. The law is very clear that it is irrelevant to Lieutenant Massie's defense. None of us can be held legally responsible for acts committed while we are deranged or insane. That is a fact. It is also a fact that the story told by his wife, true or false, was the fuel for poor Lieutenant Massie's derangement, and needed only a spark to fulfill its explosive promise. The victim provided that spark, with tragic consequences."

That "victim" he referred to in passing would still bear the cross of Thalia's fabrication—lies twisted yet again to fit the defense concocted by her husband's lawyer. It was a cold fact that Darrow would be concerned only with the welfare of his clients. That's what he was paid for.

I still felt the need to speak for Joe Kahahawai.

"I just wonder where the justice is in this."

Darrow chuckled—a rich, heartfelt sound, filled with the experience or perhaps the cynicism accumulated in a thousand courthouses.

"Justice? And that is what you came here hoping to find? No." He shook his head. "I have learned many hard lessons in my life. The hardest is undoubtedly that we are unlikely to find truth or justice in a courtroom. I do not know in what obscure corner of this planet we should look for such things, but if it is justice and truth you are seeking, I know absolutely that they are not to be found on the second floor of the Territorial Courthouse.

"Take the counsel of this old man: If you are looking there, you are inevitably bound to be disappointed."

"That's a fairly pessimistic point of view, coming from a lawyer."

"No, the lawyer's idea of justice is a verdict for his client. This is the sole end for which he aims."

Darrow stood up and began to pace. Even sitting a few feet away from him, I could feel some of the fire return to the old man, and see some of the traits that had made him the greatest lawyer of his time. His thoughts ran ahead of him, and returned with the words he framed into simple, elegant phrases that were powerful, seductive, intriguing, and wrong. Still, he expressed them with such absolute sincerity and certainty, I could have no doubt that he believed them completely.

The great Clarence Darrow delivered the closing argument in the Massie trial—the last he would ever give—six days later. It was broadcast by radio to the entire nation. He gave the next-to-last to an audience of one in a hotel room in Honolulu. In it, he outlined a philosophy that had guided him for fifty years.

"Justice?" he murmured pensively, turning the word over, trying it out. "You are not seeking justice, young sir. You are asking for punishment. You invoke, though you may not know it, the old doctrine of 'an eye for an eye and a tooth for a tooth.' All penal codes—the federal one you serve and that which charges Lieutenant Massie—are really built upon that doctrine. When you trace these codes back to the beginning, they mean one thing and only one: vengeance." His voice rang out on the last word, startling me and two doves sitting on the windowsill.

"A man has done something. He has caused someone to suffer. Therefore society will do something to him. In the early stages, if someone slew another, the members of his tribe had the right to go and take the life of any member of the other tribe in return. Perhaps that was the case here in these islands. It was the law of vengeance, the law of punishment, and punishment and vengeance have always meant the same thing in the world, no matter where it has been."

He paused, collecting his thoughts, picked up a paper from the desk as though it held some clue to his argument, then set it aside.

"It was always thus, but we are changing, my young friend. Oh, yes. Some individuals in our society—the one two thousand years ago who urged us to turn the other cheek and others since—say that punishment is bad. Not heavy punishment alone, but *all* punishment. They believe that man has no right to punish his fellow man—that only evil results from it. They believe that the theory of vengeance and punishment is wrong—that an eye for an eye cures nobody, that a tooth for a tooth does not benefit society in any way. Neither does it change the defective for the better, and none of it tends to build us up.

"And to that elusive 'justice,'" he continued, "for the victim of this terrible tragedy? There can be none. What good is justice to him now? He will still be dead." He leaned in closer, bringing his argument home. "And Mrs. Fortescue, Lieutenant Massie, and the others…how will imprisoning them bring this 'justice' to the dead?" He slowly shook his head again, visualizing this possibility, seeing the unfairness of it all.

"Imprisoning a grieving mother and a tortured husband will somehow achieve this justice you seek? No." He shook his head, his voice resigned. "Whatever visions we may form of the word 'justice,' it has still never meant anything except adjusting human claims and human conduct to the established habits and customs and institutions of the world. Justice never can be a lofty ideal. It has neither emotions nor passions. It has no wings. Its highest flight is to the Blind Goddess that stands on the courthouse roof."

He passed his hand across his forehead, and brushed aside the wisp of hair that had fallen across it. There was a long moment of silence. The echoes of his passion still stirred in the room.

"Justice. No, it cannot solve the problems brought to these lovely shores. But understanding can. It cannot rescind words already spoken, but sympathy and forgiveness can. It cannot make people live together in a climate of love and tolerance, but generosity and charity can. We have only to begin, and are given this chance. Where better to take that first step toward a better world than here, in paradise?"

He dropped back onto his loveseat. He didn't seem very interested in my reaction.

"You should have been here to represent Joe Kahahawai," I said. "He needed you."

His eyes rose to meet mine. "So do Tommie Massie and Mrs. Fortescue."

"Yeah, but Joe had the advantage of being innocent."

"I'm representing four people charged with a crime I don't believe *was* a crime. They will get the best I have. Perhaps it will be justice." He leaned forward, and his interest was obvious. "Now, can you tell me about this evidence you possess that makes you believe Thalia is a liar?"

"I've been telling other people for months now, and it never seems to mean a damn," I said bitterly. "Is it going to make a difference with you?"

"In the instant case? Not a bit. For the peace of mind of one who is expected to counsel this young spirit, perhaps quite a lot."

"I've got information—first-hand information—about other crimes she's committed."

He thought about that for a minute, and regarded me gravely. "Other crimes. Yet you don't share this information with the prosecutor. How do you propose to use it, I wonder?"

"I'm trying to convince you not to allow a perjurer to pollute this trial with another damned lie. She's told too many already."

Darrow gazed up at the ceiling, calculating—seeking, I hoped, a compromise we both could live with.

"Let us make a bargain, you and I," he said at last. "Without conceding the truth of your allegations, I will agree that, regardless of the outcome of this trial, Thalia Massie will not testify against the Ala Moana defendants." He held up his hand, forestalling my objection. "I know, I know, this does nothing for poor Joe Kahahawai. It is too late to save him; surely you can see that. But if we can come to some accord, the law will cease to trouble the lives of the others. Under the law's presumption, they will be forever innocent of any crime."

"She wouldn't pay any kind of price for what she's done. I don't care what you call it—punishment, vengeance, justice, or anything you want. She deserves some consequences for all the grief she's caused."

"Two wrongs will not miraculously make a right, Mr. Mather." Darrow's aging voice was filled with reproof. "If what you say is true, Thalia will have Kahahawai's death on her conscience. Perhaps, since it does not reside in the courtroom, this justice of yours can be found in the human heart."

"Assuming she's got one."

He looked at me with the hint of a smile on his lips. "Ah, I almost forgot for a moment that you are a policeman, after all, with the attendant attitudes and prejudices."

It was my turn to laugh. "Yes, sir. I'm prejudiced against liars, I'll grant you that. I'm new at this job, but I've already found out how hard it is to get to the truth even when people aren't lying their heads off. Somebody told me once I don't have a dog in this fight, and they're right. It doesn't matter to me how you do your job, whether some jury lets your clients off or sends them to Oahu Prison. What does matter is she's lied, and I know it. She's got to tell the truth this time."

"Or else what, exactly?"

"Or else we'll find out how many supporters the *real* Thalia Massie's got."

He mulled that one for a good half minute. What he finally said was completely unexpected. "You know, Mr. Mather, we are going to lose this case."

I must have shown my surprise, because he chuckled again. "Yes, we are going to lose. Mr. Kelley has done a good job presenting his evidence, and this jury will convict. Still, I am confident that I will ultimately prevail. But it will not be here, not now. Is it any wonder I say there is no justice to be found in a courtroom?"

"Maybe it's justice if murderers are punished."

"No...as I said, no good will come of putting Mrs. Fortescue in a prison, or Lieutenant Massie, or the others. Someone between here and Washington will see that, and reason will prevail. The men on this jury will not have the final say."

"That's not my problem, either. Like I said, whether I agree or disagree with the jury, I've got no say in the outcome."

"What is it you want, exactly?"

I squared my jaw. "What I *want* is Thalia Massie locked up. She's caused an incredible amount of damage to the people here, not to mention being the main reason Joe Kahahawai's dead right now." Now I held up my hand to stop him, because he was already protesting the idea of poor Mrs. Massie in a jail cell. "Don't worry, I know that's not going to happen. But the least she can do is tell the truth about the four who're left. They didn't rape her, and she knows it. They shouldn't have to carry her lies around with them for the rest of their lives."

"Now, really, how can you possibly know of their guilt or innocence? Because they, who have every reason to deny their crime, told you so?"

"No, actually, Mr. Darrow, because Thalia told me what really happened, where she really was. Who really hit her."

He leaned back sharply. A wisp of white hair fell across his forehead and swayed as he shook his head. He pushed it aside, giving himself a moment.

"Hmmm. Will you consider my earlier proposition? Would you be satisfied if the Ala Moana boys were not subjected to another trial?"

I thought about the offer, knowing I wasn't holding the highest hand in these negotiations, and the very high price of showing my cards. "I'd prefer it if she'd recant the statements she made before and admit the truth, but I know that isn't going to happen, either. So, yeah, I think no retrial is a fair outcome."

"There's justice in that, you think?" His words had a slightly mocking tone, but I could see that he, too, was weighing the options.

"No, there's no justice in it," I said hotly. "More like partial restitution. No matter what she does, she'll never bring Joe back. And you and I both know that whatever happens, there'll always be some people who think the boys did it."

"Yes, prejudices will continue with us, and you're right, it will undoubtedly dog the young men."

"All right. I'll go along with your proposal. But she's lied about the rape; she can't lie again."

The lion head bowed in acceptance. "I agree. *If* she testifies, we will follow the Judge's ruling and ask only what she told her husband."

Our business was almost concluded, so I changed the subject. "Fine. I hear you're supposed to be friends with Dr. Porter out at Pearl Harbor."

Now it was Darrow's turn to be surprised. "John Porter is an excellent man."

"Yeah? You talk to him about Thalia? Maybe you better give him another shout. Ask him how much opium a twenty-year-old girl should be taking, and how many doctors she should be seeing to get it. Ask him about her other doctors."

"You're not going to tell me any more."

"Nope. No, sir. You've got no reason to believe me, anyway. I'm just a cop. But maybe you'll listen to somebody you do trust."

I stood and looked around the hotel room, and at the old man in the rumpled suit. My debt to Bill Pittman was paid.

"Thanks for your time," I told the Attorney for the Damned.

Territorial Courthouse
Saturday, April 16

Everyone on both sides of the aisle agreed that Thursday's session had been extraordinarily entertaining, the highlight of the trial so far. Tommie Massie's emotional testimony was a welcome relief from Kelley's relentless procession of facts. There was hardly a dry eye in the place, at least among Tommie's many supporters. So the crowd was greatly disappointed on Friday morning when court was postponed due to the illness of lead defense counsel Clarence Darrow.

Many had spent the night on the lanai outside the courthouse doors, or arrived hours before dawn, hoping to secure one of the seats in the crowded courtroom. Others sent servants to save places in line. At least one of the bailiffs received a caution from Judge Davis for holding seats for a fee. All these best-laid plans went for naught when Darrow fell ill.

A charitable press reported that the lawyer was "exhausted," and in truth it had been hot the day before. Prayers were offered for the recovery of the old agnostic and noted anti-religionist, but that was a proposition of dubious plausibility. In a more practical vein, Judge Davis agreed to a day of rest, and assured the spectators that a Saturday session would make up for the lost time.

The savvier followers of the case, especially those who monitored Darrow's out-of-court activities, knew that the cause of the lawyer's "exhaustion" had been the aftereffects of a substantial quantity of okolehao and pineapple juice consumed with several reporters the night before. Dr. Porter came downtown to minister to Darrow's hangover, and the old lawyer recovered early enough in the day that he was able to meet with his co-counsel and their clients.

In addition to a long private conversation with Dr. Porter, Darrow spoke alone for some time with Thalia Massie, who everybody expected would be taking the stand soon after Tommie was finished. Everybody also anticipated that the lines would be far longer, and form much earlier, on the day Thalia was sworn in.

CHAPTER 37

Territorial Courthouse
Saturday, April 16

Saturday morning found Tommie back on the stand. Darrow wasted no time getting straight to the killing of Joe Kahahawai and what his client knew about it.

Not much. Tommie testified most earnestly that he had essentially slept through the important parts of the kidnapping—a prospect most viewed as approximately as likely as his wife regaining her virginity.

As Darrow had told me, Tommie readily admitted taking part in the kidnapping plot, and denied there was ever any intent to actually kill Joe. He was clear on all of the details right up to the actual moment of the shooting.

"We had him sitting on a chaise lounge," he testified, "and he kept denying everything. I told him, 'you know that isn't true, admit it,' and threatened him with the gun. I told him some of the boys from the Navy Yard were outside, and were going to give him the same that Ida got. That was when he said it, 'Yes, we done it.'"

"'*Yes, we done it,*'" Darrow repeated for effect, his sonorous tones echoing in the hush. "What happened then?"

"I don't know."

"You can't remember anything after that?"

Tommie shook his head regretfully. "No, nothing."

He came to later, he said, by the side of the road at Hanauma Bay. Everything else was gone, lost in a fog of what his alienist would later call "shock amnesia."

"It was never your intention to kill Kahahawai?" Darrow asked.

"No, never."

Clarence Darrow passed the witness to John Kelley, who hammered away for two hours on Tommie's story and scored a few points. But for the most part, Tommie Massie had "I don't remember" down pat.

Kelley did shake the witness on one issue, Tommie's sad tale of Thalia's pregnancy—the "proof" she had really been raped and not merely assaulted. He produced a report from the hospital where the dilation and curettage was performed, and called his attention to the line that read, "No sign of pregnancy was found." Tommie had no explanation for the discrepancy, and there was much talk later about how such a sensitive document found its way into the prosecutor's hands.

The document was signed by the physician who had performed the procedure, Paul Withington.

Surprisingly, Darrow next called not Thalia, but two psychiatrists, then known as alienists—a term that perfectly described the extraterrestrial nature of their testimony. For Hawaii's down-to-earth jurors, Drs. Thomas Orbison and Edward Huntington Williams might as well have been speaking Martian.

To relieve the boredom caused by the overdose of psychiatric twaddle, Darrow asked the court to allow Mrs. Massie to attend the session.

"She will be our next witness, and I would like to take this opportunity to familiarize her with the proceedings."

Thalia, of course, was intimately familiar with how a trial worked, having perjured herself at length in the Ala Moana case.

"He just wanted to give everybody something to look at besides those two idiots," Billy chuckled later when, like everyone else, he laughed at the doctors.

Both men had recently testified as defense experts in Winnie Ruth Judd's insanity plea; she was the notorious Arizona "trunk murderess" whose crime included packaging her victims in a railway shipping container. She had been convicted despite the appearance of Darrow's two experts, and was supposed to be executed shortly.

Dr. Williams, a dead ringer for the man you see today on buckets of fried chicken, right down to the white goatee, testified first and described a condition he called "somnambulistic ambulatory automatism." In this bizarre state, Massie—upon hearing Joe's "confession"—suddenly went into a "walking daze" and could neither control his actions nor remember them later. Conveniently for the lieutenant, this condition was quite curable, said the doctor, and not liable to be repeated since the cause, Joe's words, was hardly likely to be reprised.

Barry Ulrich's cross-examination quickly bogged down in an impenetrable swamp of psychiatric jargon. When he saw that the jury was just as lost as everyone else, Ulrich let Williams take his leave.

Dr. Orbison, a paunchy man with no patience for lawyers unless they were paying him, had an even more bizarre explanation for the killing. Lieutenant Massie, he said, had "shock amnesia," a "mental bomb" that had gone off at the words *"Yes, we done it,"* supposedly spoken by Joe Kahahawai. The condition had left Tommie temporarily insane and unable to remember anything he did while in this shocked state.

Ulrich wasn't buying any of it and suspected the jurors weren't, either. He set to work on the doctor. "Your testimony, Dr. Orbison, is based solely on the assumption that Lieutenant Massie believed Joseph Kahahawai was the man who attacked his wife, isn't that so?"

Orbison weighed his response carefully, then conceded, "That's true."

"Would you say it is impossible that Massie could be telling a lie—malingering in his testimony? Isn't it usual in cases of this sort for the defendant to simulate insanity and then hire expert witnesses who can testify in support of this pose?" Ulrich prodded.

"I object to that question," Orbison responded heatedly.

"Generally only counsel are permitted to make objections in these proceedings," Judge Davis countered with a smile.

"It is a mean question, too mean to deserve an answer," Orbison said.

"Well, try," Ulrich urged.

"You're implying that expert witnesses would change their testimony for money," Orbison snapped, correctly summing up Ulrich's implication. "I think attorneys are more likely to change facts for money." He lumped his own employer into his objection.

"Let's get back to the evidence," Judge Davis—also an attorney, and not smiling anymore—instructed.

"All right." Ulrich stood directly in front of Orbison. "Do you think Massie is quite sane at present?" he asked.

"Yes, of course."

"Oh, I *see*," Ulrich said in the manner of one whose view of the world is suddenly made perfectly translucent. "Just a one-killing man, then, eh?"

Territorial Courthouse
Wednesday, April 20

The moment everyone had been waiting for came on a sunny Wednesday morning, a day when the courthouse lanai was packed three and four deep, and the courtroom itself overflowed into the hallway. Thalia arrived on Darrow's arm, looking bad when she took the stand and worse when she got off, thinner than I remembered, older and paler. Her blue eyes still flashed in response to the lawyers' questions, but some of her fire seemed to be gone when she started.

I was wedged back into a corner by the jury box, but I watched as she crossed the open area in front of the bar, waiting to hear how her lawyer planned to keep his word to me.

A year before he died, I talked to John Kelley about the most famous cross-examination he ever did, one that lasted less than five minutes. He was as puzzled that day as on that Wednesday in 1932 when Thalia Massie settled herself into the witness box for Darrow's first question.

"I knew what he was going to do," Kelley recalled, "put little Miss Perfect up there to do her 'poor me' story all over again. Which is what he did, of course. And what am I supposed to do? I could only cross-examine her on what he asks her, so every question just gets more of the rape stuff in…"

Kelley paused, looking up through the smoke of his cigarette, looking back over the years at a roomful of people emptied of everyone but the young girl and the old lawyer. He shook his head. "What the hell was he thinking? He knew I had the paper. The professor told him he'd given it to us. And still, the first thing out of his mouth is the one thing—the only thing—that gives me the chance to nail her."

Darrow's first question seemed innocuous enough, but I recall seeing Kelley sit up sharply and turn toward Barry Ulrich, disbelief on his face.

"You love your husband, don't you, Mrs. Massie?" Darrow asked softly.

Thalia swore that she did, and affirmed Tommie's affection. Darrow moved on into the area Kelley feared—drawing out, over his objections, the story of September 12 and 13. Although Judge Davis told Darrow to limit his questions to "what she told him and what he told her," she got the whole story out again, and won the hearts of everyone in the room who didn't believe her to be lying like a *lauhala* floor mat. She wept, she emoted, she suffered, and she gasped out the story of the rape and how she came to report it to her husband. She turned those blue junkie eyes on the jurors, asking for their trust, and for a couple of hours, she got it.

"It was too late, though," Kelley told me. "He'd already opened the door with that first question." He waved the cigarette, acknowledging a mystery he would never solve. "He must've just slipped; he was getting old. Maybe he really was sick. That was the only mistake he made in the whole trial, but once he'd opened the door like that, there was no going back. It was almost like he wanted…"

John Kelley never knew what Clarence Darrow wanted, although I think I do. But when he stood up for his cross-examination, he gave Thalia Massie all she needed. He also gave everybody else a look at the real Thalia Massie, the one I'd seen up close and very personal.

"All right, Mrs. Massie. You have testified that your husband was always kind and considerate to you, that there were never any quarrels. Is that correct?"

"Yes, that is so." She gazed fondly in Tommie's general direction.

Kelley walked back over to his table and got a document. After looking it over, he gave a curt nod and then carried it to the witness stand.

"It was an examination paper from her psychology class at the university," he told me. "There was a lot of stuff about dreams. Some of it was pretty strange, you ask me. But the kicker was some question on it about marital relationships with one of those multiple choice answers," he chuckled. "Thalia turned it into a little essay. She even wrote some more stuff on the back." He laughed, remembering the moment when Thalia's words came circling back to bite her.

"Is that your handwriting?" he demanded.

Thalia went chalky white; even her lips seemed to drain of color as she stared down at the paper, then up at Kelley in the silent courtroom.

"Well…?"

"Where did you get this?" she hissed. "You realize, of course, this is a private and confidential matter?"

"I'm asking the questions, not answering them, Mrs. Massie. Is that your handwriting?"

Flushed now, Thalia half-stood and leaned forward. Her shrill voice climbed, glittering like a blade reaching for Kelley. "I refuse to answer. I refuse to say if this is my handwriting. This is a private matter between a patient and physician, and you have no right to bring it into open court like this!" Her fingers tightened on the paper as she gestured with it angrily.

"Oh? Is this man your doctor?" Kelley asked, knowing that he was not.

"Yes, he is."

Darrow raised himself slowly to his feet, but said nothing. Tommie looked up at him from his seat, confused. Though the room was quiet, it was one of those pregnant silences; everyone hoped something big was going to happen very shortly.

Like Kelley, they got what they were hoping for.

Thalia suddenly stood completely upright in the witness box and, holding the paper at arms' length, began tearing the document into pieces, the ripping noise rending the hush. In a collective spasm of commiseration, the haole ladies burst into applause; some also stood and cheered. Tommie joined in as others in the room stood just to see the scene unfolding.

Judge Davis slammed his gavel down repeatedly, breaking the handle as he shouted for order. Pandemonium prevailed for a long moment.

Carrying the shredded paper, Thalia walked, then ran, past an astonished John Kelley and collapsed into her husband's arms, sobbing.

"Thank you, Mrs. Massie," Kelley said over the din, "for at last appearing in your true colors."

Judge Davis quickly had this remark stricken from the record. The angry judge then turned to the crowd and told everyone to sit down and behave or he'd clear the courtroom. Kelley shook his head when asked if he had any more questions.

"I mean, how am I ever going to top that?" he asked me. "And then, *she* does it for me."

In the moment of silence that followed, Thalia's words to her husband rang out clearly, describing for the world the contents of the torn paper in her hands.

"What right has he got to say I don't love you? Everybody knows I love you," she cooed.

Clarence Darrow stepped away from his client and the girl clinging to him, and glanced back toward the spectators' gallery—looking directly, I thought, at me. "The defense rests," he intoned into a hushed courtroom. "The defense rests."

Territorial Courthouse
Tuesday, April 26

I didn't go to court for Clarence Darrow's last-ever closing argument; like everyone else, I listened to the old warrior's final four riveting hours on the radio. At times, the speaker rang with the passion of old, but all too often Darrow—aging, tired, ready to go home—spoke like the man I'd met in the hotel room…a man whose race had been run, and one who saw his competitors celebrating up ahead across the finish line.

The attorney who, for five decades, had pursued a career in the legal process now argued fiercely that the jurors should disregard "manmade laws" when "the inescapable power of the human conscience" called on them to do so. He appealed directly to the jurors' hearts, not the minds that might have been persuaded by a week's worth of John Kelley's cold, hard facts. He asked for the jurors' pity for the four people he defended—for two common seamen guilty of loyalty to their officer, for a mother guilty of loving her daughter, and for a husband guilty of trying to right a terrible wrong done to his wife.

When he was almost finished, Clarence Darrow stood in front of the jury that had stared back at him for weeks with empty expressions. "There it is, gentlemen. Take these poor, suffering people, not in anger but in cool judgment, in pity and understanding. Take it humanly. You have in your hands not only the fate, but also the lives of these poor people. What is there for them if you pronounce a sentence of doom upon them? You are in a position to heal, not to destroy; to bind up the wounds of the past. This case is in your hands, and I ask you to be kind and considerate, both to the living and to the dead."

After a short recess, John Kelley charged head-on into Clarence Darrow's appeal. He spoke for only forty-five minutes, and wrapped up the case for the prosecution with a mixture of evidence and emotion.

"For fifty years, that man there," Kelley's voice rang out as he pointed at Darrow, "has stood before the bar of justice and practiced the law he now belittles, the law he asks you to disregard." He looked at Darrow with a mixture of contempt and pity, and shook his head. "Are you going to decide this case on the law? That is your charge, your burden, and your responsibility."

He tore through Tommie Massie's testimony, pointing out the lies, the evasions, and the words of a man he called "a conceited, vain, egotistical individual who is responsible for everything that has happened since September 12th."

He ridiculed not just the gibberish of the two defense psychiatrists, but the premise behind their testimony—that Tommie Massie was temporarily insane. Calling it "the sheet anchor of the rich and influential, who can hire liars as experts and put on a defense of insanity," he asked the jurors to ignore Darrow here, too. "This defense is not insanity—it is sympathy."

Kelley's final appeal was an emotional one. He started softly, respectfully, as he faced Joe Kahahawai's mother seated in the first row behind the prosecutor's table.

"Mr. Darrow has spoken of mother love." Then he turned toward Grace Fortescue, and his voice assumed a sharp bite. "He has spoken of 'the mother' in this courtroom. Well, there is another mother in this courtroom. Has Mrs. Fortescue lost her daughter? Has Massie lost his wife?" He spun back to Esther Anito, who wept silently in her long white *holoku* gown. "But where is Joseph Kahahawai?" he thundered.

The jury got the case the next day. Judge Davis instructed them on the law and sent the twelve men off to deal with Hawaii's prickliest problem since the overthrow of the monarchy. From Honolulu to Washington, a nation held its breath, waiting for a verdict guaranteed to anger some powerful constituency or another.

After more than fifty hours of deliberation and fifteen votes, the jury came back and unanimously decided against all four defendants. Darrow had lost, just as he told me he would. The jurors had tried to find a middle ground between the competing forces, returning a verdict of manslaughter instead of murder, with a recommendation for clemency. The compromise judgment satisfied no one, outraging the Navy and disappointing those in Hawaii who saw Joe's cold-blooded killing as the murder it was. But the fact that twelve Hawaii men could resist the pressures on them and the power of Darrow's persuasiveness, and agree on the killers' responsibility, was remarkable.

With the heat off the jurors, those powerful constituencies turned their anger and attention elsewhere. So did we, still hopeful that the White Friend's trail might emerge from somewhere in the wreckage Thalia Massie had left behind.

We all went back to work.

CHAPTER 38

Kamanuwai Lane (Tin Can Alley)
Tuesday, May 3

"Let's go. Kam's got a line on Akana," Billy said, banging down the phone. We drove up to Lau Yee Chai, a Chinese restaurant just down the street from our opium den.

"Got a bird out there, the black cap," Kam said, jerking a thumb at the street outside. Billy and I both leaned out for a peek at the informer. The rail-thin Chinese man wore, as Kam had said, a black leather cap squatting over some greasy-looking hair. Henry McKeague stood a few feet away, but not close enough for people to connect the two of them.

"He says Akana's holed up in a room in Tin Can Alley, pretty far in."

This wasn't especially good news. The narrow lane that wandered off Beretania Street into Hell's Half-Acre was probably the worst in Honolulu, if not the entire Pacific. Honolulu policemen entered in pairs, and sometimes still had to fight their way out. As in most of Honolulu's slums, good people struggled for survival in a tough time, but Tin Can Alley had a high concentration of depravity. Here, rotten people preyed avidly on each other, their neighbors, and especially on any outsider foolish enough to stray into the area. Getting Akana out of that environment would be a chore.

Kam's informer said Akana's hideout was a second-floor cubicle in a wooden tenement. A set of stairs in the middle of the building provided the only access to the rooms above. Because house numbers were occasional and sometimes flat wrong in the Alley, Kam planned to have the informer precede us down the street, then stop and remove the leather cap when he was in front of the correct address. We'd be fifty feet behind, so we might not be linked to his betrayal—no small consideration in a place that could reward even the hint of treachery with a knife in the back.

Just after nightfall, we went in. The light Kona winds that occasionally wheeze into Honolulu from the south dragged a blanket of warm, humid air onto the city. People driven from the hothouse atmosphere of their cramped rooms flocked into the constricted passages, eddying in the alley, collecting in sweaty knots on the sidewalks. Their faces turned to us as we pushed forward.

Kam, of course, was well known. Those who had reason to fear him shrank from his approach, fading back into the shadows under overhanging balconies or the cramped walkways between buildings. Hooded eyes and glowing cigarettes created tiny beacons in the murky darkness and warned us away from unknown dangers. Children of the neighborhood ran up, capering around the big detective, laughing and trying to provoke some reaction.

Billy, McKeague, and I walked a step or two behind, staying in the roadway where we could see the informer up ahead as he wove through clusters of people not yet aware of our advance.

"That's it," McKeague said as the informant swept the hat from his head. The skinny Chinese piper paused a moment in front of an unpainted wooden eyesore, then moved on without looking at us. We continued our steady pace and closed the distance to the building—a tenement house with, as the informer had promised, an entrance at the center of the rickety-looking structure.

Kam veered suddenly and ducked inside, then bounded up the steps with the rest of us on his heels.

Halfway up, he met a Hawaiian girl in an orange muumuu coming the other way. Fear flashed on her face when she recognized him. "Sammy, get cops!" she squealed, before a hand the size of a frying pan swatted her aside.

She bounced hard off the wall, and rolled down the steps in a jumble of flailing arms and legs. Billy and McKeague managed to get clear, but she caught me at the knees and took me down with her. As I struggled to free myself, the sound of a door slamming echoed through the stairwell, and feet pounded down the hallway above.

Kam wasted no breath yelling at Akana to stop; he just covered ground as fast as he could. The others disappeared onto the second floor landing as I managed to shake off the squirming girl and start back up.

When I reached the top of the steps, I saw Billy and McKeague slip through a door at the far end of a narrow corridor. Rooms opened on both sides. Some people were standing in the doorways, gazing off after the pursuit. Not even a whisper of breeze visited this dank tunnel; the leaden air was thick with the smell of smoke, cooking oil, and frying fish.

As I galloped down the hallway, more footsteps reverberated back across the corrugated metal roof overhead, rolling like thunder. I stopped to stare upward past a single line of naked light bulbs and wooden trusses to the bare metal, and saw the roofing panels bouncing with every step our fugitive took.

Reversing field, I ran back along the corridor, cringing as cockroaches the size of half-dollars and geckos dislodged by the impact rained down with bits of dust and rusted metal flakes. Now the people who started emerging from rooms on either side of the passageway slowed my progress. Blue charcoal smoke, drawn into the corridor by the opened doors, gave the pursuit a hellish aspect. Hands clutched at me as I passed.

At the stairs, I glimpsed an open door at the end of the passage where a Chinese girl stood nursing a baby. I ran up to her and shoved her aside as she jabbered at me in Cantonese.

I ducked under a hanging blanket, and looked for a window in the dimly lit room. An elderly couple shrank from the trespasser and hugged each other in front of a charcoal *hibachi* brazier. A whole fish lay sizzling in a pan on the hibachi; one skeptical eye glared at the commotion overhead. Dirty gauze curtains and smoke from the fish dinner wafted outward through a square black hole in the far wall.

I crossed to the window and leaned out. A shadow passed across the clouds between the roof of our building and the next tenement. Then I heard a tremendous crash as the shadow landed heavily on the metal roof next door, tumbled toward the edge, dropping into the darkness below.

I had to get down there fast. I scrambled out of the window and hung for a moment from the sill. My last view of the room I was leaving was a frozen tableau of the elderly couple, the Chinese girl and her baby, and the fish—all gaping open-mouthed at me.

My feet scrabbled against the rough wood as I remembered too late the inevitable rubbish in the yard below. I hoped it wouldn't be too lethal.

It wasn't a long fall, and a chicken coop cushioned my landing. The coop's roof gave way and plunged me up to my armpits in a welter of wire, straw, broken slats, smashed eggs, and frenzied chickens. I panicked for a moment that I was trapped, and I floundered in the wreckage, knocking it apart as I staggered to my feet. Pale shapes, clucking frantically, scattered into the shadows, preferring even the vast terror of darkness to the whirlwind that had torn apart their flimsy little home.

I got my bearings and ran at the spot where I'd seen the shadow fall. A wobbly board fence separated the two yards. I crashed into it, flattened a five-foot section, and fell again—this time atop a groaning body. Quickly I knocked pieces of broken wood aside and looked down into Sammy Akana's anguished face. We panted at each other, too spent to speak.

Seconds later, a beaming Kwai Kam hoisted Akana to his feet and shook the former ship's steward like a rat. Akana released the left leg he'd apparently injured in his fall, clutching desperately at the fist gripping his shirt collar.

"No, no, no," Kam warned. "I got you now." He shook him again.

Billy ran up. "You okay, Jack?"

"I think so," I nodded, and watched Kam frog-march his captive toward Tin Can Alley. "I guess we got him." I rolled over and gazed up at the moonless night. "Gee, I hope it was worth it."

Billy held out a hand to help me up.

"Hooo-ey!" Kam exclaimed when we reached the parked car on Beretania Street. "What is that stink?" He peered at me in amazement. "What were you doing back there?"

Billy laughed, motioning for McKeague to drive as he climbed into the passenger seat. I was covered with chicken shit, feathers, mud, busted eggs, bits of fencing, and assorted rubbish. In short, I was not a pretty picture. Or a sweet-smelling one. Even Akana scrunched as far away from me as Kam's massive bulk would allow.

"At least I caught him," I muttered. "Where the hell were you?"

"Trying to keep up with this little *lan yeung*," Kam said. "How come you run, you dumb bastard?" He poked the still-moaning Sammy in the side with a thick finger: it was a gesture easily capable of denting a two-by-four. "And what are you complaining about? You don't wanna get hurt, you don't run from a policeman."

"I never knew you guys was cops," Akana whined.

"Right. After your girlfriend yells at you, 'Sammy, the cops,' you figured it was somebody else?"

Sammy wasn't willing to risk another poke; he just shrugged.

"Plus, too, I *know* you know I'm looking for you. Somebody had to tell you, otherwise why are you hiding out?" Kam asked reasonably, and prodded Sammy again.

"Oww! I never knew was you folks. I'm clean. I thought it was about that haole lady again."

"You were right, my friend," Kam said, settling back with a satisfied smile. "That is exactly what we want to talk to you about."

Akana, obviously surprised, thought that one over as the car pulled into the courtyard at the Federal Building. Billy directed McKeague to the back stairs. Kam jerked Akana out of the car as soon as we stopped.

"Get yourself cleaned up," Billy said, grinning broadly. "Then come on upstairs."

By the time I got to the office, the magical transformation was almost complete. The man we had hunted for three months, and the cause of my considerable discomfort, now sat easily in front of Billy's desk, fussing about his swollen ankle and talking about the Ala Moana case.

"I told you already. I stay at the wedding party, other side of the island that night. How come you don't believe me?" he whined.

"Because, you silly sonofabitch, didn't you hear me? I just got through talking to your friends," Kam gestured at the phone on Billy's desk. "They told me that was horseshit. They said they got married on Sunday, not Saturday like you said."

"Maybe I forget."

"Maybe you lied. Now you gonna tell us the truth this time, or are we gonna lock your ass up for conspiracy? Did you like McNeil Island? This time you're gonna be there for ten damn years."

"What you folks like know?"

It was my turn. "The White Friend, for starters. We already know where you were and who you were with that night," I told him. "You were with the White Friend."

Akana looked more surprised, but said nothing.

"Oh, yeah. We know all about you and that guy."

"Who told you?"

"Who do you think? Come on. You really think a white man is going to protect somebody like you?" I lied easily, as though the White Friend's treachery was as natural as eating. "He gave us everything, told us all about you."

That made him pale just a little. "What you folks like know?" he repeated.

"We want to check out his story. We think he was lying when he told us you were the key man in the hui."

"Me? I ain't no key man!"

"Not according to your pal. And you're the one who got caught with all those tins going into L.A., so it sounds like he might be right."

"No, he ain't."

"You gonna play straight with us now?"

"Sure," he shrugged. "I help out those cops in L.A. before." He looked up slyly. "And they help me."

I looked at Billy, who winked. "We'll see about that," I said. "Okay, so go back to the Ala Moana thing. Tell us about that one first."

"He never told you?"

Kam leaned in close and jabbed a big finger into Sammy's side as a sharp reminder. "You just answer the questions, quit horsing around."

"All right already." Sammy leaned away from Kam and toward me, which was exactly the reaction the detective was trying to provoke.

"What if I told you he said you were the one who busted the wahine's jaw?" Kam taunted. "How'd you like that?"

"I never did."

"So tell us what really happened, and we'll decide who to believe."

Akana hung his cuffed hands between his legs and surrendered. "He find me downtown, says, 'Come on, we gotta talk to this girl.' I knew who he meant, 'cause he bring her around a couple of times. Even the night before, we was at that place on River Street where you catch me. She can do some pills, that girl." The handcuffs rattled as he shifted in his chair.

"We're driving, got his car and a couple of his boys, and he's telling me she's gonna be trouble, she might talk about the hui. He wanted to get her to shut up. I think he told her too much before, and now he was worried."

"How did he find her that night?"

"He knew already the Navy was going to be down there. But we pull up, he never like go inside, 'cause the wahine, he don't know what she might say if she saw him. That's why he send me. Told me, get her to come out and talk."

"What did you do?"

"I went in. I knew some of the folks there, the band boys, and I talked with them. I seen the wahine, but she always stay with some other Navy people. Finally I see her by herself, and I catch her on the stairs. I tell her I want to talk to her. She get all sassy, throwing her hair around, saying she don't need us anymore. I tell her 'you only have to listen,' but she just walks away. I don't know if she gonna leave or what, but finally she comes outside."

"Then what happened?"

"I talk to her a minute in the parking lot, then she walks along. I'm in the car with the other boys. Now he's walking along behind her, trying to talk to her, but she ain't listening, I can see. We going past the park, and I see him behind her, waving to us. We pull in front of them and I get out and help him put her in the car. She never like go, but he's got her by the arm. I never had to hit her or nothing.

"In the car, he's telling her stuff like, 'Be reasonable, don't make problems,' like that. But I think she's drunk, plus she is one total bitch already.

"We get to Ala Moana, pretty dark, and she tries to get out of the car, so he cracks her a couple of times. I didn't think it was too hard, but later I seen where she had a broke jaw."

"You just let her go, just like that?"

Sammy nodded vigorously. "Yeah. He finally just says, 'Hell with it,' and tells her, 'You say anything, next time, I send the Chinese to kill you.' Then he tells us, 'Let's go.' We left her standing there."

"You sure he was the one who hit her, not you?"

"Hell, yeah. I never did none of that shit. If he said I did, he's lying. I never have nothing against the wahine. I ain't the one scared she's gonna talk. So what if she tell you folks about me? You already know about me—you just pinched me the night before. I practically never even touch her, except when we was getting in the car. I thought all we was going to do was talk to her. I didn't know nothing about the hitting, and we never rape her."

"Alright. That sounds right. Let's get back to your buddy, Mr. White Friend. How'd you meet him?" I said.

"On the ship, *Golden Star*, when we're at Shanghai. We talk and he ask if I like make some extra money. Shanghai side, he introduce me to his Chinese friends. He know a lot of people. They tell me, all I gotta do is keep an eye out on the boat if any Customs or police snooping around. I do, they give me some cash. Later on, they give me some hop, too."

"Shanghai," I said, the light finally dawning. I'd been awfully slow catching on—nine months slow. But now, finally, I had it. I finally spoke the name of the White Friend. "Yeah. This would have been in '29, right? Butler was stationed there."

Billy and Kam looked stunned, staring first at me, then at Akana, waiting for the reaction.

He didn't notice the surprise. "I guess in '29. The same year I get arrested in L.A. Yeah, Carl was on one of those river boats. He came here, after."

"So your job, you're like an escort for the load?"

"Escort? Yeah, but the first time? There wasn't no load. They was just testing me out, 'cause the hop don't come that way. I never know that, so I just went along, kept an eye out, and come Honolulu, the man—the one in jail now—meets me. He says, 'Anything happening?' I tell him not that I seen."

"In jail? This is William Lee?"

Akana nodded, and squirmed in his chair.

"If it didn't come on the *Golden Star*, how did it get here?" I asked.

He shrugged. "On the Army ship, same as always."

"Army ship?"

"Yeah. All three of the loads, they came on one of those transport ships."

"Three?"

"That's what Carl said. He bragged about it."

"The records show he only got paid for two."

"Yeah, but the one the Customs got at the dock? That one, Chin tried to run on his own without him."

"The *Madison*. Carl didn't know about it beforehand?" Billy interjected, frowning.

Akana shook his head. "Boy, he stay plenty happy after. He said they just prove how much they need him. He could jack up the price on the next one."

"He told you about the other three?"

"Yeah. Was two before the big fruit one you got, and one a long time after. Must've been right around the time you arrest me."

"How did it work?"

"The Chinese get the people in Hong Kong and Macao. They send the *hop* to Shanghai and put it in with a lot of Navy stuff. If it's official boxes, or comes on a Navy or Army ship, the Customs practically never looks at 'em. He never say, but I think things for Navy men coming back from China. Butler get the numbers on the right boxes, and he can get them after they get here. And, 'cause he's a Navy cop, he guards the ship while it's here, so no problem taking the stuff off."

"And they did one load after Customs got the dried fruit one?"

"Yeah. They wait till after the trial and the trouble is all over, then do one more using the Navy thing. I think was about the time we grab the wahine. Everything went smooth. He get pay for that one."

"How much?"

"Oh, he stay bragging big about fifty thousand. Best one ever. I think maybe he up his price to get even for the fruit one. Plus, he know he ain't gonna be here that much longer."

For what seemed like the first time in months, I had a chance to hop back onto the island of sanity my accounting records provided. I scribbled some numbers on the desk blotter, and toted up the damage Carlton Butler had done. He'd smuggled three loads and received a total of $103,000. The hui's books showed they'd paid their White Friend $10 per tin, for a total of 60,000 ounces of opium, or 3,750 pounds—almost two tons—an astronomical figure.

"That's too much hop for just Hawaii," I told Akana.

"Yeah. It only come to Hawaii 'cause Butler stay here. Once the Chinese get 'em, they send it to Frisco, L.A., Seattle, even Canada. That's how come I had the hop going up to L.A. that time."

If this was true, Hawaii was the center of an opium distribution wheel that supplied most of the West Coast, and probably Chinese communities far to the east. And as we'd always suspected, the grease on that wheel—the man who made it spin smoothly—was the White Friend.

Each of us contemplated the scope of this information, mentally diagramming the shape of the conspiracy and the role of each participant as we knew it, and plugged in the name everybody had been chasing for years. Each link in the chain represented a potential witness, each shipment an act furthering the grandest scheme any of us had ever heard.

"And that's another thing. Where have you been the last six months?" I demanded.

"L.A. I stay with some friends up there."

"Yeah? How'd you get the money to go?"

Akana looked around furtively, then flinched when Kam moved in his direction. "No, no. I tell you. Carl give me the money, five hundred bucks. He say, 'Get out and stay out.' I know he already pound the girl and try to kill the cop, so I took off." He dropped his voice as if Butler could hear. "I come back sooner, stay hiding out so he never see me."

"What cop did he try to kill?" Billy asked sharply, looking over at me.

"Some Vice who seen him and the girl one night. He thought they was gonna put one and one together, figure out it was him. One of the Chinese push the guy into the street, but never kill him."

I stared at Akana, openmouthed and speechless, remembering the slab of steel grinding to a stop next to my shoulder, the smell of burning rubber.

Billy jerked his head at the door. We needed some privacy.

We locked Akana to the chain that ran under our evidence locker, a double-door steel safe, and the three of us went out into the hallway to talk.

"He did try to kill me," I exclaimed, still disbelieving. "Twice."

"No shit," Billy scowled. "How in the hell did you come up with Butler's name?"

"I put it together. I should have seen it sooner. Thalia told us it was a Navy man. I testified for Kam at that hearing on Monday. Butler was there, remember? You introduced me to him."

"Yeah, but there were fifty Navy boys there that morning. The courtroom was full of them. They all heard you testify."

"Sure. But remember when we were talking before we went inside? Butler told us he'd been on the Yangtze before he came here. Shanghai. And then he heard me say in court I saw two men and a woman coming out of the apartment. He was right there. He heard everything."

"We were looking for somebody who'd been here when the *Madison* shipment came in," Billy said. "Somebody who'd been here even before that, in '28 or '29."

"And Butler didn't fit. Because he must have worked that first load from the other end—from Shanghai, where all of those transports started out."

Billy and Kam thought it over. Then Billy saw it and nodded. "Yeah. He thought you'd seen him that night and might recognize him."

"But I didn't. All I saw was his back."

"No wonder the sonofabitch panicked. He knew it was him and Thalia you saw, and he knows she's off the reservation. No telling what she might say. So he tries to get rid of the other witnesses. Sends Sammy to the mainland, and tries to bump you off." Billy shook his head and laughed. "Things calm down and he thinks he's put the cat back in the bag, and then we go and trap Thalia, and he sees it climbing back out again."

"And sends Gold Tooth and the boys."

"Yep. Gonna finish what he'd started. Only you're harder to kill than he thought."

"Thanks to Joe."

"And if that's not enough, we go and ask for a list of the Navy men, so he knows we're getting close. He must've been sweating. You know what this means, don't you?" Billy started fishing for his pipe.

"What?"

"This whole thing. All of it with Thalia. Joe getting killed. And Sau. It was all about protecting this bastard's identity. Dillingham and Darrow, and all this bullshit for the past six months, because that guy thought you'd seen him at an opium den."

"We've got to get this S.O.B.," I said firmly. "Sammy's the key. He knows the whole story."

"He knows some good stuff," Kam agreed.

"True. But it isn't enough," Billy countered. "And we've got no time. The sonofabitch is leaving any day. He's been transferred to California."

"What about the Ala Moana thing?" I protested. "He's up to his ass in the kidnapping!"

"What about it? The trial's over. They're going to be sentenced tomorrow, and the governor's probably going to pardon the whole bunch of 'em. Darrow told you the Ala Moana boys will never be retried. Butler and his pals could never be convicted for the kidnapping now, anyway, not after Thalia's testified twice that it was five other guys."

He stopped, rubbed his eyes with both hands, and thought hard before he spoke again. "The worst part is, we can't even make a case on Butler for the White Friend thing, not with what we've got now."

"We've got Sammy," I insisted. "He puts Butler in the business."

"Yeah? We needed him six months ago. We might've had a chance to prove this shit.

"Think about it," he said. "If we try to put Sammy on the stand with this story, we'll get blasted. He's saying Butler didn't know anything about dried fruit and the *Madison* shipment. That means we've got to try and convince a jury that Butler helped with three loads we didn't know a damn thing about, but he didn't do any conspiring on the one we caught. That's gonna be a mighty tough sell."

"We've got all the stuff Thalia told us. Why have we got her on the wire?" I objected, liking the direction of this discussion less all the time.

"You know we can't use the wire without telling everybody how we came to get it. That only would have worked if Thalia'd stayed with the program from day one.

"And Thalia's no good, we all know that," Billy went on. "We can't use her as a witness now, not with all the lies she's told, even with the recording."

"We'll get somebody else." I wasn't willing to give up that easily. "Maybe Sammy can point us at somebody who can back him up, and we go after them."

Billy looked over at Kam, who shook his head. "That puts us right back at the start line, looking for somebody who knows enough *and* who wants to tell us about it."

Some of the numbness was wearing off, and I was clutching at ever-smaller straws. "Now that we know the shipments came on the army transports, we could match them up against the hui's records. I know there was one that came in from Shanghai right before we arrested George Soon. For sure that would tie Butler into the ring."

"It's still Sammy's word against Carl's. Butler'll say, 'I don't know what he's talking about.' We got no proof he knew about the opium in the shipments. Hell, aside from Akana, we got no proof there *was* opium in them."

"But all the hui books, they show the first two payments to the White Friend. If those match up with a transport coming in, that would back up Akana. So do the witnesses from the original hui trial."

"Nobody's identified Butler, though," Billy pointed out.

"No, but they know the money was paid to *somebody*. Akana will say it was Butler, and the records confirm it. And I can get his bank records. I'll bet they'll show he got more money than he can explain with his Navy pay. Now we've got somebody who can say where that money came from!"

Billy weighed the evidence, mentally sifting through the clues stored in his head. "It's thin," he finally sighed. "In any other case, it might be enough. Not in this one, though. Not with all the other baggage we're carrying." He shook his head regretfully. "I think you should run this whole thing past C.T. Tell him about the money angle. See what he thinks. If he says go to the U.S. Attorney, then fine. But I don't think he's gonna say that, and neither do you."

Now I was a long time answering as my mind raced through the events of the past nine months. Somewhere in the building, footsteps clicked rhythmically on the marble floor, and were followed by the slamming of a faraway door. The echoes faded.

Finally, grudgingly, feeling every word being ripped from my soul, I forced them out.

"No, Goddammit, I think it's over."

CHAPTER 39

Iolani Palace
Wednesday, May 4

And just like that, it *was* over. With astonishing speed, the seemingly endless travail that had preoccupied our Territory for months ended with a flurry of photographs on the governor's balcony at Iolani Palace. Thalia was going home.

Shortly after 10:00 a.m. on sentencing day, Judge Davis cleared the courtroom of spectators and handed out the law's mandatory ten years at hard labor for each of the convicted killers. If they all looked pretty cheery, it was because the fix, as Clarence Darrow had implied to me, was already in.

Although Darrow and Governor Judd disagreed later about which of them thought up the plan, the outcome satisfied both. Judge Davis, after passing sentence, placed the four convicts in the custody of High Sheriff Gordon Ross, who escorted them and their entourage of attorneys and Navy supporters across King Street, where the governor waited in his office.

Darrow, backed by a number of Congressmen, Senators, newspaper editors, and assorted interested parties, had demanded a full pardon from the governor. Judd, who very much wanted to avoid the real threat of martial law and a military governor replacement, was also acutely aware of the growing local sentiment that everybody'd had just about enough of the Massies and their imbroglio. He drew the line at a commutation of the sentence. They'd serve one hour in the custody of the Sheriff. This meant the four killers would still be convicted felons, deprived of their civil rights, and forever guilty in the eyes of the law.

Within weeks, Grace and Thalia would be shouting about how unfair it all was, but the bottom line read that they would never spend a day in jail for killing Joe Kahahawai, which was something else Darrow had foretold to me. The old coot still had it in him. He'd lost at trial, lost again at sentencing, and been denied in his request for a pardon. But by God, he'd exited the war a winner: his clients were all free.

Billy and I stood on King Street, about fifty feet from where Joe had climbed into their car for his next-to-last ride, and watched the parade pass by. Thalia, dressed in white and clinging to her husband's arm, passed close enough to see us. She stiffened and looked away with her nose in the air.

A Honolulu police officer stopped traffic so the party could cross, and Billy nudged me. "Not exactly O.P., huh?"

"They all look pretty happy."

"They should be. They're getting a helluva deal." He shook his head ruefully. "One hour time served for killing somebody. Who'd have figured?"

"Clarence Darrow," I told him.

When they reached the opposite side of King Street, about where Mrs. Fortescue had parked her car the day she'd fingered Joe Kahahawai, the girl in white half-turned, looked back over her shoulder to our corner, then turned away again and snuggled tighter to her husband.

"Did you see Thalia?" I asked.

He snorted. "That girl's shoulder was any colder, you could freeze fish in her armpit. I get the feeling she doesn't much care for you."

"Me? Why just me in particular? You were there. Why not you?"

"Aside from the fact I'm much better looking, you mean?" he grinned. "No, it's 'cause you're the one holding her self-portrait, hoss. She's never gonna look at you and not be reminded of what she said that night, and it ain't a pretty picture she painted." He drew on the pipe, and watched the last reporter scramble across the street. The traffic cop scolded him before he waved the waiting cars into the gap.

The party wound through the palace entry's wrought iron gates, then up the broad front steps, and finally disappeared inside. Around us, the small crowd gathered around the statue of Kamehameha the Great who'd come for the sentencing began to disperse, either satisfied with the ten-year term meted out or aware that it would never be served.

Across the street, a small group emerged onto the governor's second-floor balcony. Thalia's white dress was in the middle. Photographers, their backs to us, arranged the party for a group portrait.

"Look at them," I marveled. "Like a damned wedding party or something."

Billy eyed the scene for a moment. "I'm sure glad I'm not married to her."

The little gathering broke up, and trickled back inside.

"Well, I guess it's pau," I sighed. "We lost."

"You really can't win 'em all, hoss," Billy reminded me as we headed back toward the office. "Hell, some weeks you can't win any."

"Butler killed somebody, and he got off clean, too."

"We weren't even close on him. He had us all the way."

"There's no justice in that," I muttered.

"No, I expect not."

I considered my other idea, the plan of last resort I'd thought up in the long hours after we cut Sammy Akana loose that morning. I'd run it past Billy as we'd waited for the hearing, and made my decision. "We might not be completely finished. Are you ready to think about my deal?"

Billy gave me a sideways look, fumbling in his pocket for a match. "That's a big step. I might be, hoss, but the better question is, are you?"

I glanced back across the street to the palace in which the Massie claque was serving their lone hour of "hard labor" over tea in the governor's office, and thought of Joe. "Yes," I said firmly. "Hell, yes."

Now we had a line to cross, and little enough time for the crossing.

CHAPTER 40

Naval Station, Pearl Harbor
Friday, May 6

It wasn't my scheme, really. They're never yours completely; you borrow them from other people, other cases, and other ideas. Billy recycled his trap for Thalia from Holt and Russell's swindle. I got mine from Carlton Butler and Grace Fortescue. Billy and Kam, both with reservations, agreed to see the thing through, which is how we all came to be waiting in a government car by the side of a road on the Pearl Harbor shoreline.

Darkness was falling, and white-clad figures were passing back and forth across the seventy-foot pier leading to the *USS Alton*. Since it was a Friday night, many of the sailors had liberty plans for Honolulu's clubs and speakeasies. We had baited the trap, sending a message aboard the ship: Report to the dispensary on shore and retrieve medical records left with the corpsman at the front desk. Now each person leaving the ship was carefully examined from a distance to see if our target would rise to the lure.

Just after eight, when the foot traffic had slowed to a trickle, a shadow-wreathed shape moved briskly along the wooden jetty to the shore and turned toward the naval hospital, the bait taken.

Our relief turned quickly to tension. Now luck and timing were critical.

From my vantage behind the wheel, I scanned the streets for other drivers or pedestrians who might be able to see us. There were none, so I put the car in gear. Billy, in the passenger seat, got the map ready. Kam eased the back door open a crack as I prowled up behind the walker, easing alongside only a few feet away.

"Excuse me," Billy said through the window. "Could you show me how to get into town from here?" He held up the map, blocking my view but more importantly, blocking the target's view of me.

"Of course." I heard the voice I knew so well, and the sound of footsteps approached the car. Behind the closed curtain in the back seat, Kam tensed. When Billy opened the front door, Kam waited a long beat, then pushed his own door open, trapping the target in the space between.

Kam never even had to leave the car. He just reached out and hooked the surprised victim, who reacted with one shocked "Oh!" The inspector's size and strength made any resistance futile, and in three seconds flat, both doors were closed and I was moving again. If anybody saw it, they would assume the pedestrian had stepped into the car.

We rolled past the dispensary, where lights burned brightly over the doorway, then on a roundabout path into the darkness toward Fort Kamehameha, the army post at the mouth of Pearl Harbor.

Kam pulled a pillowcase over our new passenger's head—not to hide our faces, but to keep our destination secret. I didn't want any connection made to my father, who had graciously loaned us his office, although he didn't know the purpose. Also, as Billy had said, getting yanked into a car by a bunch of unknown antagonists is bad enough, but having a sack on your head takes things all the way to terrifying. Terror had been a part of Carl Butler's scheme to shut Thalia up, and I borrowed that part, too.

Our prisoner sure sounded scared. A muffled high-pitched keening sound emanated from the bag.

Kam grunted. "He pissed his pants. It's all over back here."

"I'll bet he did," Billy laughed. "I know I would have."

I kept silent, drove the short distance to the engineers' building, pulled the car around in back, and cut the lights. After making sure no evening strollers were about, we bundled our whining captive out of the car and into the building, then shoved him down the corridor to the office.

The place was as dark as Grace Fortescue's heart. All the shades were pulled, and the only light came from a small lamp with a red filter I had rigged over the recording equipment. Kam sat the hooded figure down in a chair facing our Blattnerphone. I nodded, and Kam jerked off the sack.

Tommie Massie sat trembling on his chair, looking wildly about and blubbering incoherently. His face was ice-white, panicky, slick with sweat. He finally got out some words I could understand, and they were predictable. "Who are you? What are you going to do to me?"

"You don't look so tough now, Tommie," I said. "You're the original drowned rat."

"You!" He squinted at me. "You can't do this."

"Yeah, it's me, the octoroon…and I just did."

He didn't say anything; he was straining to see past Kam to the door.

"We're not going to kill you, if that's what you want to know. We just want to talk to you for a few minutes. Just sit there, you little bastard, and maybe you'll learn something."

Massie slumped, though whether from relief or surrender, I couldn't tell. The clock was ticking, so I kept on talking. "Tommie, we went to all this trouble so we could tell you a few things before you take your sorry ass out of the Territory. Time's short, so listen real carefully. You with me?"

He looked confused, but nodded.

"Your wife's a whore, Tommie. An opium-smoking junkie slut."

I'll give him credit; he bucked right up at that, and rose out of the chair. Whatever spine had carried him through that stupid plan to kidnap Joe Kahahawai, to defend his wife's honor by killing an innocent man, finally made an appearance.

But we had no time to admire his sand. It had to be knocked out of him, and quick. Kam pushed him down, and I slapped him once across the face. Not hard, just a caution.

"Don't even try it. I told you, we don't have time for that shit. And besides, believe me, you want to hear this."

"I don't. I don't."

"Too bad. You're gonna hear it anyway." I leaned in close to hammer in each word. "Your. Wife. Is. A. Whore. And you don't have to believe me, Tommie, because I'm going to let her tell you herself."

Billy dropped the headphones onto Massie's head, and Kam laid one hand on his shoulder to hold him seated while I turned on the recorder. Thalia's voice flowed into the earphones. As the words penetrated his fear, a procession of emotions marched across Tommie's face: recognition, surprise, confusion, disbelief, and finally something else…something deep and mean and desperate.

We can be truly certain of little enough in this world, but I know I have never seen that look on another man's face. I am also sure I never want to.

A year or two later, we borrowed the Blattnerphone for another case, and I spent a week of late nights making a transcript of the one reel of tape we'd kept from Thalia's interview. It was the more damning of the two, because she'd relaxed enough to tell us the truth about what had happened on September 13, on that dark, lonely beach road.

This is what Thalia Massie's husband heard:

> Q: When did you start smoking opium?
>
> A: I suppose it was about March or April of this year. A few weeks after Tommie introduced me to…his friend. You can find out exactly, because it was a party at the Oahu Country Club.
>
> Q: That's where you met Tommie's friend?
>
> A: Right. Tommie introduced us on the lanai. It must have been March. I was taking a class at the college.
>
> Q: What's your relationship with this friend of Tommie's?
>
> A: We are…we were lovers.
>
> Q: Were?
>
> A: We haven't been together since that night.
>
> Q: What night?
>
> A: September 13.
>
> Q: Oh. Uh, the night of the assault. The rape.
>
> A: Yes. He did that. I couldn't be with him after that.
>
> Q: Did what?
>
> A: Broke my jaw. He hit me over and over.
>
> Q: Why'd you lie about it?
>
> A: Well, I couldn't just tell the truth, could I? I'd have to admit I was something everyone knows I'm not.
>
> Q: I'm not following this. What the hell are you talking about?
>
> A: I'm a married woman. I couldn't admit I knew the man who did it. I'd have to explain everything.
>
> Q: So, you lied and blamed five boys.
>
> A: I tried not to. You've got to believe that. Tommie made me do it. I didn't want anyone to get in trouble. I told them and told them. I said to the police that night I hadn't seen anyone. I said I couldn't see anyone's face. But they had some boys, and they were so sure they were guilty. And Tommie and his friends were pressuring me.
>
> Q: How did you get the boys' license number? You couldn't have seen it that night.
>
> A: At the hospital. Tommie gave me the license number from the car. He said the police were looking for it. He was alone with me in the room and he said I had to do it. I didn't want anyone hurt.
>
> Q: But they did get hurt. They all got locked up, and Ida got the holy hell beat out of him.

> A: I didn't do it! I didn't want to go through with it. You don't know the pressure I was under. The police were bringing these awful people to my house, street hoodlums, vile, ugly people, black kanakas, pointing at them, saying 'Is that the one? What about that one?' After a while, it just seemed easier to say 'yes,' so I did. I tried later just to drop the whole thing. I told Tommie I didn't want to go to court. I said I wouldn't go.
>
> Q: But you did.
>
> A: We had a tremendous row. Tommie told me he'd be ruined if I didn't go through with it. He said it didn't matter, they wouldn't be convicted. And they weren't. They're not going to prison.
>
> Q: Not yet. There's going to be another trial, though.
>
> A: Tommie says they'll never be convicted. He's right. The people on the juries here, they won't put them in prison. Not unless they confess. And how can they do that? They don't have anything to confess to.
>
> Q: Yeah. Everybody keeps telling me that's not really my problem.
>
> A: Could I have a cigarette? There are some more in my bag.
>
> Q: Okay.
>
> A: And a glass of water. I'm getting a little dry. This is all so emotional. I don't suppose you have anything stronger.
>
> Q: Don't be stupid.
>
> A: Don't be mean.
>
> Q: Getting back to the opium. Can we do that?
>
> A: Of course. This is your office. We'll do anything you say.
>
> Q: You said your lover introduced you to opium?
>
> A: That's right. He took me to my very first opium den. It was love at first sight. You might say he robbed me of my virginity in that way. (Laughs)

As Billy flipped the switch on the machine, the echoes of the tinny little voices faded into a hush now broken only by Tommie's harsh breathing. We'd agreed that Billy would be the soft "good cop" for this interview. Like he'd said, "Massie already hates your guts, so you being the bad guy won't be too much of a stretch."

Now he spoke the cold truth gently. "That's right, Tommie. You killed the wrong man," he said, coaxing Massie toward betrayal. "But you didn't know about any of this, did you?"

Tommie, hunched over and snuffling at the floor, shook his head.

"He knows now," I said, talking down at the wreckage of what used to be Lieutenant Thomas Massie. "Joe Kahahawai never even knew your wife existed. It's Saturday night, he's just cruising around town with his pals, getting drunk and being happy, while the slut was meeting up with your dope-peddling friend."

"It can't be." This emerged as more of a moan.

"I can play it again. You want to listen to some more? It goes on quite a while."

"Why?" he croaked.

"Why what?"

"Why are you doing this to me?"

"To you? That's typical. It's always about *you*. Kelley was right in court. You *are* a conceited brat, and you're responsible for everything that's happened since September 12. Think about it. Who dragged Thalia to the party when she didn't want to go? Who called the cops when she didn't want to? Who gave her the license number? Who made her identify the boys? Who was running around hiring lawyers and nagging everybody to make sure the case got prosecuted? Who's got the whole goddamn U.S. Navy in such a total uproar they're kidnapping Horace Ida and helping you kill Joe Kahahawai? *You're* the answer every time."

Billy stepped closer and laid his hand on Tommie's shoulder. "Tommie, we brought you here because these folks put you in a box, and you needed to know how you got there. And we need to find out if you can do anything about it. Do you understand?"

Tommie looked up, confused, his eyes pleading for an explanation. "No. I don't know."

"Oh, for God's sake," I snapped. "You can't be that thick. We're talking about getting even. You understood payback well enough when you were out there kicking Shorty Ida's ass and killing Joe Kahahawai."

Massie shook his head from side to side, like a boxer trying to recover from a couple of hard shots. "Jones did it," he croaked, peering up at Billy. "Jones killed the Hawaiian."

"Well, no shit. I never thought *you* had the balls to pull the trigger. '*His hand held the gun,*'" I mocked. "I'm sure it did. You probably played with it in bed the night before. Did it impress Thalia? Get her all excited? You, pretending to be a man?"

He dropped his head and, gasping, hid his face in his hands.

"But really shoot somebody? Not a chance. Uh uh. Not you. What was it Barry Ulrich said about you at trial? '*He's just a one-killing man.*' Hell, look at you, you big baby. You don't even have *one* in you."

"That's enough, Jack," Billy said mildly. "He's got the picture now. He knows what Carl did to him. You know that's who it is, don't you Tommie? Thalia's lover? You introduced him to her at the country club, right?"

Massie looked up long enough to meet Billy's eyes, then nodded and hung his head again as Billy pressed on. "Carlton Butler. He says you two are close. He says you folks talk. Can you tell us anything about the dope? About his Chinese pals?"

Tommie swallowed hard a couple of times, then finally spoke in a half-moan. "I never knew anything. I don't know any Chinamen. We just talk about the trial. That's all."

"What about Thalia? Did she ever mention it?"

"No! No, I swear to God."

We stood around him, all three looking down at the slight figure in rumpled Navy whites who had beaten the rap for killing an innocent man—our last faint hope for getting justice for Carlton Butler. Massie stared back up at us, his eyes wide and shocked, his pale face still framed by the headphones.

Clarence Darrow had been right. I wouldn't find any justice in a courtroom. Maybe it really was just about vengeance, and you had to take it where you found it.

I reached over to the Blattnerphone and flipped the switch.

> Q: You and this friend of your husband's were lovers?
> A: I did just say that. Do you want the juicy details?
> Q: I want some of them.
> A: It's so strange, telling someone about this. (Sighs) We met at one of those awful, boring Navy parties, a lot like the one that night. Navy people are all so familiar. And dull. And Tommie introduced us. (Laughs) Isn't that ironic? It was a Saturday night and Tommie was going to sea on Monday morning, one of those five-day things. We were making love on Monday afternoon, and we kept it up until Friday morning. He has shore duty, so he doesn't have to go out in one of those dreadful boats. That was very convenient. We saw each other a lot. Tommie thought I was going to school, and sometimes I really did. Sometimes I went to his house. He lives in town, too. Sometimes he stayed at my house. We pretended to sleep in different rooms, but I don't think Beatrice—the maid—was fooled.
> Q: Your husband never suspected?
> A: Tommie? (Laughs) He wouldn't. He's a complete prude. He couldn't conceive that a wife would ever want to be with anyone

besides her husband. What an ass. And so stiff. Stiff in everything except where it matters. Do you know what I mean?

Q: I, uh, yeah.

A: He—Tommie's friend and I—used to laugh about that in bed. Is that more detail than you wanted? I think I like talking to you about it, after all.

Q: Where was this opium den?

A: Oh, you're a prude, too. How disappointing. It was in Chinatown, of course. We went on a night in the middle of the week. Tommie was at sea. The whole thing was very sensual and romantic. We had great sex afterward. The best ever. I was so stimulated. The room, hmmm. It was over a store on Smith Street, I think. There was this lovely Chinese girl, Mai, very young, who prepared the pills. I remember she presented me with the pipe as though it was some sort of precious gift. It was very quaint. Very Oriental. The Chinaman gave me that pipe later.

Q: The one we got from you?

A: Yes. Are you going to give it back?

Q: Hardly. Who is this Chinese guy?

A: I don't know his name, only that he's done some kind of business with Tommie's friend.

Q: What about if I showed you some pictures?

A: I'll try. I'll do anything you ask.

Q: Knock it off.

A: I did anything he asked.

Q: That's probably why you're here now, isn't it?

A: I fucked the Chinaman for him.

Q: What?

A: He wanted me to make love to him, so I did. Does that shock you?

Q: Where was this?

A: At a house in town. It's not a den, it's someone's house. We went there several times. The girl was there too, Mai, the one who fixed the pills. I smoked some pipes, maybe three or four pills, and Tommie's friend said the Chinaman wanted to be with me. He said it was important to him. To both of them. I didn't care. The opium made me want to do it, so we did. That's when the Chinaman gave me the pipe.

Q: And after that night, the night you were assaulted, you haven't been with him?

A: I've seen him quite often, of course. But we haven't been intimate since then.

I lifted the headphones off Massie's head, and Billy turned off the Blattnerphone for the last time as Tommie made retching sounds from inside his hands.

"Sounds like he's gonna throw up," Billy said. "Here, use the trash basket if you need to." He pushed the can over and nudged Tommie's knee.

Massie was sobbing now, bawling like a baby. All gone. What was left looked exactly like an egg you drop on the pavement in the hot sun, all messed up and runny, with bits of shell and broken pieces mixed in. Nothing valuable left, or anything worth looking at, just somebody's accident to be stepped over and avoided. Humpty Dumpty in Navy whites.

I looked at Billy and Kam. They both nodded. It was time to go.

"We're leaving now, and we're going to go back down to Pearl and drop you off outside the main gate. You can walk the rest of the way easy. I know you're not going to say anything about this because I've got this tape here, and you'll remember that."

"What am I going to do?"

"Why the hell are you asking me? You want some advice? Go talk to your mother-in-law. She's a great one for advice and plans. Thalia probably told her the truth. Or how about your lawyer? The great Clarence Darrow. I told *him* your wife was lying. He's another one who knows what a fool Butler made of you."

He looked up at me, and there was more surprise in those black pebble eyes in the whitest face I'd ever seen.

"What *are* you going to do, Tommie? That's a puzzler, all right. You just keep asking yourself that question. Maybe you'll figure out how to get even with the bastard who did this to you. I wish I could, but I can't. We've been trying for six months to nail that sonofabitch, and now Carl's going to sail away from here scot-free."

"But you know what? You aren't, are you?"

His eyes stayed fixed on mine for what seemed like a lifetime, then finally slid to the floor, wordlessly answering the question.

We drove in absolute silence along the streets of the Navy Yard and the submarine base, toward Pearl Harbor's Main Gate. Tommie would have a long walk back, and plenty of chances to think about everything he'd heard.

When we passed the Marine sentry, I pulled over in the shadows beyond the bus stop where the underbrush was thick, and told Massie to get out. Kam drew the pillowcase from his head, more gently this time.

He climbed out, and it ended as it had all begun—with a small and lonely white figure receding in the darkness.

We rode, each alone in his own thoughts, until the lights of Honolulu were bright and cheerful ahead of us, and the ugliness of the harbor lay in the darkness behind.

"Say, Billy, I was thinking," I said finally.

He jolted upright. "Oh, no. Don't you even start with that!" he warned, shaking his finger at me. "This is enough. It has to be, 'cause it's all you're ever gonna get."

"I know. I just thought I saw something, is all, and…"

"Stop the car! Pull up!" Billy was out the door, escaping as I braked, stumbling to the edge of the roadway even as the tires still crunched on the gravel. Kam followed, moved to Billy's side, and bent to his ear as I got out and walked to him.

"Billy, you okay?"

He didn't say yes or no; he just started talking in a tone almost apologetic. "I had an ambulance during the war. Drive up to the front, pick up some customers, drive back to the field hospital. 'Course the Germans are shelling you both ways, so it's hell outside. Gas, too."

He hunched his shoulders, watched one shoe trace a pattern in the gravel, and lowered his voice. "Inside ain't much better. Boys screaming for their *maman* in their masks. Blood everywhere. Get to the hospital, take the customers out, go back for some more. Kept that up once for thirty-seven days straight. On the Somme.

"My buddy Rick and me? I'll bet we carried damn near a thousand Frenchies back to the rear that time, half of 'em dead or soon to be." His voice trailed off. I looked down and saw him feverishly working the scraper deep in his empty pipe bowl. His knuckles were white in the darkness, and he was breathing hard.

"Brother Billy," Kam said softly, reaching for his elbow. "You don't have to…"

"No. He's got to know this, and I'm getting to the end." He shook himself. "So I've seen more dead men than you can imagine, killed every way you can think of.

"You want to know why I don't go home till I'm ready to drop every night? 'Cause I got nightmares to this day about the boys I carried, and all the ways they got killed. Close my eyes? I can still see every one of 'em, that's why.

"The point is, I'm the world's expert on driving dead men around in a car, and I'm here to tell you, you killed that boy deader than any German shell ever could. That was an ugly, ugly thing to see. Not the worst I ever saw, maybe, but bad enough."

He turned to face me. "And God help me, I'm glad I was there to see it, 'cause it might've been right. Now you're gonna tell me you want more?"

I shook my head.

"Good. Because that's not justice, hoss. That's obscenity. And if you can't see that, you're not the man I thought you might be."

"I guess you're right," I said after a long pause. "It's just, well, I thought I saw something there at the end."

"Like what?"

"Nothing. Probably nothing." I tried to remember. "No, it was something in his eyes. Not hope. Something else."

Billy Wells was silent for a full minute. "I hope you're wrong, son," he finally murmured, examining me as if we were meeting for the first time. "Waking dead people up is bad business. Do that, no telling what might happen."

It wasn't until hours later, at home in bed, gazing up at the ceiling and replaying the scene over and over, that it came to me. The look I'd seen in Massie's eyes had the glow of a coal the instant after the ash is knocked away, that deep cherry-red of a fire well banked. The kind of fire that devours itself, turns inward, depletes its fuel, exhausts its oxygen, so that its energy fades and fades before it dies, forgotten in the dark.

This was the death Billy had faced every night for fourteen years—the one he dreaded every time he got into a car with someone else. As long as I'd known him, Billy Wells had never driven anyone anywhere, and now I understood why: because some part of him believed that when he got to wherever he was going, that life spark would be gone from his passenger as it had been so many times for him before.

Part of me hoped it had died in Tommie Massie that night—he'd gotten Joe Kahahawai killed, even if he hadn't pulled the trigger himself. But I still heard Billy's warning: that kind of fire can also be one the firemen fear. It burns hot as hell itself, lying hidden under its ashen cloak, waiting…hoping for a chance to burst into live flame, living on to consume anything it touches.

Lying there with my hands behind my head, the cool evening breeze brushing over me, I thought about the fire that burned in Tommie Massie and what I had done to put it there. What we—what *I*—had done was nothing less than to tear a man's soul right out of his body, then make him watch while it was dirtied by everything he loved or cherished. His friends, his wife, his Navy.

We walked on the very core of Tommie Massie's being that night, and then stuffed the remains back in the car under a pillowcase and dropped them outside Pearl Harbor's Main Gate like yesterday's garbage, exactly the way I had planned it.

This wasn't rape, or murder, or even Billy's horror. This seemed somehow infinitely worse— the complete spiritual destruction of a life. Was there anything left in the ashes of Tommie Massie's world after we finished? Was there any justice in it?

Outside, moonlight cascaded down onto a now-vacant house on Kahawai Street in dream-haunted Manoa Valley. I would wait nearly two years for confirmation, but I knew already. I knew. I had just sent one more specter to haunt the darkness.

CHAPTER 41

Manoa Valley, Honolulu, State of Hawaii
Sunday, June 6, 1999

A dream may have faded, but some things followed me over the next seven decades. The memories are still strong—some painful, some poignant, some shoved way back in a corner where they don't get dusted off much. In one of these corners stands Tommie Massie.

After all, while I might have carried Thalia's self-portrait, it was her husband who carried mine. That was what I'd seen in Tommie's face that night. I'd been looking for something evil or corrupt, something that would explain why Joe Kahahawai had to die. I'd wanted an understanding of how this wretched little man could pervert his search for justice, could possibly hope to redeem his lost "honor" by such sordid means.

And I *had* seen something base and loathsome in his eyes, something more than the spark that might, indeed, have made Tommie Massie what his prosecutor sneeringly called "a one-killing man."

What I saw, but only acknowledged years later, was a picture of my own painting.

Maybe Clarence Darrow was right. Maybe we cannot possibly find the meaning of justice. Maybe it is nothing more than some passionless adjustment of claims that has no value in the more important things that matter in our lives—things like family and honor, love and death. Maybe justice is just another pipe dream. I went chasing that dream once myself, seventy years ago, and I found something. There are days, many of them, when I'm ashamed to say it might have been me.

Now, with the story told, as the long shadows fall again on the hills above Manoa Valley, I can finally put these papers on my desk with the relics of a bygone age. There is a gold badge in a Lucite square, a massive reel of rusting silver ribbon, too heavy for an old man to lift, and an ivory opium pipe, carved to look like bamboo.

That badge, in gleaming gold and blue, will be perfectly preserved in its clear plastic vault, its symbolism intact a thousand years from now. The memories of the one who carried it will all be lost much sooner.

Those in the spool of silver tape are already gone. Time and technology replaced the Blattnerphone with vinyl records and tapes and compact discs, eliminating any chance to retrieve the words that only you and I know are stored somewhere on that heavy reel. Like me, the ribbon has languished too long in Hawaii's sea air, found contentment in its present condition, and proclaims its fragile reluctance to awaken by breaking in silent protest into small, scimitar-shaped pieces. When I pick them up, I imagine that each of the little fragments contains the name of a naval officer now dead, or a snippet of a girl's voice, preserved forever but never again to be heard.

In the pipe, though, the memories still speak. I can raise the exquisitely carved tube, run my fingers along the smooth, cool ivory, feeling each delicate ridge. It was old and well used when its former owner acquired it. The opium she smoked and seven decades of time have suffused the ivory with a radiant yellow tint. The glow conjures up the image of a girl's eager face in the flare of an oil lamp, of long fingers curled around the stem, of blue eyes shining hungrily as they follow the movement of the opium cooking in the lamp's flame. I can listen again to the hiss of the yen pock as it heats on her bowl, see her body shudder as she draws in the vapors, and hear once more the tremor in her voice as she talks of crows flocking in its smoky recesses.

I pull off the hollow clay bowl and smell the lingering fragrance of opium smoked seventy years before, and I am instantly transported across space and time to a narrow room in a building long gone, to be again among faces long dead. All this comes to me clearly, as plainly as though it happened only this morning, as distinctly real as the objects I hold.

Still I find myself asking, as I look out across Manoa's serenity, and as I have each day for seventy years: Was it right, or was it just a dream?

I told you the beginning and the end. I'll tell you the rest and let you decide.

EPILOGUE

THOMAS MASSIE grew up. In the weeks after the *Malolo* left Honolulu, he received many proposals for stage contracts and other "commercial offers," which he rejected. He and Thalia went to Los Angeles to visit friends, then on to Tommie's home in Kentucky, and they were mobbed by reporters at every stop along the way. He was hailed as a returning hero in his hometown of Winchester, and Kentucky governor Ruby Lafoon restored his civil rights in an impressive—but legally meaningless—ceremony.

When the acclaim subsided, Massie returned to duty and relative obscurity in California. In 1933, he was assigned to the *USS Oklahoma*, a battleship then homeported with the Pacific Fleet's Battle Force at Long Beach. Thalia divorced him in 1934, and he remarried in 1937 in Seattle, Washington.

In 1940, President Roosevelt decided to move the Pacific Fleet battleships to Pearl Harbor as a deterrent to Japanese expansion in Asia. Massie's old ship, along with most of the Battle Force, arrived in Honolulu on December 6, 1940, nine years to the day after the mistrial was declared in the Ala Moana case. A year after that, *Oklahoma* slept with the rest of the fleet on the eve of America's Day of Infamy. She was hit hard by Japanese torpedoes, capsized, and sank with the loss of 429 of her crew.

Thomas Massie—still a lieutenant—had left the service a year before, so he missed the attack. He'd had a nervous breakdown and spent some time in St. Elizabeth's, a mental hospital in Washington, D.C. After release, he settled in California to pursue a life in business half an ocean and a world away from a tragic past. Tommie died in San Diego on January 8, 1987. It was the fifty-fifth anniversary of Joe Kahahawai's murder.

CARLTON BUTLER's next assignment after Honolulu was on a destroyer based at San Diego, California. On the night of December 12, 1933, Butler's body was found next to his car, a new Packard, in a parking lot just outside the naval station gate. He had been shot once in the head with a .32 caliber pistol. Police speculated that the officer was taken by surprise or knew his assailant, as there were no signs of a struggle. Robbery was ruled out as a motive; a large sum of cash was found on his person. No witnesses came forward, the murder weapon was never found, and no one was ever arrested for the killing.

I learned of Butler's death when an envelope postmarked "*USS Oklahoma*" arrived at the office. It contained a newspaper clipping describing the killing, and nothing more. I put it in a box of files that sat behind my desk and took them both to the Public Health incinerator on Ala Moana Road, not far from the old animal quarantine station, and sent them to join Carl Butler in the flames.

THALIA FORTESCUE MASSIE lived, by all accounts, a troubled and unhappy life after leaving Hawaii. Exactly one month after Carl Butler's death, she appeared in Reno, Nevada, and announced that she planned to divorce Tommie on grounds of "extreme mental cruelty." The couple had been separated since their return to the mainland in 1932. In a statement to the press, Thalia said, "Tommie insisted we get a divorce. It was the terrible publicity of the trial."

The divorce became final on February 22, 1934. That night, celebrating her newfound freedom in a Reno nightclub with three friends, Thalia accidentally overdosed on laudanum. The press reported the incident as a suicide attempt. Her doctor described it as a "nervous collapse."

One month later, while cruising the Mediterranean on the *SS Roma*, Thalia did attempt suicide, first declaring her intent and then slashing her wrists. She was hospitalized in a Genoa sanitarium for a month, where the doctor said, "She believes people want to kill her." The former Mrs. Massie then returned to the United States and dropped from sight. In 1951 she briefly resurfaced when, intoxicated, she "went berserk" and attacked her landlady, who sued her for $10,000.

Those crows finally caught up with Thalia in West Palm Beach, Florida, where she had gone to live near her mother. On July 2, 1963, the most famous rape victim of the twentieth century was found dead in her apartment. Police discovered a large number of bottles and vials containing drugs prescribed by several doctors in the bathroom with her body. The coroner ruled the cause of death to be an accidental overdose of barbiturates. She was fifty-two years old.

CLARENCE DARROW kept his word. He took Thalia Massie with him back to the mainland, thereby ending any chance for a retrial of the Ala

Moana case. Darrow himself eased into retirement in Chicago with his forty grand. His final bow, the Massie case, was the last time his soaring oratory and questionable logic would be heard in a courtroom.

History will always link Clarence Darrow with the underdog—a lawyer who, throughout his career, enjoyed and even reveled in a reputation as a defender of people of color. In his Hawaii case, he represented wealth, privilege, and white hegemony, as exemplified by Grace Fortescue and Tommie Massie. Thus was the world treated to a picture of Darrow, "the attorney for the damned," standing decisively on the side of lynch law, at least in the perception of those same people of color he had so long represented.

This was particularly poor timing as decent Americans, both black and white, were trying in the early 1930s to drive a last nail into "Judge Lynch's" coffin.

Darrow's argument, boiled down to its bare essence, that the law should not apply to four white murderers, left a bad smell in Honolulu for years. It would have been better for all concerned had he stayed in Chicago, where he died in 1938.

He did right by me, though.

HORACE IDA, BEN AHAKUELO, HENRY CHANG AND DAVID TAKAI, the surviving Ala Moana defendants, dropped out of the public eye. John Kelley made a sincere attempt to retry them, vowing to proceed even without his star witness, Thalia Massie. In an effort to resolve the case, Governor Lawrence Judd commissioned an independent investigation by the Pinkerton Detective Agency, which did a very thorough job and published their report in 1933. In one important conclusion, the detectives noted:

"We have found nothing in the record of this case, nor have we through our own efforts been able to find what in our estimation would be sufficient corroboration of the statements of Mrs. Massie, to establish the occurrence of rape upon her. There is a preponderance of evidence that Mrs. Massie did in some manner suffer numerous bruises about the head and body *but definite proof of actual rape has not in our opinion been found.*" (Emphasis added.)

The same report frankly doubted whether, in light of the time issues that Samuel Lau described to me, the five who were charged could have done the crime, noting:

"We believe, however, that it has been shown that *the five accused did not have the opportunity to commit the kidnapping and rape as described by Mrs. Massie* between the time she says she left Ala Wai Inn at 11:35

p.m. and the time she was picked up on Ala Moana Road at 12:50 a.m." (Emphasis added.)

This left Kelley with no complaining witness, no reasonable suspects, a crime his own investigators thought hadn't really happened, and a Territory full of people who were sick and tired of the whole mess. Accepting the inevitable, he filed a motion for *nolle prosequi*, a request that the case against the four remaining defendants be dismissed. Judge Charles Davis took less than ten minutes to grant the motion.

The people Thalia Massie had identified as her assailants got on with their lives, although Joe, of course, was gone. Horace Ida changed his name, worked for a beer company, and died in 1952. Ben Ahakuelo became a Honolulu firefighter stationed in Waikiki and in Kailua on the windward side of the island. He died in 1970. Henry Chang stayed a "police character" involved in multiple run-ins with the law over the next forty years. Most were minor—gambling, petty theft, and public drunkenness—but he did some hard time, too, and never truly put the Ala Moana case behind him. David Takai died in 1989, after having worked most of his life as an electrician for his father's company.

WALTER F. DILLINGHAM, the dean of Hawaii's business community, managed to ride the wave generated by Thalia Massie's passage through his islands. He would hang onto the power he'd accumulated, though not without some tense moments. Most observers felt that the Massie case postponed Dillingham's dream of statehood for Hawaii for at least another two decades.

On May 17, 1932, as the Massie affair drew to its sorry close, Dillingham wrote a "private memorandum" for Hawaii's congressional delegate, describing the events following Thalia Massie's reported rape:

"These rumors spread rapidly through the community. Within a few days there was common gossip to the effect that: 'she was drunk,' 'out looking for trouble,' 'was a depraved character,' 'was a sex pervert,' *'a dope fiend'*..." (Emphasis added)

This memorandum, which I think sums Thalia Massie up rather neatly, can now be found in the Hawaii State Archives. By the time of Dillingham's death in 1963, the Big Five no longer ruled Hawaii's economic and political world.

CLARENCE T. STEVENSON, who turned out to be an awfully good man to work for, left Hawaii in 1936 and took the position of Director of District 14 of the Federal Bureau of Narcotics in Seattle, Washington. On his last day in our office, C.T. nailed up a piece of black and gold cloth on the wall above his desk. It was the epaulette of a lieutenant commander in the United States Navy.

He came back to Hawaii after retiring and took a job as warden of Oahu Prison. C.T. died, too soon, in 1946.

KWAI KAM passed from the scene in 1952, while I was living on the mainland. My friend left a wife and thirteen especially promising children, all of whom fulfilled their father's dreams and were successful in their lives in Honolulu.

Kam had joined the Honolulu Police Department in 1910 and become a detective ten years later. He survived the purges that claimed Samuel Lau, continuing as the head of HPD's reconstituted Vice squad and busting opium dens, gambling operations, and illegal brothels into the mid-1930s, when he retired.

I last saw Kam just before my transfer to the Bureau's New York City office in 1947 when he invited me over to his little house for an *aloha* dinner. Miraculously, there still seemed to be roughly the same number of small Kams roaming the premises as in 1931; the happy chaos had passed to a generation of Kam's grandchildren.

Following dinner, we sat and talked about old cases and remembered faces. Those of Tommie Massie and Carl Butler always hovered in the darker corners of both our memories. Though we were both on record denying any belief in superstitions, we didn't tempt fate by speaking of dead people.

Afterward, in the car, as I was backing out onto 1st Avenue, I caught sight of a package I'd brought for Kam's wife. I grabbed the box off the back seat, and ran up to the open screen door at the top of the steps and into the house.

The distinctive scent of burning incense filled the living room, as wisps of the fragrant smoke drifted toward an open window. Inspector Kam, grayer at the temples and thicker around the middle, stood at the little altar against the far wall. On the table in front of him, colorful joss papers shaped like small boats awaited incineration and the opportunity to lift a prayer to heaven.

"Hey, I thought you didn't hold with that stuff," I laughed, pointing.

Kwai Kam regarded me steadily. "I never said that, exactly."

"No, but you always said you didn't need the luck."

"I don't. I've still got all I need." He shrugged, then turned back to fire one of the little ships. "This," he said, speaking to his offering, "this isn't for my spirit. It's for yours, Jack Mather."

William K. "Billy" Wells grew up in Honolulu, went to sea as a merchant seaman at eighteen, then volunteered as an ambulance driver in World War I. While serving with a French regiment, he participated in eight major campaigns in the space of six months, saw duty at the Somme and Verdun, and won a Croix de Guerre for valor. Marshal Petain himself awarded the honor to Billy Wells and Fedrico Biven, also of Honolulu, in February 1919.

Billy returned to Hawaii that same year. He became a law enforcement officer by accident, first joining the Prohibition Service, then becoming part of the Bureau of Internal Revenue in 1920, after being talked into it by a friend he encountered on a Honolulu street corner. He was assigned to the Narcotic Division in 1921, and retired from its successor agency, the Federal Bureau of Narcotics, thirty years later. Although he also worked in St. Paul, Minnesota, and Cleveland, Ohio, Billy spent all but one year of his career in Hawaii.

Billy Wells, who'd given me so much over the years, gave me two more things when we had lunch in 1984. The first was a lift in his station wagon. He drove me to the Moana Hotel, smoking his pipe and commenting favorably on the tourist girls in Waikiki. The second was a gold and blue shield locked in a Lucite square. The Bureau had awarded us our badges on retirement, and I'd had mine mounted on a plaque. This one was older, well worn from two decades in Billy's pocket. The styles had changed, but this was the official issue in 1931, the year I came back to Hawaii to join the opium wars.

"I want you to have it," Billy told me. "It'll mean something to you." As indeed, it did.

William Kāne Wells, who always insisted on "Billy," even at age ninety-four, died in 1986. I miss him.

Jack Mather served with the Treasury Department for thirty-seven years in places like New York, Washington D.C., and Honolulu, and as far away as Shanghai and Marseilles. After his retirement, Jack returned to his family's home in dream-haunted Manoa Valley. Among his personal effects, his grandson found a gold badge on a plaque and another set in Lucite, a big reel of silver ribbon, and an ivory opium pipe carved to look like bamboo. He also found six manuscripts describing a life in the opium wars from beginning to end. Pipe Dreams *was the last of the six to be completed, and having said everything he thought worth saying,* **John Hoʻopono Mather** *passed away in June 1999.*

AUTHOR'S NOTE

Although *Pipe Dreams* is fiction, it is based on real events of 1931 and 1932 and the actual participants in Honolulu's infamous "Massie affair." This part of the story is as historically accurate as I could make it. All of the details of Thalia Massie's rape case and Joe Kahahawai's murder case are supported by the research of other authors and original documents, trial records, and primary sources from the Hawaii State Archives. This is also true about the opium smuggling case, including the "White Friend" of Honolulu's opium ring.

Having grown up in Hawaii, I knew all about Thalia Massie and the troubles she brought with her to the Islands. I had often walked by her former home in Manoa Valley on my way to and from the stores on East Manoa Road, and as I researched *Pipe Dreams* I discovered more connections to the Massie affair.

We lived on Terrace Drive above Bill and Bertha Pittman, and my family often visited the home next door to the Kolowalu Street house where Joe was killed. As a child, I played in that yard, never suspecting the dark events of thirty years before. A friend of my grandmother had heard the shot in 1932. I once worked with a Honolulu police detective who knew Henry Chang—the last survivor of the "Ala Moana boys"—who had talked with my colleague about the case. And for the past fifty years my own family has lived in the Manoa home that once belonged to the murder trial jury foreman.

I had also read the books on the case written in 1966 and '67 after Thalia died, so like most everyone else in Hawaii at the time, I figured I knew the whole story. Then I met Billy Wells.

He was in his early nineties and had been retired from the Treasury Department longer than I'd been alive. William K. Wells, who still insisted on being called Billy, had joined the Internal Revenue Service in 1921, carrying the same official credentials that I did in my career. As a Prohibition Agent, he was assigned to the narcotics section and then to the Narcotics Division and its successor agency, the Federal Bureau of Narcotics (FBN). A part-Hawaiian, he may have been one of the first non-white federal law enforcement officers in the entire country, and he spent all but about a year of his career in Hawaii, much of that working on opium smuggling cases.

I contacted Billy to see if he'd talk to me about the history of illegal drugs in the Islands. He had some great stories to tell and was happy to share his memories. Some of his stories I knew about from my reading. Most of them he remembered by a ship's name—the *Empress of Japan* case," the "*President Hoover* case," the "*Golden Star* case." He still had some photos, one from the seizure of the *Empress of Japan*. (We in the narcotics business called these "trophy pictures." I have a few of my own.)

He had a great sense of humor and a very clear memory, and he recalled many names: doctors he'd arrested, drug sellers in Hilo and on Kauai, the black servicemen who took over the heroin/morphine business in Honolulu in the years right after World War II, and from farther back, the members of the opium hui that operated in Honolulu's Chinatown in the 1920s—including the mysterious White Friend.

These names and cases are all-but-forgotten today, but I had some FBN reports that documented some of the cases he told me about, and he gave me a couple of reports he'd written toward the end of his career, when he was Acting District Supervisor in the FBN's Honolulu office. I also had dozens of newspaper clippings from the *Honolulu Advertiser* and took these to Billy's house to remind him of the things he'd done before he retired in 1951.

Over time, we moved on to other subjects. I was particularly interested in his World War I experiences. Sixty-five years after it had ended, he still had a hard time talking about that war, and he preferred to dwell on the Hawaii friends who'd accompanied him to France with the US Army Ambulance Service—Federico "Rick" Biven and Francis H.I. Brown.

One day, I asked him about a case that everyone did remember, the one that began with Thalia Fortescue Massie.

"Oh, yeah," he said. "We knew she was yen shee quoy."

These words and the ones that followed launched *Pipe Dreams*. He said he'd told the story to a few others over the years, but nobody cared much, even before Thalia died of a drug overdose in 1963. I thought the story could best be told as fiction, but I wanted to keep it as historically correct as possible, so every character in the book is a real person except Jack Mather and the members of his family. I also changed the name of the naval officer who Billy believed was the "White Friend of the opium hui."

And yes, Grace Fortescue was just as mean and bigoted as I portray her here.

—John Madinger, Honolulu, Hawaii

ACKNOWLEDGMENTS

Like every author, I owe many thanks to others who helped bring my book to life. First and foremost is my friend Billy Wells. He knew more than I'd ever heard or read about Thalia Massie, and it led to the kinds of "who" and "what if" questions that make a good mystery story. Thanks to Billy for his inspiration, his keen memory, and his willingness to share the reminiscences of a half-century earlier. I also owe him a debt of gratitude for Thalia's pipe and the yen shee ngow pipe scraper that he gave me to remember him by—and to remember the girl whose lies started it all. I do miss him.

I'd also like to thank my family, which has been most supportive—including my grandmother and my mother, Beth Madinger, both now passed on, who taught me the love of books and reading—and Holly, Sean, and Ian.

My editors, Linda Cappel and C.J. Darling, worked very quickly and professionally to get the book ready—and made it better.

George Engebretson at Watermark Publishing in Honolulu believed, like me, that Hawaii and the world was ready for a novel about the Islands' most famous crime.

Janis Hines, who loves Hawaii and despises Thalia and Grace, was unfailingly encouraging and believed in *Pipe Dreams* from the very first. I owe her and everyone else involved in this project my deepest thanks and appreciation.

GLOSSARY

bo lau — Pool hall (Cantonese underworld slang)

boo how doy — Literally "hatchet boy," commonly a hatchet man or "highbinder," a triad member used for strong-arm protection and murder; sometimes wore a chain-mail vest and steel-lined hat to protect from rival blades

char siu — Chinese barbecue pork, often used as a filling in manapua

gee rag — Small cloth patch that fit between the bowl and the stem in an opium pipe; served as a gasket but also collected opium residue—in desperate times an opium fiend could boil the rag and drink this "yen shee suey" as tea

haole — In Hawaiian, a "foreign person" but applied only to Caucasians

hapa haole — Half- or part-Caucasian

hibachi — Small Japanese brazier for cooking with charcoal or wood

holoku — Full-length Hawaiian gown, long-sleeved, sometimes with a train

hop — Chinese slang for opium

kanaka — A person of Hawaiian ancestry—term used frequently as a pejorative in the 1930s

koa — A large native Hawaiian tree of the Acacia family yielding a valuable wood used in ancient times for canoes

lan yeung — Cantonese/Hong Kong underworld slang; literally "penis head"

lauhala	The leaf of the *hala* (pandanus) tree, woven into baskets, hats, and floor coverings or mats
manapua	A steamed Hawaiian-style bun usually containing a meat filling
O.P.	Oahu Prison, built in Honolulu's Kalihi area in 1916
okolehao	Roughly, "iron bottom," a fiercely potent, almost pure alcohol distillate made from the root of the native *ti* plant; most similar to potato vodka
H.R.T.	Honolulu Rapid Transit, the city's public bus operator
pau	Finished, done (Hawaiian)
pilikia	Trouble (Hawaiian)
sikh dai	Cantonese slang for detective
tael	Chinese and Hong Kong measurement (equivalent of 1.33 ounces or 37 grams)—opium was generally sold in five-tael tins, or 6.666 ounces
wahine	Woman, female (Hawaiian)
yen dow	Detachable ceramic bowl that fits into a metal saddle on top of an opium pipe; usually brass or pewter, some luxury pipes had saddles made of silver (Thalia's is pewter)
yen pock	Ball of heated opium prepared for smoking on the pipe; about the size and shape of a kernel of corn
yen shee loo	Opium man, a user
yen shee ngow	Also *yen gow*, a hook-shaped scraper used on the inside of opium pipe bowls (used by Billy Wells on his tobacco pipe)
yen shee quoy	Literally "opium devil," the term usually reserved for longtime users or habitués
yet toy	Small container usually made of bone or wood and holding a half-tael or less, enough opium for two smokers for an evening
young chee	Also *young gee*, the saddle on the top of an opium pipe into which the bowl fits; usually made of brass or pewter, though some luxury pipes had saddles made of silver (Thalia's is pewter, mounted on ivory carved to look like bamboo.)

ABOUT THE AUTHOR

John Madinger was raised in Honolulu and served for three decades as a state and federal law enforcement officer, mostly in America's war on drugs. Considered one of the country's leading authorities on money laundering, he is the author of *Money Laundering: A Guide for Criminal Investigators, Third Edition* and *Confidential Informant: Law Enforcement's Most Valuable Tool*. *Pipe Dreams* is his second novel, after *Death on Diamond Head* (Watermark Publishing, 2007). He has received awards for fiction, non-fiction, short stories, and even poetry, and still lives in Manoa Valley.